THE GRAFTON GIRLS

Four girls, one war to fight...

When Diane Wilson leaves Cambridge for Liverpool to work as a teleprint operator, she is intent on mending her broken heart. Her new roommate, mean-spirited Myra Stone, knows they aren't kindred spirits, but does her caustic wit belie a secret sorrow? To put food on the table for herself and her widowed mother, Ruthie endures terrible conditions at the munitions factory, where she is befriended by lively and vivacious Jess Hunt. All four women are brought together at The Grafton, the local dance hall favoured by American GIs as well as the local servicemen – will they find true love ... or heartache?

THE GRAFTON GIRLS

THE GRAFTON GIRLS

by

Annie Groves

Magna Large Print Books
Long Preston, North Yorkshire,
BD23 4ND, England.

British Library Cataloguing in Publication Data.

Groves, Annie
    The Grafton girls.

    A catalogue record of this book is
    available from the British Library

    ISBN   978-0-7505-2868-9

First published in Great Britain in 2007 by HarperCollins Publishers

Published in Large Print 2008 by arrangement with
HarperCollins Publishers

Magna Large Print is an imprint of Library Magna Books Ltd.

Printed and bound in Great Britain by
T.J. (International) Ltd., Cornwall, PL28 8RW

To the readers for their generous reception to the first of my World War Two books. I hope they will enjoy this one as much.

Annie Groves

Acknowledgements

I would like to thank the following for their invaluable help:

Teresa Chris, my agent.

Harper editors Maxine Hitchcock and Susan Opie, who has now kindly taken me under her wing.

Yvonne Holland, for making sure I got my facts right.

Everyone at HarperCollins who contributed to the publication of this book.

Tony, who as always has helped enormously with the research process.

PART ONE

Liverpool 1942

ONE

'My station's coming up next, and then it'll be Lime Street, luv, tek it from me. Done this ruddy train journey that many times, I have, since this bloomin' war began, I can tell the stops practically in me sleep. That is, of course, if a person could manage to get any sleep with the trains being that full and noisy. Not that I'm complaining, like, not about the overcrowding nor about all the place names being teken down from the stations so as to confuse any of Hitler's spies wot manage to land. Aye, and if I were your age, I'd be in uniform too. WAAF isn't it?' Diane Wilson's new-found friend said knowingly, referring to the Women's Auxiliary Air Force, studying Diane's airforce-blue-clad frame admiringly.

'That's right.' Diane smiled politely enough to be pleasant but not so warmly that she would be encouraging the woman to ask her too many questions.

'A right 'andsome lot them fly boys are. By, if I had me time again...' the older woman chuckled.

Now it was harder for Diane to force a responsive smile. Automatically, and despite the fact that she was wearing gloves, she placed her right hand over the bare place on her ring finger. The pain she thought she had under control could sneak up on her to catch her unawares and stab her with such agonising sharpness. She ought to

15

be over it by now. After all, it had been three months. Three months, two days and ten hours, an inner voice tormented her. Resolutely Diane ignored it. She had known other girls, any number of them, who had been stationed with her at Upwood, Cambridgeshire, who had gone from being desperately in love with one chap to clinging happily to the arm of another when they had lost him. So there was no reason why she shouldn't be doing the same. Only she wouldn't be clinging – not to any man – not ever again. There was no danger of her repeating that mistake. Sometimes, when she was at her lowest ebb, the horrid thought wouldn't go away, the thought that it might have been easier to accept things if Kit had been killed instead of...

'You'll be heading for that Derby House, then, like as not?' the woman leaned towards her to whisper, interrupting her reverie. 'Saw Mr Churchill himself standing outside of it one morning, I did. Smiled at me, an' all. Hitler might have 'is ruddy SS but just so long as we've got our Mr Churchill we'll be sound, mark my words,' she added stoutly.

She was a good sort, Diane recognised, a bit shabbily dressed, but then who wasn't these days, with the war in its third year and new clothes only available if one had enough coupons with which to purchase them. Luckily she had joined the WAAF before clothing coupons had come in, and so she had not had to part with any of her own precious coupons in exchange for her obligatory WAAF uniform of black lace-up shoes, grey lisle stockings, which none of the girls

16

wore during the summer months if they could help it, a skirt, a tunic, a peaked cap – which the girls loved as much as they hated the lisle stockings – an overcoat, which came in jolly useful in the winter, and even regulation underwear, with its horrid bubble-gum-pink 'foundation garments', although none of the girls wore these either if they could get away with wearing their own underwear instead.

More seriously, the whole country was now feeling the effect of the food rationing that had been brought in at the beginning of the war, but if Hitler had hoped to destroy the fighting spirit of the British by attempting to sink the ships struggling across the Atlantic to bring in the supplies on which the country depended, he had omitted to take into account the sturdiness of the nation's spirit, Diane recognised proudly.

Her recent request for a transfer was responsible for Diane's presence on this train to Liverpool and her new post at Derby House, the headquarters of the combined forces protecting the convoys coming into the port. Her life in Liverpool would be very different from that in Cambridgeshire, she knew. Several of the pals she had been leaving behind had expressed doubts about the wisdom of what she was doing.

'Liverpool!' more than one of them had exclaimed, pulling a face. 'You wouldn't catch me wanting to transfer up there. Not for anything.'

Diane had affected not to notice the sharp nudge another of her friends had given the speaker, knowing that the warning was kindly meant and intended to protect her feelings. Her broken heart.

She could feel the burning threat of tears at the back of her eyes, and was thankful for the diversion of the sudden hiss of the train's brakes and the noise of escaping steam, plus the bustle of her travelling companion getting ready to leave the train.

'Well, here's my station.'

Diane forced herself to return the woman's smile.

'Good luck, lass,' the older woman said, giving Diane a grateful look as she helped her out of the compartment with her bags. 'You'll like Liverpool once you get to know it. Of course, it's not the place it was, not since that ruddy May bombing back in 'forty-one. A whole week of it, we had, and it ripped the heart out of the city, and no mistake. There was hardly a family in the city that didn't lose someone, and there were thousands evacuated who didn't come back. But it takes more than a few bombs to knock the stuffing out of Liverpudlians, as you'll soon find out.'

The bright summer sunshine was surely enough of an excuse for her to blink, Diane reassured herself as the train pulled out of the station. And if she was also blinking away those threatening tears then who was to know but her? No one here knew anything about her or her situation. That alone was enough to make her glad that the transfer she had begged for had brought her here.

'HQ Western Approaches won't be what you're used to here, Wilson,' she had been warned when she had been called to the office to receive her new orders from her commanding officer.

'But I'll still be working as a teleprinter operator won't I, ma'am?' she had asked, uncertainly.

'Well, as to that, I dare say that yes, you will. But Derby House is a joint effort run principally by the Senior Service,' she told Diane, referring to the British Navy, 'unlike here, where it's all RAF. It will be part of your duty as a WAAF to make sure that you create the right impression on those you'll be working with.' When her CO had added, straight-faced, 'The Senior Service takes a pretty dim view of flighty behaviour,' Diane hadn't known whether or not she was cracking a joke.

'The CO joke?' one of her pals had scoffed when she had related the incident to her. 'That'll be the day!'

Diane hadn't really needed her CO's warning. Everyone in uniform knew about the rivalries between the various services, and that the Senior Service in particular tended to look down somewhat on the upstart RAF.

She could practically hear Kit's voice now – strong and filled with good humour as he laughed, 'The trouble with those Senior Service lot is that they're jealous of our success.'

'You mean because of the Battle of Britain?' Diane had asked, thinking he had meant that the navy men envied the victory the RAF had had over the Luftwaffe in the summer of 1940, when men like Kit had driven back the incoming German fighters.

'No,' she remembered Kit had told her, his eyes – fighter pilot's far-seeing eyes – crinkling up at the corners with amusement as he had leaned

19

forward and told her boldly, 'I meant because of our success with the fairer sex.'

She had pretended to be dismissive, tossing her head as they stood together at the small bar of the packed Cambridgeshire pub on that breathlessly hot summer night, but when a careless airman, overeager to get to the bar before the beer ran out, had accidentally bumped into her, she hadn't complained when Kit had made a grab for her waist. 'To protect you,' he had assured her guilelessly, but he hadn't been in any hurry to release her, and the truth was that by that stage she had been too entranced by him to want him to. With Kit, over six foot tall, broad-shouldered, with a shock of thick wavy dark hair, and the kind of good looks and easy charm that had already got him a nine out of ten rating in the WAAF canteen, there was barely a girl Diane knew who wouldn't have fallen for his charms.

But there had been another side to him, or so she had believed. A side that...

The sudden jerk of the train's brakes brought her back to the present. Already the corridor outside her carriage was packed with passengers wanting to get off. Diane reached up to the overhead luggage rack to remove her kitbag, ready to join the stream of people disembarking at Lime Street.

So this was Liverpool. The voices she could hear all around her certainly had very different accents from those in Cambridgeshire, although the Liverpool accent wasn't the only one swelling the noise in the busy station, and Diane's eyes

20

widened a little when she saw – and heard – how many Americans there were clustered around in large groups.

They would, of course, be the 'Yanks' from the American base at Burtonwood, which her fellow traveller had mentioned. American bases were being established in Lincolnshire, and at Bomber Command, in High Wycombe, and there had been American personnel at the Cambridgeshire base as well. Diane had heard from some of the other girls about the attractions of the American male and the American PX – as the stores on the newly established American supply bases were named – both generous providers of much that was unavailable or rationed, including chocolate and stockings.

The station platforms were busy with men in uniform, with the distinctively dressed women of the Women's Voluntary Service also very much in evidence with their tea urns. Diane would not have said no to a cuppa herself, but it had already gone five in the evening and she still had to find her way to her billet near Wavertree.

One of the friendly WVS women was happy to explain to Diane how to get to her billet on Chestnut Close, which was in what she described approvingly as 'a respectable part of the city'.

'It's a fair walk, but you could take the bus.'

'No, I'd prefer the walk,' Diane assured her.

The summer sunshine had enough warmth in it to make her walk a pleasant one, and to allow her to pause to stare in shocked compassion at the blitzed and bombed-out centre of the city. She could see huge gaps where it looked as though

21

whole streets had disappeared, and smaller ones, where only a single house had gone, leaving the rest of the street intact.

The city was very different from the pretty Hertfordshire village where she had grown up, Diane acknowledged. Her parents were far from well off, but their semi was one of several on a quiet leafy lane opposite the village green and duck pond. Diane had grown up knowing virtually everyone else who lived in the village. She couldn't help contrasting the pretty comfortable calm of her home village with the devastation of this powerful northern port city. Her parents had been proud but anxious when she had announced her intention of doing her bit and joining up, and they had been even more anxious when she had told them that she was seeing an airman, insisting that she took him home with her so that they could meet him. Although at first they had been cool towards him, by the time Diane and Kit's forty-eight-hour pass was up, Kit had completely charmed them. Diane had been so thrilled and proud, both of him and her parents. Of course, the minute her mother had discovered that he was virtually an orphan, having lost his mother shortly after his birth, she had taken to fussing over him. They had laughed about it together later, Kit teasing Diane that once they were married she would never be able to run home to her mother because she would always take his side. She had laughed too, telling him with the assurance that falling in love brought that she would never ever want to run anywhere other than to him.

She had been so deliriously happy, living in a

world coloured by her hopes and dreams for the future, even if her heart had been in her mouth during every mission Kit flew, her fear always that he might not make it back. Too happy, she knew now. And her fear should not just have been for Kit's survival but for the survival of their love.

She had been so busy with her own thoughts whilst she was walking that she hadn't really observed very much of her surroundings, and it came as a surprise when she realised that she must have passed the hospital she had been told to look out for and that she could now see the Picton Clock landmark she had been warned meant that she had gone too far and missed her turning.

An elderly woman, obviously having noticed her looking around, came over to her.

'Lost your way, have you?' she enquired.

'I've been billeted to Chestnut Close,' Diane explained, 'but I think I've missed my turning.'

'Well, as to that,' the other woman sniffed, 'you have, yes. This is Wavertree, not Edge Hill.' The way she stressed what she obviously considered to be the superiority of 'Wavertree' would normally have made Diane smile. A similarly petty type of snobbery existed in Melham on the Green, the village where she had grown up, with one end of it being considered 'better' than the other. Kit had enjoyed teasing her about her mother's pride in the fact that their well-cared-for semi was just over the invisible border that separated the 'better' end of the village from the 'other' end. 'And, of course, we aren't supposed to give out directions to strangers,' the elderly lady added pompously.

'No, indeed,' Diane responded with suitable

gravity. 'Actually, I do have the directions, but I've wandered off track. I believe that I should have turned off left for Chestnut Close before I got here.'

'There's some folks that live there that like to claim that it's in Wavertree, on account of it being on the border, but even if they are right, the better part of Wavertree is further up the road, past the tennis club and that. I expect you play tennis, do you? I used to play myself when I was younger.'

Diane made her excuses as tactfully as she could. The older woman's question had brought a fresh wave of painful memories. The previous summer she and Kit had just managed to snatch the mixed doubles trophy from the previous year's winners at the Cambridgeshire courts where they and other members of the RAF squadrons based locally played.

It had been at the tennis club, on a warm September night just after the Battle of Britain, not yet two years ago, that Kit had proposed to her.

If they had got married straight away then, instead of deciding to wait, would things have been any different?

It didn't take Diane long to retrace her steps and find the turning into Chestnut Close, which turned out to be a neat collection of small semi-detached homes and terraces of four interlinked red-brick houses, with low red-brick front garden walls and privet hedges.

Number 24 was about a quarter of the way down Chestnut Close, and Diane suspected that she saw several sets of net curtains twitching as she walked up its tidy gravel path.

The front door was opened the moment she knocked.

'Come in, dear,' she was instructed by the small, plump woman in her fifties who greeted her, whom Diane assumed to be her landlady. 'I've bin expecting you. Tired, are you, and parched too, I'm sure? I'll put the kettle on and then I'll take you up and show you the room. You'll be sharing, did they tell you that? Another young lady who's working at Derby House. I told them when they asked me if I'd have some lodgers that with me being a widow and liking things just so, I'd only take young ladies. Not that some of them I've had have been what I'd call "ladies", but then I can tell that you're a decent sort. I'm Mrs Lawson, by the way. It's a good-size room, the largest in the house. It was me and my Herbert's room but seein' as I'm on me own now I moved out of it, like, and I got rid of the double, had a pair of single beds put in – there was that many young couples wanting to have it, what with the furniture shortage an' all, and there's much more space in the back room now with only a single in it. It's funny, isn't it, some folks don't like sleeping in a single after they've shared, but me, I don't mind at all. I like me own space, you see, and men and marriage – well, they aren't allus what they're made out to be, take it from me. It's this way,' she continued without pausing for breath, as she started up the stairs, leaving Diane to follow her.

'Now I'm very fussy about the state of me bathroom – I won't have no makeup nor any of that fake leg stuff all over everything. Baths are once a week, unless you want to pay for extra. You'll get your breakfast, and a meal before you go out when you do your night shift. But there's to be no food taken upstairs to your room. And no followers neither,' she added firmly. 'I won't have no truck with any of that kind of goings-on.'

They had reached the landing and Diane reflected ruefully that beneath Mrs Lawson's soft outer plumpness lay a core of pure steel.

'The lady wot you'll be sharing with is married. Only bin here a couple of weeks herself, she has.'

'This is the room.' She gave a small knock on the door and called out, 'It's only me, Mrs Stone, duck, bringing up the new lady.'

Diane heard the sound of the door lock being pulled back, and then the door opened.

'I'll leave you two to get to know one another whilst I make you both a cuppa,' Mrs Lawson announced.

'Not for me, thanks, Mrs L. I've got to go soon,' said the room's occupant.

'Right you are, duck,' said the landlady, leaving Diane and the girl now seated on one of the room's two narrow single beds to study one another surreptitiously in the slightly awkward silence that followed her exit.

'I'm Diane – Di,' Diane introduced herself.

'Myra Stone,' the other girl responded.

Diane had never seen a more stunningly beautiful nor sensuously voluptuous-looking young woman. She had the kind of looks that would have turned men's heads in the street. She had glossy brown curls, and brown eyes that should have looked warm but which instead held an expression of cynical brittleness that both shocked

Diane and made her feel wary. Somehow that voluptuous body and those cold eyes just did not match up with one another.

'You'd better come in and shut the door. I've already bagsied this bed,' Myra told her, indicating the better positioned of the two beds. 'And I'd better warn you now that there's next to no wardrobe or drawer space left.'

'I dare say I'll be able to manage,' Diane responded lightly. 'It can't be worse than we had at camp. I haven't lived out before.'

'Well, you won't have to bother about curfews or anything like that,' Myra told her, 'and the social life's pretty good up here, especially now that the Yanks have arrived. Have you dated any Yanks yet?'

Diane stiffened. Already a certain amount of competitive hostility had developed between the RAF flyers and the newly arrived Americans. The readiness of some girls to accept 'dates', as the Americans called them, from the newcomers had resulted in them being branded as 'disloyal', and there had even been incidents of outright hostility, with them being accused of favouring the Americans because of the luxuries they could provide.

'You'll be working at Derby House, I expect?'

'Yes,' Diane agreed, as she removed her gloves and her jacket, and then lifted her hand to make sure that her blonde hair was still smoothed neatly into its chignon. Her fingers were slender and fine-boned, her wrist blue-veined under creamy skin. Her colouring was more Nordic than English rose, and her father had always teased her that her blonde hair and blue eyes, together with her height

27

and slender frame, were a throwback to some Viking ancestor on her mother's side of the family. Diane had learned young that her looks made her stand out from the crowd and that sometimes other girls could be wary of her because of them. That in turn had led to her developing an initial defensive calm coolness of manner with people. 'My Ice Princess', Kit had called her. Diane knew that she did tend to hide her own shyness away behind a protective front with new people.

'So what happened to him, then?'

Myra's question caught her off guard, causing the colour to rise in her face. 'What happened to who?' she responded as soon as she had recovered her equilibrium.

'The chap who gave you the ring you've taken off.' Myra gestured towards Diane's left hand and then waggled her own ring finger. 'See, I've got the same telltale white mark. I always check out other girls' ring fingers. It takes one to know one,' she told Diane drily. 'Husbands, eh...'

'We weren't married, only engaged,' Diane told her sharply.

'Lucky you,' Myra drawled. 'I just wish I could say the same. But, more fool me, I went and married mine, and you know what they say about marrying in haste? Well, take it from me it's true.' She paused and gave Diane a speculative look before demanding, 'So what happened to him, then? Bought it, did he?'

Diane could hardly believe her ears. For sheer callousness Myra's question couldn't be beaten. If Kit had lost his life – or 'bought it', as Myra had so casually enquired – Diane knew she would have been overwhelmed with grief by Myra's nosy probing. She looked angrily across and saw that Myra was waiting almost eagerly for her response. Diane had met women like Myra before, women who were so unhappy in their own lives that they fed off the misery of others. She had always taken care to avoid such types and her heart sank at the realisation that being billeted here meant she was not going to be able to now. Well, she might have to share a room with her, but she certainly wasn't going to play along and give Myra the satisfaction of seeing her upset, Diane decided firmly.

Lifting her head she told her crisply, 'No, actually, if anything, it was our relationship that "bought it".' Diane forced herself to give a small dismissive shrug. 'These things happen in wartime.' Not for the world was she going to allow Myra to guess at the pain that lay beneath her casual dismissal of her broken engagement.

Even so, she was surprised when Myra immediately pounced on her words and told her openly, 'Don't they just. Like I said, you want to be thankful that all you did was get engaged. An engagement's easily got out of, not like marriage. I can't believe now that I was such a fool. If I had my time over again, I'd know better. Three years I've been married, and I knew within three months I'd made a mistake. I told him last time he was on leave that I wanted to end it, but he wouldn't agree, so it looks like I'm going to have to hope that the war does the job for me.'

Diane couldn't conceal her shocked revulsion.

'You needn't look at me like that,' Myra told her sharply. 'You don't know what it's like. Worst mistake I've ever made – not that it doesn't come in handy sometimes, like when a chap at a dance gets a bit too forward. I just tell him I'm married and that my hubby is serving abroad, and nine times out of ten that's enough to make 'em back off. Not of course that I always want to say "no". Not now we've got all these Yanks over here. Really know how to treat a girl, they do, not like our own lads. You should see them – tall, they are, and that handsome in those uniforms of theirs... What's wrong?' she demanded, obviously sensing Diane's disapproval.

'Nothing,' Diane lied, and then admitted, 'Well, if you must know, I think it's a pretty poor thing for you to be praising American men. It seems disloyal to our own boys.'

'Oh, I see, you're one of them, are you? Have you ever met any Yanks?' she challenged Diane.

'As a matter of fact, yes I have,' Diane told her coolly. It didn't do to give away information, even to a colleague in uniform, so she wasn't going to tell Myra that she had been based in Cambridgeshire and so had had any amount of opportunity to observe 'Yanks'.

'Oh, hoity-toity now, is it!' Myra mocked her. 'Well, you can do as you please because *I* certainly intend to, and when it comes to a handsome chap wanting to take me dancing and offering me nylons and other little treats, I know where my loyalty is going to lie, and that is to meself! You can disapprove all you like,' she added determinedly. 'I've had enough of this ruddy war, and I want to have a bit of a good time whilst I still can. If you had any sense you'd do the same. After all, what have you got to lose? Anyway, I'm going now. I'm on duty at eight.' She pulled on her jacket and crammed her cap down onto her curls, then headed for the door.

Diane watched her go, relieved but feeling sorry that they had not got off to a better start. How many weeks of Myra's carping could she stand?

When she reached the door, Myra stopped and turned round. 'Look, there's no sense in you and me not getting on,' she announced, making Diane warm to her more. 'There's a dance on at the Grafton Ballroom Saturday night. It's the best ballroom in Liverpool and they have some smashing bands playing there. Why don't you come along with me and see for yourself how much fun you can have?'

Diane was about to refuse when Myra added perceptively, 'If this chap of yours has broken things off, then there's no sense in coming here and moping about, if you want my opinion. What you should do is show him what you're made of and have a darn good time. That's certainly what I'd do. There's no point looking back over your shoulder for a chap who doesn't want you when there's plenty around who would.'

'What makes you think that he was the one who broke the engagement?' Diane demanded, her pride stung by Myra's caustic words. 'As a matter of fact, having a good time is exactly what I do intend to do,' she added nonchalantly.

'Good. You'll be on for the dance, then?'

'Of course.' The acceptance was out of her mouth before Diane could summon the good sense to refuse.

'Wait until you see them Yanks. You won't be moping over your chap then, I can tell you, not if you've any sense,' Myra told her enthusiastically as she opened the door.

'I'm not moping...' Diane began but it was too late, Myra had gone, clattering down the stairs.

Half an hour later, having thanked Mrs Lawson for her cup of tea and the Spam sandwiches she had made her, Diane dutifully listened whilst her landlady went through her house rules.

'You'll be well fed, or as good as I can manage,' Mrs Lawson assured her. 'All the chaps round here have allotments and, knowing I'm widowed and that I'm doing me bit having you girls here, they mek sure that I get me fresh veggies and fruit. Mind you, you'll get some of your meals at the Derby House canteen, as well, so you won't be going without.' She gave a small sniff that wasn't quite a criticism, but Diane took the hint.

'If there's anything going spare, I'll make sure I bring it back with me, Mrs Lawson.'

She was rewarded with an approving smile.

'You're a sensible type, I can see that,' the landlady told her. 'Now, I'll give you a key, 'cos I know you'll be working shifts. I'm off out in a few minutes, once I've washed up, as it's me WVS meeting night.'

'I'll give you a hand with the washing-up, shall I?' Diane offered dutifully, earning herself another approving smile. She realised she would have to adapt so that she could get on well with both Mrs Lawson and Myra Stone if she was going to cope with life at number 24.

TWO

Left to her own devices, Diane decided that she might as well explore her new surroundings rather than stay cooped up in the room she was sharing with Myra.

She changed out of her uniform, taking care to hang it up neatly, before unpinning her hair. The trouble with being a natural blonde was that there were so many unnatural blondes around who had taken the maxim that blondes have more fun so enthusiastically to heart that one was judged automatically as being the same. It was part of the reason why she preferred to wear her hair up instead of down. But only part, Diane admitted. The other part was the fact that Kit had loved to smooth her hair back off her face and run his fingers through it, and now she just couldn't bear to look in the mirror and see it falling softly down onto her shoulders. It was horrid to love someone so much when they no longer loved you back. Diane had never imagined she would feel like this. She had grown up in a happy loving environment, with parents married nearly thirty years now, and from the moment Kit had proposed to her she had simply accepted that he loved her and that he always would do.

She wasn't to think about him any more, she reminded herself fiercely. He wasn't worthy of her tears or her thoughts, and she had had a lucky escape. Better to have found out now what he was really like...

She had said these words to herself so often these last few weeks that they had become a litany that ran ceaselessly through her head. It had been very hard to maintain the pretence of their deciding on a mutual end to their engagement in front of her colleagues, especially those young women who, like her, had RAF boyfriends and with whom she and Kit had often socialised.

Not letting the side down had become not letting herself down, just as keeping a stiff upper lip in the face of the hardships of war had become making sure that she didn't let others see how she really felt.

It wasn't unknown for engagements to be broken, and though the ending of hers had been greeted with a few raised eyebrows, the camp was a large one and everyone there knew young women who had lost fiancés and husbands to the war, and who because of that were far more deserving of sympathy than Diane.

Out of Kit's squadron only just over half of the original young pilots were still flying. One of Kit's closest pals in the squadron had been shot down and killed, leaving a distraught young widow, so distraught in fact that she had tried to take her own life. Diane shivered, remembering poor little Amy. But it didn't do to dwell on such things – the war taught everyone that. Amongst those pilots who weren't flying were the dead, the injured and those who were presumed to be prisoners of war. Diane gave another shiver. She must not think about that now, nor about the nights she had lain awake, wondering if Kit would make it back safely. That life was over now. This was meant to be a fresh start for her here in Liverpool, where no one knew her or her history.

She looked down at her left hand and her bare ring finger. When Kit had broken their engagement she had taken off her ring and handed it back to him. He had shrugged dismissively, telling her that she might as well keep it, plainly unconcerned about either it or her any more. The following weekend, having given in to a friend's suggestion that she join them at a dance, she had had the heart-stopping experience of seeing Kit dancing with another girl, holding her close as he crooned in her ear. But she couldn't think about that again. The familiar pain was building up. She must not let it take hold of her. And she would not. Girls like Myra, with her cynical determination to make the most of the opportunities the war offered, had a far better time of it than girls like her, and if she had any sense she would model herself on Myra and have a good time herself. What, after all, had she got to lose now that she had lost Kit? He plainly was enjoying himself without her, and now that she had no heart left to break she would not be in any danger of having hers broken a second time, would she? It was all very well being good and loyal, and loving one man and one alone, but when that man said he didn't want you any more where did that leave you? Diane took a deep breath. After all, hadn't she already told herself that from now on things were going to be different and that she herself was going to be different? Sharing with someone like

Myra was going to make it easy for her to keep that promise to herself. From now on she was going to go out and dance and laugh, and take all the fun that life was prepared to offer her. She reached up and tugged the pins out of her hair...

Ten minutes later, freshly dressed in 'mufti', as those in the forces referred to their non-uniform clothes, she let herself out of the house.

She might as well walk back into the city and find out the best way to reach Derby House, she decided when she had walked as far as Edge Hill Road. It was a light evening with a pleasant breeze, and she set off briskly in the direction she had come earlier.

The bombed buildings looked no less shocking this time than they had done earlier. Instinctively she wanted to look away. People had lived in those houses and worked in those buildings. Where were they now? Rehoused safely somewhere else, or had their lives been destroyed along with their homes, Diane wondered sadly, standing uncertainly at the crossroads she had come to and wondering which way she should take.

'Summat up, is there, lass?' a woman with a chirpy Liverpudlian accent asked her.

'I'm just trying to get my bearings,' Diane told her. 'I've only just arrived...'

'Aye, well, with that blonde hair of yours you'd better take care no one mistakes you for a German spy,' the woman told her forthrightly. 'I don't hold wi' bleaching, I don't...'

Diane forced herself to smile, rather than correct her.

'So what is it yer looking for then? If it's them

Yanks, yer won't have to go far; they'll find you soon enough. Not that I'd let any daughters of mine tek up wi' one, not for all the fags and nylons in the world,' the woman avowed firmly.

'Actually, I was trying to make my way to Derby House,' Diane told her.

'Derby House, is it? Got business there, have yer?'

Diane had had enough. Out of the corner of her eye she could see a policeman walking towards her. Excusing herself, she hurried over to him, asking him determinedly, 'I wonder if you could point me in the right direction for Derby House. I'm in the WAAF and I'm on duty there tomorrow.'

'Got your papers with you, have you?' he asked her.

Diane dutifully produced her identity documents for him to see.

'Come with me. I'll show you the way,' he told her once he had studied them and handed them back to her.

Derby House turned out to be a disappointingly dull-looking new office block behind the town hall, but as Diane had learned from her briefing before leaving Cambridgeshire, the government knew that Hitler would seek to target the place that was the headquarters of the Western Approaches Command, so they had protected the real heart of the operation by building it underground.

The policeman had returned to his duties, leaving Diane to study the building on her own. Liverpool was so very different from the airfield where she had worked before, but then her whole life was going to be different from now on, without Kit and their plans for the future. A huge lump formed in her throat as desolation swept over her. She forced herself to swallow back the threatening emotions. There was no point feeling sorry for herself. She had to meet this head on and stiffen her spine against her own weakness. After all, she had asked for her transfer so that she could have a fresh start away from people who had known her and Kit, away from the whispered conversations and sidelong looks to which she had become so sensitive.

She took a deep breath and straightened her shoulders. On the other side of the road she could see and hear a group of girls giggling as they linked arms. Diane watched them, envying their happiness as they strolled out of sight.

And then, just as she was about to cross the road and make her way back to her billet, out of nowhere – or so it seemed – an army Jeep filled with American soldiers came roaring down the road.

'Hey, guys,' Diane heard one of them, who was hanging out of the window, yell, 'I see dames...'

The girls Diane had been watching made their escape, breaking ranks to run off up an alleyway, laughing and squealing, whilst the Jeep skidded to a halt, then did an abrupt U-turn. Immediately Diane stepped back into the shadows. She had seen enough of the kind of high-spirited behaviour indulged in by young servicemen desperate for female company in their off-duty hours, and did not want to draw attention to herself. But it was too late: they had seen her and, deprived of their original prey, the driver of the Jeep pulled it up across the pavement, blocking off Diane's exit.

'Hey, pretty girl, how about we have some fun together?' one of the men called out to her. 'We got nylons, we got chocolate, we got gum...'

'Yeah, and we got jackass hard ons like you've never seen...'

Somehow Diane managed to stop herself from going bright red as she heard the explicit description yelled out by one of the other men.

'Hey, Polanski, leave it out, will ya?' another voice joined in, before its owner urged Diane, 'Come on, blondie, we could have a good time together. What d'ya say?'

Things were threatening to get out of hand, Diane recognised. She could smell the alcohol on their breath from where she was standing, and she was now alone in the street with them.

She forced herself to remain calm as she said as firmly as she could, 'I say that you boys are going to get in big trouble if your military police find you in this state.'

'Hey, will ya listen to that?' another of the men drawled admiringly. 'A ballsy dame. I like that...'

'But not as much as you'd like it if it was your balls she was playing with, eh, Dwight?' another man laughed.

Whilst it wasn't true to say that she was scared, Diane knew she was feeling apprehensive. She was a sensible young woman who had no intention of reacting in the kind of silly way that would cause the situation to escalate but she was also aware that she was out of uniform and thus could not command the same kind of respect wearing it would have gained her. She decided she had to get away from these men.

'If you'll excuse me...' she told them, stepping forward so that she could skirt past them.

But they wouldn't let her go, and to her shock one of them jumped down from the Jeep and started to walk towards her.

Now she *was* scared, Diane admitted as another GI jumped down onto the road.

'Come on, sweet stuff,' the first one coaxed. 'All we want is a bit of fun. We won't hurt you, will we, guys?' As he spoke he was reaching out to grab hold of her arm.

It was foolish to panic, Diane knew, but she couldn't help it. Backing off from them, her voice high-pitched with tension, she demanded, 'Stop this and let me go.'

'Sure we'll let you go, honey, once we've had our fun...'

She could hear them laughing as they started to crowd her, her fear giving them the power to be more insolent. Anger and shocked disbelief fought for supremacy inside her. This could not be happening. Not in broad daylight in the middle of the city.

'Come on, blondie. You'll enjoy it...'

'What the hell's going on here?' The authoritative voice of the uniformed officer who had suddenly appeared out of nowhere acted on them like a physical barrage, making them fall back and suddenly look more like scared boys than young men.

'Sorry, Major...'

'Gee, Major...'

Muttering apologies and excuses, the men piled back into the Jeep, leaving Diane facing the tall, broad-shouldered and obviously furious officer.

'Now, I don't know who you are, but if you'll take my advice, you'll think yourself lucky that I came by when I did, and maybe next time you'll think twice about encouraging my men to–'

Diane's self-control snapped. 'Encouraging them? I'll have you know, *Major*, that I was doing no such thing. *Your* men were behaving in a way that would have got them court-martialled had they been British,' Diane told him bitingly.

'You must have encouraged them–'

'I did no such thing! Their behaviour was inexcusable and it's no wonder that parents are telling their daughters to keep away from Americans. Your men were behaving more like some kind of occupying force than allies.' Diane had the bit between her teeth now and all the bitterness and misery of the last few weeks, as well as the fright she had had, were fuelling her fury.

The major was equally incensed. He took a step towards her, and Diane had a momentary impression of reined-in temper and sheer male physical strength as he towered over her. His hair was thick and very dark, and his eyes, she noticed, were a brilliantly intense shade of blue.

He could quite easily have been a film star, and the uniform he was wearing, so much smarter than the uniforms of the British forces, only served to add to that impression. For some reason that infuriated Diane almost as much as his accusations had done.

41

'My men—'

'Your men behaved like wild animals and you should be ashamed of them, not defending them. All I was doing was simply standing here.'

'Oh, yeah? Then you can't blame them for thinking you were waiting for business, can you?'

It took several seconds for his meaning to sink in through her anger, but once it had she drew herself up to her full height and told him icily, 'I suppose I shouldn't be shocked in view of the behaviour of your men, but somehow I am. You see, in *this* country, Major, we expect our officers to know better. Now if you'll excuse me I need to return to my billet. I'm on duty at eight, and by on duty,' she told him pointedly, 'I mean that I shall be serving my country – in uniform, just so there isn't any misunderstanding.'

Diane had the satisfaction of seeing the slow burn of colour creeping up under his skin.

'OK, my boys may have made a mistake—' he began grudgingly.

'There was no "may" about it, Major. Perhaps you should invite them to tell you about the group of girls they were pursuing and lost when they charged down here in their Jeep – or maybe that's acceptable behaviour for American servicemen?'

Without giving him the opportunity to respond, Diane stepped past him, keeping her head held high as she virtually marched up the street, away from him. Outwardly she might look fully in control but inwardly she was quaking in her shoes, she admitted, as she refused to give in to the temptation to turn round and see if he was watching her. It made her feel physically sick to think of what could have happened to her if he hadn't turned up when he had, and it made her feel even more nauseous to recognise what he had thought of her and how he had condemned her without bothering to check his facts. She knew that there was already a lot of antagonism in some quarters towards the American soldiers who had arrived in the country, but until now she had felt that they were being treated a bit unfairly. Feeling superior because they had better uniforms and equipment was one thing, but behaving as they had towards her was something else again, Diane decided angrily. Did they really think they were so important that they could get away with treating decent British women like that? By the time she had reached Edge Hill Road, she had walked off some of her temper and was feeling calmer, but it wasn't until she had closed the door of her bedroom behind her and dropped down onto her narrow bed that she realised how shaky the incident had left her feeling.

'Oh, Kit,' she whispered, wishing he could take her in his arms and comfort her. But it was no use crying for her ex-fiancé. He had made it plain that she meant nothing to him any more.

THREE

'Come on, girls, we'd better get back to work. We've overrun our break by five minutes as it is.'

'Another few minutes won't do anyone any harm, Janet,' Myra protested. 'I haven't finished my ciggy yet.'

'Huh, you're lucky to have any ciggies to finish,' sniffed the third Waaf gathered round the canteen table in the Navy, Army, and Air Force Institute – or the Naafi as all the canteen facilities provided for the armed forces were affectionately nicknamed. 'I suppose you've been cadging some off them Yanks again, have you? I saw you talking to that handsome corporal earlier on.'

'He's only a bit of a kid and he looked half scared to death,' Janet Warner, the most senior member of their small group, said drily, adding under her breath, 'Watch out – here comes Sergeant Riley.'

'What's this then, a mothers' meeting? Haven't you lot got any work to do?'

There was a sudden clatter and the scrape of chairs being pushed back as all the girls apart from Myra reacted to the sharp voice and hurried to the exit.

'We're just on our way, Sarge,' Janet assured the thickset, sharp-eyed RAF sergeant who was surveying them before turning away to head for the counter.

'Come on, Myra,' Janet urged in a hissed whis-

44

per from the doorway as Myra took her time crushing out her cigarette before starting to stroll insolently towards her friends. 'Sometimes I think you go out of your way to wind up Sergeant Riley I really do,' Janet muttered crossly.

'It gets on my nerves the way he throws his weight around and thinks he can tell us what to do.'

'He's a sergeant, Myra; he doesn't "think" he can tell us what to do, he knows he can.'

'Stone, over here.'

Myra hesitated just long enough to make the anxiety sharpen further in Janet's eyes and to have the satisfaction of seeing the red tide of anger starting to burn up the sergeant's face, before obeying his summons.

'It's your kind that give women in the services a bad name,' he told her when she eventually reached him. 'And if I had my way—'

'But you don't, do you, Sarge?' Myra taunted him. 'Have your way, I mean. We all heard about that little Wren turning you down. Shame. She's dating an American now, I hear. And who can blame her? Good-looking lot, they are, and generous.'

'You've got a husband who's away fighting for his country.'

'So I have.'

'It hasn't gone unnoticed that you've been carrying on like you are single.'

'Hasn't it?' Myra gave a shrug. 'So what?'

'You ought to be ruddy well ashamed of yourself.'

'Jealous, are you, Sarge, 'cos other people are

45

having a good time and you aren't? Well, I'll tell you something, shall I? I don't blame your little Wren for turning you down in favour of her Yank, not one little bit. In her shoes, I'd have done the same.'

'Sarge, your tea's going cold,' the Naafi manageress called out.

The sergeant turned his head, giving Myra the opportunity to escape.

She and the sergeant had clashed from the moment they had set eyes on one another. He reminded her in many ways of her father. A small shadow darkened Myra's eyes. How her mother had stuck him for so many years Myra didn't know. Part of the reason she had married so quickly had been to escape her home. She hadn't known then, of course, that her father would have a seizure in the middle of one of his furious outbursts of temper and die three months after the wedding.

Men! Once you let them get the upper hand they thought they could treat you how they liked. That was why she was determined that no man would ever control her life the way her father had controlled her mother's and had tried to control hers. She wished passionately now that she had not been stupid enough to get married and land herself with a husband hanging around her neck and thinking he could tell her what to do. Well, he could write as many letters as he liked telling her he did not want her going out whilst he was away. They weren't going to stop her doing a single thing that she wanted to do.

46

FOUR

Ruthie tensed as she opened the front door, her shoes gripped tightly in her free hand as she glanced fearfully over her shoulder into the blackout-shrouded darkness of the silent house, terrified of making the slightest sound that might wake her sleeping mother. If that happened ... but no, she mustn't think about that.

Once she was safely outside in the cold dawn air she slipped on her pair of Mary Jane shoes, polished over and over again to make them last as long as they could. It was summer now, but in the winter, wet shoes had to be stuffed with paper and left to dry out, not always successfully. Mothers did their best, warming their children's thick hand-knitted socks on fire guards in an attempt to send them to school with warm dry feet, whilst young women submitted to the sensible habit of wearing thick lisle stockings, even though they itched dreadfully...

All Ruthie had to do now was make sure she reached the appointed place in time.

Her mother would never forgive her for this; she would tell her truthfully how shocked and upset her father would have been.

Her father! Ruthie paused outside the gate of the neat red-brick semi, not daring to risk putting the gate on the latch just in case the noise might alert her mother to her departure. It hurt so much to think about the way Dad had died, crushed beneath the masonry blown apart by the German bomb that had devastated the Durning Road Technical College in the autumn of 1940. He had been on duty there as an air-raid warden. Her mother, Ruthie knew, would never recover from his loss; it hung over the small house like the pall of smoke and dust that had hung over the destroyed college. When the news had come her mother had insisted on them going down there, even though she had been advised not to do so. The rescue work had still been going on when they had arrived – what could be salvaged of once living, breathing human beings, tenderly and respectfully brought out of the carnage. Ruthie knew she would never forget what she had seen that night: a human hand and wrist – thankfully not her father's – the watch on it still going, a baby's rattle, a woman's torso, images too horrible for her to want to recall.

Ruthie had reached the Edge Hill Road now and she continued down into the area of terraced streets that lay below it, once filled with people's homes but now ravaged by Hitler's bombers' assault on the city during the first week of May 1941, when Liverpool had endured a week-long blitz that had destroyed hundreds of buildings and killed so many people.

Had she come to the right place? She wasn't sure and she started to fret, her hazel eyes darkening with anxiety as she pushed a nervous hand into her soft mousy brown hair. How long would she have to wait? She stared into the half-light, her heart thudding. She still couldn't believe she

48

was actually doing this. Her mother would be so shocked and so unforgiving. She could almost see the sad, gentle look her father would have given her if he knew.

She could hear the sound of a bus coming up the road towards her. Automatically she stiffened. She flagged down the driver and it pulled to a halt.

'Is this the bus for the munitions factory?' she asked anxiously as she stepped onto it.

The interior of the bus was packed with women, and one of them called up sarcastically, 'Course it bloody is. What does it look like – a ruddy chara trip to Blackpool?'

Ruthie blushed bright red as the women burst out laughing. A pretty redhead with a mass of curls and smiling eyes looked Ruthie over and then said determinedly, 'Give over, Mel. The poor kid looks half scared to death. Just starting, are you, love?' she asked Ruthie, making room for her on the seat next to her.

Ruthie nodded, feeling tongue-tied and uncomfortable.

A lot of people said that it was only the poorer sort of women who signed on to work at the munitions factory at Kirby, and Ruthie suspected from the coarse language and dress of those on the bus that it was probably true. But she needed a job, and not just because now that she was nineteen it was compulsory for her to do war work. She and her mother needed the money, and she had heard that the munitions factory paid good wages, even to unskilled, untrained workers like her.

'I must be daft in me head tekin' on a ruddy job

49

like this,' the woman who had mocked Ruthie grumbled. 'Up at four and working ruddy long shifts, and tekin' me life into my hands every day.'

'Come on, Mel, it isn't as bad as that,' the redhead that had offered Ruthie a seat objected. 'The wages are good, and then there's them concerts that the management put on for us, and these buses...'

'Oh, trust you to say that, Jess Hunt. A right little ray of ruddy sunshine, you are. What about the danger then? There was that girl last week had all of her fingers blown off, she did. You could hear her screaming three sheds away,' Mel announced with relish, whilst Ruthie sucked in her breath and fought back the nausea cramping her stomach.

It had been three days before they had found her father in all the rubble. Her mother had been too distraught to identify his body so Ruthie had had to do it. There hadn't been a mark on his face – he looked like he was asleep – but where his feet should have been there had been nothing. Ruthie's had been a innocent childhood, her parents loving and protective, but that single act of identifying her father's body had stripped that innocence from her.

'So what's your name then,' the redhead asked.

'Ruthie Philpott,' she responded.

'Well, I'm Jess Hunt, and that there is Mel, and sitting next to her there is Leah, and behind her, Emily.'

'Tell you what to expect, did they, when you went up for your interview?' Mel asked.

Ruthie nodded her head.

'Aye, well, it won't be owt like that,' Mel told

50

her sourly. 'A right rough lot some of them as works there are. I know of girls who've had to walk home in their bare feet on account of having their shoes pinched from them bags they give you to put your stuff in. That lot you're wearing won't be there when you go looking for it at the end of your shift,' she warned Ruthie unkindly. 'That's why we allus wear our oldest stuff.'

'I'm sorry, I don't understand,' Ruthie faltered.

'Stop scaring her, Mel,' Jess chipped in. 'It's all right, Ruthie, it's just that when you have to get changed into the coveralls they make you wear, you have to put your own stuff in this bag they give you and then you hang it up on a peg, next to the locker they give you for your purse and that. Most of the time your things are safe enough until you come off shift but there's a few there that aren't as honest as they should be and it has been known for someone to find their bag's empty. That's why we all wear our oldest things.'

Ruthie was too shocked to be able to conceal her feelings.

'Gawd, just look at her face,' Mel said derisively. 'A right know-nothing, this one is and no mistake. Green as grass, she is. You might as well get off the bus now 'cos you won't last a day.' Turning her back on Ruthie she added to one of the other girls in a voice easily loud enough for Ruthie to hear, 'If you ask me they shouldn't be tekin' on folk like her, and time was when they wouldn't have. She's the kind that would have turned up her nose at our kind of work. There's too many of her sort coming wanting jobs in munitions now on account of them having heard

51

that the pay is good.' She gave a derisive sniff. 'Seems to me that whilst her sort thinks they're too good to mix with the likes of us, as soon as there's a sniff of a bit of money to be had they can't wait to change their tune.'

Ruthie tried to pretend she hadn't heard what Mel was saying and to look unaffected by it, but she could see from the quick look Jess was giving her that she hadn't succeeded.

'Come on, Mel, there's a war on, remember,' Jess broke into her complaint. 'We've all got to do our duty.'

'Oh, aye, but I'm not daft, and if you ask me it isn't just doing their duty that's bringing her sort into munitions. Like I just said, she wouldn't be wanting to work wi' the likes of us if it weren't for the good wages.'

Ruthie could feel her face burning with self-consciousness and guilt. It was true that the only reason she had been able to steel herself to apply for a job at the munitions factory was because of the high rate of pay and because it would mean that she didn't have to leave her mother living on her own, like she would have had to do if she had joined the ATS or one of the other women's services. To her relief she realised that the bus was pulling up to the factory gates.

'Come on,' Jess said. 'We all have to get off here.'

A little uncertainly Ruthie followed the other girls towards the small opening in the factory gates. Her instructions were that she was to present herself at the factory as a new worker, but as she watched the women, who all seemed to know

52

exactly what they were doing, streaming towards the gates from the buses, Ruthie began to panic. She had lost sight of the girls she had been on the bus with already, and even though she had only known them half an hour and had not exactly been welcomed amongst them, she would have liked the comfort of their presence. She looked desperately towards the gate, trying to remember what exactly she was supposed to do and where she was supposed to go. Why had she done this? Mel was right: she did not fit in here with these girls, she was an outsider amongst them – and right now she felt sick with nerves and misery. She tensed as she felt a quick tug on her sleeve, remembering Mel's warning and half fearing that her top was going to be torn from her, but when she turned round it was Jess, her eyes crinkled up with a reassuring smile.

'It's bloody bedlam here this morning,' she puffed as she managed to stop them from being parted by the press of girls making for the gate. 'I just came back to tell you that you'll have to tell them on the gate that you're new. There'll be other girls who'll be starting today and they'll keep you back and then get you sorted out. Ta-ra, now, and good luck.' Jess wriggled back through the crowd.

'Wait, please...' Ruthie begged her. There was so much she didn't know, and Jess's jolly manner had been comforting in the alien surroundings of this frightening new world. But it was too late: Jess had already disappeared into the mass of women milling around.

'Here, you. New, are you?' a brisk voice demanded sharply, as a stern-looking woman gave

Ruthie a sharp dig in her arm.

'Yes. Yes, I am,' Ruthie confirmed.

'Name?' the official demanded, making ready to write it down on the clipboard she was holding.

'Ruthie...' Ruthie answered her, flushing when the woman demanded witheringly, 'Ruthie what? Lord save us, my cat's got more nous than this one,' she announced to no one in particular. Some of the other women, waiting by the gate, laughed.

'Ruthie Philpott.'

'Right. Next...?'

'OK, are you? Only I heard her over there mekin' fun of you, when we was waiting to be let in.'

Ruthie blinked away the tears that were threatening, to focus on the young woman who had just addressed her. She was a well-built girl with small pale eyes, and a sharp glance that seemed to be looking everywhere but directly at her, as though she was looking around for someone or something more interesting, but Ruthie was too grateful for her kindness to be critical.

'Not giving her my surname was such a stupid thing to do.'

'Aye, well, we all do daft stuff at times and anyone can see that you're a bit out of yer depth, like. Couldn't get into any of the services, like, could yer not? Same here. Tried for the ATS, I did, but they wouldn't have me on account of me having flat feet.'

'I needed work that would let me stay at home. It's my mother, you see,' Ruthie heard herself explaining.

54

'Wanted yer to tip up at home and give her wot you was earning, did she? My mam's like that, an' all. Seems to me like you and me 'ave got summat in common and we should stick together.' She gave a disparaging sniff. 'There's some right common sorts working here. Thieving and Lord knows what goes on, so I've heard.'

Ruthie could only nod her head. She wasn't used to having her friendship courted. Suddenly her new life didn't seem as threatening as it had done. 'I'd like that,' she offered shyly.

'Aye, well, my name's Maureen, Maureen Smith.'

'Ruthie...' Ruthie began, but Maureen snickered and shook her head.

'Aye, I know I heard you telling it to her wot's in charge, didn't I? Live on Chestnut Close, you told her. So where's that when it's at home?'

'It's between Edge Hill and Wavertree.'

'Oh ho, you'll be a bit posh then, will yer, living up there?'

'No, of course not,' Ruthie denied. There was something about the way Maureen was looking at her that made her feel slightly uncomfortable.

'Course you are. Anyone can tell just by looking at yer. Them nice clothes you're wearing. Got much family, 'ave yer?'

'No. It's just me and my mother.'

'Well, you're the lucky one then and no mistake. Our house is that full wi' me mam and da, and me and me sisters, two of them with kiddies of their own, living in it, a person doesn't have room to breathe. I'm going to be looking for a new billet just as soon as I've got a bit of money together from working here.'

'Right you lot, this way...'

'Let them others go first,' Maureen advised Ruthie with a warning nudge as she prepared to obey the overseer's command. 'Then we can tag on at the end, like. It don't do to get yerself too much noticed by them wot's in charge. Yer don't want ter seem too eager.'

Ruthie allowed her new friend to take the lead. She gulped as she took her first step into her new world, wondering what on earth she had let herself in for. Far from being exciting, right now this new life of hers threatened to be alien and frightening.

FIVE

Her presence on the streets of Liverpool was certainly being treated with a good deal more respect this morning than it had been last night, Diane admitted, as she walked briskly past the town hall, heading for Derby House. No doubt the fact that she was wearing her uniform had something to do with that. It was a sunny morning but cool enough for her not to feel uncomfortable in her tailored skirt and jacket. Her hair was rolled into a neat French pleat and, unlike some of the girls she knew, she was wearing her cap at the correct angle and not some jaunty and flirtatious version designed to attract male attention.

As she reached the building, the night shift was

just coming out, their faces stiff and pallid from the long hours of concentration.

'Keen, aren't you? The next shift doesn't start for another half-hour yet.'

Diane stopped in mid-step when she realised that the question had come from Myra, who was leaning back against the wall of the building, lighting up a cigarette.

'Yes. I thought I'd get here a bit earlier, just to be on the safe side. I've got to report to a Group Captain Barker.'

'Nanny Barker. She's OK but a bit of a fusspot. You'll have to watch out for her sidekick, though, Warrant Officer Whiteley – hates good-looking girls, she does.' Myra pulled a face. 'She's got a real down on me.' She stifled a yawn. 'I'm for my bed. I've got a hot date with a GI this afternoon. He's taking me to a matinée. He should be good for a box of nylons if I play my cards right.'

Diane smiled noncommittally.

'I could fix us up with a double date for later in the week, if you fancy it?'

'No, thanks.' Diane refused, adding when she saw Myra's expression begin to darken, 'I'm up for going dancing and having a bit of fun, but I don't plan to date.'

'Well, it's your loss,' Myra shrugged. 'And it means more men for me!'

'Glad to have you on board, Wilson. Know much about our ops here, do you?'

'Nanny Barker' had turned out to be a sturdy-looking woman in her early forties, with a hearty no-nonsense manner. Without waiting for Diane

57

to reply she continued, 'According to your previous CO, you're a quick learner, so I'm going to put you on one of the new teams we've set up. I'll show you round first and explain to you what we're doing.

'In January of this year Captain Gilbert Roberts established the Western Approaches Tactical Unit here. It's based officially on the top floor of the Exchange Building, which is close to here. Captain Roberts and his team study U-boat tactics and then develop effective countermeasures. The unit runs six-day training courses for Allied naval officers to help them improve the tactics they use in their escort groups.

'Over here in Derby House the Senior Service and the RAF work together on joint Atlantic ops along with some of our American allies to protect the convoys crossing the Atlantic. Senior Service has overall control, but we have an important part to play. It's our RAF reconnaissance planes that provide vital forward information – as a Waaf you'll be involved in working on that info. Follow me,' Group Captain Barker instructed Diane, leading the way to a flight of stairs.

'Down here is the nerve centre of the ops. It's bomb- and gas-proof,' she told Diane with evident pride as she led her down to what Diane guessed must be a large basement area. 'We've got all the regulation emergency areas, just in case – dorms, ablutions, the Commander-in-Chief's private quarters, in addition to the telecommunications room, and a couple of off-duty areas.' She paused to return the salute of a pair of naval ratings on guard duty in front of a large door.

'You won't be permitted to come down here without your pass, so don't forget to carry it with you whenever you are on duty,' she warned Diane as the guards opened the doors for them.

Diane had, of course, seen operations rooms before and was familiar with their set-up, but the sheer size of this one took her aback. A huge map of the North Atlantic dominated one wall, whilst filling the centre of the room was a massive table holding an enormous situation map. Around it Wrens were busily moving models of the various convoys to show their deployment. There must have been nearly fifty Wrens working in the room, as well as a good-size bunch of Waafs, Diane calculated as she watched them for a few seconds before switching her attention to the wall bearing a map of the waters around Britain. More Wrens were perched on ladders, updating the maps and the reports chalked on large blackboards.

'Over there is the Aircraft State Board,' the Group Captain told Diane, nodding to the rear of the room, where a board showed the readiness of all the RAF stations displayed, as well as up-to-the-minute information about on-going air operations, brought in from the teleprinter rooms close at hand. There was also a weather board, and the noise from the different orders being called out was so deafening that at first it made Diane wince. It would take some concentration to learn to listen only to her own instructions and blot out the rest, she acknowledged, as she watched the control room's busyness.

'We've just lost a couple of our ops room operatives, so you'll be working down here to start with, instead of going into the teleprinter communications room, which is where we usually put the new girls to start off with. Normally we don't put girls down here until we've had time to assess them, but since the powers that be have seen fit to poach some of our best girls we don't have much option. I'm prepared to take a chance on you.'

Diane tried to look suitably gratified, but the truth was that she was feeling slightly intimidated by the activity of the ops room and would have welcomed a more gradual introduction to it.

'One of your duties will be to show our training groups how the system works. We're getting a lot of American service personnel coming along to see how we do things here at the moment. Any questions?'

'No, ma'am.'

'Good-oh. I'll hand you over to Corporal Bennett, then. She's in charge of the team you're going to be on.'

To Diane's relief the young woman the captain introduced her to looked a sensible sort, around her own age, Diane guessed, although the light in 'the Dungeon' – as Myra had informed her the ops room was nicknamed – didn't do her pale skin any favours. She was also, Diane saw with a sharp pang, wearing a gleaming wedding ring. Lucky her. *Her* chap hadn't changed his mind, then.

'Good to have you with us, Wilson,' the other young woman welcomed her after the Group Captain had introduced them. 'Done much of this sort of thing before, have you?'

'No, I'm afraid not, Corporal Bennett,' Diane admitted. 'I was working as a teleprinter before I came here.'

Out of the corner of her eye Diane caught the resigned looks exchanged by the other four girls making up the team of which she was now to be part. Instantly she pulled herself up to her full height and said firmly, 'I'm willing to learn, though.'

'You're going to need a keen eye and be quick off the mark. Men's lives will depend on you. We can't afford any mistakes, not with so much at stake,' Corporal Bennett warned her. 'You'd better partner me so that I can show you what we do and keep an eye on you. I'm Susan, by the way.'

'Diane.'

Diane carefully memorised the names of the other girls on the team as they were introduced to her. Liz, Jean, Pauline and another Susan, this one to be addressed as Sue, she reminded herself as she mentally catalogued them all. Liz was the one with the serious, almost mournful expression and the short dark straight hair. Jean was tall and thin, and rather earnest-looking, with prominent blue eyes, and she was wearing an engagement ring. Pauline was small with brown curls. Sue was also engaged. Diane promised herself that she would remember them all. She sensed that these young women took their work very seriously and that they would be quick to consider her less than able if she couldn't manage to do something as simple as remember their names.

Three hours later, despite her initial reservations, when Susan gave an approving nod of her head and told her crisply, 'You'll do,' Diane felt a real glow of pride. Kit would laugh when she told

61

him... Just in time she caught herself up, the small thrill of her success obliterated. Just for a few minutes she had been so engrossed in what she was doing she had forgotten that her engagement was over, her heart was broken. She instinctively reached for the place on her left hand where she had worn Kit's ring.

'Ooh, look who's just walked in,' she heard Pauline announcing happily in a soft whisper, 'and he's coming over here.'

'Stow it, Pauline,' Susan advised firmly. 'We all know you think a certain American major is the best thing since Clark Gable, but there's a war on, remember.'

'No, I don't. Major Saunders is ten times better-looking than Clark Gable,' Pauline replied, un-abashed. The others laughed. Diane joined in, willing to be a part of the little group, and then turned her head to get a better look at the subject of the conversation. A tall, dark-haired man in the distinctive uniform of the United States Army was striding determinedly towards them, accompanied by a rather youthful-looking RAF flight lieutenant. An unpleasantly *familiar* tall, dark-haired man, Diane acknowledged, her heart sinking as she recognised that the major was the man she had crossed verbal swords with the previous evening. Instinctively she shrank back into the shadows, trying to conceal herself behind the other girls. It was unlikely, surely, that the major would recognise her. She had the advantage over him of having seen him last night in uniform whereas he had only seen her in mufti. However, although she tried to make herself as unnoticeable as possible, Diane could feel the major's sharp-eyed gaze falling and resting on her. Her face started to burn.

It was the flight lieutenant who broke the tension, saying cheerily, 'Thought I'd bring the major across so he can take a look at how we keep tabs on things. Major, you'll–' He broke off as he saw Diane and exclaimed admiringly, 'You've got a new recruit to your team, I see, Susan. Aren't you going to introduce me?'

The major *had* recognised her, Diane realised, as she was subjected to a second and very chilling visual assessment, which, unlike that of the young flight lieutenant, did not contain any scrap of male approval.

'I'm sorry, Flight Lieutenant,' Susan began formally, but to Diane's astonishment the young officer burst out laughing and then said cheerfully, 'Oh, I say, sis, give a chap a chance, won't you, and introduce me to this lovely girl?'

'Wilson, I apologise for my brother,' Susan told Diane ruefully. 'Teddy, I am sure that Diane does not want to have some barely-out-of-short-pants and still-wet-behind-the-ears, just-made-up flight lieutenant pestering her.'

'Oh, I say, that's not fair, is it, Diane? I'm sure you're just the kind of girl who is kind enough to take pity of a poor young officer.'

Blond-haired, with laughing blue eyes and an engaging smile, he was very amusing, Diane acknowledged, and a type she knew very well from Cambridgeshire. Helplessly young and brave, hopelessly full of high spirits and idealism, he couldn't be a day over twenty-one, Diane guessed.

She had seen so many of them, and seen them too after the reality of war had driven the youth from their eyes and replaced it with desperate bleakness. Her own Kit had been one – once.

Susan rolled her eyes. 'Diane, once again, I do apologise for my ridiculous little brother.'

Diane laughed and shook her head, exchanging an understanding look with Susan. 'I know all about younger brothers from my time in my previous posting,' she assured her, deliberately not naming her previous post, in accordance with wartime regulations. As the posters had it, 'Careless Talk Costs Lives.' Not, she suspected, that there were likely to be any German spies here.

'You promised the folks you'd take care of me and here you are refusing to introduce me to the most stunning girl I've ever seen.'

'What happened to that redheaded Wren you were raving about last week?' Susan teased him, relaxing when she saw that Diane was neither going to take offence nor read anything into his flattery.

'What Wren?' he demanded, looking injured.

'I don't want to break up the party, *Flight Lieutenant,* but if you don't mind...' The major's voice had a hard edge to it for all the softness of his American accent. Susan looked uncomfortable and her brother crestfallen, whilst Diane was con-scious of the condemning look the major was giving her. Well, let him think what he liked. She didn't care. She knew the truth about herself. Diane lifted her chin and returned his look with one of her own – the kind she used to make it plain to overeager young men that she

64

was not interested.

To her satisfaction she could see first disbelief, then incredulity followed by anger in the major's eyes. That would teach him to look down on an Englishwoman, she decided sturdily.

'Thanks for letting my wretched brother down lightly, Diane.' They were in the canteen, having their break. Susan offered Diane a cigarette, which she refused. Diane had been horridly sick the first time she had smoked a cigarette – illicitly, of course, behind the church after Sunday school – and she hadn't really smoked very much since apart from the odd social cigarette.

'Bill, my husband, swears that Teddy is a danger to himself. None of us can believe he's actually been made up to flight lieutenant. His CO must see something in him that we can't.'

'Is your husband in the RAF as well?' Diane asked her.

'No, Senior Service. But Dad's an ex-RAF man – that's why Teddy and I joined up. Bill's posted to convoy duty. It doesn't always do to be working so closely. I'm always on edge when his convoy is due back. The two girls we're missing at the moment both had husbands in the navy. They were on the same ship – we were all here when we got the news that she'd been torpedoed. The girls kept on going until the end of their shift, even though they knew what had happened. It broke them, though. One asked for a transfer, the other...' Susan sighed. 'She was expecting their first baby. She lost it three days after we heard the news that he'd been killed. I hate this war so much sometimes.'

There was a small pause – the kind Diane was familiar with – during which one mentally paid silent respect to those comrades lost, and then Susan rallied, saying determinedly, 'That's enough about me. What about you?'

'Oh, there's nothing to tell. I'm single and fancy-free, and that's the way I intend to stay,' Diane told her lightly. And meant it.

Myra took a sip of her drink and then leaned back in her seat, pretending to be absorbed in studying her fingernails.

'Aw, come on, doll, I brought you the nylons, didn't I, and there's plenty more where they came from. You play ball with me and I'll play ball with you, right?'

Myra took her time about lifting her gaze from her nails to the face of the young American seated opposite her. 'Wrong,' she told him, then stood up. They had gone to the matinée, which Myra had sulked through when her date had tried to get fresh with her, and in an effort to 'make it up to her' he had suggested they go on to Lyons' Corner House for something to eat.

A brisk assessing glance round the chandelier-lit room had quickly informed Myra that there were some far better options open to her than remaining with her dull date.

'Hey, where are you going?' he demanded when she started to walk past him.

'To the ladies' room, and then back to my billet. I'm on duty in an hour.' She had to raise her voice to make herself heard above the orchestra. Out of the corner of her eye she saw that a slightly

66

swarthy-complexioned, very handsome GI, who looked both older and more experienced than her present companion, was leaning against the opposite wall, lazily surveying the room and its female occupants. He was, Myra saw, staring straight at her, very meaningfully, making it obvious that he was attracted to her. Not that she was surprised by that. Myra was used to her stunningly voluptuous figure and her dark lush beauty attracting male attention. Men's desire for her normally left her cold. She was not a highly sexed or even a moderately sensual woman. Her childhood had left her with a deep-seated need to be in control within a relationship, rather than be controlled by it. Knowing that a man who had something she wanted desired her gave her a feeling of power. She was bored with the raw young GI seated opposite her. She noted the silver cigarette case the man watching her was using, and his expensive wristwatch. He was American; he had money; he wanted her and he had the confidence to let her know it.

'You can't just walk out on me like that,' her companion was objecting loudly.

'No? Watch me,' Myra told him.

Angrily he made a grab for her, banging into their white-clothed table as he did so, sending some of the cutlery flying.

'Let go of me,' Myra hissed. She hadn't been prepared for this. Bloody Yank. Was he really stupid enough to think that a girl like her would drop her drawers for a box of stockings?

'Having trouble, ma'am?'

The other GI had levered himself away from

67

the wall and was now standing in front of them.

'Your countryman doesn't seem to understand the meaning of the words "get lost",' Myra complained. Her date had released her wrist but she made a play of rubbing it as though it was hurting her a good deal more than it actually was.

'I gave her a whole box of nylons,' he was complaining loudly to the newcomer, 'and now she's making like she doesn't want to know!'

'Like the lady just said, pal – get lost. Unless of course you want I should call in the MPs.'

Cursing under his breath, her date flung some money down on the table and then took himself off.

'Thanks for rescuing me.' Myra batted her eyelashes and gave him a limpid-eyed look.

'My pleasure.' Now he was close up she could see that there was a hardness about this GI, an echo of something she instinctively recognised without having to put a name to it. And he wanted her. She could see that too. He wanted her and if she played her cards right he might be the man who could provide her with what *she* wanted. What a fool she had been to tie herself up to Jim, who could never make her dreams come true, but then she hadn't known that men like this one would be coming into her life. Men who could give her the life she longed for in the country where she longed to live. America. Just thinking the word was enough to make her heart thud with longing and excitement. She gave the young nippy who was inexpertly clearing the table and who had bumped into her a scalding look. Catch her waitressing, Myra thought contemptuously. At least when you were in a services uniform you got a bit of respect.

'Pity you're going on duty. Otherwise I'd have asked you out to dinner,' her new acquaintance was saying.

Myra gave him a slow smile. Did he think she was going to fall over herself with gratitude and drop everything to date him? His sort enjoyed the chase, even if they didn't normally have to do very much of it.

'Oh, well, if you want to see me again, I'll be going dancing at the Grafton this weekend,' she told him airily.

Pity she wasn't already wearing her new nylons, she thought regretfully as she sauntered slowly towards the exit, mimicking the slinky walk she had seen film stars like Vivien Leigh, Rita Hayworth and Greta Garbo using to such good effect. She had better make sure that that new billetee kept to her promise to go dancing with her. Myra wasn't very popular with the other girls, who tended not to include her in their off-duty outings. Not that she cared about that. But she could hardly turn up at the Grafton on her own. She'd wear that sateen halter-neck top that set off her creamy skin and dark hair. Jim had complained that it was cut too low, but so what, she would wear what she wanted now. With a last coy look over her shoulder, she walked out of the tearoom, eagerly anticipating Saturday night.

Ruthie was exhausted. She could feel her head dropping down towards her chest as she sat on the bus. Her nostrils were still full of the now familiar distinctive metallic smell of TNT from

69

the munitions factory. It seemed to cling to her like an invisible extra layer of skin, even though she had changed her clothes. She had found everything so frightening and overwhelming. All the more so when she had discovered she had been posted to work in one of the most dangerous areas of the factory, where shells were filled with liquid TNT. The workers had been given a brisk no-nonsense lecture about the rules and the danger of breaking them. Ruthie had learned that the danger areas were known as 'cleanways' and were subject to strict regulations. She had also learned that everyone working in the TNT sheds was served with a glass of milk and a bun shortly after starting their shift, because the milk put a lining on their stomach that prevented it from being damaged from TNT fumes. Nothing metallic of any kind was allowed anywhere within the cleanways because it could cause the TNT to explode if it came into contact with it, and this included such things as hairpins and even metal rings on shoe lace eyelets. For this reason those girls working in cleanway areas were provided with special leather shoes.

The day had seemed to go on for ever, filled with confusing instructions and experiences. Ruthie had been set to work on a production line filling shells. Initially she had been told to watch the other girls working, and the speed with which they filled the shells had dizzied her. She had felt almost sick with fear at the thought of trying to copy them, knowing that she would be all fingers and thumbs and terrified of arousing the foreman's ire.

When eventually one of the girls had told her

comfortingly, 'Don't worry you'll soon get the hang of it,' she hadn't recognised Jess at first, under her overalls and with her red hair concealed by the protective cap she was wearing.

'Who was that you was talking to?' Maureen had demanded to know when they had finally been told to stop work for their dinner break.

'She was on the bus this morning,' Ruthie had answered her.

'Well, just remember that you're my friend, not hers,' Maureen had told Ruthie sharply.

'Jiggered, are yer, Ruthie?' Jess asked Ruthie sympathetically as the bus made its way slowly along Edge Hill Road. 'It gets everyone like that on their first day.'

Ruthie forced her eyes open, nodding her head. 'I've been trying to memorise the rules they told us this morning,' she said tiredly, repeating, 'No jewellery of any kind but married women can wear their wedding rings so long as they are bandaged up, no hairpins or metal hair adornments, no cigarettes, matches or lighters, and nothing that could ignite or cause an explosion.' She knew she ought to feel more scared about the work she would be doing, only she was far too tired.

'Like milk, I hope, only yer going to be drinking a lot of it. I reckon if I'd knowed in time I could 'ave told them I can't stomach milk. Then they would have put me somewhere else,' Jess told her with a grin.

'I don't mind the milk,' Ruthie admitted, 'but I don't know how you can pack the shells so quickly.'

Jess laughed. 'Oh, you'll soon get the hang of it.

You wasn't too bad at all – better than that girl you was chatting with over dinner. Bit of an odd sort, if you ask me. Know her well, do you?'

'No. She was new today too. She said that we should pal up because we'd both started together on our own.'

'You wasn't on your own, you're with us,' Jess told Ruthie stoutly. 'Look, we all go down the Grafton Ballroom on a Saturday night – why don't you come along with us?'

'Oh, that's very kind of you but I couldn't...'

'Don't be so daft. Of course you can. We meet up outside at about half-past six, then we can get in early and get a decent table. And we allus stick together so that none of them lads start thinking they can get away with any funny business. Having a dance is all right, but that's as far as it goes.'

'Sez you,' one of the other girls chipped in. 'Like you wasn't smooching wi' that soldier the other week.'

'What? Charlie?' Jess tossed her curls. 'I'll have you know that him and me was at school together. Like a brother to me, he is. Gone off to serve abroad, he has now.'

Wide-eyed, Ruthie listened to the talk. She would have loved to have gone to the Grafton. She had never been to a dance hall, but it was impossible for her to go. How could she leave her mother? But she couldn't tell anyone about her mother, of course. It would be disloyal.

Half an hour later, having got off the bus, Ruthie turned the corner from Edge Hill Road into Chestnut Close. She could see the slim figure of a young woman several yards in front of her. Sighing

72

enviously over the smartness of her WAAF uniform, Ruthie realised that she must be one of Mrs Lawson's billetees. Mrs Lawson had complained vociferously at first when she had learned that she was to have service personnel billeted on her, but Mrs Brown, Ruthie's mother's neighbour, had confided to them that Mrs Lawson was doing very nicely indeed out of her billetees.

'It's not just the money – they bring her all sorts of extras from the Naafi canteen, they do.'

Mary Brown was a bit of a gossip but she had a kind heart and Ruthie was grateful to her for the way she tried to cheer up her mother. She was standing in her small front garden when Ruthie walked past, so Ruthie stopped to say hello to her.

'How did it go, Ruthie love?' Mrs Brown asked. 'Only your mam got a bit upset at dinner, like, wondering where you was.'

'Oh dear, I was worried that something like that would happen. I've bin explaining to her all week about all women between the ages of twenty and thirty being called up by the government to do war work, and that with me coming up for me twentieth birthday I needed to get meself a proper war work job so that I could stay at home with her, instead of being sent away to work somewhere or go into uniform, but I could tell last night, when I was talking to her about it again, that she didn't really understand. I thought there'd be ructions. I'm really sorry that you've had to deal with it, Mrs Brown,' she apologised guiltily.

'There, Ruthie lass, there's no need for you to go feeling bad about anything,' Mrs Brown told her firmly. 'You've bin a good daughter to your mam, and I'd have summat to say to anyone who tried to say different. Not that folks round here would do that. They can all see how hard you've had it with your mam since your dad died.'

Ruthie gave her neighbour a grateful look, but she couldn't relax.

'You didn't ... you didn't say anything to Mum about me working on munitions, did you?' she asked hesitantly. 'Only, with Dad dying in the way he did...'

Her neighbour's vigorous shaking of her head stopped Ruthie continuing.

'No, Ruthie, you needn't worry about that. The minute your mam started fretting and asking why you hadn't come back from getting in the rations, I did what you'd said and reminded her that you'd had to go to work because Mr Churchill had said so, but I didn't say nothing about it being in munitions.'

'Oh, thank you. Mum thinks such a lot of Mr Churchill that I was hoping that that would stop her from worrying,' Ruthie admitted. 'It's difficult for her to understand the way things are.'

'No, she's not bin the same since she lost your dad. Took it hard, she has, and no mistake. I've done a bit of bubble and squeak for me own tea and there's plenty left, if you fancy some. It will save you having to cook.'

Ruthie smiled her thanks. All she wanted to do was crawl into her bed. She hadn't realised how tired she was going to feel but she would have to get used to it, she told herself firmly.

'You're a good girl, Ruthie, like I just said, but

you should be having a bit more fun, like other girls do, going out dancing and that,' Mary Brown told her kindly.

'I've been asked out dancing by some of the girls I'm working with,' Ruthie told her quickly, not wanting her to feel sorry for her.

'Well, I'm right pleased about that.'

'I won't be able to go, though,' Ruthie felt bound to point out. 'Mum wouldn't understand and she'd fret.'

'Well, I can go and sit in with her for you, don't you worry about that. It will give us both a bit of company, what with my Joe going off and doing his ARP stuff.'

'Oh, I couldn't ask you to do that, Mrs Brown,' Ruthie protested.

'Who said you was? It's me as is doing the offering, not you doing the asking. And don't you go telling me that you don't want to go. Of course you do – any young girl would. And if yer mam was in her right senses she'd be wanting you to go as well. There's a war on, Ruthie, and you young ones have to have your fun whilst you can, that's what I say. It's different for us; we've had our lives, but you...'

Ruthie shivered as she heard the sadness in their neighbour's voice. It was true that she longed to go out and have fun as she saw other girls doing but she felt that it was her duty to take care of her mother now that her father was dead.

As though she had guessed her thoughts, Mrs Brown said gently, 'It would break your dad's heart if he could see you and your mam now, Ruthie. Thought the world of you, he did, and the last thing he would want is for you to be tied to your mam like she was the little 'un.'

'Mum doesn't understand ... about the war,' Ruthie defended her mother quickly. 'She thinks if I'm not there that I might not come back like ... like Dad.'

'I know, lass. I've heard her crying and calling out when she's having one of her turns. It's just as well sometimes that we don't know what life holds for us. And that's all the more reason why you should do as I'm telling you. The more you molly-coddle your mam, the worse she's going to be when you aren't there. Settles down quite happily wi' me once I've given her a cup of tea wi' drop of Elsie Fowler's special home-made elderberry cordial in it. Calms her down no end.'

Ruthie managed to give their neighbour a brief smile, but the last thing she felt like doing was smiling. Was it her imagination or was her mother getting worse? Was she becoming more and more like a small frightened child who could not understand the workings of the adult world? Some days she could be so much like her old self – the self she had been before Ruthie's father's death, that Ruthie couldn't help but feel her hopes lifting that her mother was returning to full normality, but then something would happen, like Ruthie having to do her bit for the war effort, and her mother's reaction would force her to recognise that her hopes had been in vain.

It was her screaming, sobbing fits of despair that were, for Ruthie, the worst times, when her mother called out again and again for the husband she had lost, like a small child crying for a parent. Ruthie felt so afraid herself sometimes, not just because of the war, but also for the future, after the war. What would become of her mother and herself in that future?

Sometimes Ruthie felt as though that fear was all she was ever going to know of life.

After saying goodbye to Mrs Brown, Ruthie hurried up the front path and unlocked the door. She found her mother sitting in the back parlour, listening to the wireless. The moment she saw her, her mother's face lit up.

'I've missed you,' she said.

Immediately Ruthie went over to her and hugged her lovingly. 'Just let me get my coat off and then I'll put the kettle on, and then we can settle down and listen to the wireless together,' she told her.

'I didn't know where you'd gone.'

Ruthie's hands trembled slightly as she filled the kettle when she heard the almost childlike confusion in her mother's voice.

'I've missed you too, but I had to go to work to help with the war effort,' she told her gently.

'Yes,' her mother agreed. 'Mary Brown told me. She said I should be proud of you, and I am, Ruthie. I'm very proud of you and I know that your dad would have been as well.'

Only now, hearing her mother refer to her father in the past tense, could Ruthie allow herself to relax a little bit.

'Mary Brown said that she knew that I'd be pleased that you'd be working with girls of your own age, with there not being many of them living here on the Close. And I am pleased, Ruthie. Pleased and proud.'

'Oh, Mum,' Ruthie responded, her voice muffled as she left the kettle to go over to her mother and give her another gentle hug.

SIX

'Shift's over, girls, thank goodness. My Bill's back – walked in this morning just as I was walking out.' Susan stifled a yawn. 'Said they'd been waiting out over the other side of Liverpool bar for the pilot boats to bring the convoy in for unloading for nearly five hours, on account of them not letting them into the docks until the early hours just in case the ruddy Luftwaffe takes it in their heads to come over and bomb them.'

'Has he got a decent leave this time, Susan?' Jean asked.

'No such luck. Forty-eight hours, that's all. He should have had more but he's got "new orders".' She paused significantly. All the girls knew better than to ask what those orders might be. All round Derby House notices were pinned up, as they were everywhere throughout the whole country, warning people 'Walls Have Ears' and the like. It was strictly forbidden for there to be talk about troop movements, even between close friends and family. 'But at least he's home and we can have some time together. Have you got any plans for the rest of the weekend, Diane?'

Diane was grateful to Susan for going out of her way to be friendly towards her, and encouraging the others girls to do the same.

'Not really,' she answered her. 'I've promised to go dancing at the Grafton tonight with my fellow billetee.'

'Who's that then?' Jean asked.

'Myra Stone, one of the teleprinters. You may not know her.'

'Everyone knows Myra,' Jean told her drily. 'She's got a bit of a reputation for having a sharp tongue and an even sharper eye for the chaps. You want to be careful about how friendly you get with her, Diane. I don't want to be a gossip but she isn't very well thought of around here. Has she told you that she's married?'

Diane took this as a warning and suppressed a small sigh. She really wished that she hadn't agreed to go out with Myra. She could only spell bad news.

Thank heavens the summer nights, with their extra daylight-saving hours of light, meant that she could walk to and from work every day without having to worry about the blackout, Diane reflected, as she stepped out of the shadow of Derby House and into the warmth of the early evening sunshine. The natural light and fresh air felt wonderful after being underground for so long. Sometimes some of the girls scared one another by coming up with ghoulish stories of what it would be like if the citadel, as it was sometimes nicknamed, was ever bombed and they were trapped inside. Diane didn't join in these conversations. She had her own nighttime horrors to haunt her.

She looked up at the clear sky, remembering how, in the late summer of 1940, the September skies over the south of England had been speckled with squadrons of RAF fighters, the sound of racing engines all too quickly interspersed with the stomach-churning rat-a-tat-tat of machine-gun fire as the RAF pilots engaged in fierce battles with the Luftwaffe. It was then, shortly after she had first met Kit, that she had started to have terrible nightmares of a blue sky raining blood and destroyed aircraft. She had witnessed at firsthand the devastation caused by the fierce battle fought overhead in the British skies. Twenty-nine British planes had been lost – a terrible toll of young lives, but nowhere near so terrible as the sixty-one planes lost by the Germans. Diane had seen things then she never wanted to see again: the shattered bodies and white lifeless faces of the young men who only hours before she had seen alive and well, familiar to her and yet horribly unfamiliar in their death. When she had confided her bad dreams to a friend, her friend had told her that nearly every woman who worked at the airfield in a supporting role had her own version of the same kind of nightmare.

In the end the RAF had won the battle for England's skies. Diane knew that the reason that Susan's young brother had been made up to flight lieutenant was probably because of the number of men that had been lost. Kit had been made up to squadron leader in the space of a few short months that summer. She had been so proud of him, but he had told her bitterly that his promotion had come at the cost of the lives of his friends and comrades.

'Diane, do you mind if I have a word with you?'

Diane swung round at the sound of Susan's voice, glad to be brought out of her sombre reverie.

'Of course not.'

'I don't want to be a spoilsport, but if I were you I really wouldn't get too involved with Myra Stone. It's bad enough that she behaves as though she isn't married, but there was a bit of an incident a while back; a silly young newly married chap who fell for her hook, line and sinker. She'd encouraged him, of course, but his poor little wife was heartbroken. The chap was transferred, and Myra got a ticking-off, but these things leave a bad taste in everyone's mouth and as a result the other girls have tended to give her a bit of a cold shoulder. I appreciate you're in a bit of a difficult position with the two of you sharing a billet, but I thought I ought to let you know the way things are. For your own sake you might want to consider not getting too pally with her.'

'Yes. Thank you.' Diane hesitated. 'I appreciate you telling me. The problem is that I've already agreed to go dancing with her tonight, but if she were to suggest it again...'

'There's nothing you can do about tonight now, I agree, but it's something to bear in mind next time. We're a close-knit bunch in the Dungeon, working as closely as we do, and I don't want members of my team being at odds with one another. You see the thing is, that silly young fool I was telling you about, well, he was Jean's cousin and his wife was her best friend. Jean asked Myra to back off, but she just laughed at her. Anyway, I'd better get on. Bill will be wondering where I am.'

She could now understand why Myra wasn't popular with the other girls, Diane acknowledged as she walked up Edge Hill Road. After tonight she would have to put as much distance between them as she could, otherwise the other girls were going to think she and Myra were two of a kind.

Mrs Lawson was just coming out of the front door as Diane walked up the front path.

'I'm off to my WVS meeting so I've left you a bit of summat keeping warm on top of the oven. Oh, a couple of letters came for you. I've left them on the hall stand.'

'Did Myra mention to you that we're going out tonight?' Diane asked after she had thanked her.

'Yes.' Mrs Lawson's mouth pursed disapprovingly. 'Going dancing, she said you was. It don't seem right to me, not with her married, but she said as how she felt she ought on account of you asking her and you being on your own.'

The sly cat! Diane reflected grimly as she stepped into the hall, picking up her letters from the oak hall stand as she did so. One was from her parents. She recognised her mother's handwriting immediately. The other was from Beryl, a girl who had been one of her closest friends at her previous posting. She had written her name on the back of her envelope.

Pushing wide the kitchen door, Diane started to open her mother's letter, wrinkling her nose at the smell of boiled cabbage emanating from the stove.

'*There* you are. We've got to be ready to go out at seven, you know, otherwise we won't get a table. I reckon you won't get much of a hot bath. Mrs L must have turned off the geyser, mean old bat.'

Diane didn't bother looking up from her letter. If she did have to have a cold bath it would probably be because Myra had used all the hot water, she suspected. Her mother's letter was cheery and loving, wanting to know how she was settling in and when she thought she would have enough leave to come home for a visit. The notepaper was scented with her mother's favourite rose-water scent, and Diane felt a wave of nostalgia sweep over her. How much simpler and safer her life had seemed when she had been a young girl still living at home.

'Gawd, I'm not staying down here. What's that stink?' Myra complained.

'My tea, I expect,' Diane answered, refolding her mother's letter and putting it in her bag before she opened her friend's.

'Can't you leave that until tomorrow?' Myra said irritably. 'You're going to have to rush as it is, unless you're planning on going out in uniform.'

'No ... I'm not ... I'm on my way,' Diane assured her.

Beryl had written that she was missing her, but that she understood why she had felt she had to go.

'To be honest, I think you've done the right thing. I don't want to tell tales out of school, but you might as well know the truth.' Diane gripped the letter tightly. Her stomach had started to churn in anticipation of a blow to come.

Kit isn't the man I thought he was, Di, dropping you to go chasing after one girl after another, and getting them and himself talked about by keeping them out late, driving them all over the countryside. You're better off without him and that's a fact. I've heard that he never dates the same girl twice and it's been all over the camp that, last weekend, he was found rip-roaring drunk in a country pub with a girl he'd picked up from somewhere. The landlord threw them out and threatened to call the police, and it was only because of his pals that Kit managed to get back to camp safely. Seems that someone asked him about you and where you were and he said he neither knew nor cared, and that he wanted to have some fun with the kind of girls who knew what fun was. He's getting himself a reputation for being a real party man, if you know what I mean. You were right to give yourself a fresh start.

Diane closed her fist over the letter, crumpling it up, willing herself not to give way to her emotions in front of Myra. So Kit didn't care about her, did he? Well, she already knew that and she certainly didn't care about him. And when it came to having fun, they would see which of them could do the most of that, she decided fiercely, as she headed for the stairs.

SEVEN

'Do you think I'll be all right going dancing like this, Mrs Brown, only I haven't got anything else?' Ruthie asked uncertainly as she stood in the kitchen waiting for her next-door neighbour's verdict. Her mother was in the parlour listening to the wireless, lost in the world to which she had retreated. Ruthie did not know which she dreaded the most: her mother's blank silences when she hardly seemed to know her, or her tearful clinging pleas not to leave her.

'I don't look right, do I?' she guessed as she saw the uncertainty in the older woman's face as she studied her heavy shoes and ankle socks teamed with the only pretty dress she had, a school-girlish pink gingham cotton with white collar and cuffs.

'Well, you look very nice, love, but p'raps more like you was going to Sunday school than a dance. But there,' she continued hastily when she saw Ruthie's face fall, 'I'm sure it doesn't matter what you wear. They go in all sorts these days, so I've heard – uniforms an' all. You just go and enjoy yourself.'

Ruthie was the last to reach the Grafton, anxiously hurrying down the queue waiting for the doors to open, when a hand suddenly came out and grabbed hold of her.

'Oh!' she exhaled in relief when she realised it belonged to Jess.

'Where've you bin?' Jess scolded her good-naturedly. 'We was just beginning to think you wasn't coming.'

'Well, whatever she was doing, it wasn't worrying about what to wear,' one of the other girls quipped quietly, causing a ripple of laughter to run through those near enough in the queue to hear her. 'Did you tell her it was fancy dress or summat, Jess?'

'Don't take any notice of them,' Jess comforted Ruthie. 'They don't mean any harm. Your frock's a pretty colour. Suits you, it does.'

'I didn't know what to wear. I haven't got...' Tears filled Ruthie's eyes.

'There now, don't go getting yourself all upset. Your frock isn't that bad, and if you had a different pair of shoes and took off them ankle socks and put a bit of rouge and lipstick on...'

'And took them slides out of her hair and undid that plait and tried to look like she were eighteen and not fourteen. They'll never let her in looking like that, Jess,' Mel warned sharply.

'Of course they will. If she's old enough to be working on munitions then I'm bloody sure she's old enough to go dancing,' Jess defended Ruthie stoutly, adding, 'Here, Polly, you always bring a spare pair of shoes wi' you. Hand 'em over here, and let's see if they fit Ruthie.'

'I'm not giving her me best heels,' a pretty blonde girl with large blue eyes protested sulkily.

'Well, give me them you're wearing now and you put the heels on,' was Jess's response, and somehow or other, Ruthie found herself persuaded out of her lace-ups and ankle socks and into a pair of scuffed white sandals.

'Now for your hair. Lucy, you're a dab hand with a comb. Come and see what you can do,' Jess commanded.

There was no use her objecting, Ruthie could see that; a crowd of young women had gathered round her giggling as they enthusiastically offered their advice.

'Anyone got any scissors?' Lucy called out. 'Only if I'm to do a decent job, I'm going to have to cut her hair.'

'I've got a pair,' someone called up. 'Allus tek 'em wi' me when I go out just in case some chap tries to get too fresh.'

'Go on with yer,' another girl laughed. 'What yer going to do wi' 'em – cut it off?'

Ruthie could feel her face getting redder and redder from a combination of trepidation and embarrassment.

'Don't worry,' Jess assured her, giving her hand a small squeeze. 'My, but I bet you never thought this'd be happening to you when you decided to go working on munitions,' she laughed. 'You'd have run a mile if you had, wouldn't you? How come you're still going out dressed like a Sunday school kid, anyway, Ruthie?'

It was impossible to resist her questions or to be offended by them, and somehow or other Ruthie discovered that she was telling her what she had thought she would never be able to tell anyone.

'My dad was killed in the May bombing and ... well, my mother...' She paused, feeling guilty about discussing her mother to someone who was still relatively a stranger, no matter how easy

87

she was to talk to.

'You don't have to talk about it if you don't want.'

'Hold still, will yer?' Lucy was complaining. 'How am I expected to give her a decent style if she keeps moving her head around, Jess? See, that fringe I just give her has gone all lopsided.'

'You'd better get a move on, Lucy; they're opening the doors,' someone further down the queue warned.

Ruthie looked so apprehensive that Jess couldn't help but laugh. She was such an oddity, so obviously not the sort to be working on munitions, that Jess's tender heart had gone out to her the minute she had seen her.

Jess might be an only child but she had grown up surrounded by the busyness of a large extended family. Her mother was one of ten and her dad one of thirteen. The whole family lived close to one another on the same narrow streets off the Edge Hill Road, but nearer to the city centre than Chestnut Close, where Ruthie lived and which was considered to be a 'better' working-class area, because of its proximity to Wavertree. But although there may not have been much money around whilst Jess had been growing up, there had been plenty of love. Her father had been a jolly, good-natured man, always ready for a joke and a laugh. He and his brothers were rag-and-bone men, and he'd been proud of the fact that his patter had housewives favouring him rather than anyone else.

'Got to 'ave the right touch, our Jess,' he had often told her, giving her a saucy wink. 'That's how I managed to steal your mam away from under your Uncle Colin's nose. Mad for her, he was, but it were me she married.'

'Give over, do, Samuel Hunt,' her mother had always chided him. 'Don't you go filling her head with all that nonsense. And as for your Colin – all he ever did was ask me out the once.'

There had always been a lot of banter between her parents, both of them able to give as good as they got, but it had been good-natured, and when her father had fallen ill after he had slipped on an icy street and broken his leg, her mother had become as thin and sick-looking as he.

Jess had been taken away to stay with one of her aunties when the doctor had said that her father was going to die.

'Got poison in that broken leg of his, he has, lass,' her Uncle Tom had told her. 'Can't do nowt about it.'

She had been taken to see him one last time, but he hadn't looked like the dad she remembered, lying there in bed, his face oddly swollen and his breathing harsh.

She had been ten then, and could well remember walking behind the coffin when they went to bury him, and she could remember the wake afterwards as well, when his brothers, her uncles, had got drunk and started telling tales about when they had been lads together.

Her Uncle Colin had never married, and a year and a day after they had buried her dad, Jess's mother had told her that she was going to marry him and that they would be going to live in his house. That was the way things were done in their community, and both sides of their extended family had looked approvingly on the marriage because of the security it gave a widow and her child. But, conscious of the child's feelings both Jess's mother and her new stepfather to be had been at pains to explain that her dad would never be forgotten and that the love all three of them had for him would never die, but would always keep him alive in their hearts.

Her uncle had provided her with as loving a home as her father had done and, as a child, just as her father and his brothers had brought home the flotsam and jetsam of their trade, sifting through it to rescue and nurture the 'treasures' they found, so Jess had learned to rescue her own flotsam and jetsam, normally in the form of some living thing. A singing bird that someone was throwing out because it wouldn't sing, a stray kitten with a piece of string round its neck tied to a brick, a dog with three legs and cross-eyes – whatever it was, it only had to present itself to Jess as unloved and in need for her to take it to her heart and embrace it. There was nothing Jess liked more than bringing a smile to people's faces, and happiness to those who didn't possess it. She had an unerring instinct for those in need of her special touch, and she had recognised Ruthie as one of them the minute she had set eyes on her. Not that Jess analysed things as practically as that. She just knew that something made her feel sorry for Ruthie.

When the other girls took her to task for inviting Ruthie to go out dancing with them, Jess had told them firmly that Ruthie needed bringing out of herself a bit.

'Have you done yet, Lucy, 'cos if you haven't we're going in without you? Otherwise we'll lose our place in the queue and we won't get a decent table,' Elsie Wiggins, one of the older girls, who hadn't wanted Jess inviting Ruthie along, shouted up.

'We're coming now,' Jess responded, turning to smile at Ruthie. 'Quick, have a look at yourself.' She dived into her bag and produced a small mirror. 'Proper smashing, you look. All you need now is a bit of lipstick. I'll lend you mine when we get inside, and you'll be turning all the lads' heads and no mistake.'

Ruthie wasn't listening to her. She was staring instead at her reflection in the mirror. She lifted her hand to touch the short fringe curling onto her face, her eyes widening. She looked so different, so grown-up.

'Come on ... Jess.'

Grabbing hold of Ruthie's hand, Jess put the mirror away and hurried her along the street. Ruthie could feel the prickle of bits of hair sticking to her skin inside her frock. How much had Lucy cut off at the back? She had been snipping away for a very long time. Ruthie had never had her hair cut, always wearing it scraped back off her face in its neat plait. She reached behind her head and froze when her fingers encountered a soft mass of loose hair. Short loose hair.

'Got a real nice wave to it now,' Lucy was saying. 'Though I say it meself, I've done it really nice. Mind you, them scissors I was using was that blunt it was like cutting it wi' a knife and fork.'

'All right, girls, how many of you are there then?' one of the men on the door asked jovially

'Eight,' Jess answered him. 'Eight of the best-looking girls in Liverpool. In fact, we're that good-looking you should be letting us in for free,' she told him, winking at Ruthie. ''Cos once the fellas see us they'll be paying double just to get a closer look.'

'Oh aye, well, you can tell that to the boss, if you like.'

'I don't know why you bother. It's the same every week,' a chubby ginger-haired girl protested.

'Well, you never know, Andrea, one week he might let us in for nowt. It's always worth a try. Him wot don't ask don't get – that's what my dad allus used to say,' Jess responded cheerfully, still holding Ruthie's hand she led the way up the stairs to the ballroom.

Ruthie's eyes widened as she followed Jess inside.

'It's Ivy Benson's lot playing tonight,' Lucy commented, glancing up at the gallery from which people could look down on the dance floor, and where the band played. 'Ever so good, they are. They've got a good dance floor here too. Properly sprung, it is, not like some. Modelled it on some Russian dancing place.'

'I think I remember reading that the building was designed after the Kirov Ballet Theatre,' Ruthie supplied timidly, causing them all to stare at her.

'Coo, proper schoolbook learning you've got, Ruthie, and no mistake,' Lucy exclaimed admiringly.

92

'Hmm.' Carmen, another of the girls, with smouldering dark eyes and equally dark hair, pouted, unimpressed. 'I like a proper band with a proper male singer.'

'That's only 'cos you want to give him the eye whilst you're dancing,' Elsie chirped up.

'Look at them GIs over there,' Lucy breathed. 'You have to hand it to them, they look really well turned out. Ever so tall and handsome, they are...'

'Aye, and ever so keen to get into a girl's knickers, from what I've heard,' a girl whose name Ruthie thought was Cathy sniffed.

'Well, that good-looking one over there can try getting into mine any time he likes,' Lucy answered her back.

'Oooh, Lucy...'

'I only said he could *try*,' Lucy pointed out. 'Come on, let's go and grab that table over there, right by the dance floor, before anyone else does.'

'I knew we should have got down here earlier,' Myra complained as she and Diane joined the end of the queue. 'Pity you haven't got something a bit more dressy to wear,' she added critically, before glancing down smugly at her own red sateen halter-neck top, obviously comparing it to the plain dark blue taffeta dress that Diane had on. Diane didn't say anything. She was still brooding on the content of Beryl's letter. She might not have dolled herself up like Myra, with her tight-fitting top and her red lipstick, but tonight she was going to show the world that she could have as good a time as anyone – especially Kit.

93

'I knew it,' Myra grimaced as soon as they were inside the ballroom. 'There's not a free table to be seen.'

'We can share with some other girls, can't we?' Diane responded.

Myra gave her a withering look. For all her good looks it was plain to her that Diane knew very little about the art of attracting men. If they went and sat at a table with plain girls they'd be overlooked along with them, and if they went and sat at one with pretty ones, then they'd be vying with them for the best-looking men, which was why... She searched the room with an expert eye, and then dug Diane in the ribs.

'Come on, over there, three from the band, and be quick about it in case someone beats us to it.'

She was pushing her way through the crowded ballroom before Diane could say anything, leaving her no option than to follow her. But when Diane saw the table she was heading towards, she stopped and made a grab for Myra's arm.

'What is it?' Myra demanded impatiently.

'We can't sit there.'

'Why not?'

'Because it's full of men.'

'Oh – so it is. Fancy me not noticing,' Myra agreed, making big round eyes and then giving Diane an exasperated look. 'Of course it's full of men. Why do you think I'm heading for it? Come on.'

'No,' Diane told her firmly.

Myra's mouth hardened in a thin line. 'All right then. Wait here.' Determinedly she made her way to the table, saying something to the eager-looking GI who turned to her, and then calling out to Diane, 'Come on, these nice boys are going to give us two of their spare chairs, so that we don't have to sit at a table with men we don't know.'

Diane was so angry with Myra for the way she had drawn attention to her that she was tempted to turn on her heel and walk out, except she felt that doing so would make her look even more foolish. She would have something to say to her later when they were on their own, though – like she wasn't going out with her again.

The Grafton was obviously a popular venue, the tables set round the dance floor all filled and men standing several deep at the bar. The tables in the part of the ballroom Myra had made her way to seemed to have been taken over by the Americans, whilst the men seated at the tables on the other side of the room were wearing British uniforms or civvies. As she made her way to join Myra, Diane felt almost like a traitor. In Cambridgeshire she would never have gone to sit with a crowd of Yanks. The young women she could see sitting with the Americans seemed to have no qualms about making them welcome, though. There was a desperation in the eyes of some of the girls, which made Diane look away quickly. What was it they were desperate for? The luxuries that their American boyfriends could give them? Or did their need go deeper than that? The country had been at war now since 1939. Some women had not seen their men for a very long time; some women would never see them again. Was that the cause of the angry, bitter hunger Diane could see in their eyes? Despite the heat of the ballroom Diane gave a

95

small shiver. The war had turned so many girls into women, its urgency breaking down all the old rules that governed relationships between the sexes. Girls who would never normally have let their young men give them more than chaste kisses had become desperate to send them off to war with 'something to remember them by'. What did preserving one's virginity for tomorrow mean when there might not be a tomorrow, when all one might have was tonight? And then with their men gone and their senses awakened, was it any wonder that those girls-turned-women yearned for the warmth of a pair of male arms to hold them?

Diane shivered again, remembering the stolen nights of pleasure she and Kit had shared under the thatches of remote quaint village pubs, where the landlord had been prepared to turn a blind eye and accept their self-conscious claim to be a married couple. Would her body, deprived of what it had known, eventually fill her with a hunger and an anger that would take her into the arms of a stranger to seek oblivion? Pushing her disturbing thoughts aside, she made her way towards Myra.

Myra patted her hair and cast a discreet look over her shoulder. Not that she was looking for anyone in particular, of course. She leaned down and pretended to check the seam of her stockings. She was pleased with the amount of attention she was attracting. The red halter-neck top showed off the smooth skin of her bare arms and shoulders, although it was on the shadowed valley between her breasts that she could see male glances lingering. She hid a triumphant smile. Next to her

Diane looked nothing special at all, despite that blonde hair. That frock she was wearing was the dullest thing she had ever seen and you wouldn't catch her wearing something so boring. Her own skirt followed the curves of her hips and her bottom; she had had it altered, to make it tighter and shorter, determinedly ignoring Jim's comment that he didn't like her wearing her clothes like that. 'Supposed to be saving on fabric, aren't we?' she had told him, tossing her head. 'At least that's what the government says. Shorter skirts, we have to have.' Jim had shaken his head but he hadn't said any more. He was a real softie.

Myra's smile disappeared at the thought of her husband. The British Government had done her a favour sending him out to fight in the desert, and Hitler would be doing her even more of one if he never came back. She checked the surrounding tables again. Where was he? Hadn't he picked up on her message? She'd made it plain enough, telling him where she was going to be and when. It wasn't as though he wouldn't be easy to spot either, never mind that the Grafton was packed out tonight. Not with those good looks of his.

The young fair-haired GI who had found her the chairs on which she and Diane were seated was gazing at her like a dumb puppy, all pleading eyes and eagerness to please. Myra put out her cigarette. She might as well dance with him. At least that way she'd get away from disapproving Diane and her haughty looks. Who did she think she was? Sticking her nose up in the air and refusing to let the GIs buy her a drink. Myra shot Diane a baleful look. She was sitting facing the dance floor, nursing a glass of lemonade.

Myra looked at the fair-haired GI. 'Well?' she asked provocatively. 'Who's going to ask me to dance then?'

It had been a mistake to come here with Myra, Diane admitted as she watched her dancing with a young GI who looked as though he couldn't believe his good luck. The GIs had been drinking heavily, passing around a bottle of what Diane suspected must be spirits and adding some of its contents to their beer, as a result of which they had started yelling out encouragement to their friend. Already the table was attracting hostile looks from the British servicemen on the dance floor. The initial mood of the evening, which had been one of high but good-natured spirits, had somehow developed a darker, unpleasant undertone. Some of the comments being called out by the GIs as they assessed the girls who were dancing were going well beyond what was acceptable, and Diane was not totally surprised when a short, red-faced man in civvies left the dance floor, dragging his uncomfortable-looking partner with him and marched self-importantly up the table to remonstrate with them.

'Hey, bud, if you don't like it then go tell Uncle Sam. Seems to me you should be treating us with a bit more respect, seeing as how we've come to win your war for you.'

The slurred voice of one of the GIs caused a surge of angry mutters from those near enough to hear it.

To Diane's relief Myra was returning to her seat.

Standing up, Diane told her, 'I think we should find somewhere else to sit.'

'Why?'

'Because I don't like the way things are developing.'

'Oh, don't be such a bore. They're only having a bit of fun.' Myra said tetchily. Where was he? She had been so sure he would be here. She'd been depending on it. The only reason she'd danced with the clumsy farm boy with two left feet had been to make sure that she was seen. 'Relax and have another drink,' she advised Diane. If they moved away from this table right beside the dance floor she'd have no chance of catching his eye. The Grafton was well and truly packed with an influx of fresh American troops from their camp at Burtonwood, and naval men on twenty-four-hour leave from their convoy escort duties.

'You can do as you please, Myra, but I'm not staying here,' Diane replied sharply.

Myra looked over her shoulder. She had sent her dance partner to get them fresh drinks and she could see him weaving his way back through the crowd. Like Diane, she had seen the bottle being passed round the table, and she too had guessed it contained spirits. There was no way she intended to leave, but she knew she couldn't stay without Diane. Somehow she would have to find a way to make her stay. An idea suddenly came to her.

'Clem's bringing us some drinks. We can't just walk off,' she protested, standing up herself. 'Stay there, and I'll get them.'

She intercepted Clem a few yards from the

table, taking the tray from him and telling him, 'Go and get some of whatever it is your pals are putting in their drinks, will you, Clem? My friend wants to try it.'

'Are you sure? It's pretty strong. Not a lady's drink...'

'She isn't a lady,' Myra told him sweetly. 'Go get it.'

He was back within a few seconds, brandishing a bottle.

'What is it, anyway?' she asked him when he removed the top.

'It's genuine American bourbon,' he told her proudly.

'Give me the bottle,' Myra demanded, pouring a good measure into one of the glasses.

'Hey, not so much,' Clem objected. 'That stuff's lethal. It fries your brains. It's not for girls,' he protested, but it was too late.

Myra handed him back the bottle and walked towards Diane, carrying their drinks.

'Goodness, it's hot, isn't it?' she commented as she handed Diane one glass whilst taking a drink from the other one.

'Yes. Yes, it is,' Diane agreed, lifting her own glass to her lips.

'Drink up,' Myra urged, 'then we can have a dance together, seein' as how you don't want to stay here.' She could see that Diane was looking for somewhere to put her glass. 'You'll have to finish it,' she told her quickly. 'There's nowhere safe to leave it, not with this crowd. Someone's sure to pinch it.'

She didn't really want to dance with Myra,

Diane admitted, but in view of Myra's attempt to pacify her, she didn't feel able to refuse. Myra had already finished her drink and was waiting for her so Diane hurriedly swallowed her own.

'That didn't taste like shandy,' she told Myra.

'Didn't it?' Myra gave a dismissive shrug. 'Maybe Clem misunderstood. Shandy was what I told him to get. Mine was OK. Come on, let's go and dance.' She grabbed hold of Diane's wrist, almost pulling her on to the dance floor.

Heavens, but she felt dizzy, Diane admitted. Her head was spinning. It must be the heat and the noise. She really felt quite odd; not herself at all.

Myra looked uncertainly at Diane. All she had wanted to do was get her to loosen up a bit, and relax, but instead, Diane was swaying unsteadily on the dance floor and there was a unfocused look in her eyes. People were beginning to stare pointedly at her but Diane was oblivious to their disapproval. She had lifted her hand to her forehead as she stopped dancing and simply stood in the middle of the dance floor. Myra began to panic. Why on earth was she behaving like this? She hadn't poured that much spirit into Diane's drink, she reassured herself. It wasn't *her* fault if Diane couldn't take her drink, was it? *She* couldn't have been expected to know that! As she struggled to wriggle out of any blame, she felt a tap on her shoulder.

'You dancing, gorgeous?'

She whirled round, her eyes widening in recognition, only too happy to push her guilt about Diane to one side as she smiled up into the eyes of the man from Lyons' Corner House.

'I might be,' she told him coquettishly. 'It depends how good you are.'

'Oh, I'm very good, honey. In fact, I'm better than good, I'm the best,' he told her.

'Says you,' Myra returned.

'Well, there's only one way you're going to find out if I'm right, isn't there?' he told her boldly, as he stepped towards her, taking her acceptance for granted. Right on cue the music changed to a slow smoochy number. Myra hid her feeling of triumph as he pulled her into his body, one hand caressing her back whilst the other made its way down to the curve of her behind, making it plain how attracted to her he was.

'So what's your name then?' she asked him.

There was something about all Americans, but this one in particular that made her long to be different, and increased her frustrated resentment of her own life and marriage. They came from a different world – a better world – and it was one she herself longed to be part of. She had seen it in films at the cinema: sophisticated elegant women living lives she could so easily see herself living. She had grown to feel so envious of those women; and, through them, of all American women. She hungered for a life in which she hailed New York 'cabs' and drank 'martinis', a life in which she shopped on Fifth Avenue, and went to shows on Broadway. She had studied the actresses on the screen, bitterly convinced that her own beauty was just as great as theirs if not greater, becoming increasingly discontented and resentful. Until the Americans had joined the war all she had been able to do was dream, but now, with American servicemen coming over to England, she wanted more than just dreams. Now she had a definite ambition she wanted to fulfil, which was to become what the newspapers and magazines were referring to as 'a GI bride'. Magazines such as *Good Housekeeping* might caution young British women to recognise the problems they would encounter if they decided to marry their American sweethearts; so far as Myra was concerned the only problem she would be encountering was that of her now unwanted existing husband. What could Jim have to offer her, she asked herself with inward contempt for her husband, compared with this man she was now dancing with? She greedily noted his beautifully laundered uniform, his clean-smelling skin, his knowing eyes and equally knowing way of dancing, not to mention his obviously superior financial status as evidenced by his watch and the gold ring, with its small diamond, he was wearing on his little finger.

'Nick,' he answered her question. 'What's yours?'

'Myra.' She refused to let him see just how much he impressed her, or what she was thinking. Myra was no fool: she knew that men liked to do the chasing and that they valued what they couldn't get easily far more than what they could.

'Well, Myra, what's a smart broad like you doing in a place like this?'

Where was Myra? Diane stared at the dance floor, trying to focus on the dancers. The music seemed to be roaring inside her head in waves, mingling with the sound of people's voices. She wanted to go to sit down but she couldn't seem to find her way off the dance floor. She blundered into a dancing couple, earning herself a disgusted look.

'Some people,' the girl muttered.

'Looks to me like she's had too much to drink,' her companion commented.

Diane didn't hear them. Her head was beginning to pound. She felt hot and sweaty and decidedly unwell. Where *was* Myra? She could see couples dancing cheek to cheek all around her. Just like *she* had once done with Kit. Kit... It was his fault she was here on her own without him. Her alcohol-muddled emotions filled her eyes with tears.

'Kit...' She had no awareness of saying his name out aloud as she twisted and turned on the dance floor, looking for a familiar face. Myra was forgotten; it was Kit she wanted. Through the blur of her tears she could see the back of the familiar RAF uniform in front of her. Unsteadily she made her way towards it, reaching out to put her hand on the arm of the airforce-blue jacket, as she pleaded, 'Kit...'

'Hey, what the...?' The man looking at her was a stranger. An angry-looking stranger. Diane backed away from him, cannoning into another couple.

'Well, really. How disgraceful.' The woman's coldly disapproving voice made him turn to look at her. She was dancing with a man who looked vaguely familiar. He was wearing an American uniform. His gaze flicked disparagingly over her.

'I think you should go and sit down,' he told her curtly.

104

'I can't find Kit,' Diane told him, hiccuping loudly.

'Ignore her, Lee. She's drunk. Her sort brings disgrace on all of us. She ought to be made to leave.'

'Can't leave,' Diane answered her, her voice slurred. 'Not without my friend... I know you and I don't like you,' she told the man, suddenly recognising him. 'You're that American major that I don't like...' She hiccuped and staggered away into the middle of the crowded floor. Her eyeballs hurt and so did her head and her stomach. She needed to go somewhere cool and quiet and lie down. Unsteadily she started to make her way to the edge of the dance floor.

'Just look at that woman,' Emily commented contemptuously. 'She can hardly stand up straight.'

'Poor thing,' Jess commiserated. 'She doesn't look at all well.'

'She's drunk,' Emily said sharply.

'Oh, no, look, if she's not careful she's going to fall over.' Jess pushed back her chair and hurried to where Diane was on the point of collapsing. 'Come and give us a hand,' she called out to the others. 'We need to get her into the ladies'.'

Immediately Ruthie rushed to join her.

'You get under that arm, Ruthie, and I'll take this one...'

'Why don't you leave her? Why should we help her?' Emily demanded.

'Well, it doesn't look as though anyone else is going to, poor soul. Come on, Em, and you too, Lucy. She's in a bad way.'

'Well, it's her own fault.'

Somehow between them they managed to get her into the ladies' – and only just in time.

'Gawd, if she don't stop heaving soon, I'm going to be doing the same meself,' Lucy complained.

'Go and tell them at the bar that we need some water, Lucy,' Jess commanded.

'It's all right, you've just had a bit too much to drink, that's all,' she tried to comfort Diane, who was now moaning weakly.

'A bit too much!' Emily muttered firmly. 'More like a bloody hell of a lot too much.'

Diane shivered. Her stomach and her throat ached from being sick, but her head was starting to clear. She heard what Emily said and she shook her head. 'All I had was a shandy,' she told her.

'A shandy? Give over, a shandy never got anyone in the state you're in, staggering all over the dance floor and then trying it on with that RAF chap. No wonder that GI was giving you a right dirty look.'

Diane stared at her. She had no memory of any of that. 'I can't ... are you sure it was me?' she protested.

Emily laughed. 'Hark at her. Of course it was bloody you. Why the hell do you think Miss Save the World here,' she nodded in Jess's direction, 'forced us to bring you in here?'

'You and your friend was sitting with a table of GIs and they was passing a bottle around,' Jess offered, seeing how distressed Diane was becoming. 'Maybe they slipped summat into your shandy.'

'I ... I don't know. My friend brought me the drink...'

'Here, I've got her some water,' Lucy announced breathlessly, bursting into the cloakroom. 'There's a real to-do going on out there, wi' some folk saying as how she ought to be told to leave, and others saying it were them GIs fault for giving her the drink in the first place.'

Diane looked apprehensively towards the door. How could she show her face out there? She was so ashamed.

'How are you feeling now?' Jess asked her as she handed her the glass of water.

'A lot better.'

'We came here to have a good time, not stand around in the cloakroom playing at nurses,' Elsie complained.

'If you're feeling a bit better, then why don't you come and sit wi' us for a while? Your friend must be wondering where you are.'

The last thing Diane wanted was to go back into the dance hall, but she didn't have the energy to protest.

Five minutes later she was being urged into a chair, with Jess standing protectively at one side of her and Ruthie uncertainly at the other.

'Mind you drink plenty of water to flush your insides out. That's what my dad always used to do when he'd had a skinful,' Jess told her firmly. 'And no dancing neither.'

Diane shuddered and closed her eyes. She never wanted to see a dance floor again, never mind take to one, not after what she had been told she had been doing. Vague flashes of memory were starting to seep back: an RAF uniform, an angry male face, an angry American male voice. The major...

Jess reached across and gave Ruthie's hand a shake. 'There's a GI on that table over there bin watching you for the last five minutes, Ruthie. Bet you he comes over and asks you to dance.'

'No,' Ruthie protested in a panic. 'No, he mustn't. I can't dance.'

'Don't be daft, of course you can. He looks a nice lad, an' all.'

The girls turned to look at the table in question, where upwards of a couple of dozen GIs were crowded together, either seated or standing.

'Give him a bit of a smile, Ruthie,' Jess urged her.

Tongue-tied and blushing, Ruthie could only shake her head.

'Well, he's coming over anyway,' Jess laughed.

'And he's not on his own. He's bringing another chap with him as well,' Lucy announced.

Ruthie could only make a small breathless sound when she realised that Jess was right, and the earnest-looking young GI in front of her, with his clean scrubbed face and tow-coloured hair was actually asking her to dance.

'Of course she'll dance wi' you. She's just a bit shy, that's all,' Jess answered for her before turning to smile warmly at his companion.

'If you'd be kind enough to do me the honour, ma'am...?' he asked Jess hesitantly.

Jess smiled at him with almost maternal approval. His manners were as meltingly flattering as the look in his eyes.

'I certainly will,' she told him.

Diane watched as one by one the other girls were asked up to dance. One of the men looked as though he was about to ask her, but Jess told him pleasantly, 'She isn't feeling very well – no offence.'

This was her chance to slip away unnoticed, Diane decided, if only she could find Myra to tell her that she was leaving. Where on earth was she?

'What do you mean, no?'

Myra looked up into Nick's face. When he had suggested they slip outside 'for a bit of fresh air' she had nodded her head, letting him take her down a quiet side street, where, in its shadows, he had placed his hands on her arms and pushed her back against the wall. Now those hands were resting on the wall either side of her head, virtually imprisoning her. She smiled inwardly. Nick might think he knew all the moves and had the advantage, but she wasn't stupid enough to let him have what he wanted out here up against a wall, like some floozie. Oh, no, all he was going to get tonight was a little taste of what he was after. Just enough to keep him eager for more, Myra decided smugly.

'I'd better go back. My friend is going to wonder where I am.'

'Let her wonder,' Nick told her as he moved closer to her and bent his head towards hers.

Quick as a flash Myra ducked under his arm and moved away from him.

'What the...?' he began angrily.

'Like I said, I'd better go back. After all, we only

came out for a breath of fresh air, didn't we?'

'What is this?' Nick demanded roughly, trying to grab hold of her arm. 'Don't you go playing games with me, honey. You were coming on to me like there was no tomorrow.'

'Coming on to you? Is that what you thought?' His anger had her body tensing warily but Myra wasn't going to let him see that. 'No such thing,' she told him, shaking her head. 'I was just being friendly, that's all.'

'Like you were being friendly to that sucker who gave you the stockings,' Nick challenged her.

Myra drew in her breath. This wasn't the way she had expected things to go. She had expected her refusal to encourage Nick to press her for a proper date, not make him angry.

'Like I said, I was just being friendly,' she insisted. 'It's our duty to welcome our allies.' Conveniently she was choosing to forget just how she had come by her stockings. They didn't matter now, nor the man who had given them to her, not now that she had met Nick. But he mustn't be allowed to think she was some sort of pushover. Men like Nick didn't respect women they thought would give them everything they wanted the first time they asked. That was something she knew instinctively.

'I'm going in,' she told him.

She started to walk away from him, knowing he would catch up with her and prepared for him when he did, softening in his hold as he grabbed hold of her and swung her round to face him.

'Just a kiss,' he said.

'No,' Myra refused. 'It's too soon. I don't give

110

my kisses out so freely.' She could see a look in his eyes that was a mix of resentment and grudging respect.

'Tell that to all the guys, do you?' he demanded.

'Yes I do,' Myra agreed tartly. She knew that she wanted to see him again. A quick glance at his companions had told her what she had already guessed – that he was very much their leader – and Myra had already decided that the rightful place in the new life she dreamed of for herself was as the wife of just such a man, rather than as the wife of one of those he led. But she knew too much about men to go openly chasing after him, no matter how tempted she was to do so, to make sure that no other girl got her hooks into him.

Ruthie could hardly believe what was happening and that she was here dancing with an American. An American, what was more, who had lost no time in telling her earnestly that he had been watching her all evening and that he thought she was 'real cute'.

'I'd like to walk you home,' he began awkwardly, 'but, see, we've been told not to do that.'

'Oh, no, you couldn't anyway,' Ruthie told him, both horrified and excited by the suggestion.

'Well, will you let me see you again then? I mean here, perhaps ... or I could come and call on your folks ... introduce myself to them...'

Ruthie stared at him whilst her heart turned over inside her chest.

'What I mean is that, well, I can see you're not the sort of girl ... that is...'

111

'Hey, buddy,' another GI called out in a loud voice. 'Quit whispering sweet nothings in her ear and get your ass over here. Sarge says we've got to leave in five. And you can go and tell Walter over there,' he jerked his head in the direction of Jess and her partner, 'the same.'

'Oh, poor you,' Jess was saying sympathetically to the young GI who had asked her to dance. 'You must miss her so very much.' He had spent virtually the whole time they had been dancing together telling her about his 'girl back home' and how miserable he was about the fact that he hadn't had the courage to propose to her before 'shipping out'.

'You can write to her, though,' Jess tried to comfort him.

'Yeah, I know that, but it ain't exactly the same. A guy can't tell a girl he loves her nearly so well when she ain't there for him to hold. Would you like to see her photo?' he asked Jess eagerly.

Nodding, Jess peered dutifully at the photograph of the pretty but very young-looking brunette.

'Her folks kinda hinted to me that they thought we was too young to get serious.' Walter was telling her, when Jess saw Ruthie hurrying over with her partner.

'Jerry said to tell you it's time to go,' Ruthie's partner told Walter.

'Poor boy,' Jess commented to Ruthie as they watched the two men go to join their comrades. 'He misses his girl at home.'

Diane glanced at her watch. Her head was throbbing dreadfully.

'Isn't that your friend over there?' Jess suddenly asked her, nudging her and pointing to the other side of the dance floor. 'Wi' that GI who looks like he thinks he's God's gift.'

'Yes, it is,' Diane confirmed.

Myra was laughing at something her companion had said and looked in no hurry to leave, Diane noted. Nor did she seem at all concerned about *her* whereabouts. Somehow Diane wasn't surprised. Her instincts had told her right from the word go that Myra was only striking up a friendship with her for her own benefit.

'I'd better go over and join her,' she told Jess, adding warmly, 'I really am grateful to you all for helping me the way you did. Heaven knows what would have happened to me if you hadn't. Something tells me that I certainly wouldn't have made it back up Edge Hill Lane in one piece.'

'Up Edge Hill Lane? Is that where your billet is?' Jess asked. 'Only Ruthie lives up there, don't you? That's good, then. You can walk back together.'

'I don't know how far up you live, but we're on Chestnut Close,' Diane told Ruthie.

'Yes, that's where I live as well.'

'There you are then. Funny how things work out, isn't it?' Jess beamed, looking as pleased as though she personally had arranged for them to live so conveniently close to one another.

'There you are. Now you'll have someone to walk home with,' she told Ruthie happily before telling Diane breezily, 'Ruthie here's not so used to looking out of herself as me and the others. Looked like she was scared to death, she did,

113

when she got on the bus for the munitions factory for the first time.'

Diane gave Ruthie a sympathetic smile. Her head still hurt but she was beginning to feel much better than she had done.

'We don't stay on until the end,' Jess continued informatively, 'on account of the way some of the lads hang around looking for a girl. It gives them the wrong idea, if you know what I mean.'

Diane knew exactly what she meant.

'I'd better go over and tell my friend that I'm ready to leave then,' she told Jess.

'Oh, I thought you must have left,' Myra greeted her unenthusiastically, immediately turning her back on Diane to move closer to the GI standing next to her. Myra said something to him and when he turned round to look at her, Diane recognised immediately what sort he was. He might be tall and good-looking but he was also a thoroughly unpleasant type, she decided as he subjected her to open appraisal, whilst draping one arm casually around Myra. It wasn't just Myra who was hanging on his every word, Diane noticed. He also seemed to be the ringleader of a group of noisy GIs.

'We must go, Myra,' Diane told her crisply. 'I've arranged to walk home with another girl, and I don't want to keep her waiting.'

'Well, don't then,' Myra told her sharply. 'You go ahead and leave. Nick here will walk me home, won't you, Nick?'

'I sure wish I could, doll, but the MPs will have me by the balls if I did. Uncle Sam doesn't want

114

us getting ourselves into trouble with you Brits.'

'*You* get into trouble?' Myra pouted.

'Yeah, that's right, isn't it, guys?' he demanded.

Diane winced as she heard the loud chorus of assent.

'Sarge says to tell you the transport is about to leave.'

There was something about the coldly venomous look that the man with Myra gave to the young GI who had approached them that shocked Diane back to full sobriety. Poor boy, what on earth had he done to provoke a look of such openly vicious dislike? She watched in silence as Myra's companion turned on his heel without saying a word and strode off in the direction of the other GIs, leaving the now red-faced younger man to trail behind him.

What on earth, Diane wondered, could Myra possibly see in a man like that?

EIGHT

'So you walked home with young Ruthie Philpott last night, did you?' Mrs Lawson commented as she poured Diane a cup of tea, and then continued without waiting for Diane to answer her. 'Feel sorry for her, I do. Well, you can't not do really, not after what happened to her dad, and then her ma taking it so badly, like. Tell you about that, did she?'

'She said that her mother was a widow,' Diane

115

answered, 'but she didn't go into any details.'

'No, well, she wouldn't. She's not that sort of girl. Her dad was in the ARP; got killed in a bomb blast, he did. A real shame it was 'cos they was a nice little family. Kept themselves to themselves, mind you. You'd see them walking to church together every Sunday. But Ruthie's ma, she took her husband's death real bad. Not bin the same person since she lost him, she hasn't. One minute she's out looking for him and won't have it that he's gone, and then the next she's crying her eyes out and refusing to let young Ruthie leave her side. Dr Barnes has had to come out to her a fair few times, to give her something to calm her nerves. I'm surprised young Ruthie went out and left her. Not like her, that isn't.'

'I think, from what Ruthie said, that a neighbour was with her mother.' Diane felt obliged to defend the other girl.

'Oh, yes, that'd be Mary Brown. Her hubby, Joe's, in the ARP as well. You was in later than I was expecting.'

'I'm sorry if I disturbed you,' Diane apologised automatically.

Mrs Lawson gave a small sniff. 'Well, as to that, I'm a martyr to not being able to sleep, I am, and that's no mistake. Still, at least you're up at a decent hour this morning. Unlike some people,' she added, giving a significant look towards the ceiling.

'Myra should be down soon.'

'I should hope so. In my day a married woman didn't go out dancing for all the world like she didn't have a husband. I suppose there was a lot of them Americans there, was there?'

'The dance hall was very busy,' Diane responded obliquely.

'Causing a lot of trouble, them GIs are, from what I've heard. Turning girls' heads with their fancy uniforms. Mind you, it's the girls I blame. They ought ter have a bit more respect for themselves. I don't approve of girls who get themselves involved with Americans, and that's a fact.'

Mrs Lawson would certainly not have approved of the way Myra had been behaving last night, Diane acknowledged as she forced herself to eat a small slice of toast with a scraping of margarine on it. Neither her stomach nor her head were fully recovered yet, and she was thankful that it was her day off.

It was another half an hour before Myra finally appeared in the kitchen.

'I thought I'd wait until the coast was clear and Mrs L had gone to church,' she told Diane as she lit up a cigarette.

'I rather think she was expecting us both to go with her,' Diane told her.

Myra gave a dismissive shrug. 'Tough. I'm not wasting my day off going to church. I've got better things to do with my time. You could have gone, though. Why didn't you?'

'Because I wanted to have a word with you about last night. Somebody must have put something into my drink and I was wondering if you happened to see anything.'

'No, nothing,' Myra lied, adding quickly, 'Look, if I were you, I'd forget about it. OK, so you made a bit of a fool of yourself, and Nick said–'

117

She broke off as she saw Diane's expression, demanding suspiciously, 'What are you looking like that for?'

'I know it isn't any business of mine,' Diane told her steadily, 'but–'

'But what?' Myra drew heavily on her cigarette and then exhaled angrily.

'He's arrogant and he's a bully, Myra, the way he behaved to that young man.'

'That's their business, isn't it? You really messed up the evening for me. You know that, don't you?' she burst out angrily, stubbing out her cigarette.

The last thing she wanted was to be lectured. She had decided that Nick was perfect, the kind of man who, if he was hers, could transform her life. Already she was fantasising about how different her life would had been if she had been lucky enough to be born an American. And surely the next best thing to being born an American was to marry one. Especially one like Nick. He had talked to her last night about New York where he lived.

'You want to see Times Square,' he had told her. 'And the shows on Broadway. You Brits don't know what life is all about.' He had laughed then. 'Jeez, you'd never catch a New Yorker putting up with your blackout, rationing and wearing hand-me-downs.'

'New York must be wonderful,' Myra had sighed enviously

'It sure is,' he had agreed. 'The best place on earth, and I can't wait to get back there.'

Myra's sharp comment had made Diane's face burn a little, but before she could defend herself Myra continued critically, 'I thought you were someone who knows what life's all about, Diane, not some stupid kid like the one we walked home with last night, all stars in her eyes and still believing in Father Christmas. You and me could have been well in with those GIs if you'd played along with them instead of acting the way you did. What's the point in going to a dance if you're going to behave like you don't want to be there, and you don't want to have any fun?'

'Getting picked up by GIs might be your idea of fun but it certainly isn't mine,' Diane responded firmly.

'Then more fool you. This bloody war makes me feel like I deserve every bit of fun that comes my way. We could all be dead tomorrow,' Myra reminded her.

'Oh, come on, that's the argument every man in uniform who wants to get into a girl's knickers comes up with,' Diane protested. 'You must know what's said about girls who chase after GIs, Myra. The Americans themselves are calling them little better than prostitutes. In my last post, some of the GIs were saying some pretty unpleasant things about our girls.'

'Save the moralising for someone who needs it,' Myra stopped her rudely. 'After all, the state you were in last night you aren't in any position to go telling others how to behave, are you?' Myra conveniently forgot the part she had played in Diane's downfall.

'The fact that I was in that state, and through no fault of my own, should tell you all you need to know about your precious GIs,' Diane shot back, as angry now as Myra. 'Is that really what

119

you want, Myra? A man who thinks it's acceptable to tamper with a girl's drink?'

'What I want is a man who's got something to
offer me. I'm sick of everything about this war,
and I'm sick of everything about this country as
well. It's all make do and mend, pull together, put
others first, make sacrifices. They don't have to do
that in America. God, I'd give anything to get
away from this wretched country and live there.'

Diane was too taken aback to know what to say.
'Well, perhaps when the war is over you and your
husband could think about emigrating,' she
began, but Myra cut her off with a bitter laugh.
'Jim? Go and live in America? There's no way
he'd do that, and even if there was... No, I've got
other ideas,' she finished smugly.

'I've got some letters to write,' Diane told Myra
when it became obvious that she didn't intend to
tell her what her 'ideas' were, 'but if you feel like
going out for a walk later...?' she suggested, trying to restore peace and anxious not to be
cooped up in the house on such a glorious day.

'I can't, I'm afraid,' Myra said carelessly. 'I've
got plans.'

Myra was anxiously aware that Nick hadn't
asked her for a date last night. He would have
asked her, of course, if Diane hadn't come over
when she had, Myra was sure of that. He'd been
keen enough, after all, when they'd gone outside.
A shiver of excitement gripped her body. No one
had ever made her feel like this before. It was
strangely exhilarating, dangerously so. She had
lain in bed last night, unable to sleep, recalling
how she had felt when she had let him take her

outside, knowing what he wanted. There had been a hunger in him for her then, just like there was hunger in her to escape from the greyness that war had brought to the country and to make a new life for herself. If she played her cards right, he could be her ticket to that new life.

Diane looked at the two letters she had just written. The first, to her parents, had been the easier to write. She had simply told them what she knew her mother in particular wanted to hear: that she was comfortable in her billet and happy in her work. She had mentioned last night's dance very casually, knowing that her mother would be searching her letter for telltale signs that she was 'getting over Kit' and, equally, telltale signs that she wasn't.

The second letter had been more difficult to write. She had thanked Beryl for what she had told her, and assured her that she knew she was acting in her best interests in disclosing to her that Kit was seeing other girls. She had also told her, though, that she wanted to put Kit and the past behind her and that she no longer considered him important enough to want to hear about him. How could she ever forget him if she was constantly being reminded of him and the love she had lost? She couldn't tell her friend that, though. Not without either making her feel guilty or running the risk of her telling others that she was pining for him. It had been hard to strike what she hoped was the right note, and she had read the finished letter through half a dozen times, anxiously checking that she hadn't said anything she would regret nor omitted to say everything that needed to be said. She had finished her letter with a cheerful few lines about the Grafton and going dancing there and the fun she expected to have in her new life in Liverpool.

Now all she had to do was go to post the letter before she could have second thoughts.

'Just going to post my letters Mrs L,' she called out to her landlady as she opened the front door.

The afternoon sunshine revealed the dust dimming the green of Chestnut Close's front garden hedges. A legacy of the heavy bombing the city had endured, the dust was everywhere, coating everything in a thin fine film that Liverpool's inhabitants no longer seemed to notice. No doubt when you had come through a bombing blitz as heavy as that endured by the city, a bit of dust was easy to ignore, Diane decided as she strolled towards the postbox.

She was not looking forward to going in to work in the morning. She suspected that by now everyone would, in the way of such things, know about last night. She could explain what had happened, of course, but it would still be embarrassing. She had seen the disapproving looks she and Myra had been attracting before she had been given that wretched drink. It made her writhe in horrified embarrassment to think about the way she had behaved to that poor RAF man, mistaking him for Kit. So much for her determination to prove that she could have a good time without him. Buck up, she chided herself sternly. You've just got to get on with it.

She had just posted her letters when she saw

Ruthie crossing the road several yards away.

'Hello, there,' she called. 'Was your mother all right when you got in? I know you were worrying about her.'

'Oh, yes. She was fine, thank you,' Ruthie confirmed, looking shy. 'Mrs Brown, our neighbour, said that she hadn't asked for me once. In fact, she said she could see no reason why I shouldn't go out dancing more often, because she could see that it had done me good. She wanted to know all about it and if I had danced with anyone.' A soft pink tinge had crept up under Ruthie's skin and her eyes were shining. 'I told her all about dancing with Glen and she said that he sounded really nice. I never thought when Jess persuaded me to go with them that I'd be asked to dance by a real American GI.'

Had *she* ever been that young, Diane wondered ruefully.

'Jess said that she knew he was going to ask me to dance, but I never thought... I mean, why should he want to dance with me? Didn't the Americans look handsome in their uniforms? And he had such lovely manners, calling me "ma'am" and asking for permission to call me Ruthie,' Ruthie rushed on breathlessly, so plainly aglow with delight that her naïvety made Diane feel a hundred years her senior, rather than a mere half-dozen.

What could she say to her, Diane wondered wryly. She ought to warn her not to take her GI or his compliments seriously in case she got hurt, but the shining look of delight on Ruthie's face made it impossible for her to do so.

'I don't suppose I'll ever see him again,' Ruthie told her, betraying an unexpectedly practical streak. 'But I'll know that I'll remember last night for the rest of my life,' she breathed, before asking sympathetically, 'Are you feeling all right now?'

'Yes, apart from an aching head, and my bruised pride,' Diane told her. 'I can't believe I was silly enough to let something like that happen. Just let it be a warning to you, Ruthie. Young men about to go to war and risk their lives don't always remember to be gentlemen.'

'No, I know. Jess told me that you have to be careful and that when a man asks you to prove how much you love him, you have to tell him to prove that he loves you.'

Diane laughed. Jess certainly had her head screwed on the right way, and Ruthie was un-likely to come to much harm if she heeded Jess's words of wisdom.

'I'm just on my way back from the allotments,' Ruthie told her. 'Mr Talbot from number eight looks after Dad's allotment now and he always makes sure that me and mum get plenty of fresh veg, so I've just been down to thank him.'

'You and Jess and the others work on muni-tions, Jess was saying,' Diane prompted as they fell into step.

'Yes. We all have to do our bit for the war effort, don't we?'

'You didn't fancy joining up and wearing a uniform, then? Not that it's any of my business, of course.'

'I did think of it,' Ruthie admitted wistfully,

'but I didn't feel I could leave Mum. I'm all she's got now...' The happiness had disappeared from her face, leaving her looking uncomfortable and tense.

Remembering what Mrs Lawson had said about Ruthie's mother's mental condition, Diane didn't pursue the matter, saying lightly instead, 'Well, I think it takes a very brave person to work in munitions.'

'I was really frightened at first,' Ruthie admitted. 'But Jess says that you just have to make sure that you do things properly.' She gave a small soft sigh. 'I didn't want last night to end. I didn't even want to dance at first. I was afraid that I'd fall over my own feet, but Glen just made it all seem so easy, even jitterbugging.'

Poor little Ruthie, Diane reflected wryly, she had got it bad and was totally infatuated with her GI already, by the sound of it. Her heart was bound to be broken, just like hers had been. That was what war was all about for their sex, wasn't it? Love and death. Both of them equally painful. She certainly never wanted to love again, but nor, Diane realised, did she want to be another Myra, and filled with bitterness. What was there, though, for woman like her, who had loved and lost and who carried their own wounds of war deep inside themselves?

'I'd better go in, I don't like to leave Mother for too long.'

Diane had been so deeply involved with her own bleak thoughts that she hadn't realised they had reached Ruthie's house. They said goodbye, and Diane made her way slowly back to her

125

billet, vowing to stop thinking about her broken heart. At least working helped to keep her most private thoughts and emotions at bay.

Myra had dressed as carefully for her afternoon out as though she had actually been meeting Nick rather than having no one's company other than her own. Her white silk dress, with its scattering of rich scarlet poppies, might have been bought second-hand, but it still clung seductively to her curves, whilst her hat, with its matching trim, was tilted at exactly the right angle to draw attention to her mouth, painted with her precious red lipstick. She was perfectly well aware of the looks she was attracting as she walked towards Lyons' Corner House, even if she was behaving as though she wasn't. The café was very busy, filled with men in uniform and the women they were escorting. Half a dozen or so people were standing outside the door. They could have been queuing but Myra decided to take the view that they were simply thinking about whether or not to do so, dodging past them and going inside. A couple of nippies were busy resetting recently vacated tables. One of them, set up for four people, was in full view of the door, and Myra headed for it.

''Ere, you can't sit there,' the indignant nippy told Myra. 'This here is a table for four.'

'I'm going to be joined by some friends,' Myra told her determinedly, sitting down. If Nick should decide to come in on the off chance that he might find her here – and she was saying 'if', mind, and not that he would – then it made sense for her to be seated somewhere where he could

126

see her.

'I'll have a pot of tea, please, and look sharp about it,' she told the nippy.

The girl glowered at her, obviously not believing her claim to be waiting for friends, but unable to challenge her over it. The two couples who she had walked past were also now inside the café and looking crossly at her, but Myra didn't care. She opened her handbag and removed the copy of *Picture Post* she had brought with her. Then she carefully crossed her legs and posed herself so that she was on view to anyone coming in through the door, before pretending to be engrossed in reading it.

'I thought you said you was meeting friends, only we've got people waiting for these tables.'

Myra lifted her gaze from her *Picture Post* and blew out a cloud of smoke, narrowing her eyes as she looked at the nippy.

'My, you're sharp, aren't you?' she told her. 'You'd better be careful you don't cut yourself. My friends have obviously been delayed. You'd better bring me another pot of tea.'

From behind her magazine, Myra watched as the girl made her way determinedly towards a supervisor, saying something to her that made her look over in Myra's direction. She didn't care what they said, she wasn't going to move.

'Waiting for anyone special?'

Myra nearly dropped her cigarette.

Nick. How had he managed to creep up on her without her seeing him?

'Not really,' she managed to answer. 'I just

127

came in for a cup of tea. What about you? What brings you here?' she asked, striving to appear only casually interested.

'I'll give you three guesses,' he told her softly, pulling out one of the chairs and dropping into it, leaning towards her, his long legs stretched out in front of him. 'I've been thinking about you. You have a hell of a way of keeping a guy from his sleep at night, making him think thoughts he shouldn't be having, do you know that?'

The nippy was returning with her tea. It gave Myra a great deal of satisfaction to see the look on her face when she saw Nick.

'Bring another cup, will you?' Myra directed her coolly.

'I thought you said you was expecting three friends,' the nippy returned sharply.

'Hey, you should have said that you were expecting friends to join you.' Nick made to stand up.

'No. I mean... I was, but they must have changed their minds.' Myra told him. Damn the wretched waitress and her big mouth.

'It's a bit of luck me running into you like this,' Nick said when he had sat back into his chair. 'A few of the guys have been thinking of driving over to Blackpool next Saturday. They say the Tower Ballroom there is a good place for dancing. How about coming along with us?'

'Well, they do say that there's safety in numbers,' Myra acknowledged. 'Will these other guys be inviting girls to go along as well?' Officially she wasn't off duty on Saturday night but she would wangle the evening off by persuading one of the other girls to change duties with her. The chance to spend an evening at the Tower Ballroom alone was worth parting with a couple of pairs of the nylons she had had from Al, never mind going there with Nick. Not that she had any intention of letting Nick himself see how much his invitation had thrilled her.

'Sure they will,' he said easily. 'We'll make up a party, guys and their girls. We'll organise the transport – pick you up outside Lime Street Station. What do you say?'

'I suppose it will be a change from the Grafton,' Myra answered with a small careless shrug.

The overofficious nippy was still hovering, and the look she gave Myra as she stood up to leave was only just short of open contempt.

'Pity it's not dark yet,' Nick murmured to Myra as they left, 'otherwise I'd offer to walk you home.'

'Who says I'd let you?' Myra countered. Pure excitement was running hotly through her veins, so hotly that she felt also dizzy.

'Oh, I'd find a way of making sure that you let me, sweet stuff,' Nick promised.

'Hey, Mancini, get a move on.'

'Sorry, sugar, but I've got to go.' Nick held up his arm in acknowledgement of the shouted command from the sergeant standing beside the waiting Jeep. 'Otherwise Sergeant Polanski is gonna shoot me out of tonight's crap game.' Before Myra could stop him, he leaned down and kissed her hard and purposefully full on the mouth. Myra could hear the roar of approval from his waiting comrades.

'Outside the station, say five o'clock next Satur-

129

day afternoon,' Nick told her as he stepped back and then strolled arrogantly towards the Jeep.

At last she had found a man who was a real man, Myra acknowledged; an American man; a man who could give her the kind of life she wanted.

The city centre was busy with people coming and going, and groups of men in American uniform passing the time whilst they waited for their transport back to their base at Burtonwood, watching the girls who walked past them. The Americans, with their immaculate uniforms and their pockets full of money, had brought a buzz of energy and excitement to the grim bleakness of the war-ravaged city. It was no wonder that women were drawn to them, Myra decided, eyeing the dull uniforms and war-weary pallor of a small group of British Army men with disdain. They looked shabbier and smaller than the Americans, bitterness in the looks they were directing towards the smartly dressed GIs, who were laughing and joking as they flirted with the girls whilst the British were ignored. Too bad, Myra decided unsympathetically, turning her own back on the men as she crossed the street, her mind full of plans to ensure that she would be able to get the coming Saturday evening off.

'Well, if it isn't the street's prettiest girl. Now there's a welcome sight for a poor weary soldier to feast his eyes on.'

'That's enough of your nonsense, Billy Spencer,' Jess half scolded the tall, dark-haired man who had caught up with her as she walked home.

Billy was five years her senior and Jess had

known him all her life. His family had lived in the street as long as her own. Now she eyed him critically, firmly refusing to be impressed by the breadth of his shoulders or the handsome face beneath the thick shiny hair that any girl would have killed for. It was no good her rebellious heart complaining because she wasn't going to allow it to moon over Billy. He had more than enough girls soft on him without her joining the queue. The truth was that Billy was a heartbreaker, and that teasing smile of his, like those twinkling blue eyes, had coaxed many a girl into giving him her heart – and more than her heart, if the gossip Jess had heard was anything to go by.

The very fact that he continued to flirt with her even though he knew she was aware of the tricks he got up to only went to prove just what a fool she would be even to think about letting down her guard around him.

'Fancy taking pity on a poor soldier who's only got twenty-four hours' leave before he has to go back and risk getting himself killed for his country?' he asked her.

Jess gave him a derisive look. 'Risk getting yourself killed? That's a good one. Your regiment's on home duties,' Jess reminded him.

'It's very dangerous, keeping an eye on them barrage balloons,' he told her, straight-faced. 'Anything could happen, what with you girls being that desperate to get your hands on a bit of silk to make yourselves a few pairs of new drawers.'

'Oh, trust you to come up with something smutty like that, Billy Spencer,' Jess replied scornfully.

'Come on, you know you like me really,' he coaxed her, giving her a broad wink. 'I bet you go to bed every night hoping that I'm going to ask you out.'

'What? I'll have you know I do no such thing. I'd have to be out of me wits to go fancying someone like you,' she told him wrathfully. But she was all too uncomfortably aware of the way her heart was beating far too fast and of the betraying colour that was slowly seeping up under her skin, despite her attempts to control it. Determined not to let him get the better of her, she fanned herself vigorously with her hand and complained, 'It's too hot to stand out here listening, to you talk a load of rubbish.'

'Rubbish?' He gave her a mock injured look. 'I'll have you know them was me best girl-catching lines.'

'Don't give me that. I've heard about how you've bin boasting you had a different girl for every day of the week.'

'Ah, but that's only because you won't be my girl, Carrot Top.'

Jess flashed him an indignant look.

'Say the word and I'll pack them all in and be true to you and no one else. I can see us now. Number eighty-one's empty, right next to your Auntie Jane. We could be married and moved in there in next to no time. Allus on at me to settle down, my mam is. Mind you, I don't know as she'll be too keen on gingernut grandkids.'

'Me and you married?' Jess had to steel herself against the shaky feeling in her stomach. 'As if!'

'Why not?'

Suddenly he wasn't smiling any more and there was a look in his eyes as he stepped closer to her that made Jess feel far too vulnerable.

'Because...' feverishly she hunted round for something to say that would bring this dangerous conversation to an end, and quickly, '... because I'm already seeing someone else, that's why not,' she told him triumphantly.

'Someone else? You mean you're walking out wi' someone?'

'Yes.'

'Who?'

Who? Jess thought frantically. She'd got herself in a fine mess now, and it was all Billy's fault, tormenting her like he had, but she wasn't going to back down now and let him win.

'You don't know him,' she told him airily. 'He's an American.'

'A GI? You're going out with a GI?' Billy looked very different without a smile on his face. 'I thought better of you than that.'

'And what's that supposed to mean?'

'Work it out for yourself, Jess. An ordinary decent British soldier isn't good enough for you. You'd rather have a GI, who throws his money around and boasts about how he can have his pick of the girls just by offering them a few pairs of stockings. Well, good luck to him. Personally, I'd rather have a girl who thinks a bit more of herself than to give her favours away so cheaply.'

He was turning away before Jess could retaliate, leaving her to shout down the street after him, 'Well, Walter isn't like that. He's a gentleman ...

133

and ... he'd never say anything to a girl about her drawers.

'Oh, blast you, Billy Spencer,' she muttered angrily under her breath as he continued to walk away from her without turning round.

NINE

'Group Captain wants to see you. She said you were to report to her the moment you came on duty.'

Diane tried not to look as worried as she felt as Susan delivered the message in a clipped and very cool voice. Even so, she couldn't help asking anxiously, 'Did she say what it was about?'

'No, but I doubt there's many people working in the Dungeon who haven't heard about Saturday night.'

Diane could feel her face burning.

'I must say that you fooled me. I didn't have you down as that type at all.'

'I'm not,' Diane protested. 'Someone must have put something in my drink.'

Susan's eyebrows rose.

'It's the truth,' Diane persisted.

'Well, you'd better hope that Group Captain Barker believes you, and if I were you I wouldn't keep her waiting.'

'No. I'd better cut along now,' Diane agreed.

Her heart was thumping as she walked down the corridor that led to the Group Captain's office. Thank heavens she had taken the time to polish her shoes last night and iron her tie. She knocked briefly on the door and then smoothed her hands nervously over her skirt as she waited for permission to enter.

'Ah, Wilson.' Group Captain Barker's voice was as cool as Susan's had been. She didn't invite Diane to sit down, or even to stand at ease, and Diane was acutely aware of the warrant officer standing beside the captain.

'Stand up straight when the captain speaks to you,' the warrant officer bawled out, 'and straighten that tie.'

'You will be aware, I am sure, of the reason you are here,' Group Captain Barker began coldly.

Willing her voice not to betray her, Diane said quietly, 'If it's about what happened at the Grafton on Saturday night, ma'am...'

Group Captain Barker reached for her glasses and put them on before looking down at her desk.

'On Saturday night you visited a dance hall where you were seen in the company of several American soldiers. Certain insulting remarks were made about our own servicemen, and you, it seems, were so drunk that you were unable to stand up properly. Furthermore, you accosted an RAF officer whilst he was dancing with his wife, and...'

Listening to the allegations read out by Group Captain Barker, Diane bit down so hard on her bottom lip that she could taste blood. She was desperate to put her side of the story and defend herself but at the same time she was very aware of Warrant Officer Whiteley's coldly disapproving presence and her own training, so instead of rushing impetuously in she managed to request formally, 'Permission to speak, please, Ma'am.'

'And your behaviour was such as to bring discredit not just on yourself but on the uniform you wear,' the captain continued, ignoring her request.

Diane was nearly in tears. Nothing, not even losing Kit, had reduced her to such shamed misery.

'So,' Group Captain Barker demanded, 'what have you to say for yourself?'

Diane took a deep breath and prayed that she would remain calm enough to tell her side of things properly.

'I was drinking shandy, that's all. I believe that something stronger must have been added to my drink without my knowledge. I know that doesn't excuse my behaviour. I should have been on my guard and realised–'

'Indeed you should. If spirits of some sort had been added to your drink surely you should have noticed this?'

Under normal circumstances Diane knew that she was right, but Myra had practically forced her to empty her glass at speed so that she hadn't had a chance to taste it properly.

However, an unwritten code she refused to break made it impossible for her to involve Myra in the trouble she was now in.

'I was hot ... I assumed it was shandy in the glass and I drank it so quickly that by the time I realised it was too late...'

'You do realise how serious an issue this is, don't you?' the lieutenant demanded harshly. 'We are very proud of the good name the WAAF has here. Things may have been different at your previous posting.'

Diane swallowed back her longing to defend herself.

'You realise, of course, that this kind of behaviour cannot be tolerated?'

'Yes, ma'am,' Diane agreed woodenly.

Was she going to be dismissed, drummed out of the WAAF and sent home in disgrace? She could hardly bear to think of the shame that would cause her parents. With every word of criticism she was having to endure, her angry resentment against the GIs was growing.

'You say you believe that spirits were added to your drink by the American soldiers you were with?' Group Captain Barker queried.

'Yes,' Diane confirmed.

'You are ready to swear to this on oath?'

'Yes. There can't be any other explanation.'

'Well, I have to say that I was extremely surprised to learn about what had happened. You hadn't struck me as the sort of young woman who would behave so foolishly and irresponsibly – quite the opposite. And...' Group Captain Barker paused and then stood up, 'unhappily this isn't the first time we have had reports of American soldiers behaving in a less than chivalrous way towards British women both in and out of uniform, although I must say I would have expected one of my own girls to have recognised the danger of getting too friendly with soldiers so far away from their own homes and families. Having said that, since you have given me your word that you believe your drink was interfered with, I am prepared to overlook what happened – on this occasion. Should something of this sort happen again–'

'It won't, ma'am,' Diane stammered as the lieutenant gave her a look of angry incredulity for forgetting herself and interrupting the captain.

'I also intend to have a word with the C-in-C here and ask him to speak to his opposite number at Burtonwood with regard to the behaviour of his men.

'Now whilst you are here there is something else I wish to discuss with you.' Although the captain's voice had warmed slightly, the lieutenant was still looking at Diane as though she wanted to put her on a charge.

'Take a seat,' Group Captain Barker instructed.

Diane was glad to obey. Her legs were now trembling so much she wasn't sure she could continue to stand stiffly to attention for very much longer.

'Our C-in-C considers it important that we establish good working relationships here at Derby House with our American allies. Men's lives depend on the success of our convoys, and monitoring and protecting them from our base here is work that we all know demands the utmost dedication and concentration. The smallest error in detecting enemy activity can result in convoys being torpedoed, and ships and men's lives lost. We are all aware that some of the American airmen coming over feel very much on their mettle and determined to prove themselves. They are arriving in a country whose airmen have proved themselves as saviours, and naturally some of these young American airmen may feel that they are being looked down on and might, therefore, be inclined to behave recklessly in an attempt to match this bravery. The C-in-C feels that by welcoming them we can impress on them the necessity for calm, controlled behaviour from those who fly the planes that protect our convoys. With a view to fostering such good relations, he has decided to invite some of our American allies to welcome parties at Derby House and he has asked me to put forward the names of those of my girls whom I consider to be suitable for such an important and delicate assignment. What the C-in-C wants is for our American allies to feel they are welcome, but he is aware that they will be missing the female company of their own wives and families, and what he does not want is to encourage the wrong kind of behaviour. Prior to hearing about the events of Saturday night I had put your name forward.'

Diane gave a small start and was frowned back into place by a withering look from the warrant officer.

'Since you have given me your word that you were in no way responsible for what happened, I am prepared to let my recommendation stand. I was in two minds about giving you this second chance, but in view of your previously unblemished record and the excellent report from your previous posting I have decided to err on the side of generosity, on this occasion. However, let me make it plain to you that there must be no repeat of Saturday night's behaviour.'

Somehow or other Diane managed to scramble to her feet, salute, thank the Group Captain for giving her a second chance and get herself outside and into the corridor without making a total fool of herself. She was in no fit state to go back to the ops room, though. Instead she hurried down to the ablutions block, where she locked herself in one of the lavatories and gave her nose a good blow to stem her tears, whilst making a vehement and silent vow to show the captain just how worthy of her second chance she truly was.

Back in the ops room she was conscious of her slightly pink nose and overbright eyes, and equally conscious of the cool hostility of the other girls as she took her place at the chart desk.

When it was time for them to go for their lunch break she hung back, not wanting to force her company on them or run the risk of being deliberately ignored.

'Buck up,' Susan told her briskly, adding not unsympathetically, 'Hiding away in here won't help. You're going to have to face everyone at some stage and it might as well be sooner rather than later.'

'It isn't that,' Diane told her. 'I just wasn't sure you'd all want me with you now.'

'We're all in this war together, and we owe it to one another to stick together. I dare say the captain gave you a pretty rough time?' Susan enquired with pity.

'It was only what I deserved,' Diane admitted honestly, 'and at least she accepts that my drink was tampered with.'

'Well, I can't say I'm surprised. There've been

140

rumours about some of the Americans from Burtonwood and the way they behave towards the girls who are foolish enough to get involved with them. Like I said earlier, I wouldn't have thought you were the type. It didn't go unnoticed, though, that you were with Myra, and it's well known amongst the girls what she's like.'

'You know I'd agreed to go to the Grafton with her and I didn't feel I could let her down. I did let her know that I wasn't happy about ... certain things...'

Diane gave a small unhappy sigh. Perhaps she wasn't as cut out to be the kind of woman who threw herself into flirtation and loving men and then leaving them as she had thought. Saturday night had left her feeling grubby and shamed, and it hurt that others obviously thought the same thing and were now blaming her for bringing shame on them all.

'The best thing to do is to put the whole thing behind you,' Susan told her. 'You won't be the first girl in uniform to make a bit of a fool of herself and you certainly won't be the last. One word of warning, though. The girls here tend to think of themselves above the kind of vulgar hanging around outside dance halls and fish-and-chip queues, hoping to get picked up by GIs, that some of the local girls go in for. In fact, they tend to give the Americans a bit of a wide berth and only go out with our own chaps. That way we don't get branded as cheap. You'd be wise to follow suit.'

'Enemy sighted at...'

As the staccato voice, tense with deliberately

141

controlled urgency, called out the grid references coming in from a naval corvette on convoy duty in code, the Wrens moved swiftly to check the convoy's position whilst Diane and the other Waafs double-checked the position of the nearest aircraft.

It had already been an eventful day in a personal sense, Diane acknowledged, what with her interview with Group Captain Barker this morning, and now it looked as though the rest of her shift was going to be even more eventful, albeit in a far more important way.

'Surely they're too far north for Canada,' Diane whispered worriedly to Susan, who was standing motionless whilst she watched the U-boat sightings being chalked up on the blackboard.

The atmosphere in the Dungeon had suddenly become very tense; even the air they were breathing tasted different somehow, Diane recognised, whilst the temperature had risen with the tension. There seemed to be a collective holding of breath whilst everyone waited for the next staccato burst of radio communication.

'They aren't going to Canada,' Susan told her without moving her gaze from the blackboard. 'They're heading for Iceland and then from there, they're going on to Murmansk.'

'Well, if you ask me, it's bad enough asking a man to risk his life to bring essential supplies into this country, never mind having him take even more of a risk with it to get tanks to them Ruskies,' a small dark-haired young woman burst out angrily.

Diane's heart lurched against her ribs whilst

her stomach churned sickly on behalf of the convoy and the families they had left behind.

'It's all been hush-hush. Poor sods, if they get torpedoed in those seas they won't stand a chance; they'll freeze to death in minutes. Normally my hubby's all in favour of everything Winnie wants to do, but you should have heard him when he learned about this. Talk about the air turning blue! We aren't supposed to know,' one of the Wrens told Diane, 'but how can we not know when we can see the ships leaving Loch Ewe, where they assembled, and then heading out to Iceland? The convoy will sail from there to Murmansk. My hubby said he'd been talking to a sailor who told them about the kit they'd all been fitted out with: lambswool blankets, and lambswool waistcoats and even extra Calor oil heaters for the cabins, and of course they've been told to communicate with one another using flags instead of radio so that their messages can't be picked up by the Luftwaffe or the U-boats. I'm just thankful that my John isn't sailing with them, that's all.'

The teleprinters had fallen silent. A naval officer, pale and hollow-eyed from lack of sleep and fresh air, was studying the new information, whilst Wrens moved swiftly to translate it onto maps and the chart, the whole room exhaling a sigh of relief when it became clear that the U-boat threat had been a false alarm and that, for the moment, the convoy was still safe.

'We lost a plane up there a couple of months back,' one of the girls chipped in starkly. 'One survivor, but he'd got frostbite so badly they had to amputate his hands and feet. He died in the end. He was engaged to a girl I know. She didn't recognise him when she went to see him in hospital. His face had turned black.'

'That's enough of that.' Susan stopped the conversation quietly, and Diane remembered that Susan's husband was on escort duty with the Arctic convoys.

'Yes, Pat?' Susan greeted the uniformed Wren hurrying towards her.

'Can you lend us one of your girls, only we're a couple short,' she begged.

'It depends how long you want her for.'

'Only for the rest of the shift. We need someone to go up the ladder and write down information as it's called out.'

'You go, Diane,' Susan instructed. 'But I'll need her back tomorrow,' she warned.

'Don't worry if you haven't done this before,' the Wren reassured Diane as she hurried her to the huge information blackboards filling one wall. 'All you have to do is write down what's called out to you. You'll need a quick hand and a decent head for heights, that's all. You can take that ladder over there.' She gave a brisk nod in the direction of the ladder, over twenty foot, closest to the door.

Obediently Diane did as she had been instructed, climbing up the ladder very cautiously, and listening out for the commands shouted up to her as she and the other girls worked to keep the blackboard information up to date. It wasn't so very different from what she had been doing with her own team, except that they didn't have to climb such high ladders, and of course she was dealing with the convoy itself rather than its air cover.

You certainly needed a good head for heights, Diane admitted, responding ruefully to the girl on the next ladder as she mouthed across, 'It seems strange at first, but you soon get used to it. Just don't look down too much.'

Although with a constant stream of personnel coming in and out of the ops room, and the work she had to do, she should have been far too busy to be aware of one unwontedly familiar voice amongst so many, somehow Diane recognised the major's voice the moment he stepped into the room. The shock of hearing it had her forgetting not to look down, and determinedly she put the fit of dizziness that swamped her down to vertigo than it having anything to do with the major himself. He was standing with his British counterpart, discussing the deployment of the reconnaissance craft, and surely far too involved in that to be aware of her, Diane acknowledged in relief. And yet whether because she was looking at him and he sensed it, or for some other reason, he suddenly looked up at her, catching her off guard so that their gazes locked. The contempt in his made Diane's face burn. She was glad of a new instruction shouted to her for the opportunity it gave to turn away. And yet even with her back to him she was still somehow conscious of his every movement. Because of the humiliation she felt at knowing he had witnessed her drunken behaviour on Saturday night, that was all, Diane reassured herself. Behaviour that had been caused by his men.

Her ladder was positioned so close to one of the doors that the door itself had been pinned back to prevent anyone coming in banging it into the ladder. With so much going on no one had noticed that someone had inadvertently let the door close. The first Diane knew of the danger she was in was when she felt the door thud into her ladder, causing it to start to slip sideways.

'Christ! Lookout!' she heard someone yell, and then everything was happening so quickly that it all became a blur. Instinctively she knew she had to escape from the falling ladder.

'Jump,' a harshly familiar voice demanded. 'Jump.'

Automatically she obeyed, gasping with shock as a pair of strong arms caught hold of her and the air whooshed out of her lungs, whilst the stiffness of gold braid on a uniform jacket scratched at her face.

The major.

She could feel the fierce, fast thud of his heartbeat against her own. She could feel too the hard grip of his hands on her body as he held her and then slowly lowered her until her feet could touch the floor. She looked up at him and then forgot what it was she had been about to say – forgot everything, in fact, as her heartbeat picked up and matched his frantic race with a swift fierce pulse. The second turned into a full minute and still neither of them moved. *Was* this what happened when your body missed its physical contact with a man? Was this why it was so forbidden for young women to know the intimacies of sex before they were married; because of the need it might awaken within them? How could she even think about need and this man together?

A violent shudder went through her just at the same moment as the major released her, saying harshly, 'Next time I suggest you try taking more water with it before you go climbing ladders.'

His comment made her gasp in outrage but it was too late for her to defend herself: he was already walking away whilst the other girls were crowding anxiously around her, demanding to know if she was all right, and the white-faced Wren who had been the cause of the accident apologised over and over again.

TEN

'I thought you and me was going to be best friends, Ruthie, but it seems to me that you've got more time for that lot you're going to the Grafton with,' Maureen grumbled that morning at the factory.

'Me going out with them doesn't stop us being friends,' Ruthie tried to reassure her.

'But you'll be going to the Grafton again wi' 'em tonight I'll bet,' Maureen challenged her.

Guiltily Ruthie nodded. She hadn't stopped thinking about last Saturday all week and she had been thrilled to bits when Jess had asked her if she fancied going to the Grafton again this week. Mrs Brown had been almost as excited for her as she was herself, proclaiming archly that she

147

wouldn't be at all surprised if a certain GI wasn't going to make a beeline for Ruthie the minute he saw her.

'Oh, I don't know about that,' Ruthie had felt bound to protest. 'He may not even be there.' But of course she was hoping desperately that he would be.

She did feel bad about Maureen, though. She had told Ruthie earlier in the week that there was no chance of her ever going out dancing because she was needed at home to help look after 'the little 'uns'.

'Well, seein' as you keep on sayin' that you and me are friends, will you do us a favour then?' Maureen asked.

All too relieved at the thought of being able to do something to alleviate her guilt, Ruthie agreed.

'I'm trying to get some bits and pieces together for the little 'uns – a surprise, like, for Christmas – and I was wondering if you would keep hold of it for me, tek it home wi' you, like, until I ask you for it.'

'For Christmas?' Ruthie asked surprised. 'But that's months away yet.'

'Yes, I know that.' Maureen sounded impatient. 'But like I said, it's to be a surprise and I don't want the little 'uns cottoning on. It's not much, just a few tins I've managed to save up to get on the black market and some bits and pieces.'

'The black market! Oh...'

'There! I knew it! You say you're my friend but when I ask you for a bit of help you go all hoity-toity on me. It's all right for the likes of you wot can manage on the ration, but my mam's got her

148

own kids and we've got our Fanny and our Mabel's kids living wi' us as well. Poor little mites are starving, crying half the night for their mams, their little bellies half empty on account of this bloody war. All I want to do is give them a bit of a treat for Christmas, but if you don't want to help me...'

'No. I mean yes, of course I'll help you,' Ruthie assured her sympathetically.

'Well, that's all right then. I'll tell you wot: if you give me your locker key then I can put the stuff in your locker without anyone else seeing. Then you can tek it home wi' you.'

'Well...'

'Well what? What skin is it off your nose?' Maureen demanded almost aggressively.

'All right then.' Ruthie gave in. She wasn't sure she felt comfortable about handling black-market goods, but she couldn't refuse to help; not when Maureen had described the children's hunger so vividly. It was bad enough being grown up and feeling hungry all the time, but it must be truly awful for the children, who couldn't really be expected to understand why there wasn't enough for them to eat. Everywhere you went people talked longingly about the food they would be able to eat once the war was over. Sometimes it occupied people's minds as much as the war itself. That aching, gnawing feeling of hunger was always there, and no amount of Lord Woolton's pie, or Spam brought all the way across the Atlantic by the convoys, could banish it. Everyone talked longingly of proper fruit cake, and Victoria sandwich cake with real cream and dripping with jam; of chocolate, of roast beef Sunday dinners, rich meaty stews with light-as-air dumplings, of proper bread, and as much of anything as you wanted.

'It's all right us talking about food like we all had everything we wanted to eat before this war,' Jess had told them all at dinnertime earlier in the week when they had sat down together for their canteen meal of thin watery stew and boiled vegetables, 'but, like my Auntie Jane says, there's many a family now getting more to eat than they've ever had, and more money coming in as well.'

'Well, we might have more money coming in,' Lucy had sniffed, 'but we ain't got anything to spend it on, 'ave we?'

'It will be different after the war.' Those were the words on everyone's lips and the hope in everyone's heart, the belief they were all clinging to now with the war in its third year and the struggle of the last three years showing in people's faces.

Liverpool, more than any other city outside London, had been savaged by bombing raids, the heart wrenched out of it with the destruction of its streets and buildings. Or at least that was what Hitler hoped. The reality was that the people of Liverpool were using their well-known sense of humour to keep them going.

'We can't do owt but go on,' Ruthie had heard their neighbour saying. 'Hitler won't give up until he has us by the throat or we've beaten him, and I know which I'm putting my money on. Our lads can do it and, by golly, I intend to make sure that I do all I can to help them here at home.'

His were sentiments that Ruthie knew many of

150

her parents' generation supported. They had sons fighting for their country, after all, and daughters praying for their safety. Some of the younger generation, though – especially the girls who were having to live with the reality of rationing, and the absence of the country's young men – were beginning to chaff resentfully against the restrictions the war had brought. And now with the Americans arriving in increasing numbers, the gulf between the way they were having to live and the way their allies were able to live sometimes seemed to be dividing the women of the country into two opposing camps: one that welcomed the arrival of the Americans, and one that was bitterly opposed to it.

Ruthie knew which camp she belonged to, and besides, it was more the older generation that disapproved of the Americans, she suspected, fearing the effect they might have on young women having to live without their own men.

'Give us your key this afternoon, when we go off shift, then. I'm volunteering to work overtime on Sunday, so I can put me stuff in your locker then and I'll give yer your key back on Monday morning.'

Ruthie nodded. The foreman was looking at them, and she didn't want him coming over. Only yesterday he had praised her for the speed she was developing at filling the shells. His praise had given her a warm glow of pride. It bucked a person up no end to know they were doing their bit. Every shell she filled was helping their men to do their job, and every one they didn't fill properly was making it harder for them to do that job. That

151

was what the foreman was constantly telling them, and Ruthie had taken his words to heart. But when she imagined someone using 'her' shells, that someone was wearing an American uniform not a British one. Would *he* be there again this Saturday? And if he was, would he ask her to dance again? She could hardly breathe for the bubbles of excitement fizzing inside her tummy.

'So you won't be coming to Blackpool this evening, then?'

'No. I won't be off duty until eight and, to tell the truth, Myra, I really don't want anything to do with the Americans. Not after what happened last Saturday.'

'If I was you, I wouldn't make so much of it,' Myra told Diane carelessly. 'It was just a bit of fun, that's all.'

'Just a bit of fun that nearly cost me my job and certainly cost me the respect of the other girls,' Diane pointed out quietly.

'Oh, don't be so prissy. So you had a bit too much to drink? So what?'

Diane shook her head. Myra's attitude underlined how very differently they felt about things. But they were billeted together, and being in the WAAF taught one to stick by one's colleagues, even when you didn't agree with what they were doing.

'You were lucky to get someone to give up their Saturday night off and switch shifts with you,' Diane commented, as she checked her reflection in the small mirror in their shared bedroom.

'Well, as to that,' Myra paused, 'the truth is that

I couldn't get anyone to change with, so I've decided to play wag and just not go in.'

'You can't mean that!' Diane said incredulously.

'Why not? Other girls are off sick all the time.' She picked up her hairbrush and started fiddling with her hair, avoiding meeting Diane's appalled look.

'Off sick, yes, but you aren't sick. You can't just pretend that you are so that you can go off to Blackpool, Myra. It's wrong.'

'Oh, for goodness' sake, I might have known *you'd* start moralising.' Myra banged down her hairbrush. 'Look, I'm going to Blackpool with Nick, and nothing and no one is going to stop me. I've *got* to go, Diane. If I don't ... well, Nick isn't the type who is going to hang around waiting for a girl when he can see there are plenty of others willing to take her place.'

'And that doesn't tell you anything about the kind of man he is?' Diane challenged her.

'Of course it does. It tells me that he's the kind of man who knows what he wants and who makes sure he gets it. My kind of man. I'm going to Blackpool and that's that.'

Diane wanted to stay and talk her out of what she was doing but she knew if she did she would be late for her own shift.

'Look, why don't you change your mind and come too?'

Was that a note of pleading she could hear in Myra's voice? Why? Because she wasn't as sure of herself as she liked to make out?

'I'm sorry but no.'

'Well, suit yourself,' Myra told her dismissively. 'It's your loss. I've heard that the Tower Ballroom is really something special.'

'How are you going to get there and back in an evening?' Diane couldn't stop herself from asking uneasily. 'You can't rely on the trains.'

'Who said anything about going on a train?' Myra smirked triumphantly. 'No, Nick said he would fix everything and that includes the transport.'

Diane frowned, her unease growing. Myra was placing a lot more faith in her GI date than she would have in her shoes. Meeting up with someone at the Grafton was one thing, going AWOL from her shift and agreeing to visit somewhere as far away as Blackpool with him was a different thing altogether, but according to Myra a crowd of girls and GIs were going. And, of course, the Americans, unlike their British counterparts, were not limited as to the amount of money they had to spend or, it seemed, the amount of off-duty time they had to spend it in.

'Here I am, duck,' Mrs Brown proclaimed as she knocked briefly on the back door and then came bustling into the kitchen. 'Whatever's to do?' she asked when she saw Ruthie's worried expression. 'I thought you was looking forward to going out tonight.'

'I am ... I was...' Ruthie admitted, 'but I'm worried about my mother.'

'Well, you must stop worrying. I'll look out for her right and tight, you needn't fret about that. Where is she? Listening to the wireless, I'll bet.

She loves them wireless programmes.'

Ruthie shook her head. 'She's in the parlour, but ... she isn't her normal self at all. She's hardly spoken all day, and when I talk to her she looks at me as though she doesn't know me.'

'She'll be having one of those little turns of hers, Ruthie love, that's all,' Mrs Brown said comfortingly. 'Thinking about your dad and the happy times they had together, I'll be bound. She'll be back to her normal self by the time you come back tonight, I reckon. Anyone would think that you don't want to see that handsome GI of yours,' she chuckled.

Ruthie blushed hotly. 'He isn't my GI, Mrs Brown. He only asked me for one dance, that's all.'

'Well, that's enough where young love is concerned. More than enough sometimes. You stop worrying about your mam and think about yourself instead.'

Ruthie gave her a wan smile. She didn't think she could bear not to go to the Grafton tonight, but her conscience was pricking at her, telling her that it was her duty to stay here with her mother when she was in this worryingly withdrawn mood.

'Go on.' Mrs Brown shooed her towards the door, flapping her apron at her and laughing. 'Off you go and enjoy yourself. Your mam will be fine.'

'I'll just pop my head round the door and say goodbye,' Ruthie said, hurrying into the narrow hallway, her heels tapping on the lino.

When Ruthie opened the door she saw that her mother was sitting in the fireside chair that had

155

always been Ruthie's father's chair. She looked up but her gaze was unfocused and unseeing and it caught at Ruthie's heart. Perhaps she *should* stay...

She was just about to take a step into the room when Mrs Brown bustled up, calling out, 'Here I am again, Mrs Philpott, come to sit with you and have a nice chat whilst your Ruthie goes out with her friends. See, I told you she wouldn't mind,' Mrs Brown told Ruthie firmly when her mother made no response. 'Off you go otherwise them friends of yours will think you aren't coming.'

Myra looked anxiously at the station clock. Five o'clock, Nick had said, and now it was nearly ten past. Had something happened to make him have to change their plans? If so, couldn't he have got a message to her? He knew where she was working and American servicemen were in and out of the Dungeon all day long.

She would wait until a quarter-past and not a minute longer. She had her pride, after all. But what if he arrived after that and she wasn't here? He'd think she wasn't interested. And she... She tensed as she heard the screech of tyres and a Jeep came barrelling down the road, scattering pedestrians.

Nick! She was making her way towards him even before it had stopped, ignoring the irritated looks of the people she was pushing past.

'What happened?' she demanded when she reached him. 'You're so late.'

'Sorry, babe... A bit of last-minute dickering with one of the guys.' He winked at her. 'Had to

156

collect my winnings to spend on my best girl.'

'Where's everyone else?' Myra asked him. 'You said there'd be a crowd of us going.'

He winked again. 'I decided that it would be more fun if we were on our own. Come on, jump in.'

Myra didn't hesitate. It was flattering to know that he wanted her to himself.

'You must have felt a bit let down when the others decided not to come along?' she commented archly as she settled herself beside him in the Jeep.

'Sure I felt let down, about as let down as if I'd won the platoon crap game,' he answered derisively, grinning at her. 'Hold on to your hat, babe. Blackpool, here we come.' And then he leaned across and kissed her exultantly.

'Coo, just have a look at all this lot in here,' Lucy demanded admiringly, staring round at the Stars and Stripes-bedecked dance hall.

'It's on account of it being the fourth of July and American Independence Day,' Jess told her knowledgeably.

'I know that, ta very much,' Lucy came back smartly. 'Done it up really, really nice, they have,' she added approvingly.

The dance hall owners had made a big effort to make their American allies feel welcome and that Liverpool was ready to help them celebrate their important national day.

It made Jess happy inside just looking at the flags and feeling the good mood of the crowd. Not that everyone shared her happiness, she decided, glancing across at Ruthie.

'Come on, Ruthie,' she chivvied her. 'Cheer up. You look as miserable as if you'd lost half a crown and found a sixpence. What's up?' she demanded as they handed over their money and were swept up the Grafton's staircase in the swell of eager would-be dancers, all laughing and exclaiming excitedly about the Stars and Stripes banners and decorations.

'Nothing,' Ruthie denied, summoning up a bright smile.

'Don't give me that. It's as plain as can be that something's worrying you. Come on, you can tell me,' Jess coaxed.

'It's my mother. She ... she's...' Her voice died away as she struggled between her longing to confide in Jess and her natural desire to protect her mother's privacy.

'She's bound to feel a bit low at times,' Jess comforted her. 'My Auntie Fran's just the same. Her Alfred was on a tram that got hit by a bomb during the May blitz. Only this week she was saying as how he would have been sixty-five this month.'

Ruthie hesitated. It wasn't like her to talk about her mother to others, but she felt that she just had to unburden herself, and who better to talk to about her feelings than Jess? There was something about Jess and the kindness and warmth she had shown her that told Ruthie that her new friend would understand and not sit in judgement on her poor mother.

'It's a bit different with Mum,' she told her sadly. 'She and Dad were so close that it's as though sometimes she can only get by by pretending that he's still here. It's not that she isn't right in her head or anything,' she told Jess, anxious not to give her the wrong impression of her mother's condition. 'The doctor has told us that she is, but that sometimes she just needs to pretend that Dad's still here. Not that she knows what she's doing or why. She can be as right as rain one minute and then the next something sets her off...' Ruthie broke off, shaking her head in bewilderment at the change that had overcome her much-loved mother. 'She doesn't mean any harm, but she doesn't realise. If I'm not careful she slips out and starts to go looking for Dad. Luckily we've got lovely neighbours and they keep an eye on her for me. I was that worried when we heard that this call-up for women to do war work was going to come in. That's why I decided to get a job in munitions ahead of it, so that I could stay at home and look after her. I do so worry when I have to leave her. And ... and I feel guilty as well.'

'Aw, Ruthie...'

The touch of Jess's hand on her arm and the sympathy in her voice made Ruthie's eyes fill with tears.

'You mustn't feel like that. I'm sure it's the last thing your mam would want. And my guess is too that your mam would want you to go out and 'ave a bit of fun.'

When Ruthie continued to look uncertain, Jess reminded her firmly, 'Anyway, I thought you said that a neighbour had offered to sit in with your mam?'

'Yes, yes, she has.'

159

'There you are, then. There's nothing for you to worry about, is there?'

'No, I suppose not,' Ruthie agreed doubtfully.

'Come on, you two,' Polly urged them. 'I'm gagging for a drink, me throat is that dry.'

'That's because you never stop talking,' Mel teased her.

Laughing and ribbing one another, they made their way to one of the tables, quickly settling themselves down around it and then divvying up one and sixpence each for their drinks 'kitty'.

'No, Ruthie, you only need to put half of that in.' Jess stopped Ruthie before she dropped her one and six into the empty tobacco tin Lucy had produced. 'You only drink lemonade, after all.'

'Perhaps we should teach her to drink summat a bit stronger,' Mel suggested. 'That way she'll practise and so not get herself into the state that Diane got into last week.'

'No, it's all right. I'd rather have lemonade,' Ruthie assured her hastily.

She could well imagine how horrified her father would have been to have her coming home smelling of drink. He had been so old-fashioned that he hadn't even approved of women smoking. Now, with her tummy cramping with nervous flutters of anxiety both in case Glen appeared and asked her to dance and in case he didn't, Ruthie admitted that she would have welcomed the soothing action of lighting up a cigarette. She had watched enviously the previous week as the other girls lit theirs. They had looked so sophisticated, drawing on the cigarettes and then exhaling.

She watched as Mel removed one from her

packet now and put it to her lips, quickly winking at them all before leaning across to the table behind them, which was rapidly filling up with a group of young men in Royal Navy uniforms, to say in an exaggerated drawl, 'Sorry to bother you, but could one of you give me a light?'

The speed with which the whole of the table immediately leaped to offer assistance was almost comical.

Mel certainly thought so, because she was grinning when she turned back to the girls, exhaling in triumph as she told them, 'Like taking sweeties from a kid. They'll all be over here when the band starts up again, asking us to dance, you watch.'

'You'd better watch it, Mel,' Leah warned her. 'If your Pete gets wind of you behaving like that you'll be in big trouble.'

'Huh, Pete Skinner doesn't have any rights over me, and nor will he do until he puts a ring on me finger,' Mel announced sharply. 'It's all right him saying that him and me are going steady and then disappearing off with the Eighth Army to bloody Egypt.'

'Look, here comes the band.' Jess, along with everyone else packed into the dance hall, started to clap enthusiastically.

The girls' drinks of port and lemon had arrived, and the volume of the conversation rose from all the tables, not just their own, mingling with male and female laughter.

They might be at war but they were young and alive, and here tonight they could let their hair down and have fun, even if it was *only* for tonight.

'Psst. Ruthie – over there,' Jess whispered. 'Isn't

that your Glen?'

'Where? Oh...' As she swung round and saw him, Ruthie ducked her head, not wanting the young GI to think she was trying to attract his attention.

'Walter's with him as well.' Jess had no such inhibitions. She stood up and waved, calling out enthusiastically, 'Walter, Glen, over here...'

'Jess, you shouldn't have done that,' Ruthie hissed, pulling on her arm to make her sit down.

'Why not?'

'What if they didn't want to come over?'

'Then they won't do, will they?' Jess told her practically. 'But they do, because look, here they are.'

It had been a long busy shift, and it was hard for Diane to switch her mind away from the grim battle going on in the Arctic that was more of a massacre than a true battle, with the helpless merchant ships being picked off with ease by the Germans at a rate that had brought a tense silence to the Dungeon and an edge of bleak despair to the voices of those calling out the names and positions of the damaged ships.

She might be walking up the Edge Hill Road in the evening sunshine that was an advantage of double summer time, her body warmed by the sun, but her mind was still numbed by the thought of the icy chill of the Arctic seas in which a man could only survive for a maximum of fifteen minutes without freezing to death. So many ships lost and so many men, and all for what? some of the girls were asking bitterly. So that the Russians could have their tanks? What about the needs of those seamen and their families? What about the needs of the British people, living with constant dread and constant hunger, not knowing what their future would be or if they even had one?

Diane had overheard a couple of the RAF men talking about the recent bombing raids on Germany and her heart had lodged in her mouth when she had heard the name of Kit's squadron.

'Good show, by all accounts, although they lost a couple of planes and their crews had to bale out over France,' one of the men had told the other.

Diane had to stop herself from rushing over to beg for more details. Kit wasn't part of her life any more. Easy words to say, but much harder to obey. How was she ever going to mend her broken heart if she reacted like this every time anything remotely connected with him was mentioned? Perhaps she should have gone to Blackpool with Myra. Perhaps only by plunging into the kind of life Myra led could she drown out the past. Maybe tonight if she had gone to the Grafton *she* might have been the one ordering herself a strong drink. She had seen that happen to other young women although it was seldom talked about. Young men might drink to excess to drown out the reality of war, but it was not acceptable for young women to do the same. Nevertheless they did. Diane shuddered inwardly. What was happening to her? She should be getting over Kit by now, but instead she seemed to be sinking deeper and deeper into her own misery.

For once she would have welcomed even Mrs Lawson's voluble company and her never-ending questions. The small house was pin neat but empty, her cold supper left for her in the pantry with a meat safe cover protecting it.

Spam salad. Diane looked at it without interest. The Spam, pink and marbled with fat, looked flabby and unappetising, even if the salad was fresh from the allotments. The smell of the tomatoes reminded her of her father's greenhouse. Suddenly a wave of homesickness washed over her. Tears burned the backs of her eyes. She was just about to wipe them away when she heard someone knocking on the front door.

She looked at her watch. It was nine thirty, and Mrs Lawson wasn't due back from her WVS meeting until well gone ten. It was too early, surely, for Myra to be returning unless she had had a fallout with her GI, but anyway, they both had their own keys. Uncertainly, Diane went into the hall, and looked warily through the stained-glass panel in the front door.

A man in army uniform was standing outside. Bare-headed and dark-haired, he had his back to the door and was moving impatiently from one foot to the other.

A little hesitantly, Diane opened the door and asked cautiously, 'Yes?'

'Is this where Myra Stone is billeted?' the soldier asked tiredly. 'Only I'm her husband, Jim.'

PART TWO

Summer 1942

ELEVEN

'Well...' Uncertainly, Diane looked back over her shoulder into the hallway.

'Look, this is the right address, isn't it?'

'Er, yes,' Diane was forced to admit. 'But I'm afraid that Myra isn't here at the moment.'

'On duty, is she? Just my luck.' He gave Diane a tired smile. 'Only got a forty-eight-hour pass at the last minute. Didn't even know I was coming back to Blighty until we got on the transport plane.'

Diane could see the Eighth Army insignia on his battledress and her heart ached for him.

'You'd better come in,' she told him, holding open the door. 'You see, the fact is that Myra's gone out tonight ... with ... with some friends.'

Diane was glad that she had her back to him when she told him this edited version of the truth.

'What time will she be back?'

'I'm not sure. You see, the thing is, I think they may have gone over to Blackpool.'

'Bloody hell. Oh, sorry. It's just–'

'It's all right. I understand,' Diane assured him as she led the way into the kitchen. 'I'm Diane, by the way,' she added, turning and holding out her hand to shake his. 'Myra's co-billetee.' She was praying he wouldn't ask her exactly where Myra had gone in Blackpool and who with, and she was praying too that he wouldn't take it into his head to follow her there.

'So she's gone out enjoying herself, has she? Well, I suppose I shouldn't be surprised. That's Myra all over. Never has liked missing out on a good time. I suppose it's understandable in the circumstances. Told you much about her mam and dad, has she?'

Diane shook her head. 'Like I said, I don't know when she's going to be back,' she told him, adding, 'She did say something earlier in the week about them maybe staying over and making a bit of a holiday of it, if they could find somewhere.' What on earth was she doing, lying like this for Myra? It wasn't her job to safeguard Myra's marriage, but then she wasn't doing it for Myra, was she? She was doing it for the exhausted battle-weary-looking man standing in Mrs Lawson's kitchen, who was so plainly desperate to see his wife. She couldn't let him know the truth.

'I've got meself a bed for the night with a mate who flew back with me. Comes from Liverpool, he does. He even reckoned a sister of his would let me and Myra have her spare room for the weekend.'

He pulled out a packet of Woodbines and lit one, taking a fierce drag on it. 'Sorry... Do you...?' he offered.

Diane declined. 'Look, why don't you sit down for a few minutes and let me make you a cup of tea?' she offered.

The gratitude she could see in his eyes touched her deeply. Myra ought to have been here to do this for him – this and so much more. Diane

168

could actually see the grains of sand sticking to his battle-dress, along with the lines burned into his skin by the heat of the desert sun.

'There's a bit of salad here as well, if you're hungry,' she offered him.

'I'm not taking your supper,' he told her.

'No, I ate at the canteen before I came in,' she fibbed, going to get the salad and putting it on the table for him.

From the way he wolfed it down, it looked as though he hadn't stopped to eat before catching his transport home, Diane thought, as she went to make a pot of tea.

'I'm really sorry Myra isn't here. You must be so disappointed.'

'Just a bit,' he agreed. He looked more relaxed now he had eaten, and Diane could see that behind the grimness of the soldier there was a solid kindness about him. 'It's my own fault, though. I should have got in touch with her first.' He removed a hip flask from his pocket and unscrewed it, offering it to Diane. 'Want some?'

When she said no thanks, he poured a measure of brandy into his own tea.

'Mind you, if I had told Myra I was getting leave she'd have probably decided to take herself off so that she couldn't see me anyway. Told you much about me, has she?'

'She said that she was married,' Diane assured him tactfully, 'but we tend not to talk about personal things.'

'No? I'll bet she told you that she was fed up with me, though, didn't she? She's allus telling me that. Keeps on saying she wishes she'd never married me, although she was glad enough to at the time. Of course, her dad was alive then and she reckons the only reason she wed me was to get away from him. Treated her ma real bad, her dad did. Allus knocking her about – and Myra too if he got the chance, I reckon, although she won't admit it.'

Jim's revelations shocked Diane. Her own parents were so happily married, and her father so devoted to her mother that Diane had begun to think of their relationship as a handicap to her own future happiness, because she could never hope to match it. It certainly gave more of an insight into Myra being the way she was.

Not that Myra's past excused her current behaviour. Diane felt desperately sorry for her poor husband who, despite his attempt to be cheerful, had looked so cast down when he had learned that she wasn't here. Poor man. Diane hoped that he would never discover the truth about the way Myra was carrying on in his absence.

'Course, Myra always did have big ideas about what she wanted. Allus going to the flicks and banging on about film stars and wanting to live in America, she was. Even tried to persuade me to go and live over there. I'd never heard of anything so daft. What would I want to be going to America for? But when the war broke out it brought her to her senses ... a bit.'

Had it, Diane wondered uneasily, or had Myra simply stopped telling her husband what she wanted and decided to look for another man to supply it instead; a man who understood her longing to live in America, because he was American?

They both turned towards the kitchen door as they heard the sound of a key in the front door lock, but it was Mrs Lawson returning, not Myra.

'And what's this, if you please?' she demanded sharply as Jim got clumsily to his feet when she came into the kitchen. Ignoring his outstretched hand, she turned to Diane. 'No male visitors, that's what I said and that's what I mean. I won't have no carrying-on here in my own kitchen, giving the Close a bad name, never mind using the rations to feed him with,' she told them, looking pointedly at the table with the now empty supper plate and the tea cups.

'Mrs Lawson, this is Myra's husband,' Diane explained calmly. 'He's got a forty-eight-hour leave and he called round hoping to see Myra.'

'Oh, well. Husband, is it?' Mrs Lawson studied him frowningly.

'I'm sorry if I was breaking the rules,' he apologised immediately.

'It's my fault, Mrs Lawson,' Diane broke in. 'I offered him the supper you'd left for me because I'd already eaten at Derby House, which reminds me... Cook said she had some spare tins of fruit, so I've brought back a couple for you.' Talk about being ingratiating, Diane recognised, but she felt obliged to placate her landlady, who wasn't as bad as some she had heard about, even if Cook had not so much offered the tins as had her arm twisted by one of the girls who had savvily remarked that she suspected that food intended for those working at Derby House was finding its way into the pantries of those who were in charge of it. As a result, Cook had let it be known that there were some damaged tins in the storeroom that those who wanted them could have if they wished. 'Damaged tins' was the standard code-name for those tinned food stuffs that were on ration but somehow miraculously available.

'Tins of fruit?' Mrs Lawson allowed herself to be distracted.

'Only a couple, I'm afraid,' Diane warned her. 'I got the fruit salad because I remembered you saying you liked it for your Christmas trifle.'

'Well, yes.'

'I'm sorry to have taken up so much of your time,' Myra's husband continued to apologise. 'If you'll just tell Myra that I'll call back in the morning...'

'Do you want to leave the address of the friend you're going to be staying with?' Diane asked him.

Jim rubbed the side of his face wearily. 'Yes. Thanks for reminding me about that. I must say that I'm looking forward to sleeping in a proper bed. You'd be surprised where that ruddy sand can get and how cold it can be in the desert at night.'

Mrs Lawson made a small clucking noise. 'Never let it be said that I turned one of our fighting boys away. Jack Williams down at number forty-five has a spare room. I dare say he'll be willing to give you a bed for the night. Lives on his own now, he does, since he lost his wife, and his daughter took her kiddies off to the country. I'll walk down with you and introduce you to him.'

'I don't want to put you to any trouble,' Jim was

saying but Mrs Lawson shook her head. Along with most of the country, she wanted to do whatever she could to help the brave men who were fighting for them all.

Most of the country, Diane reflected. Myra, for instance, didn't seem too troubled by the thought of how her behaviour might affect her husband, and it was impossible to be in one of the women's services for very long without hearing the whispers about women who sent Dear John letters to their men because they had found someone else.

'I've been thinking about you all week.'

Ruthie's face flooded with pink as Glen bent his head to whisper the words in her ear. The tips of his ears had gone bright red and the hand that was holding her own so tightly as they danced together felt slightly damp. He was almost as nervous as she was, Ruthie recognised with a small surge of compassion and joy.

'I wanted the ground to swallow me up when Jess called you over like that,' she told him shyly.

'And I want to sing Hallelujah,' he told her. 'But I should have asked. Have you ... is there ... is there someone else?'

'No, no, there isn't.'

'You know what? Those are just about the best words I have ever heard in the whole of my life,' Glen responded, as he squeezed her tightly.

Things were moving so fast it was no wonder she was feeling giddy, breathless, and most light-headed with joy and disbelief, Ruthie admitted. From the moment he had come over to their table, Glen had stuck to her side like glue. Not that she was complaining. She looked across to where Jess was dancing with Walter. Jess was laughing at something Walter had said to her.

'You haven't come with those other men you were here with last time,' Ruthie commented.

'No, we're all in the same platoon but some of the guys ... well, I guess we just see things differently. I'm just a farm boy from Iowa.'

'Iowa? Where's that?' Ruthie asked him dreamily. She could stay here like this in his arms, where she felt so safe and happy, for ever, she decided.

'It's in the Midwest. Farming country. Mostly crops. The granary of America, they call it,' he told her proudly. 'Not that you'd think so now after the Depression in the thirties, and the winds that blew. You don't know how glad I am that you're here tonight, Ruthie. I've been racking my brains wondering how I could see you again.'

His fingers entwined with hers and a small rush of fierce happiness suffused her.

'You see ... well, I guess what I'm trying to say is that you're a very special girl and I'm head over heels in love with you.'

'Oh, you mustn't say that,' Ruthie protested, secretly thrilled.

'Why not when it's the truth? And my mom and dad brought us kids up to always speak the truth. I've already written to them to tell them about you.'

'Oh, you haven't!'

'Yes I have. I've told them I've met the girl I want to take home to them as my wife.'

'But they'll think I'm dreadful, stealing you from some American girl.'

'There is no American girl for you to steal me from. Not that they haven't tried to match me up with someone, but I guess I kinda knew all along that you were somewhere waiting for me. I've got some photographs of my folks in my pocketbook. I'll show you them later.'

'They'll think that I'm a ... a money-grubber,' Ruthie told him, looking uncertainly at him when Glen threw back his head and laughed.

'My parents are poor farming folks, Ruthie. The Depression hit the Midwest hard, and that's why my mom wanted me and my kid sister to get good grades in school and go on to college. My mom teaches Sunday school back home and plays the piano in church, and my kid sis is in college right now training to be a teacher. Me – I guess I'm more like my dad, and when this war is over I'll be going back to the farm, and when I do, what I want more than anything else is to take you with me.'

'You mustn't say things like that,' Ruthie repeated breathlessly.

'Why not?'

'We've only just met. You may think that ... that you ... you like me now...'

'Nope, I do not think I like you at all,' Glen stopped her, mimicking her accent. 'I *know* that I love you.'

'How are you feeling now, Walter?' Jess asked sympathetically as he steered her hesitantly around the dance floor. 'Have you written to your girl yet, like I told you?' she demanded in a semi-scolding motherly tone.

'Yes. And I've told her that I love her and that I want her to wait for me,' he admitted, bashfully.

Unlike the other GIs who were dancing, Walter didn't look as though he was exactly enjoying the experience. In fact, he looked so uncomfortable that Jess's sympathy for him increased. He hadn't had very much to do with girls prior to coming to England, she guessed. Well, she might as well take him under her wing and make sure that by the time he rejoined his girl 'back home', he could at least dance without falling over his feet, and talk to a girl without sounding as though he was about to choke on his own words, Jess decided firmly.

'There's no need to hold me as though you think I'm going to break, you know,' she told him.

'No, ma'am,' Walter apologised earnestly.

'Walter, there's no need to call me "ma'am", either,' Jess reminded him. 'I thought we'd agreed on that.'

'Yes, ma'am.'

Jess burst out laughing. She felt so sorry for Walter. It was so unfair that the other GIs, apart from Glen, whom anyone could see was a real softie, didn't seem to include him in their conversation or treat him as one of their group. Walter's plight aroused all her protective instincts and she was determined to show him that British women knew how to treat the men who were risking their lives on their behalf.

'Hello there, Carrot Top.'

Jess gave an indignant glower in the direction of the familiar voice. 'Billy Spencer, how often have I told you not to call me that?' she told him as he steered his own partner close enough to her and Walter to grin down at her. Billy was equally as tall and broad-shouldered as Walter, and it was plain from the look on her face that the girl who was dancing with him was more than happy to be in his arms. Talk about looking like the cat that had got the cream, Jess thought irately.

'Aren't you going to introduce me?' he asked, ignoring her rebuke.

Walter was giving Billy a hesitant, wary look that caught at Jess's tender heart. Poor Walter, why should he look as though he had done something wrong when if anyone was at fault it was Billy for butting in like he had?

'Why should I do that–' she began.

But Billy was speaking as well, drowning out her question as he announced firmly to Walter, 'Sorry to barge in, only I promised her dad I'd look out for her. She doesn't mean any harm, but what with her being a bit flirty, like, some lads can get the wrong impression. Not that you're one of that sort. I can see that.' Releasing his partner, Billy extended his hand to shake Walter's, causing Walter to release Jess. As he did so, his wallet slipped from his pocket, but it was Billy who retrieved it from the floor, where it had landed, closing it and handing it back to him.

By this stage Jess was almost hopping up and down with fury. If she and Billy had been on their own she'd have given him a piece of her mind and no mistake but they weren't, and what with Walter looking all self-conscious, and Billy's dance partner throwing daggers at her, she had no choice but to content herself with a murderous look in Billy's direction and a warning.

'You know, Billy, I could swear that nose of yours is getting longer by the minute.'

'Don't mind her,' Billy told Walter with a smile. 'I've lost count of the number of times I've had to get her out of some trouble or other. Grown up together, we have, and she's like a sister to me.'

'Don't pay any attention to him, Walter,' Jess warned her partner angrily, forgetting her decision not to react. 'He's off his head and talking rubbish. And if he was my brother, I'd have asked me mam and dad to drown him long before now.'

'She loves me really,' Billy told Walter genially, going on to ask, 'Walking her home, are you, only if you are we might as well walk back together?'

'Well, I–' Walter began uncomfortably but Jess's blood was up now.

No way was she going to have Billy thinking she didn't have a chap to walk her home when he was with someone, so standing in front of him with her hands on her hips she announced fiercely, 'Yes, he is walking me home and we won't be walking along with you.'

'It's your choice but don't forget what happened to you the Christmas you were fourteen and you refused to let me see you home safely.'

Jess stared at him blankly. 'Nothing happened the Christmas I was fourteen.'

'You see,' Billy appealed to Walter. He reached up and patted Jess on the head. 'I'm sorry I brought it up. I should have realised that you wouldn't want to talk about it.'

'Talk about what? There is not anything to talk

178

about.' Jess was almost yelling, she was so furious. What on earth did Billy think he was doing? Couldn't he see that he was scaring Walter half to death? The poor boy now looked as though the last thing he wanted to do was walk her home, and who could blame him?

'Where are you sitting?' Billy asked casually. 'Only we might as well come and join you.'

'No!' Jess burst out, thinking angrily, over my dead body, but it was no use, Billy was already sweeping them all off the dance floor and heading for the table where Ruthie and Glen were sitting holding hands, looking like a pair of wide-eyed kittens and oblivious to everything and everyone else.

'Jeez, I thought this tower was supposed to be high?'

'It is,' Myra confirmed

She and Nick were standing on the pavement looking up at Blackpool Tower. A crowd of RAF men hurried past them, causing Nick to reach out and put a possessive arm around Myra's shoulder. She smiled secretly to herself. It wouldn't do him any harm to recognise that other men found her attractive.

'Well, the Empire State Building sure ain't got anything to worry about if this is what you call high,' Nick boasted.

'Tell me more about New York,' Myra begged him. 'I'd love to go there.'

'Everyone wants to go there, sugar.' Nick was eyeing a gang of young men pushing their way through the crowd gathering outside the Tower.

Heads down, and their hands in their pockets, their swarthy complexions marked them out as being different.

'They'll be from the gypsy families who run the fairgrounds,' Myra told him, sensing his interest.

'They look like hoods,' Nick told her as he chewed on his gum.

'Hoods?'

'Yeah, hoods, gangsters, the men who run the real show behind the men who like to think they're running the show.'

Myra looked uncertainly at the group slouching down the road. She would never have thought of them in that light, seeing them instead as outsiders, which in turn led to her feeling angered by them and her own feelings of reluctant pity for them.

'Come on, let's go inside,' she urged him.

They had arrived just over an hour ago and had walked along the front, arm in arm, buffeted by the wind before queuing to eat a fish-and-chip supper.

'Where's the steak?' Nick had demanded irritably when the waiter had shown him the menu. Whilst the waiter had been explaining that there was no steak, the RAF men at the next table had looked over at them a bit grimly but Myra had affected not to notice.

'What the hell is this?' Nick had demanded in a loud voice when their fish and chips had eventually arrived, adding, 'Jeez, I wouldn't give this to my worst enemy.'

'It's because of the shortages,' Myra had had to explain, although personally she had thought that their fish and chips were tasty and had felt that they were a bit of a treat. Perhaps they didn't eat fish and chips in New York, she had thought, acknowledging that she certainly couldn't remember ever seeing any of her favourite actresses doing so. Well, in future she wouldn't eat them either, she had decided. Not if it wasn't the 'done thing' to eat them in America.

It would be exaggerating to say that Nick's reaction had scared her, but it had left her feeling on edge. Only because she so desperately wanted him to fall for her and take her back to America with him, she had assured herself.

The Tower Ballroom seemed enormous after the Grafton, all decorated with Stars and Stripes in honour of the Fourth of July, and Myra could not help but be impressed by its décor and the famous Wurlitzer organ, although she was disappointed to learn that Reginald Dixon, the famous organ player, wasn't going to be there, because he'd joined the RAF.

'Well, this certainly beats the Grafton hands down,' Myra enthused. 'What's wrong?' she asked uncertainly when she saw the contemptuous glance Nick flicked round the room.

'Nothing, sweet stuff. If you like it, then that's fine.'

'But you don't like it, do you?' Myra persisted.

'Well, it ain't exactly Times Square.'

'Times Square? Why? What's that like?'

'It's the heart of New York, the city that never sleeps. Me and the guys used to go up from the Bronx to have some fun there. There's this diner

where you can get the best pastrami on rye...'
The animation that had glowed from his face left
it as he shook his head. 'They'll be having Fourth
of July parades there like you just can't imagine.
The whole city will be celebrating Independence
Day with everyone having themselves a good
time. Come on,' he demanded reaching for
Myra's hand, 'let's go dance.'

He was an excellent dancer, light on his feet but
powerful enough to guide her, and Myra could
see the looks they were attracting from other
dancers. They could tell that she and Nick were
different; and that they belonged somewhere
better than this, Myra decided, quickly losing
herself in a wonderful daydream in which the war
was over and she and Nick were paying a senti-
mental visit back here before leaving for New
York and the Bronx, wherever that was. Myra
pictured it as somewhere breathtakingly wonderful, peopled by men and women who all looked
like film stars, and where everyone had more
money than they knew what to do with.

'What do you say we turn tonight into something special?' Nick murmured in her ear, causing
Myra's heart to turn over with excitement and
triumph.

Things were working out just as she had hoped.
Nick was falling for her. They hadn't known one
another long but everyone knew how quickly
people fell in love in wartime. You could see it
everywhere; no one wanted to delay or wait just
in case...

'What kind of special?' she demanded breathlessly. What was he going to suggest? If he pro-

posed to her then she was going to accept, she decided fiercely, husband or no husband. She'd worry about getting her divorce later.

'Well...' Nick whirled her round so fast that she had to cling to him.

'Yes?' Myra pressed him impatiently, clutching at the sleeve of his jacket.

'Well ... how about instead of going back tonight we find somewhere to stay ... somewhere where we can be together...?'

'You really don't have to do this, you know. I mean, I don't want to take you out of your way, or–'

'I'm walking you home and that's for sure. You're my girl now, Ruthie.' Glen lifted her hand, clasped tight within his own. He had such strong capable hands, with square fingers and nice clean nails, working man's hands, but the hand of a working man who took a pride in himself. The kind of man her dad would have approved of.

Tears pricked at Ruthie's eyes as she remembered the way her dad used to scrub his hands under the kitchen tap when he'd come in from his work at the grid iron railway yard. He'd been promoted to foreman at the beginning of the war – on account of so many of the young men going off to fight, he had always said modestly, but Ruthie and her mother had known differently and had shared their delight in this official recognition of his capacity for hard work.

'Hey, what's this?'

'Nothing,' Ruthie choked back her tears when she saw the concern in Glen's eyes. 'I was just thinking about my dad.'

'I sure would have liked to have met him, to thank him for producing such a lovely daughter. But at least I'll get to meet your mom so that I can ask her permission properly to date you.'

Ruthie shivered slightly. She hadn't told Glen anything about her home life other than that her father had been killed in the blitz.

'Now I've got even more reason to win this war,' he had told her fiercely.

She looked across the table to where Jess was sitting close to Walter, whilst the handsome man she had introduced as Billy was sitting on her other side. The girl who had originally been with him seemed to have disappeared. Did Jess realise how hungrily Billy looked at her when he thought no one else was looking? Ruthie could see that Jess seemed very taken with Walter, but Glen had already told her, stumbling uncertainly over the words, how difficult it would be for them to 'date'.

'Are you two ready to leave?' Jess asked now, leaning across the table towards them. 'Only Walter says that their transport is coming to pick them up at one o'clock and if he and Glen are going to walk us home and get back for it, we need to go soon.'

'Glen, there's no need for you to walk back with me,' Ruthie began. 'Not if–'

'It's only right and proper that I see you home safely. 'Sides,' he admitted softly, 'I want to see where you live so that I can picture you there when I'm back at camp. It will make me feel closer to you. Then next time I can come and collect you so

184

that I can introduce myself to your mom and get her permission to date you. We know you do things differently over here on account of these books they gave us to read, coming over,' he told her earnestly.

'What books?' Jess demanded curiously.

'Well, there were these little books,' Glen explained, suddenly looking bashful, the tips of his ears glowing bright red as Ruthie had already grown to expect when he was embarrassed. 'They said how we were to remember that the British do things different from us and that we weren't to grab hold of folk or shake them by the hand unless they shook ours first. There was lots about rationing and how when we went visiting we should remember this and take something with us if we'd been asked to stay to eat. Just stuff like that.'

'Nothing about British girls, then?' Jess asked innocently.

'No...' Glen's ears had gone even redder.

'I think we'd better let the girls have the dope,' Walter told him uncomfortably.

'Well, OK then, there was a bit...'

'Saying what?'

The two men exchanged looks.

'Oh, nothing much, just a reminder to those of us who had girls and wives back home to remember where our loyalties are, you know that kind of thing.'

'You mean you're not supposed to get involved with us?' Jess guessed.

'Stop giving the poor chap a hard time, Jess,' Billy intervened. 'Of course they've been warned to watch it. The USA forces will have heard all

185

about girls like you. And as for them that's got a girl at home...' Billy was looking at her, Jess knew, but she refused to return his look. Why should she? Besides, he couldn't know about Walter's girl, and even if he did she wasn't doing anything wrong. Far from it.

Ruthie knew they were all only joking but she was feeling more worried by the moment. What if by falling in love with Glen and letting him talk to her as she had she was getting him into trouble?

She looked uncertainly at him, and as though he had read her mind he told her firmly, 'There's no rules that say anything about a guy falling for a girl if he's free to do so.'

'Well, there's already been a lot of talk about some GIs making out that they are when they aren't, if you know what I mean,' Jess told him forthrightly. 'A shocking thing to do a girl, that is: lead her on and then leave her to find out that she's been told a pack of lies. Not that it takes an American GI to lie to a girl,' she added darkly, looking at Billy. Let him see how he liked being 'looked at', she decided firmly.

TWELVE

'You're going to love Iowa, Ruthie, and my folks are going to love you. I can't wait for them to meet you.'

They had left the others now to continue their walk back to Ruthie's alone. It was a clear balmy

186

night, the ack-ack guns silent, and the sky filled only with stars and a soft moon.

'You know, I think I could get to like this black-out of yours,' Glen chuckled as he drew Ruthie into the shadows.

She was so nervous. She had never done anything like this before nor even imagined that she ever might. What if they bumped noses or she did something wrong? She felt Glen's lips touch her own and she drew in a sharp breath.

The kiss they shared was slightly clumsy but totally satisfying, filling Ruthie's heart so brimful of joy that she could feel it spilling over inside her. When Glen took her back in his arms, she lifted her face to his this second time with shy eagerness. It was quite amazing how quickly a person could get used to this kissing business, Ruthie decided happily as she hugged Glen back as tightly as he was holding her.

'Come on, I'd better get you home before I take you back to camp with me and ask the padre to marry us straight away.'

Ruthie was still laughing as they turned the corner into the Close, but her laughter stopped when she saw the figure standing desolately in the middle of the road, wearing a dressing gown, her feet bare. She was looking vacantly around herself.

'Say, what's this?' Glen queried in concern. 'She looks–'

'It's my mother,' Ruthie interrupted him quickly not wanting to hear him say what she knew he was going to say. Shame and guilt brought an ache of misery to the back of her throat. Why had this had to happen tonight of all nights?

'Your mom?' She could hear the shock in Glen's voice but what else was there with it? Disgust? Horror? Was he regretting saying what he had said to her now?

'She does this sometimes,' she told him with quiet dignity. 'She hasn't been herself since my father died. And ... and sometimes she ... she forgets what happened and she goes out looking for him.' Tears were pricking the backs of her eyes. 'I must go to her,' she said, stepping back from him and hurrying into the Close without looking to see if he was standing watching her or if he had turned his back on her and was walking away.

Myra looked at Nick without saying anything. She wasn't naïve. She knew exactly what he was suggesting. She also knew that the answer she gave could change her whole life.

'We can't do that,' she told him. 'It wouldn't be right.' She could see the angry impatience in his eyes and added coyly, 'It would be different if we were going steady, and you'd said that you wanted me to be your girl.'

'I've brought you here to Blackpool, haven't I?' Nick challenged her.

'For all I know you could have a steady girl back home,' Myra pointed out, ignoring his irritable challenge.

'If I had then I wouldn't be here with you, would I?'

'Some men like to act like they're free to make up to a girl when they aren't. And, like I said, if you'd asked me to be your girl before you'd suggested we stay over then it might be different. After all, no girl wants to think of her chap going off to war without her having shown him how much he means to her, does she? Just like no chap who really cares about a girl would ask her to show him how much she cares if he wasn't serious about them being together for always. I'm not saying that I agree with those couples who fall in love one night and rush out to get a special licence the next, but when there's a war on, no one wants to wait for their happiness, just in case of what might happen.'

They had stopped dancing and it was obvious to Myra that Nick wasn't very pleased about what she was saying but she was not going to give in. No way was she going to allow Nick to use her and then leave her. He needed to understand that she wanted to have a future with him; the future he could provide for her – in America. And if he refused to understand and accept that? A fierce surge of determination spiked through her. He *must* accept it. She could feel Nick watching her, waiting for her to succumb to his silent pressure and change her mind. She refused to look back at him whilst the tension between them stretched as tightly as her nerves. How much did Nick really want her? Enough to pursue her and go on pursuing her, giving her time to work on him to give her what she wanted, or was his desire for her not strong enough for that? If he did want her as much as she hoped then holding him off and making him wait could only work in her favour, she reasoned.

'Listen, babe.'

The coaxing note in Nick's voice told her all she needed to know. Very slowly Myra exhaled an unsteady breath.

'You *are* my girl,' Nick continued. 'I was kinda taking that for granted, otherwise I would never have suggested what I did.' He reached for her hand, sliding his fingers between her own, his voice soft and husky as he added, 'I've been thinking about you and me being together all week, thinking about it... All I'm asking is that you let me show you how good we would be. Who knows how much time we'll have together? I don't want to waste a minute of it. We could be seeing action any time now. You don't want to think of me dying without knowing the sweetness of being with you, do you, babe?'

Even if she hadn't already experienced sex and known that for her it was simply a means to an end, nothing he was saying to her would have persuaded her to drop her guard, Myra decided. Instinctively she sensed that Nick was the kind of man who would use every ounce of charm and power of persuasion he had to get what he wanted but that, once he had it, it would lose its value. He would have to give her far more tangible evidence of his commitment to her before she gave in to him. He might have picked up her cue and said that she was his girl but she wanted more than easily retracted words.

'We can't stay over, Nick,' she told him. 'For one thing I'm on duty tomorrow, and for an other ... well, I want to believe what you're saying about me being your girl, but how do I know that you mean it? I'm not saying that I don't believe you. But if I am going to be your girl, then we don't need to rush, do we?' Myra darted a quick look at him, wondering how far she dare go. There were plenty of other GIs around, she reminded herself practically, but since there was no saying when the war might end, it made no sense wasting time on one who wasn't going to give her what she wanted so much. Her mind made up, she gave Nick a soulful look, reaching out to touch his arm as she said softly, 'After all, when you take me back with you to America to meet your family, I don't want them thinking that I'm not a respectable sort of girl.'

She could feel the tension gripping him. What was he thinking? Was she scaring him off by letting him see what she had in mind? It would be a pity if she had. Although she was reluctant to admit it, there was something about him that appealed to her, though she disliked the thought of being vulnerable to him through that feeling.

They had stopped dancing whilst they talked, too engrossed in what they were saying to leave the floor, and now the dance floor was filling up again with eager couples.

A group of young men and women, the boys in RAF uniform, were hurrying onto the floor, in a colourful surge of airforce-blue uniforms and party frocks. Engrossed in their own fun, they didn't see Myra and Nick standing in the shadows with their backs to them until it was too late and one of the boys had bumped into Myra.

As she turned round he gave her an admiring look and invited, 'Dance with me, lovely lady?'

'Hey, buster, butt out. She's with me,' Nick told

him furiously.

The young man laughed and turned his back on Nick, saying to Myra with a wink, 'Ignore him and come and dance with me instead.'

Nick's reaction was immediate. He swung round, grabbing the lapels of the young man's uniform jacket and then lifted him clear off the ground before smashing him back against the pillar he himself had been leaning against while he and Myra talked.

'That's my girl you're coming on to, buddy,' Nick warned the young airman. Triumph surged through Myra. But then, as she saw the young man's friends rushing towards Nick, the reality of what he was doing came home to her.

'Nick, don't. Leave him alone. Let's go,' she protested, but it was too late. The RAF men rushed at Nick, who immediately swung round, throwing a couple of ferocious low stomach punches, which caused the two men they connected with to double over.

Some of the girls that were with the airmen had started to scream, whilst others burst into noisy tears. Nearby dancers stopped to see what was going on. Three GIs came running over to join in the affray and within seconds a full-blown and sickeningly violent fight had broken out.

Myra had grown up witnessing physical violence. She had seen her father return home drunk from the pub and then lay into her mother; she had learned young to keep her distance from him when he was in a bad mood. Now, watching Nick, she did what she had always done as a child, which was to shut herself away from what was happening in a safe place deep inside herself, so that whilst physically she was present, emotionally and mentally she was not. Then someone blew a whistle, a shrill warning sound that jerked her out of her self-imposed trance.

'Nick, stop it,' she screamed, alerted to the potential danger to the future she wanted for herself. 'The police will be coming...'

Like snow on a summer's day those on the periphery of the fight melted away, leaving Nick and a couple of the RAF men. Nick's fellow GIs were pulling him off the young man he had first attacked, and who was now on his knees beneath the blows Nick was raining down on him.

'Are you with this guy?' one of the GIs asked Myra tersely.

She nodded.

'Well, you'd better get him back where he came from, because if the MPs get here and find out that he's half killed that kid, he's going to be in the slammer for the rest of the war.'

The other GIs finally succeeded in restraining Nick and dragging him away from the boy, whose face was now a pulped mess of bloody flesh.

'Get the hell out of here whilst you still can, buddy,' the biggest of them warned Nick, giving him a push in Myra's direction.

Grabbing hold of his arm, Myra tugged him in the direction of the exit, only too glad to have the silent watchful escort of the pair of GIs alongside them as they made their way towards it.

'Think he'll be OK, Tex?' one of the GIs asked when they had finally reached the parked Jeep.

'Sure,' Tex responded laconically, 'but I ain't so

sure about the poor bastard he was beating up.'

Nick wasn't saying anything, and he wasn't looking at any of them either. He swung himself into the driving seat of the Jeep, leaving Myra to struggle into the passenger seat as best she could.

The GI named Tex was huge – tall and broad-shouldered, with close-cropped fair hair and a slow drawl of an accent she could hardly understand because of the cigarette dangling from the side of his mouth.

'Where you from, buster?' he asked Nick.

'New York – not that it's any of your business.'

'When I see a GI beating up some kid still wet behind the ears, I kinda make it my business, buddy. Where I come from we don't do that to kids.'

Myra tensed as she saw the feral glint in Nick's eyes.

'He was coming on to my girl, and where I come from we don't forget an insult – not ever,' Nick told him through gritted teeth. 'And we repay it with a bullet and a block of concrete.'

Through the open window of the Jeep Myra could hear one of the other waiting GIs saying under his breath, 'Let's get out of here. This guy's connected. Mafiosa,' he explained to his companion meaningfully, whilst Myra frowned, not understanding what was going on.

The tall fair-haired GI stepped back from the driver's window as Nick started the engine and put the Jeep in gear.

The protective bubble Myra had created around herself earlier had gone, leaving feelings of nausea and fear she would once have connected with her own father. But her father was dead, and she was with Nick. Nick, who was going to make her his girl, his wife, and take her to America.

She made to snuggle closer to him, but he shook her off, telling her curtly, 'Stupid bitch, that was your fault, winding me up and then dropping me flat. And as for that Texan asshole...' Nick spat out of the window of the Jeep.

Myra shrank down in her seat, her stomach churning with a mix of dread and angry resentment. But she couldn't afford to be angry with Nick, she reminded herself, comforting herself with the assurance that things would be different once they were married and the war was over and they were living in America.

'Ruthie, love, I'm that sorry,' Mrs Brown apologised as she puffed her way up to where Ruthie was trying gently to coax her mother home. 'I dunno how she managed to slip away wi'out me seeing her. One minute she was there and then the next minute she'd gone! Given me ever such a bad turn, she has.' Their neighbour's kind face was flushed and anxious, and despite her own misery and embarrassment Ruthie hurried to reassure her.

'It's all right, Mrs Brown. It isn't your fault. There's no way of stopping her when she gets her mind fixed on going looking for my dad.'

'Well, that's true enough. Like I said, though, I dunno what sparked her off. Nodding off in her chair, she was, and so I thought I'd just nip to the lavvy and then when I got back–' She broke off and stared down the dark street.

195

'Where's that handsome young fella I saw you with when I come out of the door?'

'He had to get back to his camp.' Ruthie was astonished at how easily the lie slipped from her lips.

'Well, at least he saw yer home first,' Mrs Brown commented comfortingly. 'Pity he couldn't come in and mek himself known to me and Mr Brown, though, proper, like.'

'There's no reason for him to have to do that,' Ruthie told her with forced dignity. How it hurt her to say those words after the joy she had known so intensely and so very briefly earlier. Tears pricked at her eyes. Had it been seeing her mother that had scared him off or had he just been heartlessly flirting with her without meaning a word of what he was saying all along?

'Well, I know that it's none of our business, Ruthie,' Mrs Brown was saying, 'but I wouldn't feel right in me mind if me and Mr Brown hadn't acted like we know your dad would have acted himself if he'd been here. Stands to reason that your dad would have expected us to look out for you and your mam, us being close neighbours all these years. Yes, that's it, Mrs Philpott dearie,' she coaxed Ruthie's mother sturdily. 'Soon have you home now, love. My, but you give me a shock. Shivering, she is now, an' all, Ruthie. I'll mek up a couple of hot-water bottles for you to put in her bed. That'll help tek the chill off of her a bit. So you had a good time at the Grafton, did you?'

'It was very nice,' Ruthie said quietly. She could feel the pain burning its way right through her poor breaking heart. But she couldn't really blame Glen, could she? Even if he had fallen for her like he had said, she couldn't expect him to understand how it was with her mother. Perhaps what had happened was for the best. Now, more than ever, she realised she would never be able to leave her mother to live on her own without her.

Nick hadn't spoken one word to Myra since they had left Blackpool, and now they were back home. What was Nick thinking? It was all very well for him to blame her for what had happened but it hadn't been her fault, she assured herself virtuously.

A part of her quite liked knowing that he was so mad for her, and it was that that she intended to focus on and not that sickening feeling that had gripped her stomach, or the childhood memories that had gone with it. In fact, knowing that he was mad for her had done wonders for her confidence in her ability to get what she wanted from him. And she certainly wasn't going to have him thinking that she intended to let him get away with speaking to her the way he had. No, not for a minute she wasn't. Fighting was one thing but speaking to her like that...

Myra had perfected the art of the sulk long ago, and she used it to good effect now, matching Nick's silence with her own, refusing to turn her head to look at him. The minute he turned into Lime Street and brought the Jeep to a halt, without giving him the chance to say anything, she opened the door and jumped out. Although it was nearly two o'clock in the morning the station was still busy with people coming and going.

Myra took a deep breath and then started to walk away from the Jeep – and Nick – without looking back. Let him drive off in a sulk, as she knew he would; he would soon come round once he realised what he was about to lose.

Confidently she set off to walk back to her digs. She had got as far as the end of the street and had just turned the corner into unwelcome darkness when she heard the sound of the Jeep being driven slowly behind her. All at once her confidence deserted her. Fear filled its place. She desperately wanted to run but she refused to let herself, despite the images now flooding her mind: Nick hitting the defenceless young man; her father laying into her mother as she curled up in a corner trying to protect herself. The entrance to a narrow passageway loomed alongside her. Quickly she turned into it. It was too narrow for the Jeep, and darkly shadowed by its buildings, except for the gap midway down where a bomb had hit two of the houses.

She couldn't hear the Jeep any more. She started to relax and then stiffened as she heard the sharp slam of its door and then the sound of footsteps following her.

Now she really did want to run but before she could do so, Nick had reached her, his hand on her shoulder, spinning her round.

'No dame ever walks out on me,' he told her furiously, giving her a fierce shake. 'And if you're going to be my girl you'd better understand that.' He pulled her into his arms and kissed her angrily, forcing her lips apart and grinding his mouth down on hers whilst she stood unresistingly in the darkness, feeling the heavy pounding of his heartbeat against her own body. It felt like a lifetime before he stopped kissing her.

'I'll pick you up at the station Tuesday evening. We'll have dinner.'

It wasn't a request, Myra recognised, it was a command.

'No guy cuts me out with my girl and gets away with it,' he told her, and then added, 'and no girl of mine gives out to another guy if she knows what's good for her – *capisci?*'

Myra nodded, too weakened by her own overwhelming relief to be able to speak. He wasn't going to hurt her – hit her – after all. And in fact he was offering her what she had wanted.

'I guess what happened back there in Blackpool kinda scared you, did it?'

His words caught Myra off guard. She hadn't expected him to speak openly about what he had done. Her father certainly would not have done. He had liked to pretend that nothing had happened. There was a certain sense of extra relief in being able to tell herself that Nick wasn't like her father.

'Well, it was all down to you, sweet stuff. Because, you see, I'm a jealous kinda guy, Myra, and I don't like to see another guy looking at my girl and having her look back at him, especially when she's just made me as mad as hell and as wrought up as an angry bull.'

Her relief made her smile up at Nick and then smile again when he squeezed her hand. A heady sense of power filled her.

'See ya Tuesday, honey bun,' he told her, after

199

they had walked back to the Jeep. 'And remember, keep away from those other guys, if you don't want to make me mad again. You're my girl now.'

Diane sat up in bed as Myra opened the bedroom door. She had woken up when she had heard the other girl come in.

'You're late,' she told her tiredly.

Myra gave a dismissive shrug. 'So what if I am? It's no one's business but mine.'

'Yours and your husband's,' Diane corrected her. 'He was round here earlier. He's on a forty-eight-hour-leave pass and he came here looking for you.'

Jim was home? Myra sat down abruptly on her own bed. 'What did you tell him?' she demanded sharply.

'I said that I thought you'd gone to Blackpool with some friends and that you might be staying over,' Diane informed her evenly. It confirmed everything she already thought about Myra when she didn't bother to thank her for covering up for her.

Instead she asked, 'So where is he now?'

'Down the road at number forty-five.'

'What? What's he doing there? Whose idea was that?'

'Not mine,' Diane replied. 'Mrs L came in whilst he was here and she suggested it.'

Myra thought quickly. The last thing she needed right now was a husband, but at least he was only on a forty-eight-hour pass. It was a pity that their interfering busybody landlady had taken it upon herself to get him a bed so close by. That meant she had no excuse for pretending she couldn't get to see him.

THIRTEEN

'I don't care what you say, Jim. I've made up my mind. I want a divorce.'

Myra and her husband faced one another across the small shabby parlour, with its smell of disuse and past sadnesses.

'That's crazy talk, Myra, and you know it.'

'You're the one who's crazy if you can't see that the pair of us should never have got married in the first place and that the sooner we go our separate ways the better.'

'Maybe we shouldn't have got married but we did. And even if I *was* willing for us to be divorced, which I'm not, you can't get divorced without proper grounds, you know that.'

'As to that, if it's grounds you want, then I'm willing...' Myra began recklessly, and then stopped when she saw the way he was looking at her. Why couldn't fate be kind to her for once? Any number of soldiers got themselves killed and left their wives widowed with a pension – why couldn't that happen to her?

'There's no point in saying you won't divorce me,' she announced fiercely, 'because there's no way I plan to go on being your wife. At least that way you would be free to find someone else.'

'Like you are? Is that what this is all about, Myra? You finding someone else? Or have you already found him?'

Myra's heart started to thump uncomfortably fast. Jim was getting far too close to the truth.

'What if I have?' she challenged him. 'You can't do anything about it. I've told you, Jim, it's over for you and me. If you want the truth it was never that much of a marriage anyway,'

'And whose fault is that? It's not as though I haven't tried to please you.'

Another woman hearing the misery and the frustration in his voice might have been moved to compassion but Myra wasn't like that. She wasn't prepared to be compassionate about anything or anyone who stood in the way of her own ambitions.

'There you are, you see,' she answered triumphantly. 'You're more or less saying yourself that we aren't suited.'

'Suited or not, we *are* married,' Jim retaliated, 'and married is what we are going to stay. Myra,' he called, when Myra pulled open the parlour door, ignoring him. 'Myra.' But it was too late. She was already halfway through the front door.

Jim watched her hurrying down the street, without giving him so much as a backward glance, and then thumped his closed fist on the arm of the sofa. A cloud of dust rose up from the horsehair filling, making him sneeze. Myra was the very opposite of everything he longed for in a wife, but what could he do? He loved her so much. And he knew that he always would.

Diane could feel the tension the minute she walked into the Dungeon.

'Any news?' she asked Pauline quietly.

There was no need for her to specify what kind of news she meant. When she had gone off duty on Saturday the whole of the Dungeon had been seething with rumours and counter-rumours following the news that the long-awaited and dreaded German naval attack, codenamed 'Rösselsprung' or 'Knight's Move', was finally about to take place, and that the Arctic Convoy PQ-17 was to be its target.

'Plenty,' Pauline confirmed grimly, 'and none of it good.' She nodded in the direction of the huge chart table surrounded by grim-faced naval personnel, whilst harassed Wrens were calling out positions and logging incoming information.

'Just after twenty-one hundred hours thirty last night the First Sea Lord gave orders for the Arctic convoy to scatter following the discovery that the German support ships had moved into Altenfjord ready for Rösselsprung.'

'And?' Diane pressed her anxiously. Everyone working in the Dungeon knew about the threat from Operation Rösselsprung. It had been hanging over them ever since it had been discovered that the German Navy's Commander-in-Chief, Admiral Raeder, was planning to destroy one of the Arctic convoys using his largest battleship, the *Tirpitz*, which was based at Trondheim, supported by numerous other warships, though it was not known which convoy would be the target. For that reason, the movements of convoys were always times of extreme tension in the Dungeon.

By the time Diane had finished her shift on Saturday, the ops room had been humming with the long-awaited and dreaded news that the German support vessels had joined the *Tirpitz* in Altenfjord, ready for their 'knight's move', though at that stage the intelligence sources had not been able to confirm whether or not Convoy PQ-17 was to be the target.

'It seems the *Tirpitz* and the others are still in Altenfjord.'

'So the convoy is safe?' Diane asked with relief.

'No,' Pauline told her shortly. 'Like I said, the First Sea Lord gave the order for the convoy to scatter, and each ship to make for the nearest Russian port as best it could, thinking that Rösselsprung was underway, when it wasn't. That left the whole convoy vulnerable to U-boat and air attack with no support vessels to protect it. So far we've lost nine ships, all sunk.'

'And the men?' Diane asked shakily, once she had absorbed this shocking news.

'We don't know, but the chances are...' Pauline shook her head, unable to say the words.

'Oh, no,' Diane protested, well aware of how slim the chances were of anyone surviving in such cold seas.

'Oh, yes,' Pauline confirmed wearily.

'How's Susan taking it? Her husband's ship was with the convoy, wasn't it?'

Pauline nodded. 'She's doing her best, of course, and she says she'd rather be here where at least she can get first-hand info on what's happening.'

Diane turned to look round the room. No wonder people were only speaking in terse whispers, their faces set and expressions withdrawn. A list of the ships sailing in the convoy had even been written on a new board, and Diane could now see the nine names that had been struck through.

The Commander and the rest of the top brass were leaning over the chart tables and the telephones, whilst messengers rushed in and out carrying transcripts of Morse code messages. As Diane watched, a new order was given and a young Wren crossed through another name, her hand shaking. She had barely finished doing so when someone called out again. It was impossible not to be aware of the mute, shocked horror gripping everyone in the room as more losses were chalked up.

The long day wore on without any respite, as vessel after vessel was sunk. It was pitiful and cruel. The merchant ships were defenceless targets and the U-boats and German planes were picking them off as easily as though they were targets at a fairground shooting range.

Shock had now given way to a low murmur of angry bitterness that such an ill-judged order should have been given, and at one point the Commander himself bowed his head, and they could all see the trickle of tears as he wept for the loss of so many brave and unprotected men.

Through the short dark hours of the July night the losses mounted relentlessly until the air inside the Dungeon was thick with unshed tears and heavy with a grief too terrible to voice.

Susan, white-faced and as stiff as though she were a puppet, held them all to the line with a professionalism Diane suspected she could never have emulated when the news came in that her husband's ship had been torpedoed. Only the merest tremble of her hand betrayed what she had to be feeling.

As though she sensed Diane's thoughts she told her jerkily, 'At least with the almost constant daylight they have up there at this time of the year there'll be more chance of any survivors being picked up.'

Diane couldn't bear to say anything. Her throat closed up with compassion for Susan, knowing, as they all did, that the chance of there being any survivors was pitifully small.

When the new shift came on at 4.00 a.m. on Monday morning, Diane was barely aware of having worked a double shift. Over twenty ships had now been lost, the Germans free to torpedo and bomb the helpless vessels whilst the RAF looked on helplessly, knowing that the ships lay beyond the range of their planes. Several of those working in the Dungeon had loved ones with the convoy – some on naval vessels and some on the merchant ships. One young Wren had fainted when the news had come in that the ship on which her new husband was sailing had been sunk, whilst one of the senior naval officers had had to bear the news that his only son had been on another of the lost vessels.

It was the worst kind of tragedy because it was one that those who had had to deal with it believed could have been avoided.

'Not seeing Walter tonight then, Jess?'

'No, I'm not. Not that it's any of your business, Billy,' Jess answered with a toss of her head.

'I was telling your uncle this dinnertime that he seems like a decent sort – for a GI.'

'You've no business talking about me and Walter to my uncle or anyone else.'

'Going steady now, are you?' Billy asked, ignoring her.

'You mean like you and Doreen Green?' Jess demanded stalwartly, determinedly ignoring the sharp pain that thinking about the two of them gave her.

Billy frowned. 'Who says that I'm going steady with her?'

'She does, for one,' Jess informed him pithily, 'and so does that cousin of hers. The one that does all the boxing,' she added meaningfully.

To her chagrin Billy laughed. 'You don't want to listen to everything that folk tell you, young Jess. That Doreen Green has had her eye on me since we was at school together,' he told her smugly, 'but that doesn't mean she's going to get me.'

'No, I dare say it doesn't,' Jess agreed hardily. He took the biscuit for cheek, did Billy. 'After all, she's got to get all them other girls out of the way first, hasn't she? But then, like I said, she has got their Malcolm to help her.'

'I'm surprised at you, speaking like that,' Billy told her sorrowfully. 'I thought better of you than that you'd go round listening to silly gossip. There's only one girl for me. Allus has been and allus will be.'

Did he really think she hadn't heard that kind

of line before?

'Oh, yes,' she challenged him, 'and we all know who that is, don't we? It's the next girl you come across wot's daft enough to believe you when you tell that line to her. Anyway, shouldn't you be on duty, seeing as you've got such a responsible job an' all, guarding them barrage balloons?'

'It's not them we're guarding tonight, Jess. We've had reports of an unexploded bomb being found in one of them bombed-out houses down near Pickering Street. Seems some kids found it so we've been called in to take a butchers at it.'

'Take a butchers at it? You? What do you mean? That's a job for the bomb disposal lot and you aren't one of them.'

'You mean that I wasn't,' Billy agreed. 'Seems like they've got short of men, so our sergeant asked for volunteers to mek up their numbers. You and you and you, he yelled out, and just my luck I happened to be one of them he picked.'

Jess struggled for something to say but all she could think about was the danger he was going to be in. She had heard tales from her uncle of the bomb disposal teams and the terrible death toll of the men who worked on them.

'Well, that's just typical of you, isn't it?' she burst out as she tried to calm her thudding heart-beat. 'Going and getting yourself involved wi' summat daft and dangerous like that. It will serve you right if you get blown up straight off, it will.'

'Thanks for that. I can tell that you won't be shedding any tears for me if I do.'

Jess could hear the harshness in his voice and immediately she felt ashamed of herself. There had been no call for her to say what she had. She couldn't explain to herself how her fear for him had made her say it, and she certainly wasn't going to try to explain it to him, and have him laugh at her and guess... Guess what, exactly? Guess nothing, she told herself sternly. She looked up at him silhouetted against the blue sky, and her heart seemed to turn over inside her chest.

'Billy...'

'Yes?'

She hadn't really been going to reach out and grab hold of his hand and beg him not to put himself at risk, had she?

'Nothing. Just don't you go talking to my uncle about me and Walter, that's all.' She began to walk on and then stopped and turned back. 'When are you going to be doing it?' she asked him, unable to hold back the question. 'When are you going to be looking for this unexploded bomb?'

'I'm on me way now. What do you want to know for? Want to come along and watch me blow meself up, do you?'

Jess could feel the blood draining out of her face, and then storming back in again, the ferocity of it making her feel sick and dizzy.

'That's a wicked thing to say,' she told him shakily, turning away from him again before he could see how close she was to tears, and hurrying down the street, ignoring him when he called out to her to wait.

FOURTEEN

The papers were full of the news of the loss of the convoy. Two-thirds of the ships had been sunk: twenty-three merchant ships and one rescue ship out of the thirty-six merchant ships and three rescue ships that had sailed.

Some of those ships had sailed originally from Liverpool, and many of the seamen on board them had been from the city. The weight of that loss was apparent in the grim faces of the people stopping to buy their newspapers and read the headlines.

'Bloody First Sea Lord – what the 'ell does he know now about the life of them wot sails under the Red Duster?' Diane heard one man saying bitterly as she paid for her paper. 'Ruddy nowt, that's wot.'

A pall of bleak disbelief filled the corridors and offices of Derby House. Susan had been given leave of absence because her husband had now been officially reported as missing in action and Jean had taken over the team temporarily.

'Captain said to remind you that you're to stay on after your shift finishes today for this welcome party she and the C-in-C are giving for the new lot of Americans. Not that anyone is going to feel like smiling nicely at a load of green-as-grass young Americans after what we've all just been through.'

'No,' Diane agreed sombrely. 'Do we know yet how many...?'

'We know that four ships have made it to Archangel harbour,' Jean told her grimly. 'I don't envy you having to attend this do tonight, I really don't.' She shook her head. 'There's already a lot of resentment at the fact that the last shift had to cope with a group of Americans down for tactical training who couldn't stop talking about their Fourth of July celebrations and didn't seem to understand why none of us feel like celebrating right now. I even heard one of them boasting that they'd been showing our RAF a thing or two by piloting British planes on a daylight raid on some Dutch German airfields.'

'Yes, I saw that in the papers,' Diane replied. 'They lost two of the planes, and a third was damaged, so that hardly suggests they have a lot to boast about.'

Too late, Diane realised that her sharp words had been overheard, and by her personal *bête noire*, Major Saunders. She shrugged inwardly. What did it matter what the major thought of her?

'I wonder if the Wrens' favourite American pin-up will be there tonight,' Jean commented, giving Diane a nudge and looking pointedly at the major's broad back.

'The Wrens' what?' Diane queried in disbelief.

'They're all mad for him,' Jean assured her, 'and I have to admit I can see why.'

'Well, I can't.'

'It wouldn't do you any good if you could,' Jean said. 'Word is that he's married and that he's let

211

it be known that's the way he intends to stay. So it's definitely hands off that particular piece of US property.' Jean pulled a wry face. 'I don't suppose we should blame him for feeling he has to make the point. The way some girls are acting around the Americans, it's no wonder they think that we're all cheap and easy. My fiancé is in radio ops up at Burtonwood where they're stationed, and he says you wouldn't believe the things some of the local girls are getting up to: standing at the roadside waiting for the GIs to drive past, calling out to them...' Jean shook her head. 'You think they'd have more respect for themselves. I wouldn't mind so much, but thanks to them we're all getting tarred with the same brush. It makes me glad that I'm hooked up to a decent British chap.'

'Yes,' Diane agreed heavily.

'I'm surprised you haven't got someone, Diane,' Jean ventured. 'Not that I'm wanting to pry, of course,' she added hastily.

'It's all right. There was someone,' she admitted. 'We ... we were engaged, but ... but it didn't work out. He ... he changed his mind...' She didn't know now what on earth had made her speak so openly to Jean about something she would normally have kept a secret. Perhaps it had to do with the tragedy they had witnessed. What she did know, though, was that her grief for the men who had lost their lives weighed as heavily on her right now as her grief for her own loss. She gave Jean a bleak look, unaware that Jean wasn't the only person who had heard what she had said.

'I'd better go and get ready for the welcome party.'

'Rather you than me.' Jean shook her head.

Diane had brought a clean blouse with her, and she went to the ladies' cloakroom to change into it and redo her hair, unpinning it from its chignon, then brushing it before pinning it up neatly again. She had no heart for the evening ahead, but it was not the fault of the young Americans. It was going to be her job to help make them feel at home, she reminded herself as she reapplied her lipstick and dabbed some of her precious Yardley's toilet water on her wrists.

The welcome party was being held in the Commander-in-Chief Admiral Sir Percy Noble's private quarters, and several other girls were already making their way there when Diane joined them.

'What exactly are we supposed to do?' Diane asked one of them.

'The Group Captain just told me that she wants us to make the Americans feel more at home.'

'They don't need encouraging to do that,' another girl informed her grimly. 'If you ask me, they're making themselves far too much at home here as it is. I had to go to one of these dos last month, and I ended up pinned in a corner by a young airman who couldn't seem to understand the meaning of the word "no", and kept on telling me how he was going to win the war for us. Bloody Yanks.'

Two Royal Navy men in full dress uniform were standing either side of the double doors leading into the Commander's private office sitting room, whilst a senior Wren was waiting with a checklist to tick off the girls' names.

'Good,' she said when everyone had been ticked off. 'Now before our guests arrive, I'd just like to say a few words. You've all been put forward for this duty because you are considered to be the right sort of people for it. And make no mistake about it, making sure our American allies are made welcome is an important duty. But just as important is your duty to your uniform, and that duty commands you to remember that you may well become the standard by which these young men will judge your fellow country-women. Young American men behave in a manner which to us seems far freer and easier than we are used to from our own men. American men and women go on dates with one another from a young age, and are used to having friends of the opposite sex. It is easy sometimes for us to misunderstand this behaviour and to read into light-hearted comments something that is not meant. An American serviceman may pay you compliments and call you "sweetheart", but that is just his way. It does not mean that he is ready to call any marriage banns.'

Dutifully the listening young women laughed.

'Unfortunately there are some young women in this country who have not properly understood the differences between American ways and our own, and because of that they have earned for themselves a rather bad reputation. Suffice it to say that here at Derby House we expect our young women to reflect only the very best kind of behaviour. You are here this evening to represent your service and your country.'

She gave them a brisk nod and then turned to the two naval ratings, instructing them to open the doors.

Diane took a deep breath and then, keeping her head up, followed the other girls into the room.

A group of senior officers was standing in the middle of the room, engrossed in discussion, the braid on their uniforms shining dully in the overhead light.

'Lord, look at all that egg yolk,' the girl next to Diane, who had introduced herself as Justine, murmured wryly, referring to the gold braid that denoted the seniority of the officers. 'Not many Senior Service in evidence,' she added. 'Mind you, it's hardly surprising in view of what's been happening over the weekend. Plenty of RAF, though, and a good few American top brass as well.'

'What are we supposed to do now?' Diane asked uncertainly.

'You'll be allocated a naval rating to act as a waiter and then it will be up to you to circulate, make sure all the invitees have a drink and someone to talk to. If you get stuck for something to say just ask them about their mum – much safer than asking if they have a girl,' Justine advised.

Diane started to nod in response when her attention was caught by the familiar features of Major Saunders. Her heart sank.

Justine, seeing the direction in which she was looking, told her, 'That's Major Saunders with the Commander. He's the main liaison officer for the Americans. Have you met him yet? If not, I'll

215

take you over and introduce you. You'll see him around here quite a lot. He co-ordinates the groups of Americans coming from Burtonwood to see the way in which the Western Approaches Tactical Unit, works,' she added.

'No, no, it's all right. I ... I have met him,' Diane stopped her quickly.

'Good-looking chap,' Justine commented. 'Pity that he's married.'

The doors were opening again, this time to admit the young Americans who had been invited to the party.

'It looks like it's the aircrew lot tonight,' Justine told Diane. 'Pity, I'm not really in the mood for American fly-boy bragging at the moment.'

'Surely they don't do that? Brag, I mean?' Diane queried. 'After all, if they're only just arriving they won't have flown any real missions yet.'

'That doesn't stop them,' Justine assured her. 'You wait and see.'

Diane was beginning to suspect that her companion wasn't very keen on their American allies, but before she could say anything to her the other girl had turned away to speak with someone else.

'Ah, Wilson, there you are, good.' Diane turned when she heard Group Captain Barker addressing her, and then wished her superior had approached someone else when she saw that one of the uniformed men with her was the major.

'Diane, by all that's holy, it is you, isn't it?'

Diane's eyes widened in surprise as she focused on the familiar face of the man who had stepped out from behind the major.

'Charles! Oh! I mean, Wing Commander,' she

216

managed to correct herself, her face burning.

Charles Seddon Gore, or 'the Wing Co', as Kit and the other flyers had called him, was a hugely popular character amongst the men, and Diane knew that Kit admired him tremendously. He had first seen action in the First World War as a seventeen-year-old, and had been shot down over the Channel during the Battle of Britain. The last Diane had heard of him was that he had been rescued but had been badly injured and his days of flying missions were over.

'Oh, I say, you *are* a sight for sore eyes.' He was beaming at Diane now. Turning to the men with him, he explained, 'This young lady worked at the base in Cambridgeshire where I was stationed before I had to bale out over the Channel. Probably glad to see the last of me, and quite right too. A flyer who has to ditch his plane and jump into the drink is a damned nuisance.'

'We were all delighted when we heard that you'd been rescued, sir,' Diane told him truthfully. 'You were missed very much by all those who knew you.'

'Mm. And that young man of yours – still flying, is he?'

Diane felt her heart do a steep dive. 'So far as I know,' she confirmed woodenly.

'Must say that I'm surprised he's let you come so far away from him. Would have thought he'd have had that wedding ring on your finger by now. I know I would in his shoes.'

This was awful. Diane kept the polite smile plastered on her face, desperate to avoid further talk of Kit.

'So you were saying, Wing Commander, about the risks involved in daylight bombing raids on German cities...'

Five minutes ago she had been hating the fact that the major was here, but now she was more grateful to him than she could ever have imagined, even if his timely rescue of her was totally inadvertent.

'What? Oh, yes. Risky business. Even with our new Lancasters.'

'But, sir, the American Air Force has some new strategies and equipment, and with those and the surprise effect of daylight bombing raids...' one of the young American airmen burst out eagerly. 'I mean, look at the success of the American raid on the German-held Dutch airfield over the weekend.'

'Two planes lost and one damaged out of six.' The wing commander looked grave. 'Too much show and not enough result, if you ask me, Airman.'

Diane couldn't help but feel sorry for the young American, who was now blushing. Sympathetically she moved closer to him when the wing commander turned away to talk to someone else, chatting lightly to him whilst he composed himself.

'I guess I said the wrong thing, didn't I?' he admitted ruefully as the wing commander and the other top brass – including the major, much to Diane's relief – moved away.

'Daylight raids are a bit of a sore point for us.' Diane explained. 'We've lost a lot of good men that way.'

'I guess you Brits aren't too pleased about us coming here and trying to tell you how to run your war.'

'You're our allies, we need your help, and we are grateful to you for it,' Diane answered him tactfully, changing the subject to ask him, 'What part of America are you from?'

Fifteen minutes later she knew everything there was to know about Airman Eddie Baker Johnson the Third and his family. She had heard about his parents, especially his father, Eddie Senior, and his mom and his two sisters. She had heard too about the small town in New England where the family lived, and the fact that Eddie had planned to follow his father into the family business before the war had come along. It hadn't been hard for her to recognise Eddie's homesickness and loneliness, and so she had let him pour out his heart to her whilst she listened, and in listening realised that she felt immeasurably older than this young man, who was, in reality, less than half a dozen years her junior. But then that was what war did to you.

'I guess I'll feel better once we start flying proper missions,' Eddie confided. 'Gee, I can't wait.'

Diane could see and hear the dreams of heroism and glory in his eyes and voice and her heart felt heavy. He had still to learn what so many thousands of their own young men – and women – had had to, and that was that war brought devastation and death, ruined bodies and ruined lives; that it brought far more pain and fear than glory. It changed your life for ever. But she could not tell him any of this, she knew. It was something he would have to learn for himself. Nevertheless, she couldn't help comparing him with the young men she had known in Cambridgeshire, young men with old eyes and searing memories. She grieved for them and she grieved for him too, and for the innocence he would surely lose.

'Sir...'

The speed with which Eddie suddenly saluted and the respectful tone of his voice caused Diane to turn round to see who he was addressing, her expression giving her away, she suspected, when she realised that it was the major.

His 'Dismissed, Airman,' had Eddie giving her an apologetic look before obeying him and heading off in the direction of the bar, leaving her on her own with the major.

'I thought it was the US cavalry that rode to the rescue, not its army,' Diane commented grittily, before adding, 'There wasn't really any need, you know. He was perfectly safe, if a little homesick.'

'I'm sure he was but, as it happens, *he* wasn't the one I came over to "rescue".'

His comment was so unexpected that Diane was shocked into looking up into his face, something she had tried to avoid doing since her unfortunate experience with the falling ladder. Now that she was looking at him, though, she realised that he had the most unusually intensely focused and compelling gaze. So much so that she couldn't seem to drag her own away from it.

'I can't imagine why you should think it neces-sary to rescue *me*,' she managed to say. The single raised eyebrow made her continue defensively, 'I was enjoying listening to him talk about his family. He's homesick and unsure of what the future holds. If I had a younger brother his age I'd like to think that someone, somewhere would take the trouble to listen to him—' She broke off when she saw he was frowning.

'You're saying that,' he told her, 'but it's no secret to those of us who have been here for a while that you Brits resent our presence.'

He was looking at her as though he was waiting for her to deny that. Well, she wasn't going to. Listening to Eddie had brought home to her something she hadn't recognised before, and it was something that her own innate sense of honesty was compelling her to admit.

'Yes, in many ways we do,' she agreed. 'People talk a lot about how war unites those fighting on the same side, but they don't often talk about the way in which it separates us. You are our allies, we know we need your support, but at the same time...' She paused and shook her head. 'At first when you came over, I admit that listening to you Americans irked me. Your manner seemed boastful and arrogant; you seemed not to know or care about what this war meant to us and had done to us. Where we feel like a ... a doomed generation, you all act like ... like victory is just going to drop into your hands. But now I realise that I felt like that because I was envious; envious of your confidence your enthusiasm, and your energy. You still have something that we've lost,' she sighed. 'This war has drained the youth and optimism from us. Whilst all of us were in the same boat it didn't matter because it wasn't noticeable, but now that you are here we can see it and it makes us feel–' Diane broke off, her face suddenly flushing with self-consciousness. She had said far more than she had intended to, but talking with Eddie had brought home to her how very much the war had changed her and her perceptions, and inwardly she was mourning that youthful part of herself that she, along with so many of her peers, had lost.

'Makes you feel what?'

She had been so lost in her thoughts that the major's prompt startled her. How on earth had she got involved in a conversation as deep as this with him – a man she barely knew, whom she certainly did not like and who she was pretty sure despised her? She shook her head and would have walked away if he hadn't reached out and put his hand on her arm. Even through the fabric of her jacket she could feel the strength of his hold. In another life, a life before Kit had broken her heart, she might have interpreted the sensation his touch was causing her as one of interest and approval. But that was impossible. He was a married man and she was a woman with a broken heart.

'Tell me.'

How commanding he sounded. And yet his voice was so low she had to lean towards him to hear it.

She wanted to refuse but instead she heard herself saying unsteadily, 'I don't know. Tired and old; envious of your energy and enthusiasm, resentful of the loss of our own; angry because you think you can do better than we have without knowing what we have done and how much it has cost us. Oh, so many things. In comparison to you we look and feel so tired and old, even though in terms of years we're still young. It's as though we've lost something. Somehow we've become separate from one another, in so many different ways, our men away at war, whilst we are here, those who are engaged in the business of war here at home, and those who aren't, men and women, children and parents, husband and wives...'

'Is that why your engagement broke up?'

Her head jerked up her eyes widening. 'How do you—'

'I overheard you talking about it earlier in the Dungeon.'

'I don't know. You'd have to ask my ex-fiancé,' she told him curtly, pulling away from him. Somehow their conversation had taken an unexpected and very dangerous turn.

She knew that this was not the sort of behaviour or the sort of conversation Captain Barker had had in mind when she had told her that she was putting her name forward for this extra duty. A sense of despair and loneliness filled her. She felt wretchedly aware of how alone she was, something that the major, with his wife waiting at home for him, would never be able to understand.

'Your wife must miss you,' she said, recognising immediately from his expression that he hadn't welcomed her comment.

'She knew she was marrying a soldier.' His voice was clipped, warning her that she had overstepped the mark.

'You don't like it when I ask you personal questions – well, that works both ways,' Diane told him.

'You were happy to talk to your colleagues about your engagement,' he responded.

'That's different,' Diane protested. 'I was talking to a friend, you and I aren't...'

'You and I aren't what?' he challenged her.

Something very odd was happening, something totally unexpected. Something she needed to bring to a halt right here and now before it went any further.

'You and I aren't anything,' Diane answered flatly, 'and now, if you'll excuse me, I must go and mingle.'

She didn't give him the opportunity to stop her, slipping away before he had time to respond.

FIFTEEN

'Who's the broad, Mancini?'

Myra flicked a deliberately snooty look at the airman who had asked the question. When Nick had announced within a couple of minutes of them meeting up that he had arranged to see 'a couple of guys' at a bar close to Lime Street Station, she hadn't been too pleased but she had hidden her displeasure. However, whilst she might be keen to make a good impression on Nick, she certainly did not feel similarly inclined where his fellow American friend Tony was concerned.

The minute the other man had come swaggering into the bar, Myra had experienced a sharp sense of antipathy towards him, and she had sensed from the look he had given her that it was one that was returned. Now, with his back to her, he was talking about her as though she wasn't there, and if it hadn't been for the fact that she was still not one hundred per cent sure of Nick, she would have made it clear to both of them that Tony's company was not something she wanted. Tony was short and square, with sallow skin and a hooded, somehow reptilian stare that made her want to shiver.

'She's my new girl, aren't you, babe?' Nick answered, grinning at Myra as he put his arm round her and gave her a hug. 'The other guys in the platoon understand when a guy has the hots for a girl and wants to get a bit of time with her, and they don't mind covering for me,' he told his friend.

'The MPs are pretty keen,' Tony commented.

'They ain't too bad if you know how to handle them,' Nick responded with a wink, before removing his arm from Myra's shoulder and telling her, 'Why don't you go and powder your nose or something, sugar, whilst Tony and I discuss a bit of business? We won't be too long – just fifteen minutes or so – and then I'll take you out for dinner.'

She was being told to make herself scarce, Myra recognised, and she could guess why. She wasn't so dim that she hadn't heard about some of the Americans supplying black marketeers with goods from the American bases' PX stores. Personally, she didn't give two hoots about Nick being involved with the black market. She had already noted the spivs clustered round the bar and had guessed that this must be one of their favoured meeting places.

There were two other girls in the small ladies' room already, both peroxided blondes with over-made-up faces, one chewing gum whilst the other smoked a cigarette.

'...And I told him straight that there was no way I were putting up with being treated like some cheap tart–' one of them broke off from saying as Myra walked in. 'Here on yer own, are yer, duck?' she asked Myra in a decidedly unfriendly voice.

'No. I'm here with my date,' Myra answered her deliberately, letting her know what her own status was.

'GI, is he?' the other girl asked, drawing deeply on her cigarette.

'Yes.'

'Well, you mek sure he treats you right,' she warned Myra, suddenly becoming almost motherly. 'They've got the money to give a girl a good time, and it does none of us any favours if you don't mek sure they learn how to spend it. Too many girls are going out with GIs and letting them treat them cheap, if you ask me.'

'How come he's brought you down here, though? This ain't an American bar,' the gum-chewing one asked.

'He was meeting a friend.' Myra kept her answer deliberately vague.

'Business friend, is he?'

'Another American,' Myra answered. She glanced discreetly at her watch. Fifteen minutes,

Nick had said, and so far she had been here for just over five.

'So how long 'ave you been datin' this GI of yours, then?' the gum chewer asked, whilst the smoker blew out a cloud of smoke.

'Not long.'

'Well, let me warn you that there's them wot will have it in for you for walking out with him. Found that out yet, 'ave yer? Stuck-up bitches,' she continued without waiting for Myra to reply. 'Give me a GI over one of our own lads any day of the week. Mind you, you've got ter watch out for some of them. I heard of a girl last week wot got herself knocked up by one of them. Swore blind to her that he was going to marry her and tek her home with him, but then when she tells him she's having his kid he didn't want to know. Daft bugger,' she said scornfully. 'All she knew about him was that his name was Joe.'

Fourteen minutes... Myra started to head for the door.

She exhaled in relief as she looked across the bar and saw that Nick was on his own.

'Want another drink?' he asked her.

She shook her head. 'Is Tony from the Bronx, like you?' she asked him curiously. Immediately she knew that she had said the wrong thing.

Nick stiffened and put down his drink. 'What do you want to know that for?' he demanded sharply.

'No reason. I just noticed that he speaks like you do,' Myra told him truthfully.

'Tony doesn't like people asking questions about him, and if I was you I'd forget about ever seeing him.' Nick looked at his watch, and Myra reflected again that it looked expensive. 'Look, I've got to get back to the base.'

'But you said you would take me out for dinner,' she protested.

'Aw, come on, babe. You don't want me to get into trouble for getting back late, do you? Look, I'll make it up to you. How would you like a trip to London?'

'London?' Myra stared at him. 'I'd love it,' she said truthfully, 'but we won't be able to get train tickets.'

'Sure we will. Leave it all up to me.' He put his arm around her and squeezed her. 'We could take in a few sights, have some fun together, and now that you're my girl...' He paused meaning-fully.

Myra looked at him, weighing up her alternatives. She couldn't keep him dangling for much longer, without risking losing him and she didn't want to do that. And, after all, he had publicly acknowledged her as his girl to a fellow American. But even so...

'Saying I'm your girl's one thing,' she told him firmly. 'Proving it's another.'

'Meaning what?' Nick challenged her, his good humour fading.

'The best way to show that you're serious about a girl is to give her a ring,' Myra informed him, adding pointedly, 'especially if you're thinking of taking her away to a hotel.' She wasn't going to let herself think about that other ring she ought to be wearing and she certainly wasn't going to think about the man who had given it to her. She and Jim should never have got married, and Myra, with the mental facility for letting herself see and know only what she wanted to see and know, had convinced herself that they were as good as divorced already. Jim, who had gone back to North Africa now, would come round to her way of thinking. After all, he always had done in the past, hadn't he?

Ruthie's back was aching, from bending over her bench filling shells with liquid TNT, which had to be carried from the large mixer that contained the hot TNT, back to the bench in a container shaped something like a watering can. But the pain in her back wasn't anything like so bad as the pain in her heart.

It was Wednesday now, four whole days since Glen had walked away from her, leaving her standing in the middle of the Close. Not that she could blame him for what he had done. Seeing her mother like that must have shocked him. Ruthie could feel her eyes filming with tears but she dared not lift her hand to her face to wipe them away because of the risk of getting the TNT in them. Normally she quite enjoyed her work, despite the danger and the dreadful smell of the TNT, which filled the air and clung to everyone's skin and clothes, but today the time just seemed to drag.

Maureen who had borrowed her locker key again and had promised to return it had forgotten it, and as a consequence of that Ruthie had had to leave her going-home clothes tied up in a cloth bag hanging from a coat peg in the cloakroom.

With theft rife in the factory, she was already worrying about whether or not her things would be there at the end of her shift. Only yesterday one of the other women had complained that she had had to walk home barefoot twice in one week on account of having had her shoes stolen.

Some of the women had even been talking about setting up their own vigilante group to track down the thieves.

'That's daft talk, that is,' Jess had pronounced earlier during their dinner break. 'They'll never find them.'

'That friend of yours wants to be careful what she says about it being daft to look for them wot's bin thieving,' Maureen warned as she returned to the bench with a freshly filled can of TNT. 'Otherwise folk might start thinking that she's one of them.'

'That's ridiculous,' Ruthie protested.

'That's typical of you – allus sticking up for them new friends you've made. Wot's up wi' that Jess anyway? Got a face as long as a fiddle today, she has.'

'I don't know,' Ruthie admitted, looking over to where Jess was working, her head bent as she filled the shell in front of her and then deftly inserted the tube that would contain the detonator, before shaking the shell to make sure the TNT was at the correct level, then going on to the next shell. Her movements were so practised and quick and Ruthie acknowledged to herself how much slower she was in comparison. She wondered what it was that was causing Jess to be so quiet and unlike her normally fun-loving self.

As she turned back to her work, out of the corner of her eye, Ruthie noticed one of the women further up the line stick her foot out into the aisle right in the path of another woman, who was returning to her own bench with a freshly filled can of TNT. Ruthie started to call out a warning but it was too late. The woman carrying the TNT tripped and was starting to fall.

The one who had caused her fall called out sharply, ''Ere, watch where you're going, will yer?' But there was no time for Ruthie to worry about what she had seen. Instead, along with all the other women working nearby, she rushed over to the woman who had fallen.

'Get out the way,' the foreman was yelling as he came rushing over, cursing and shouting instructions to the two men following him, whilst Ruthie stared in shocked horror at the woman who had slipped. Her face was covered in the TNT, turning it into a horrific mask, the strong metallic smell of the spilled liquid so strong that it was making them all cough and gag.

'Get her on that trolley,' the foreman was instructing the other men, 'and look sharp about it. Shift out of the way, you lot,' he told the other girls, as the two with the trolley took the woman down to the medical centre.

'What will happen to her?' Ruthie asked worriedly.

'She'll have to wait for the TNT to set and then they'll take it off for her,' Mel, who had left her own work and was peering over Ruthie's shoulder, answered.

'She'll be dreadfully burned,' Ruthie whis-

231

pered, still in shock and unable to blot out her mental image of the woman sticking out her foot and deliberately trying to trip her up.

'It won't be too bad. She'll have a red face for a few days, that's all. And happen it will teach her not to go nicking other folks' stuff in future,' Mel added matter-of-factly.

'There you are, Ruthie. That's what happens to folk who go stealing,' Maureen told her when they were both back at their benches, 'and if you was to ask me then I'd say it serves her right,' she added. 'Life's hard enough without having them as you're working with nicking yer stuff.'

Ruthie couldn't bring herself to say anything. No matter what the woman might have done, surely it wasn't right that she should have been treated so cruelly?

'Get on with yer,' Maureen mocked her. 'Just look at yer, wi' yer hands all trembling and yer face whiter than that ruddy milk they mek us drink. Anyone'd think you were stealing yerself.'

'Of course I'm not,' Ruthie protested.

'Then don't go acting so guilty, otherwise folk'll think that you're ter blame next time summat goes missing,' Maureen advised her sharply.

'But how did they know it was her?' Ruthie asked.

'Found some stolen stuff in her locker was what I'd heard,' Maureen replied with a small shrug.

'Then surely they should have reported her and not–'

'Lor', but you're a softy at times. What's the point of doing that? This way she's bin taught a lesson she won't forget in a long time, an' she'll

232

have to explain to folk how she come by that red face she's going to have. Now give over trembling like that, will yer, otherwise you'll be having hot TNT all over yer hands.'

Jess observed the incident of the woman being punished for her crime of stealing without any real interest. Her thoughts were fully occupied with a different kind of crime. The crime against common sense and self-protection committed by Billy.

How could he have done such a daft thing as volunteer for the bomb disposal lot – and he *had* volunteered, she had now found out, despite him making out to her that he had been forced into it. Everyone knew that the life expectancy of anyone stupid enough to join was measured in days rather than years.

Billy's reckless lack of regard for his own safety was still filling her thoughts to the exclusion of everything else when she got home.

'What's up wi' you?' her uncle asked her good-naturedly. 'You've bin in ten minutes and hardly said a word. Not that I'm complaining, like,' he teased.

'It's that Billy Spencer,' Jess told him angrily. 'Going and joining up for the bomb disposal lot. He must be off his head. Just because he wants to play the hero for some girl. Well, he'll be a dead hero, and what use will he be to her then?' Jess's voice had risen sharply, and now she put down her knife and fork, her appetite for her tea swamped by her emotions. 'What does he know about bombs?' she asked.

'Well, he was allus tinkering with stuff and taking it to bits when he was a kiddie,' her mother offered. 'Happen he'll be better at it than you think.'

'He'll kill himself,' Jess pronounced starkly, oblivious to the looks her mother and uncle were exchanging as her mouth started to tremble betrayingly.

'If you feel that strongly about it, lass, happen you'd better go and have a word with him,' her uncle suggested gently.

'What for? He won't listen to me, not when he's got some girl mooning around after him, telling him what a hero he is. Well, I hope she likes her heroes dead because that's what she's going to get if he goes ahead with this.'

'It may not be as bad as you think, Jess,' her mother tried to comfort her.

'How can you say that? The only reason they're recruiting men is because they've lost that many. Liverpool is chock-full of Hitler's bombs that haven't exploded. Every time you open the paper there's talk of someone finding another one. There was those kiddies wot found one down by the railway sidings last week, and the week before that...' Jess couldn't go on.

'Seeing that chap of yours tonight, are you?' her uncle asked her, trying to lighten the mood.

Irritably Jess shook her head. 'He's a soldier, come to fight a war. He's not been sent here to take me out.'

'All right, keep your hair on, girl. I was only asking.'

Again her mother and uncle exchanged looks,

this time more anxious ones. It was so unlike Jess to be so irritable.

'Well, if you aren't seeing him, and seeing as how you're worrying about young Billy, why don't you slip down the street and have a word wi' him?' her uncle suggested.

'I'm not worrying about Billy Spencer – why should I be? He means nowt to me.' Jess stood up, pushing back her chair, her face hot with temper and misery. 'I'm going upstairs,' she told them. 'One of the girls fell and slipped this after-noon, and dropped TNT all over the place. Stank to high heaven, it did, and it's given me a rotten headache.'

'All right, love, you go up and I'll bring you a nice cup of tea later,' her mother offered her comfortingly.

Did they really think that Billy would listen to her? Angrily Jess climbed the stairs. Of course he wouldn't. No! He'd rather kill himself trying to show off to some girl he wanted to impress. And to think that there were folk living in Liverpool who said that the GIs were show-offs.

SIXTEEN

Tiredly Ruthie turned into Chestnut Close. After her shift had finished she had gone up to Waver-tree to collect their meat rations – not that there had been much left at the butcher's when she had finally got there. Only a bit of neck end of lamb and some heart. She had been hoping she might be able to get a bit of chicken to tempt her mother's meagre appetite. She had heard the girls at work talking about the things they had got on the black market, and even though a part of her had been shocked by this, another part of her had envied them, especially when she had heard one of them talking about the meat her brother had got from a friend of a friend who worked down on the docks.

'Come from one of them American ships, it did. I've heard as how the men up at Burton-wood leave enough food on their plates to feed a whole family for a week.'

Ruthie knew that that must be an exaggeration, but she had heard and understood the resentment in the other woman's voice. Sometimes, like now when she was tired and feeling low, it felt like she had been hungry for ever. And it was no good trying to kid herself that a thin stew made up out of a bit of stringy meat and some vegetables was just as good to eat as a proper roast because it wasn't. Her father had always enjoyed his Sunday roast. She could see him now, beaming with pride as he sat in his chair, his shirtsleeves rolled up as he prepared to carve the joint. There were delicate slices for her and her mother, and thicker ones for himself, over which he would pour the thick gravy her mother had made to go with the roast potatoes and Yorkshire pudding. Ruthie could feel her mouth starting to water. But it was no good longing for what she knew they couldn't have. Every extra scrap of food she could get had to go to her mother, who was so frail and in need of nourishment. She herself could always get a meal at the factory, she reminded herself.

One of the girls there had commented only that morning that it made no difference the government bringing in sweet rationing since there were no sweets to be had the length or breadth of the country.

'Not unless you're walking out with a Yank,' another woman had pointed out curtly. 'They've bin handing out chocolate along with nylons and the like to them as doesn't mind betraying our own brave lads and going out with them.'

'Well, that's the thing, isn't it?' another woman had spoken up angrily. 'Some of us have no choice who we go out with, because the Yanks are here and our lads aren't.'

'All the more reason not to have anything to do wi' 'em, if you ask me. Come over here, they 'ave, bragging and showing off – aye, and earning five times wot our boys are getting for digging up a few fields to make runways for their ruddy planes whilst our boys are getting killed in ruddy Africa.'

'Well, it stands to reason that they're gonna need runways, otherwise how are they going to fight? I've heard they're doing that much work up at Burtonwood you'd think the whole of the ruddy American Air Force was going to be there.'

'I expect it is,' another girl had joined in. 'Least-ways from what I've heard. Seems like they're going to be bringing in their men and equipment through Liverpool and that they'll be based at Burtonwood first off before they get sent to their proper bases.'

'I've heard that they've already got some of them big bombers of theirs there,' someone else had chipped in. 'Huge ruddy great things, they are, about ten times the size of our Lancasters.'

Glen had told Ruthie all about the huge American bombers they had been preparing the new runways for. She shivered now, thinking about them, admitting how relieved she was that Glen would not be flying in them but would instead be based at Burtonwood as a member of one of the support teams. Not that she should be thinking about Glen. Not now. Her steps slowed as she drew closer to home...

Her mother was over her funny spell now, but there would be others – Ruthie knew that, and she also knew that her mum was having them more frequently. The doctor had told her to try not to worry because there was nothing he could do, but how could she not worry? She loved her mother, of course, but sometime she felt so afraid; so worried about what was happening. And so very, very alone now that she had lost Glen. She may not have known him for very long, but her love for him was as strong as though she had known him all her life. She would never love anyone else. She knew that. And even though he had hurt her so badly she would not have wanted to change things so that she would never have known him. There was such a bitter sweetness in her memories of what they had shared. She would cherish those memories in her heart for ever.

She put her key in the front door and unlocked it, stepping into the hall, and then stopping as she heard the sound of voices coming from the kitchen. Her mother's, and Mrs Brown's, and... and Glen's voice: the voice she had been hearing in her dreams at night and her longings during the day as she clung to every tender word he had said to her. Now she was hearing it here; but she couldn't be!

Feeling dizzy with disbelief, her legs trembling as though they were about to give way, she hurried down the narrow hallway – where her father's coat still hung on its peg under the stuffed deer's head, with its branching antlers – and pushed open the door to the back parlour, her eyes widening at the scene in front of her.

Her mother, her face flushed with happiness, was seated at one side of the small, square table, whilst Glen was seated opposite her with Mrs Brown at the other side. There were tea cups on the table and what looked like a large slab of fruit cake with proper icing on it.

It was Glen who saw her first, breaking off from something he had been saying to her mother to get up clumsily, the tips of his ears betraying his nerves as he looked at her.

'There you are, Glen! Here she is. I told you she wouldn't be long,' Ruthie could hear their neighbour saying chirpily before she turned to Ruthie and told her, with an arch look, 'Just look who has come looking for you, Ruthie. Been here over an hour, he has, waiting impatiently to see you. Entertained your mum and me a treat, he has, telling us all about his family in America.'

'Oh, Ruthie, why didn't you tell me about you and Glen?' her mother chimed in reproachfully. 'I apologise for my daughter, Glen. I dare say she

239

wanted to keep you to herself for a little while before she brought you home to meet us, although her dad would have had something to say about that. He wouldn't have liked at all her seeing you without him knowing. I wish you could have met him, Glen...' Tears had started to fill her mother's eyes.

'There, Mrs Philpott, don't you go taking on now,' Mrs Brown was comforting Ruthie's mother whilst Glen was also insisting, 'It isn't Ruthie's fault. You mustn't blame her. Like I was telling you, I would have come in and introduced myself to you after the dance on Saturday, but it was getting late and I didn't want to end up getting put on a charge and being confined to camp.'

Ruthie couldn't stop looking at him. She wanted to fill her hungry gaze with the sight of him and go on filling it.

When he came towards her, all she could do was offer him a tremulous half-smile as he took hold of both her hands, squeezing them emotionally.

There was so much she wanted to say to him and so much too she needed to know. Like why he was here after the way he had turned his back on her and walked away.

'I'll tell you what, Mrs Philpott,' Mrs Brown was saying warmly to her mother, 'why don't we let these two young ones go for a bit of a walk together whilst you and me get on with clearing up?'

'But Ruthie hasn't had her tea yet,' her mother objected in that little-girl voice that Ruthie had learned to recognise and dread.

'It's all right, Mum. I had something to eat before I came home,' Ruthie fibbed quickly, hating herself for the small deceit but knowing that it was necessary if she was to have the opportunity she desperately needed to talk privately with Glen.

Mrs Brown gave her an approving look, and urged, 'Off you go then, you two, whilst me and your mam clear up and have a bit of a natter.'

'Oh, but I want Glen to stay,' Ruthie's mother was protesting.

'He'll be coming back once he and your Ruthie have had a bit of a chat,' Mrs Brown soothed her firmly. 'It's nearly time for that wireless programme you like, and I reckon that since Glen has bin so generous and bought you such a lovely slab of fruit cake that we might put the kettle on and have another slice.'

'Oh, yes. I like fruit cake. It was always Mr Philpott's favourite – did I tell you that?'

It seemed an age before Ruthie and Glen were finally outside, and she was able to release the anxious breath she had been holding. She had determinedly put at least a foot between herself and Glen as they stepped into the Close, but when he reached for her hand, clasping it in his own, she didn't resist. His hand was so large compared with hers – so very large, in fact, that her hand was lost in it. Lost and yet at the same time somehow so very, very safe.

'It wasn't true what you said to my mother, was it?' she asked him quietly, unable to look at him, and instead studying the tired dullness of the shabby pavement. 'About not coming in with me,

241

I mean.'

'No.'

Relieved tears stung her eyes. She would have hated it if he had lied to her.

'It was because of Mum, wasn't it?' she continued in a low voice.

Immediately his hand tightened on hers.

'I ... I can understand what you must have thought when ... when you saw her like that. It's Dad's death that did it. She was never like this before. They were so close, you see,' she explained earnestly, 'and she depended on him so much. The doctor says that she's gone this way because she just can't bear him not being here any more. She knows that he's gone really but sometimes she has to ... to pretend that he hasn't.' She felt another squeeze on her hand.

'I ... I would have told you.' Somehow it was important that she made him understand that, and that he didn't think that she was the kind of girl who would have kept something so important from him. 'I don't blame you for walking away like you did, but–'

'I wanted to stay,' Glen interrupted her gruffly, 'but I kinda thought that you didn't want me there, and then there was your mom. I guess I was afraid that having a stranger around might upset her even more. My dad had this cousin – she's dead now, God rest her soul – well, she was more of a second cousin really. When she was little she and her kid brother used to play a game of dare, running across the lines down at the railyard where her pa worked, only one day little Joey got his foot caught, and they couldn't get him out in time. She was fine most of the time, but every now and again she'd get it into her head to go down to the railyard to look for him. Some folks round our town used to reckon she was off her head.'

Ruthie winced.

'But my mom always used to say that it was God's way of shielding her from her own pain, and that you never knew what something like that would do to you unless you had to go through it. I guess, in a kinda way, your mom feels the same about your dad as Cousin Laura did about Joey.'

Ruthie made a small choking sound of agreement through the tears that were streaming down her face.

'Aw … sweetheart, don't…' Glen begged her rawly. 'I can't bear to see you cry.'

'I can't help it,' Ruthie sobbed. 'Your poor cousin. What a truly dreadful thing to have happened, Glen. At least my mother had all those years with my dad. Some days, though, she's worse than others. The doctor says that he doesn't know whether or not she'll ever get properly well,' she admitted.

Glen squeezed her hand again, and gave her an understanding look before saying, 'I'm sorry I haven't been in touch before now, but I was waiting for this to arrive.' As he spoke he released her hand to reach into his jacket pocket for an envelope, which he handed to her.

'What is it?' Ruthie asked uncertainly without taking it.

'It's a letter from my folks, welcoming you to the family,' he told her quietly. 'You know I said

243

that I wrote to them telling them that I'd found the girl I wanted to marry?'

Ruthie nodded disbelievingly.

'Well, I knew they'd write back, and Mom put this letter for you in with mine. She said to tell you that you're to write back and send her some photographs so that she can get to know you ready for when the war is over and I take you home with me.'

'Oh, Glen.' Fresh tears filled her eyes and flooded down her cheeks. She had felt so lost and broken-hearted these last few days. They had showed her how deep her feelings for him were, but they had also showed her something else. Something that hadn't really mattered when she had thought he had walked away from her, but which mattered very much now. All the more so in the light of what he had just been saying to her about his mother.

'Aren't you going to open Mom's letter?' he urged her.

'I can't marry you, Glen,' Ruthie told him miserably. 'I just can't.'

'You can't say that,' he protested. 'You don't mean it. You love me. I can see it in your eyes.'

She shook her head. 'That doesn't matter. At least it does, because I know I will never ever love anyone else. Oh, Glen, don't,' she protested breathlessly, but without any real conviction or denial in her voice when he took hold of her and tugged her into the protective shadow of an over-hanging tree and kissed her fiercely.

'You love me. You've just said so,' he told her thickly when he had stopped. 'And I sure as hell love you.'

'I know,' Ruthie agreed wretchedly, 'but can't you see? I can't marry you and go back with you to America when the war's over, Glen. What would happen to my mum?'

They had walked as far as the allotments and although she tried to object when Glen pushed open the gate that led to them she still let him walk her through it and down to a small wooden bench he had spied from the road.

'We shouldn't be here,' she protested. 'It's Mr Taylor's allotment and—'

'There's no one here, and if this Mr Taylor should come and ask us to leave, then I'll explain to him that I needed somewhere to talk to my girl. The only girl for me, Ruthie, because that is what you are.'

She could feel herself trembling as he wound his fingers between her own and then clasped his in her palm.

'Handfast, my mom told me this is called,' he whispered to her. 'It's what people used to do if there was no church for them to be married in. Don't worry about your mom. We'll take her with us.'

Ruthie gazed up at him. 'Can we do that?' she breathed unsteadily.

'Sure we can,' he told her firmly. 'Now promise me there won't be any more talk about you not marrying me, and then read my mom's letter.'

'Yes, Glen,' Ruthie told him demurely, before exclaiming in delighted shock, 'Glen, no, you mustn't kiss me, not here!'

'Then quit looking at me like that,' he told her,

ignoring her command, to take her in his arms and kiss her very thoroughly indeed.

Naturally it was quite some time before she came back down to earth enough to open Glen's mother's letter, reading it slowly and with growing joy, breaking off every now and then, to exclaim, 'Oh, Glen, your mother has written the kindest things, about how she can't wait to meet me and to welcome me properly into your family. Oh, and look, she says that she's going to send me some photographs of you when you were a baby, and she asks if I will send her some of me. Oh, Glen ... I'll write back to her tonight,' she vowed emotionally. 'How kind she is, Glen, to welcome me, a stranger, like this, as though she loves me already.'

'Of course she loves you already. She knows that I love you,' Glen told her sturdily. 'She sent me this too,' he added, reaching into his jacket and suddenly looking both very serious and at the same time very bashful. 'It was my grandmother's.' He opened the small box and showed Ruthie an old ring with a small diamond. 'She gave it to me before she died and told me that it was for my wife-to-be. I guess it's a bit old-fashioned-looking, and maybe you'd rather have something different ... but–'

'Oh, no, Glen,' Ruthie assured him fervently. 'I love it.'

She did not know whose hand was trembling the more when he slipped the ring onto her finger. It looked so narrow that she held her breath, half afraid that it would be too small, but to her relief it fitted her finger perfectly.

'There,' Glen said triumphantly. 'We're engaged now, Ruthie. Nothing can part us now. Just as soon as I can arrange it, you and me are going to be married. Come on.' He got up and, reaching out, drew her to her feet. 'We'd better get back and tell your mom.'

'Oh, Glen, I still can't believe this is happening. I never thought I would *ever* be this happy,' Ruthie told him, looking down at her hand where the tiny diamond was reflecting all the colours of the rainbow through her happy tears.

'Well now, engaged, is it?' Mrs Brown beamed. 'I must say that I can't say that I'm surprised. I had my suspicions right from the first time Ruthie met you, Glen, and I told my hubby as much, didn't I, Joe?' she asked her husband, who had been summoned from his allotment and commanded to bring a bottle of elderberry wine with him to toast the newly engaged couple.

'And Glen says that Mum will be able to come to America with us. Oh, and, Mrs Brown, you should see the lovely letter Glen's mother has sent to me, telling me that she knows already that she's going to love me because Glen does.'

'Well, I should think she will love you, an' all, Ruthie lass. A good girl you are and allus have been.'

'Glen wants us to get married as soon as we can. But he'll have to get permission from the army first.'

'It's time we had a wedding in the Close. And think on, young man,' Mrs Brown warned Glen, giving him a serious look, 'in love or not, and war

247

or not, there's to be no hanky-panky goes on before the pair of you are wed, otherwise Mr Brown will have something to say to you, just like Ruthie's dad would have done if he'd been alive.'

Ruthie blushed peony pink, and then gazed adoringly up at Glen when he told her neighbour with great dignity, 'Ruthie's going to be my wife and there's no way I'd ask her to do anything her folks wouldn't like, or that we couldn't tell our own kids about when they're grown.' He turned to Ruthie and gave her a look that, as she told him half an hour later when she had been allowed to go to the front gate with him to say good night properly, had made her tingle all the way down to her toes.

SEVENTEEN

Diane put down her hairbrush and turned to stare at Myra in angry disbelief.

'I can't believe you're even thinking about risking doing something like this. Not after last time.'

Myra gave a dismissive shrug and lit a fresh cigarette. It was no business of Diane's what she did but she had her own reasons for telling her about her plans to spend a weekend in London with Nick.

'What risk? There isn't one. I've got a legitimate weekend pass coming up, and a week's holiday left to take, so what's to stop me spending it in

London, if I want?'

'You're a married woman with a husband,' Diane pointed out grimly. 'And if you think I'm going to cover for you a second time if he comes home and catches you out you've got another think coming.

'I'm not asking you to cover for me. I'm just asking you to lend me your silk blouse,' Myra told her, drawing on her cigarette. 'Honestly, from the fuss you're making anyone would think that Jim was your ruddy brother or something. Look, my marriage is over. Jim knows that – I've told him often enough. It might be a good thing if he *did* turn up and find out I'm with Nick. He'd have to accept that I'd drifted then.' she said bluntly, using the forces' slang for a woman who was unfaithful to her husband in his absence.

'I don't know why you're doing this, Myra, not when you've got a decent man like Jim,' Diane protested.

'No, I dare say you don't,' Myra agreed, stubbing out her cigarette without finishing it. 'Women like you never do. But I'm not like you, Diane. I want better than what I've got here. I want more from life than a "decent husband". I've always wanted more. I want to live like they do in the films.'

'But, Myra, that's just in the films–'

'No, it isn't. That's how it is in America. Anyway, how would you know? Who the hell would really want to live here if they didn't have to?' Myra demanded angrily. 'You've only got to listen to the Americans to know what they think of us and this country. They're used to better and they don't mind saying so.'

'Bragging about it, you mean,' Diane corrected her, tight-lipped.

'You can call it bragging if you want. I call it speaking out and saying it like it is. Nick can give me everything I've ever wanted. A new life in America, as his wife.'

'You're already someone else's wife. Have you told him that?'

'My marriage is over,' Myra repeated, ignoring her question. 'Probably isn't even a proper marriage in America, anyway,' she added dismissively. 'They do things differently over there,' She gave Diane a hard-edged look as though daring her to contradict her.

She couldn't possibly believe that, surely, Diane thought, but she could see that there wasn't any point in trying to reason with her.

'So can I borrow your blouse, then?' Myra pressed her. 'Only Nick said as how he was going to book us into this posh hotel.'

Diane didn't really care for the idea of her best blouse being used as an accessory to adultery but the war had brought a new mood of pulling together and sharing what was available, and even though she couldn't approve of what Myra was doing, neither could she refuse her.

'I suppose so,' she agreed reluctantly.

Somehow the summer air seemed to accentuate the shabbiness of the city and its people, Diane thought as she made her way down Edge Hill Road, past bombed-out buildings and a church with the now familiar notice pinned outside asking people to donate money 'to buy a sick child a banana'. No wonder their American allies were so critical and contemptuous of the country and the people they were boasting openly they had come to save. And no wonder too that those who had lived through so much within that country felt bitter and angry when they heard those boastful comments. She felt a small pang for Myra and then quickly dismissed it – she was still behaving terribly.

'Hello, there.'

She had been so lost in her own thoughts that she hadn't seen Ruthie hurrying across the road towards her.

'Hello,' Diane smiled back. 'Your day off, is it?' She noted the basket Ruthie was carrying and the summer dress she was wearing.

'Yes. I'm on my way to the allotments. Mr Talbot, who minds the allotment Dad had, sent word to say that there's some strawberries ready and that he's got a bit of salad for us as well. Then Glen's coming round for tea later.'

'Glen? Oh, the American you met at the Grafton?' Diane remembered.

'Yes.' Ruthie beamed, and then said in a rush, 'He's asked me to marry him and we're engaged now.' Proudly she held out her hand to show Diane the ring she was wearing.

Diane could hardly bear to look at it, remembering her joy and pride in her own engagement ring, but she knew that for the sake of good manners she had to. Her heart felt as though it was being squeezed in a giant vice.

'Oh ... it's lovely,' she told Ruthie truthfully,

somehow managing not to let her voice betray her feelings.

'And Glen's mother has written me the nicest letter, welcoming me into the family. Glen wants us to get married soon. He's one of them working on the new runways at Burtonwood, and whilst he doesn't think he'll be posted somewhere else for a while, like he says, you never know, and it's best that we get married just as soon as we can,' she explained earnestly.

There was no need for Diane to ask if the younger girl was happy. Ruthie's joy was spilling out of her with every word she said. Diane could remember a time when she had felt just the same. Now, though... If only some of Ruthie's happiness could spill into her life, on to her.

Just as Diane reached Derby House, the bus that brought in the other girls from the school in Hyatt, where they were billeted, for their 'watch', pulled up alongside her, disgorging a crowd of uniformed young women, including Jean.

'You don't know how lucky you are to be living out,' she grumbled to Diane. 'No barracking your bed every morning, then having to run all the way to parade for you, I'll bet.'

'No,' Diane agreed. She certainly didn't miss the morning routine of stripping her bed, and then folding the sheets and the blankets separately before stacking them up on top of the 'biscuit', as the narrow beds were named, but she did miss the camaraderie she had shared with the other girls at her previous post, and she would have much preferred to be billeted with someone

252

other than Myra.

'We were late on parade this morning and there was a CO's inspection so we've been given jankers,' she told Diane, referring to the routine punishment of things like washing up and peeling potatoes that was given for such an offence.

'Poor you,' Diane sympathised, before changing the subject to ask anxiously, 'Have you heard from Susan at all?'

Jean shook her head. 'Only that her hubby hasn't been found as yet, and that she's been warned to expect the worst.'

Not unnaturally, the whole of Derby House was still in the grip of an angry grief but nowhere more so than down in the Dungeon, where those working had seen the devastation at first-hand.

Breaking off their conversation to salute a Senior Service captain emerging from the building, Diane checked to see that her cap was on straight before reaching for her pass and heading for the door.

'It's all right for you,' Jean continued to grumble. 'You've got such lovely long hair that you can put it up. Somehow I always manage to end up with mine touching my collar, if I have to wear my greatcoat.'

It was against WAAF rules for a girl's hair to touch her collar, and Diane took a quick look at Jean's hair before suggesting, 'Have you thought of rolling it round a sausage?'

'What's that when it's at home?'

Diane laughed. 'It's a ring of stuffed cloth that you put on your head, a bit like a tiara, and then you tuck your hair into it. I think I might have one somewhere. I'll bring it with me tomorrow, if you like, and show you.'

'Would you? Anything that stops me from getting put on another charge would be welcome. Watch out, here come the Brylcreem boys,' Jean laughed as three small reconnaissance planes screamed overhead, the first one doing a small victory roll.

'Now that's something the Americans will never be able to do in those huge bombers of theirs,' Jean commented with satisfaction. 'Hear about Middlesbrough being bombed the other night, did you? I've got an auntie living there. Let's hope these new Lancasters we've got that are supposed to be so wonderful can persuade Hitler to give in.'

Diane smiled, but she suspected that Jean knew as well as she did herself that the war was still long from over.

'Is Myra still seeing that GI she was dancing with at the Grafton?' Jean asked her suddenly.

'I'm ... I'm not sure,' Diane felt obliged to fib. 'Why?'

'Oh, no reason really. Only that I was out with a pal of mine and her brother the other night. He's something secret in the police – I don't really know what – but he took us into this place for a drink for a bit of a joke. He told us it was where all the black marketeers – and worse – meet up, and who should be in there but that chap Myra was with. Ray – that's my pal's brother – reckons that Myra's GI and the chap he was with could be a real bad lot. He said that they've had a tip-off that a lot of new black market stuff is coming straight from stores intended for the American base PXs, and that the set-up is being run by gangsters who–'

'Gangsters?' Diane protested, suspecting that Jean's rather vivid imagination and dislike of Myra were getting the better of her.

'Well, that's what Ray said, but don't believe me if you do not want to,' Jean told her huffily.

'It isn't that I don't believe you,' Diane reassured her. 'It's just that it sounds like something out of a Warner Brothers film.'

'Maybe it does, but Ray says that some pretty bad eggs have been caught up in the American conscription draft. You know,' she lowered her voice, 'Mafia and that.'

They had reached the doorway into the building now, both of them automatically presenting their passes for inspection, whilst Diane digested what Jean had told her. It seemed too far-fetched to be true and, even if she were to pass it on to Myra, she sincerely doubted that the girl would listen to her.

'The C-in-C's office door's open,' she commented to Jean, to change the subject. 'That means he's in. I heard that he's been sleeping here these last few days.'

Their Commander-in-Chief took his duties towards the convoys, of which he was in charge, very seriously indeed, as everyone working at Derby House knew.

'I heard that he'd had a real run-in with the First Lord of the Admiralty over what happened,' Jean agreed, as they made their way to their cloakroom. 'Someone said that they saw Winnie up

255

here last week. I don't know if it's true but I do know that he does come to Derby House. Not that we're supposed to know, of course. I reckon that's part of the reason why the Germans would have given anything to have hit us when they were bombing Liverpool, but with the real business part of the building being so deep underground they didn't have a chance. Thank goodness.'

Diane grimaced as she looked down at her shoes, and then went over to the box in which the girls kept a shared collection of 'essential items' necessary for keeping their uniforms smart. Watching her giving her shoes an extra polish, Jean exclaimed, 'Lord, I nearly forgot I've got a button coming loose. I'd better sew it on whilst we're in here otherwise I might get another set of jankers.'

Within a couple of seconds both girls were busily occupied in their chores, their shared silence broken when Jean asked Diane, 'What are you on today?'

'Wireless Operator in signals. They're a girl short. I just hope my Morse speed is up to it.'

Jean pulled a sympathetic face as she finished sewing on her button and snapped the thread with her teeth. 'I can still remember my course,' she agreed. 'I was terrified I wouldn't pass the exam at the end of it, with all that stuff about Ohm's law, the stratosphere, the Appleton layer and then Morse code. Finished?'

Diane studied her shoes and then nodded. Companionably they walked out of the cloak-room together until they reached that part of the building where they had to go their separate ways,

Jean into the Dungeon, and Diane into one of the signals ops rooms.

As she walked in, the girl in charge came over to her.

'Captain Barker wants to see you,' she told Diane without taking her attention from the girls working on the keyboards, translating the Morse messages they were receiving.

Diane's heart thumped uncomfortably. The instruction she had just received was unpleasantly similar to the one she had had after the humiliating evening at the Grafton. Then, though, she had known what she was being carpeted for. This time she had no idea.

Thankfully there was no sign of the lieutenant when she knocked on the captain's open door five minutes later.

'Come,' Captain Barker called out, glancing up from the papers on her desk and then smiling when she saw Diane.

'You wanted to see me, ma'am?'

'Yes, Wilson. Stand easy. We've had a request from our allies for a stenographer to accompany Major Saunders on an inspection of various properties that may be used to house some of the officers of the Eighth Army who are due to arrive here in the next few weeks. Normally, of course, the major would find someone from their own staff to accompany him, but since on this occasion that is not possible he has asked for our help.'

Diane's spirits sank lower with every word Captain Barker said, but of course it did not do for a Waaf, or indeed anyone in the armed forces, to show any reaction to the orders they were being given by a superior officer, and Diane prided herself on her professionalism when it came to her duty.

'I see from your records that you are a trained shorthand typist,' Captain Barker continued. 'Is that correct?'

How Diane longed to say 'no', but of course she couldn't. *Why* had this happened to her? Why couldn't the major have written up his own notes? But of course she knew the answer to that, she decided crossly. The Americans must have everything they wanted – or at least that was how it sometimes seemed to the hard-pressed British forces personnel, struggling to cope with their own work and provide assistance to their allies as well.

The requirements of the Eighth Army seemed to grow with every day that passed, and Diane thought it was no wonder that the British forces were growing increasingly resentful of the priority accorded to their allies. Sometimes it seemed as though the Americans were behaving more like an occupying force than an ally.

'I appreciate, of course, that this is outside your normal duties,' Captain Barker told Diane, almost as though she had seen into her head and read her thoughts. 'But needs must, I'm afraid. Please report to the major at ten hundred hours, outside the main entrance to the building.'

'How long–' Diane began, unable to stop herself from voicing the question uppermost in her turbulent thoughts, but the captain shook her head, telling her crisply, 'For as long as the major needs you. He hasn't specified how long that will be.'

Diane was too well trained to do anything other than salute smartly. She knew better than to imagine that the major could have specified that he wanted *her* to accompany him. Group Captain Barker wasn't the sort to sanction *that* sort of request. However, half an hour later, when the major drew up outside the building in a US Army Jeep, if he was surprised to find her waiting for him he didn't show it.

Diane stepped forward, saluting formally before saying crisply, 'Leading Aircraft Woman Wilson reporting for duty, sir.'

Somehow she managed to withstand his silent cool-eyed scrutiny without betraying how on edge he was making her feel. What was he thinking behind that impenetrable look that shut her out as effectively as a steel door? Never mind that, what was *she* doing, allowing herself to think of him in such personal terms?

'Jump in, soldier,' he told her with a brief inclination of his head as he reached across to push open the passenger door of the Jeep.

Soldier. Was he desexing her deliberately or was his term of address simply American custom? Burying her self-consciousness beneath an outer air of professionalism, Diane approached the Jeep. It surprised her that the major should be driving himself. Taking aside the fact that most of the high-ups used staff cars with drivers, she wouldn't have thought that he would want to drive on English roads. Those who had heard their allies' scathing comments about their roads knew the irritated contempt in which the Americans held the narrow winding country lanes and the main roads choked with men and war machinery on the move.

'Have you been told what this is all about?' Major Saunders asked her when she had climbed into the Jeep and closed the door.

'Captain Barker said that you needed a stenographer, sir.'

'That's right. We've got a shipload of army personnel, including officers, about to arrive, and since the word "liaison" happens to appear in my title, someone has got it into their head that that means I'm the best person to sort out billets for the officers.' There was an open mix of irony and irritation in his voice, and this time when he looked at her she could see his annoyed impatience quite clearly in his eyes. That too surprised her. She wasn't used to hearing an officer express his or her feelings so openly to someone of a lower rank. But then they had all noticed the different and far more relaxed behaviour within the US forces, where the ordinary servicemen never stood to attention when they saw a senior officer, unless they had a specific reason for doing so. No British officer would lean back in his seat in the casual way the major was now doing, but no amount of relaxed deportment could take away the fact that everything about the major warned that he could be a very formidable opponent. Opponent? They were supposed to be allies, Diane reminded herself, wondering if she would have been so on edge if he hadn't witnessed her making such a humiliating fool of herself.

Somehow she had to forget that, and focus on the reason why she was here. She couldn't blame him for finding the task he had been given unappealing. It was not going to be an easy assignment, she could tell.

'The good news is that most of the ground work has been done already,' he told her, 'and I've been given a list of the places I need to go and check out. The bad news is that they seem to be spread over half of Cheshire, and by my reckoning it's going to take us the best part of a week to get round them all.'

A week! Diane dipped her head, not wanting him to see how horrified that made her feel.

'So I guess we'd better make a start otherwise the Eighth is going to find its officers sleeping under canvas in a Burtonwood field. How well do you know this area?' he asked her.

'Not well at all, sir,' Diane replied, sitting bolt upright in her seat and looking straight ahead.

'OK then, how well can you read a map?'

Now she did look at him. 'Group Captain Barker said you wanted a stenographer.'

'So you can't read a map.'

The irritation in his voice stung Diane into saying fiercely, 'I *can* read a map but–'

'Yeah?' He pulled in to the side of the road, bringing the Jeep to an abrupt halt, and then turned to her, commanding, 'Show me.'

As he reached across to remove a map from the shelf in front of her, he was so close that Diane could smell the clean fresh smell of soap on his skin. Immediately she recoiled from it and from him, appalled by the unwanted ache of yearning that had suddenly and violently seized hold of her. Kit ... Kit... She closed her eyes. She must make herself remember that what she was feeling was because of *him*, and not because of this man, who was, after all, nothing to her and never would be. But Kit didn't want her, he didn't love her; she was nothing to him now, so she might as well... She might as well what? Throw herself at another man who didn't want her, just because he made her remember that she was a woman? Did what she was feeling now help her to understand what happened to those women who took up with men to whom they were nothing? Because if it didn't then it should, she told herself fiercely. This, what she was feeling right now, was surely happening to her because she had lost Kit. Because she was a woman, and there was a war on, and no one knew what the future might hold, and she was filled with an urgency to live whilst she still could. But not through a man like this one, Diane warned herself.

When she opened her eyes she discovered that her unease was causing the major to give her a hard look as he settled back in his own seat and unfolded the map.

'OK, now show me where we are now.'

She knew perfectly well how to read a map, but his proximity, coupled with what she had just been thinking, was making it a struggle for her to focus.

'Are you sure you can read a map?' she heard him asking drily. Damn him, why couldn't he leave her alone?

'We're here,' she told him, exhaling in relief as she finally managed to pinpoint where they were, and then realised that her relief had been too soon when he leaned across to look at the map, his thigh touching hers, his arm resting on hers as he moved his finger over the map and told her, 'The first place we need to look at is here … so we need to drive up toward Burtonwood along this road here that goes to Warrington. Have you got that?'

'Yes.' She'd have said anything to get him to move away from her.

'And once we get to this place here then you'll need to call out the directions to me. Think you can manage that?'

'I'll do my best, sir,' Diane replied, almost lurching into him as he swung the Jeep round to face the opposite direction.

'Cut the sirring, soldier – and that's an order.'

'Yes, sirrrr,' Diane threw at him through gritted teeth.

It was six o'clock in the evening but no way was Diane going to point out to the major that her eight-hour shift had ended well over an hour ago. So far they had 'checked out', as the major called it, over a dozen of the properties on his list, and with each one, or so it had seemed to Diane, the major's expression had grown grimmer and his silence more condemnatory. Now, with her stomach aching with hunger, she was beginning to wonder if the major was even human. The joke in the British Naafi canteens was that being on parade for the Americans meant slouching off to the nearest PX to stock up on Hershey bars and the like, but the major had shown no inclination to stop to eat at all. She, on the other hand, was beginning to feel so hungry that she was afraid her stomach would humiliate her by starting an audible protest.

The billets they had seen had ranged from an empty girls' school – where the major had studied the instruction pinned up on a dormitory wall, 'Ring for a Mistress if Required' without betraying even a flicker of amusement – to pin-neat bedrooms in private homes. But the thing the rooms all had in common was their war-weary shabbiness. It was evident everywhere: in the eyes of the people, in the way they walked and talked and the very air they breathed, Diane admitted, and it was in stark contrast to the vigour and smartness of the American forces, in their 'pinks and greens', as their dress clothes were known.

The major had certainly been thorough, both in his inspection and his reportage of each potential billet. As the day wore on, his dictation speeded up rather than slowed down so that Diane's wrist was now aching from the unfamiliar shorthand writing, and she groaned inwardly at the thought of its transcription and typing-up.

'It's coming up for eighteen hundred hours,' the major informed her, glancing at his watch. 'I guess we should break for something to eat before heading back.'

'There's a village a few miles down the road,' Diane told him. 'It should have a pub but I don't know if we'll be able to get something to eat.'

The look she could see in his eyes rubbed painfully against the raw patch of misery that was her pride in her country and her feelings of shame for what it had become, and her equally intense feeling of anger against the man who was forcing her to see it through his own eyes.

The village, when they came to it, was a straggle of houses either side of the road, surrounded by the fields in which Diane assumed the original villagers had once worked. A garage, its solitary petrol pump forlorn and unattended, marked the boundary between fields and village, the houses old and huddled together, the paint flaking off the doors and windows. A group of boys, old enough in reality to be wearing long trousers, but forced by the war to remain in shorter ones to save on cloth, who had been aimlessly kicking a ball around in the road, scattered at the sight of the Jeep, only one of them brave enough to stay where he was and yell out, 'Got any gum, chum?'

Diane curled her fingers into her palms when she saw the way the major's mouth tightened as he flicked a grim look at the boy. No doubt in *America*, that land of plenty, children did not beg from passing strangers. She could feel the pressure of her own defensive tears against the backs of her eyes. 'This isn't how we really are,' she wanted to tell him 'This isn't what this country is really about,' but she knew there was no point.

Typically they found the pub virtually opposite the church, its sign swinging in the evening breeze.

Diane glanced up at it as the major stopped the Jeep, and read the name – the Traveller's Rest. The village didn't look as though many travellers passed through it, but then looks could be deceptive.

The major had already got out of the Jeep. A

sign of his hunger, or his dislike of her company?

She reached for the handle to the Jeep's passenger door, cursing herself inwardly for not being more speedy when the major stepped round the Jeep's bonnet and opened the door for her.

She didn't look at him as she thanked him, but she could once again smell the scent of his skin, more his skin than his soap now, she recognised. She had no right to be aware of the major as a man. And no desire to, either? She was glad that the necessity of following him into the pub gave her an excuse for not answering her own question.

Inside, the pub was low ceilinged with heavy dark beams and the kind of bar she was familiar with from her days in her previous posting. The usual group of elderly 'locals' were grouped round the bar and occupying the wooden settle close to the huge open fireplace, and with a good view through the old-fashioned mullioned window.

The silence that followed their entrance could have been because she was a woman – the only woman in the place – or it could have been because the major was American. Diane suspected it was probably caused by both.

'Looking for Burtonwood, are you?' the landlord asked affably, but Diane had seen the looks the locals were exchanging and knew that his comment masked disdain.

'I guess you get pretty tired of Americans coming in here to ask the way,' the major answered him easily, adding, 'We'd like something to eat, first.'

All the men exchanged looks.

266

'Sorry, mate,' the landlord answered. 'But no can do. I'm afraid you and your lady friend will have to try somewhere else.'

Diane saw the way the major stiffened. She felt like doing the same herself. It was plain that the landlord thought she and the major were a couple, and of course he would disapprove of an English girl taking up with an American whilst young British men were away fighting for their country.

The major's silence was lasting just that little bit too long. Diane could feel the growing tension, and diplomatically she told him untruthfully, 'I'm really not very hungry. Do let's go and find somewhere else.'

For a second she thought he was going to ignore her and challenge the landlord, but then he looked down at her and gave a small shrug.

They had just reached the door when Diane heard one of the men at the bar telling the landlord, 'You missed your way there, Pete. I reckon you could have charged him a tenner to let him have that spare room of yours for the night.'

'Bloody Yanks,' the landlord swore angrily. 'I don't want no truck with them, nor their fancy pieces, not when I've got a lad fighting in ruddy Africa.'

The major stopped moving. Quickly Diane yanked open the door, her palms damp with nervous sweat. She walked out into the street and headed for the Jeep without looking to see if the major was following her, not wanting to give him an excuse to stay and challenge the men at the bar.

When he followed her to the Jeep she wasn't

sure if it was relief or hunger that was making her feel sick.

They travelled several miles before he finally broke the silence, demanding coldly, 'Tell me something. Does everyone in this country hate our guts, or–'

'It's your own fault that people react to the American forces the way they do,' Diane stopped him defensively, suddenly all her own pent-up feelings rushing to be voiced. 'You're supposed to be our allies but you behave more as though you're some kind of occupying force. You treat us with contempt, and you brag about how much better you think you are than us. You call us shabby, and badly dressed, you hate our food and our roads, and our weather. We've all heard GIs calling our soldiers cowards for running away at Dunkirk, and we've heard you saying our flag should be red, white and yellow. You talk about winning the war for us, as if we haven't done anything or achieved any victories. Well, for what it's worth, what we think of you is that you're a bunch of arrogant and ignorant idiots, that you're boastful braggers who don't even know what it's like to fight, and who don't have what it takes to see that if we look poor and down at heel, if we don't have much food, and our homes are shabby, it's because here in this country we believe actions speak louder than words, and what we're doing, why we're going without, is because of what we believe in. We don't need Americans to tell us the importance of freedom, as though it's something they invented, and we don't need people like you looking down your nose at us with contempt ...

sir!' she finished as she ran out of breath.

Now, with the adrenalin rush of anger that had fuelled her outburst depleted, she recognised miserably that she had behaved dreadfully and broken every rule in the book, which would no doubt now be thrown at her, resulting in her spending the rest of the war on a charge. But she didn't care. It would be worth it, Diane told herself defiantly.

'Finished, have you?'

Diane looked away from him.

'Because if you have, here are one or two things I'd like to say to you, *soldier*. First off, I'm one man, not the whole of the American forces. Second, no way have I ever considered myself to be part of an occupying force. Third, for what it's worth, what I personally think of the British people and their country is–'

'None of my business – I know,' Diane cut in smartly.

'What I think of the British people and their country is that their bravery grabs me by the throat and humbles me; that every time I see a person in the street, wearing clothes that look worn and shabby, it brings home to me the sacrifices this country and its people are making in the name of freedom. Fourth, if you ever, ever speak to me like that again, your backside will be so sore you won't sit down for a week.'

Outraged, Diane spun round. 'You have no right–' she began, but he would not let her continue.

'I have every man's right to defend myself and my honour.'

'By physical violence to a woman? Your wife may–'

'My wife would never soil her pretty painted lips with the kind of talk I've just had from you, nor her head with such aggressive thoughts,' he told her brusquely. 'She's a Southern belle, who never forgets that fact. And another thing...'

Diane waited warily.

'I'm getting a little tired of calling you "soldier" – Diane, and since it looks like we're going to be working together for the next week or so, you'd better call me Lee.'

'Yes, sir... Lee...' Diane amended huskily. She couldn't believe now that she had ripped up at him in the way she had, and she certainly couldn't believe that he had let her get away with it. As for his comments about what he thought of Britain and its people... She blinked quickly. She wasn't going to make even more of an idiot of herself, was she?

'Right, *food...*' the major announced firmly.

It wasn't until Diane saw the base looming up in front of them that she realised where he was taking her.

'But this is–'

'Burtonwood,' he finished for her. 'I guess it seemed easier to come back here than to keep on searching for a pub to serve us.'

The checkpoint was in front of them, the men on guard duty saluting as he stopped the Jeep.

'Major Saunders,' he told them, showing them his pass. 'The soldier here is my guest.'

Diane's hand was trembling as she produced

her own ID, but neither of the soldiers on guard showed by so much as the flicker of an eyelid that they found anything strange in her presence with the major.

Even so, she still protested, 'I'm not sure I shouldn't be doing this,' as they were waved through.

'You're forces personnel and since I'm vouching for you there's no problem with you being on the base.'

Although, of course, like everyone else, she had heard about the work being done at Burtonwood to prepare it for the arrival of the Eighth Army, and equip it as an operational headquarters, which would include a combat crew replacement centre, a gunnery school, a quartermaster's depot, and a supply and maintenance depot – in other words, a major support base for men and machinery – she hadn't realised just how huge the base was going to be.

In the clear light of the summer evening it seemed to stretch for miles, with its runways and its buildings, and although she didn't want to admit it, Diane felt slightly overwhelmed by its size, and its Americanness. It had only been in the aftermath of the attack on Pearl Harbor that America had sent over men, its own engineer battalions and their equipment, to help the British working to build the new airfields from which the Eighth Army would bomb the enemy. The results of their arrival and the work they had done were certainly plain to be seen here.

It seemed an age before Major Saunders finally pulled up outside a newly built, anonymous-looking building – anonymous, that was, until Diane saw the words 'Officers Only' above the doorway.

'We can get something to eat here,' the major told her. 'I'm not saying how good it will be – how good it tastes is likely to depend on how hungry you are.'

'I can't go in there,' Diane protested.

When he frowned she pointed out stiffly, 'It says "Officers Only".'

'You'll be going in as my guest,' he told her curtly. 'Officers are permitted to take guests in.'

Maybe they were, but that didn't stop what looked like a roomful of men in American uniform bearing high-ranking insignia turning to look at her as she and Major Saunders walked. in, their curiosity making her feel very much an interloper. Without realising she was doing so, Diane moved closer to the major, but it was only when he put his hand beneath her elbow to guide her across the room that she realised how intimate and inviting her own gesture must have seemed. It was too late to regret it now, though.

'Lee!' a tall man with grey grizzled hair called out, leaving the table where he had been playing cards to come over to them.

On his jacket Diane could see the stripes denoting his status, and consequently wasn't surprised to hear the major respond to his greeting with a respectful, 'Colonel, good to see you again.'

'No need for any of that colonel stuff, Lee. I'd heard you were based here. Long time no see. How's Carrie?'

'She's fine thanks, Dwight. She's decided to see

the war out in Charleston with her folks.'

'Mimi's doin' the same. She's taken the kids to Virginia; her folks have a farm there. So how are you doin'? I'd heard you've been made up to major, by the way. Congratulations.'

'Thanks. Let me introduce Diane Wilson to you. She's with the British WAAF and based at Derby House in Liverpool. I've been dragging her all over the country today, taking notes whilst I checked out the accommodation we've been offered for the top brass, and now I've brought the poor girl back here for a canteen meal.'

'Sure nice to meet you, Diane.'

Diane was caught off guard in mid-salute when he extended his hand to shake hers.

'Dwight here is an old buddy of mine,' the major explained.

'Not so much of the old, if you don't mind,' the colonel joked.

'He was my platoon major when I started out.'

'Yeah, and, fool that I was, I went and gave you top marks. Don't let him sweet-talk you any, Diane. This guy's a soldier first, second and third. Ask his wife.'

Diane wasn't quite sure exactly what kind of warning she was being given, but the smile that accompanied it seemed genuine enough.

'The last I heard you were on reconnaissance, Lee, so how come you're sorting out accommodation; missed too many Luftwaffe have you?' the colonel joked.

'I'm in charge of organising the reconnaissance training for our pilots, as they come over. What about you? I didn't know you were over here.'

273

'Well, I'm not really. They've put me with the Ninth out in the field, but I had some leave so I thought I'd spend a few days in London. Have you been there yet?'

The major shook his head.

'Well, you must go. Look, I'll give you the address of this hotel where I stayed... Have you got a pen?'

As the major reached into his jacket and removed his wallet, opening it, Diane caught a glimpse of the photograph it held. If that was his wife, and it must be, she certainly was very beautiful – and maybe it was the photograph that gave that hardness to her eyes that belied her smile. Whatever the case, it was none of her business, and it was foolish of her to feel such an instinctive dislike for a woman she didn't even know.

'More coffee?'

'I couldn't,' Diane told the major truthfully, putting her hand on her stomach. 'I'm too full.' No wonder the Americans derided British rations if they ate like this every day, she reflected, thinking of the huge steak she had been served, along with fried onions, tomatoes, mushrooms, sweetcorn and chips – or French fries, as the Americans called them – followed by apple pie and ice cream.

'Fine. Well, if you're ready to leave, I'll go and organise some transport for you.'

'Don't go to any trouble. Anything will do, just so long as it gets me back.'

Not for the world was she going to let him think she was disappointed because he wasn't driving her back himself.

'I'll sort out a Jeep and a driver. Wait here.'

'There's no need for that. Surely there's a bus, or...' she began, but the major was already walking away from her.

When he returned five minutes later he was accompanied by a young private.

'Charlie here will drive you back,' he told her. 'I recognise that you've worked well over your hours today. I'll have a word with your captain and let her know that you'll be owed some extra leave.'

Diane nodded. What was the matter with her? Anyone would think that she wanted to stay here with him, the way she was hanging around.

'Hey, Lee, wanna come and join us for a hand of poker?'

Diane exhaled unsteadily when she saw Dwight coming over to clap the major on the shoulder and draw him away with him. She was glad really, of course. The kind of enforced intimacy they had shared today wasn't something she wanted with any man other than Kit, much less an American.

EIGHTEEN

'So the wedding's all arranged then, Ruthie?' Jess asked.

They were on their dinner break, and Ruthie pulled a face at the watery stew they had been served before shaking her head.

'We've seen the vicar and we've sorted out the church hall, and Glen has asked Walter to be his best man, like I told you he was going to do. And, of course, you're going to be my bridesmaid, and we're all going to meet up in town to talk about everything. Not that we'll be able to have the banns read or anything yet, though.' She pulled a small face. 'I hadn't realised, but with Glen being an American we've got to be given permission to get married by the US Army and that means that I've got to go to Burtonwood and be interviewed by his CO or the army chaplain.'

'Interviewed – to marry a ruddy GI?' Mel cut in, outraged. 'That just shows what this country's coming to. I've said all along that the Yanks act like they're doing us a favour by being here and now you're saying that you've got to go and be inspected before they'll let you marry one of them.'

'It's not that,' Ruthie told her pacifically. 'Glen explained it all to me. It's because the army doesn't want the men to jump into marriages because they're overseas and alone, and then wish that they hadn't, so we both have to see his CO together so that he can make sure that we know what we're doing.

'Oh, and did I tell you, Jess, that I've had the loveliest letter from Glen's sister, telling me how much she's looking forward to meeting me and saying that she's always longed for a sister?' Tears filled Ruthie's eyes. 'I can't tell you how happy I am. It's like a dream come true, and when I think that, but for you, Jess, I'd never have met Glen in the first place.'

'So when do you have to go and have this inspection, then?' Mel asked.

'I'm not sure yet. Glen has put in a request to his CO and now we have to wait for him to tell Glen when he will see us.'

'Aye, well, you'd better hope he sees you before this second front happens that everyone's going on about, otherwise your Glen could find himself overseas and you left here without a wedding ring.'

'Oh, no! You don't really think that could happen, do you?' Ruthie protested, white-faced.

Jess shook her head. 'She's only winding you up, Ruthie. Mind you, she does have a point, so no anticipating them wedding vows or your wedding night, you think on. Just in case...'

Ruthie immediately went bright red and protested, 'Glen would never ask me to do anything like that.'

The other girls exchanged looks.

'Give over,' Mel objected bluntly. 'We all saw the way he was looking at you at the Grafton. I reckon he'd have carried you off to bed then if he thought he could have got away with it.'

When Ruthie struggled for the right thing to say, Mel carried on firmly, 'There's no call to look like that about it, anyway. There's nowt wrong wi' a lass and a lad feeling like that for each other. In fact, it seems to me that there's more likely summat wrong when they don't. Even doing it's OK once you're engaged, but you've got to make sure you don't get caught out and left up the spout...You mustn't let him get you pregnant,' she explained in exasperation when Ruthie looked blankly at her. 'And if he tells you that you won't if you do it standing up then tell him to get lost, 'cos that doesn't work. At least not according to my cousin Alison. A friend of hers got caught that way and left with the kid when her chap did a runner.'

'What are you going to do about your frock? Only you can't get them for love nor money unless you know someone who's got one?' Jess interrupted, seeing the mortified look on Ruthie's face.

'The Red Cross are lending out wedding dresses to girls who are marrying GIs,' Ruthie told her happily. 'We'll have to go and look together, seeing as you're going to be my bridesmaid.'

Jess gave her a wan smile and tried to appear enthusiastic. She wouldn't have hurt Ruthie's feelings for the world, but the truth was that she had felt her heart sink a little when Ruthie had told her that Glen had asked Walter to be his best man. Naturally that meant the two of them would be paired up at the wedding, especially with everyone thinking that she and Walter were a couple, but the truth was... Jess bit down hard into her bottom lip. She wasn't prepared to admit even to herself exactly what the truth was. She liked Walter – of course she did – but she had been more relieved than disappointed when Walter had told her during their first dance about the girl he was in love with 'back home'.

Mind, it might be for the best if folk did continue to think that she and Walter were together. She knew one person who wouldn't hesitate to make fun of her if he thought that Walter had dropped her. Not that she cared what Billy thought, of course. But she wasn't going to have him thinking that she couldn't get herself a chap if she wanted to. Not with him always showing off about the number of girls that fell for him. They wouldn't be falling for him if he went and blew himself up, though, would they?

'And Glen says that there's no need for us to worry about the food for the wedding breakfast, because the US Army will provide that,' Ruthie chattered happily to Maureen without taking her attention off the shells she was filling.

'Oh, do stop going on about your ruddy wedding, will you? Me ears are aching with hearing about it,' Maureen told her rudely, before adding, 'Anyway, it's that Jess you should be going on about it to, since she's the one as will be your bridesmaid.'

Concern clouded Ruthie's gaze. 'I asked you as well,' she pointed out quietly. 'You know I did.'

'Oh, yes, you *asked* me all right, but that was only because you felt you had to. Anyone could see that.'

'That's not true,' Ruthie protested, even though a part of her knew that was the truth.

'Besides, how do you think I'd be feeling, wi' 'er,' she jerked her head in Jess's direction, 'there wi' her fancy GI chap, and me there on me own, especially when it comes to the dancing?'

'It won't be like that. Glen will be inviting his friends and I'm sure they will be delighted to dance with you.'

'Oh, I see, so that's it, is it? You only want me there on account of your Glen's friends needing a dance partner. Well, like I've already told you, if you really was my friend like you said you were going to be, I'd be the only one you'd want as your bridesmaid.'

Ruthie tried not to feel upset by Maureen's antagonistic comments. It was true that her first choice had been Jess. Jess had been responsible for her meeting Glen and had been so kind to her, unlike Maureen, who was possessive and made her uneasy sometimes, even though she felt guilty for doing so.

She said gently, 'I really do want you to be one of my bridesmaids, Maureen.'

'Well, you can want all you like because I'm not. It's all right for you, talking about borrowing frocks and that from the Red Cross, but you'll have to pay to borrow them, you mark my words, and there's no way I can afford that kind of thing. Not with me having to help at home.'

Guilty colour burned up under Ruthie's skin. Oh dear! How insensitive of her not to have thought of that. No wonder Maureen was so cross with her.

'I wouldn't have expected you to pay out anything,' she hurried to assure her. 'I would have paid for the frock.'

'Oh, well ... maybe I'll think about it then, but I'm not saying that I'll do it, mind. Just that I'll think about it.'

NINETEEN

August already, the month Kit had proposed to Diane, and the month they had planned to marry this year. But at least there was one patch of blue about to break through her otherwise miserably grey unhappiness. The major, or 'Lee', as she was finally beginning to think of him, had told her yesterday that he thought another few days would see an end to his inspection of potential billets. And that meant she would see an end to having to work with him. And nothing would please her more than that, she told herself, as she struggled to confine her normally obedient hair into a businesslike chignon, and envying the young mother she could see from her bedroom window, free to wear a cool summer frock, whilst she was obliged to wear a thick heavy uniform.

'You haven't forgotten that you said you'd lend me your silk blouse, have you?' Myra demanded, emerging from the bathroom and into their shared bedroom. 'Only it's this coming weekend that I'm off to London.'

'No, I have forgotten,' Diane replied quietly.

'All right, I know you don't approve of what I'm doing,' Myra told her angrily, 'but it's my life, and no one is going to stop me. And before you start going on about me having a husband, well – not that it's any of your business – I've written to Jim telling him that I'm going to America with Nick, whether or not he gives me a divorce, so he might as well make up his mind to giving me one.'

Diane forced herself not to let her face betray how appalled she was by Myra's callous action in sending that kind of letter to a man who was fighting in the desert for his country. Instead she warned her quietly, 'You might find it isn't going to be as easy to go back with Nick as you think. From what I've heard, the American authorities are clamping down on British girls trying to marry GIs so that they can go back to America with them after the war is over.'

'Oh, that's typical of you. You're just saying that because you disapprove of me being with Nick because I'm married. Well, for your information, me and Nick have already talked about that, 'cos I can read a newspaper as well as the next person, and Nick's told me not to pay any attention to any of that. He says it's all a load of rubbish, and that there won't be any difficulties, especially with him having the right kind of contacts. Besides, with his family having their own business in New York, there'll be no problem with the money side of things. Set up for life, I'm going to be, just you wait and see,' Myra finished with a self-satisfied smirk. 'If I was you I'd start looking round for a GI of you own,' she added. 'And not a married one like that major.'

'I'm working with the major, that's all,' Diane reminded her sharply. She hated how working at Derby House meant everyone knew everything a person was doing. Living and working with Myra meant there was no escape.

'I reckon the US Army really knows how to

treat people. Nick gets paid five times as much as a British soldier,' Myra boasted, ignoring her comment.

Diane's mouth tightened.

'Nick gets an eight-day furlough every six or seven months and no messing. Like as not the next time we go away it will be more than for just a weekend. And the American Army is putting on special trains for its troops so that they can visit London on their weekend pass outs.'

'But you won't be able to travel on that with him,' Diane pointed out.

'That's all you know. Nick's had a word with someone he knows who owes him a favour and he's got me a seat. The train goes from Lime Street tomorrow dinnertime and we're meeting up for a drink first.'

Diane had finally got her hair into its chignon and, as she slid in the last of her precious store of grips, she turned to look at Myra. She didn't like passing on gossip, but Myra's own boastful comments about what Nick could do seemed to confirm at least to some extent what Jean had told Diane. Myra wouldn't take kindly to any criticism of him, Diane knew, but her own conscience was still urging her to warn the other girl.

'The kind of favours Nick seems to be able to call in aren't given for nothing, Myra,' she told her quietly.

'Meaning what, exactly?' Myra demanded, bristling.

Diane took a deep breath. 'I have heard that Nick could be involved in some pretty dishonest stuff.'

'You mean a bit of dabbling on the black market?' Myra challenged her, tossing her head. 'Is that supposed to put me off?' She laughed. 'Good luck to him, is what I say.'

Myra's attitude told Diane that there was no point in her saying anything more.

'That silk blouse of yours...?' Myra was repeating.

Repressing a small sigh, Diane opened the wardrobe door and removed her best blouse from its padded hanger.

Bright sunshine bouncing off the pavement made Diane grateful for the fact that her mother had insisted on loaning her her precious pair of pre-war sunglasses. She stood waiting for the major to arrive. Her experience of the first day she had worked for him had taught her to make sure she always made herself some sandwiches to take with her, carefully preserving the precious grease-proof paper in which they were wrapped to reuse each day.

Today's sandwiches were tomato with a thin shaving of cheese, but she considered herself lucky to have a landlady with access to an allotment.

'Off out with the handsome major again today, Di?' Jean grinned as she hurried across the road towards her. 'Phew, it's hot,' she added, removing her cap. 'I'm not sure whether I should thank you or curse you for giving me this thing,' she added, touching the roll Diane had given her for her hair. 'My hair looks better, but it's dreadfully uncomfortable in this heat, and it's making me itch like mad. Oh ho, here's the major now, you lucky thing,' she grinned enviously.

Giving her a brief smile, Diane stepped forward, hurrying round to the passenger door of the Jeep, but as always the major was there before her, holding the door open for her. Today, like her, he was wearing a pair of sunglasses – aviators, she had heard the airmen calling them – and something about the darkness of the lenses added an extra strength to his air of command. Sometimes she felt that this small act of his of managing to open the Jeep door for her before she could get out by herself had become a silent but fiercely fought battle between the two of them, and a battle in which he had the unfair advantage of longer and more powerfully muscled legs. But winning the skirmish of who could get to the door first didn't mean that he would win the war, Diane told herself. She had her own battle tactics, one of which was to thank him with freezing politeness and then ignore him, thus, she hoped, making it plain to him that as service personnel she did not welcome being treated to his American gallantry. His wife might enjoy his acting as though she were as delicate as a piece of rare china, but she, Diane, was different. His wife? *Why* was she comparing herself to her?

To punish herself for this weakness, Diane refused to allow herself to look at him, sitting face forward and bolt upright in her seat until she heard him exhale and say drily, 'I thought it was a stiff upper lip you Brits were supposed to have.'

Now she had to turn to look at him. 'It is,' she agreed coolly.

'Then relax. The way you're sitting right now is

making *my* spine ache, never mind what it must be doing to yours. These Jeeps aren't the most comfortable things to ride in. Or is this another way to prove how superior a tough Brit is to us mollycoddled Yanks?'

He was laughing at her, Diane recognised, and the truth was that she could feel her own lips wanting to curve into a responsive smile, but of course she couldn't let them. That would be giving in, although she wasn't sure she knew what exactly it would be giving in to, other than her own dangerous desire to let herself enjoy his company.

'OK, let's get this show on the road,' he said. 'We're going to be heading out towards Knutsford today, home of the late Mrs Gaskell.'

Diane shot him a surprised look.

'What's wrong?' he queried. 'Surprised that an ignorant Yank knows about a British writer?'

'No,' Diane denied. 'If I was surprised it was because I would have thought that Knutsford is a fair distance from Burtonwood.'

'Uncle Sam's orders are that the top brass mustn't risk their necks by bunking down too close to the airfield, just in case Hitler decides to come over and drop a few bombs on them,' he told her lightly, but Diane knew that he was not deceived by her answer and that she *had* been surprised by his reference to Mrs Gaskell. Why was it that he kept on managing to catch her out and make her look, if not stupid, then certainly prejudiced?

'What will you do when this is all over, Diane?'

His question startled her. They never discussed anything that wasn't 'business', and this was the first personal question he had asked her.

'I ... I don't know,' she admitted. 'I haven't really thought about it. What about you? What did you do before you were conscripted?'

'Drafted, we call it, not conscripted, but I wasn't drafted. I'm a career soldier. I joined the army straight out of high school. My dad had been a farmer. It's a tough life and in the end it killed my mother, then him. They lost everything in the Depression. My mom died of hard work and lack of money, and my dad died of shame because of it.'

His voice was clipped and low, empty of emotion, but Diane knew better than to believe that he wasn't feeling any. She had known too many men use the same defence mechanism – including Kit.

'Joining the army was my way out,' he told her. 'It was the best decision I've ever made. The army's the most important thing in my life.'

'Apart from your wife,' Diane murmured.

The look he shot her made her heart slam into her ribs.

'You're putting words into my mouth that I didn't speak,' he told her curtly. 'Career soldiers shouldn't marry.'

'That's crazy,' Diane objected. 'You can't mean that.'

'Why not? If my wife were here she'd tell you straight that the worst thing she ever did was marry a soldier. Hell, she's told me often enough, and anyone else who will listen. If a soldier does marry then it should be a woman who understands what the army means to him and accepts

287

that, not a–' He broke off, his mouth compressing so grimly that Diane guessed he had said far more than he had intended.

Well, his silence now suited her, because she certainly didn't want to discuss his marriage with him, or start exchanging cosy stories of love affairs gone wrong.

An hour later, when the major still hadn't broken the silence between them, Diane acknowledged that if she had wanted to find a way to get under his skin she had certainly succeeded, but then she had noticed that he had become increasingly snappy and irritable with her over the last couple of days. Because he couldn't wait to get rid of her? So what if he did feel like that? She didn't care. After all, she felt exactly the same way about him, didn't she?

Diane squirmed uncomfortably in her seat. She was spending far too much time thinking about the major and what he might think about her. Far, *far* too much time.

'OK, we're just about finished here.'

Here was an Edwardian house just outside Knutsford, set in a couple of acres of grounds. It had originally been requisitioned by the British Government, who were now offering it to the Americans. That it had once been a family home was still evident in the small beds and the cot they had found in the attic bedrooms.

'What is it with you Brits that you shut your kids away in the attics?' the major muttered under his breath in between calling out the measurements he was taking to Diane.

'We don't shut them away, and anyway, it's only the rich who can afford staff and have proper nurseries,' Diane told him shortly. There was a battered teddy bear on the floor underneath the cot. Automatically Diane bent down to retrieve it, unaware of the way the major was watching her, as she straightened its legs and smoothed the place where the fur had been rubbed away. Poor bear. He looked so neglected and unloved, so forlorn and forgotten somehow. She could well imagine what would happen to him once the military moved in here. Once he must have been some child's much-loved toy.

A rush of emotion seized her, a combination of her own childhood memories and the knowledge that she would never now hold in her own arms the children she had hoped to have with Kit. They had talked about them together, laughing and teasing one another. 'A boy for you and a girl for me,' Kit had whispered lovingly to her, that first time they had been intimate together, as she lay in his arms beneath the low ceiling of the small hotel where they had been able to get a room, self-consciously registering as 'Mr and Mrs Smith', whilst Diane had toyed guiltily with the 'wedding ring' she had been wearing. 'No, a boy for you and a girl for me,' she had corrected Kit before he had taken her back in his arms.

The bear emitted a soft growl under the pressure of her tight grip on him, making her jump.

The major had his back to her. Diane looked at the bear. By rights she ought to leave the bear here... But those bright button eyes were looking so reproachfully at her. Half ashamed of her own sentimentality, she stuffed the bear inside her bag.

'Ready?' The major was holding open the door. Nodding, Diane turned to follow him.

The next house, strictly speaking, was too far out of the way, since it was situated close to the market town of Nantwich, but the major told Diane that they might as well take a look at it since it was close to a small RAF airfield, which some of the smaller American planes could use in an emergency.

They were on the outskirts of the town, just driving past a school playing field where children were playing in their summer holiday; when a light plane, its engine stuttering and whining as it plunged into a steep dive, dropped down to earth so fast that it was easy to see the American insignia on the fuselage, and easy to see too the two young men in its cockpit. Diane felt her stomach roil with foreknowledge and sickness. She had spent too much time around airfields and airmen not to know that the plane was out of control and that it would be impossible for the pilot to pull out of the dive, even if by some miracle the engine restarted.

The major pulled the Jeep to an immediate halt, yelling to Diane 'Keep down' as the plane skimmed the top of some trees on the other side of the playing field.

'Christ, he's going to hit the field,' Major Saunders swore. Diane could hear the children screaming and scattering in every direction whilst someone blew shrilly on a whistle.

'He's trying to clear the field,' she whispered

without taking her eyes off the small plane.

'Down, get down,' the major yelled at her as, by some miracle, the plane missed the playing field, only to lose speed and drop several feet, crashing through the trees, snapping off branches with a raw tearing sound that made Diane think of an agonised scream, before hitting the ground and skidding nose on into the trunk of one of the trees.

For a few seconds an unearthly silence and stillness seemed to stop time. Then Diane started to run towards the plane, ignoring the major's furious command to her to stop.

She had known it would be useless, pointless, but she was a woman after all, and her instincts were those of any woman who had loved a fly boy. It could have been Kit in that plane ... it could have been one of a hundred or more men she knew ... men who had gone to war and not come back, men who had come back, but so changed that no one could reach them any more, men who had been boys until they had given themselves up to the sacrifice that was war.

The plane had come to rest with its nose crushed up to nothing by its impact with an oak tree. Some of the branches lay on the ground like severed limbs, whilst from those branches that remained attached, leaves fluttered down onto the gunmetal object that was twisted around it and into it; tree and plane clasped together in a deathly embrace.

The passenger side of the plane had been ripped open like a tin can, a huge branch leaning against it so that it was impossible to see inside the plane. The co-pilot had obviously tried to jump out – and failed.

His body was pinned lifelessly to the ground by the torn branch that had speared through him. That he was already dead was obvious, but still Diane would have paused to close the sightless eyes staring up at the sky if it hadn't been for the low moan she heard from the cockpit.

Behind her she could hear the major making his way through the debris.

'Get the hell out of here, and that's an order, soldier,' he told her angrily as he caught up with her. 'This thing could go up at any minute.'

Diane knew he was right. She could hear the steady drip of aviation fuel, its smell burning the back of her throat.

'The pilot's still alive,' she told him.

'Fine – let's keep you that way as well, shall we? Now get out of here.'

Diane shook her head as the major made to push past her to get to the cockpit. The pilot's side of the plane lay at an angle, the door pressed against the ground so that the only way into the cabin was through the knot of metal and tree that had been the co-pilot's side. Anyone could see that it was impossible for a man of his size even to think about trying to squeeze through that tangle of branches and metal to get to the pilot. A man of his size, yes, but a woman of her size might just do it.

'Soldier, I order you to go back to the Jeep,' the major told her.

'There's a pilot inside there who is still alive,' Diane told him quietly. 'You can't go to him to see how badly he's injured. I can. That's another thing you Yanks need to learn about us British females, Major. We may not have the latest fashions or the latest lipstick but we are up to date on the correct procedure for dealing with something like this. That pilot in there is someone's son, and maybe someone's husband and father. So far as I'm concerned that's enough to make me believe that I have a duty to go to him.'

Without waiting to see how he was reacting to what she had said she started to scramble through the twisted wreckage, fighting her way past broken branches that scratched at her skin, and refusing to give in to the fear cramping her stomach as the smell of fuel grew stronger and the foliage closed in behind her. They would be sending help out from Nantwich; the school would have alerted the authorities to the crash in the unlikely event of no one in the town having noticed it.

She closed her eyes as she crawled past the body of the dead airman. The low moans were louder now. She held her breath as she managed to squeeze through the narrow gap between one of the branches of the tree and the side of the plane. She could see the pilot as he lay hunched over the controls, his face turned towards her. Her heart twisted inside her chest, as even in the shadows cast by the tree she recognised that it was the young pilot who had confided in her about his homesickness at the C-in-C's welcome party.

'How is he?' she heard the major demanding. Tears filled her eyes. The whole of the front of the plane was stoved in and somewhere trapped in that mess of twisted metal were the pilot's legs.

She could see and smell the blood that had soaked the bottom of his tunic, and she *knew*... She could hardly bear to acknowledge what she knew as she swallowed against her anguished grief.

The pilot opened his eyes and looked at her.

'Mom,' he whispered painfully. 'Mom, is that you? It's so dark here that I can't see so well.'

'Yes, it's me,' Diane whispered back.

'Gee, I'm glad you're here. I don't feel so good, you know...'

'I know.'

Diane reached for his hand. It felt icy cold. He was so young. The tears she couldn't shed burned the back of her eyes and throat.

'The pain is real bad, Mom.'

'I know, sweetheart, but it will be gone soon,' Diane told him gently.

Somewhere in the distance she could hear anxious voices, and the sound of activity, but they didn't matter. All that mattered right now was here, in this cramped place with the smell of blood and death all around her and a young man's need for the comfort of his mother in his dying moments.

'Stroke my forehead, will you, Mom? It feels so hot.'

He still had his flying helmet on but Diane reached out anyway and stroked his face, putting her arm around him to support him.

'Do you remember when I first started grade school?'

She had to lean very close to him now to catch the slow painful words.

'I felt real bad because I didn't want to go. Well,

I kinda feel like that now, you know ... like I have to be someplace I don't want to be. But I guess it will be OK when I get there.'

His breathing had slowed to almost nothing. Diane turned to try to look down at him and make him more comfortable, supporting him with one arm as his head lolled against her shoulder.

She could hear men working their way towards her, chopping branches, removing debris. She could even hear one of them cursing as he called out, 'Ruddy well hurry up, will you, before the bloody thing goes up,' but she didn't move.

The boy in her arms gave a small sighing breath. 'It's so dark, Mom...'

'It's all right, darling,' Diane whispered against his ear. 'Everything's all right ... just ... just go to sleep now.'

He took another breath and struggled in her arms, his eyes opening. 'Mom...?'

She could hear the fear in his voice, and she reached out to comfort him, pressing her lips to his cold forehead as the breath rattled in his throat and he was gone.

'Diane?'

She looked up to see the major crawling towards her. 'He's dead,' she said emotionlessly.

'And so will we be if we don't get out of here, and fast,' he told her grimly, reaching for her hand and half dragging her out of the cockpit.

They only just made it in time.

'Run,' the major told her once he had dragged her free of the plane, and, 'Get down,' he yelled, pushing her to the ground in front of him as the plane exploded with a dull crump, only a couple of hundred yards away from them.

Diane could feel the heat of the flames as she lay winded on the ground. A second explosion followed the first.

'Spare fuel tank,' the major muttered, as he got to his feet. Shakily Diane did the same, as the men who had taken cover from the explosion came towards them.

They were escorted into the town and offered baths and clean clothes by the grateful towns-people – as though they had been the ones who had managed to avoid crashing into the school playing field, Diane recognised numbly, after the WVS had provided her with something to wear, and she was sitting in the church hall, drinking the cup of tea she had been given, whilst the major was talking to the local police. Her uniform, folded up in brown paper, was torn and stained with blood. She could still smell it all around her, still see that poor boy... She started to tremble so violently that her teeth chattered against the cup. Unsteadily she put it down.

'Here's your bag, love,' a WVS helper told her. 'One of the ARP lads picked it up for you. This fell out,' she added, giving Diane a small smile as she held out the teddy bear to her.

Tears filled Diane's eyes. Somehow the sight of the bear brought home to her that on the other side of the ocean a mother would soon be mourning her child.

The major had refused to let them be driven back to Burtonwood, stating that he was perfectly able to drive himself. They had left the town behind them and were travelling down a country lane bordered by fields, when he suddenly pulled up.

'What is it? What's wrong?' Diane demanded uncertainly.

'The next time I give you an order, soldier, you obey it. Is that understood?' he told her harshly.

Diane stared at him. 'I had to do it. I had no choice,' she told him fiercely.

'You could have been killed,' he yelled back at her. 'You could... Oh hell,' he swore suddenly, and then to Diane's shock, he took hold of her, gripping her upper arms tightly as he bent his head and kissed her with angry passion.

It was just shock that was holding her immobile in his embrace, just shock that was keeping her lips on his ... just shock that was coursing through her, making her match angry passion with angry passion until she was holding on to him as tightly as he was holding on to her, returning his kiss angry pressure for angry pressure.

TWENTY

Myra could tell from the way Nick came swaggering towards her that he was in a good mood.

'Hiya, baby cakes,' he greeted her, pulling her to him and giving her a possessive kiss, and then grinning at her triumphantly as he released her, and cast a swift assessing look at her.

'The other guys are sure gonna be envying me when they see you on my arm, sweet stuff.'

297

Myra had never seen him so ebullient before, and her spirits lifted to match his.

'Well, if you want to keep me there, then you'd better make sure they know I'm yours, hadn't you?' she smiled daringly.

'What, you mean with something like this?' he suggested nonchalantly, digging into his pocket and producing a small leather ring box.

Excitedly Myra reached for it.

'Oh, no,' he teased her, stepping back and keeping it out of her reach. 'We're gonna do this the right way.' Holding on to her left arm, with one hand he flicked open the box in his other hand.

Myra stared in disbelief at the shiny glittering diamond ring he was holding. The diamond was bigger than anything she had dreamed of owning, bigger, she was sure, than anything she had seen in the windows of any of Liverpool's jewellers.

'Like it?'

She couldn't bear to take her gaze away from it, not even to whisper breathlessly, 'Yes...'

'Come here, then,' he said, taking hold of her left hand.

Myra stared down at her left hand as he slid the ring on to her wedding finger. It felt cold and heavy, and it was slightly loose, and now that she could see it close up she could see too that it wasn't new and that the gold was slightly worn. Had he bought her something second-hand? She started to frown and then checked herself. It was still the largest stone she had ever seen, of the size only usually on the fingers of Hollywood stars.

'It's beautiful,' she told Nick fervently.

'A beautiful ring for a beautiful girl,' he responded. 'My girl... I hope you're going to keep that promise you made to me about what you'd do if I gave you a ring.'

Myra affected to look demure and slightly affronted.

'Don't give me that look,' Nick warned her, his voice hardening. 'A deal's a deal where I come from, babe and–'

'Oh, Nick, don't go and spoil things by being cross with me. Not when we've just got engaged,' Myra pouted. She reached for his hand and moved closer to him, leaning in to him and smiling with secret triumph when she felt his body's response to her. 'Of course I want to be with you ... properly. And now that we're engaged ... and especially since we're going to London...' She gave a small shiver as her excited triumph gripped her.

'Oh, Nick, it's going to be so wonderful.'

'It sure is, babe. Let me tell you about the hotel I've booked for us.'

Myra started to tense.

'One of the guys told me about it, some place name of the Savoy.'

'The Savoy? You've booked us into the Savoy?' Myra exclaimed in shocked excitement. 'Oh, Nick, that's just about the best hotel in London. Oh, Nick...' Her face started to fall. 'But what will I wear? My clothes...'

'Trust a dame to start worrying about her clothes, when all a guy is thinking about is getting her out of them,' Nick answered.

'But this ring ... the Savoy ... it must be costing such a lot,' Myra ventured. She didn't care how much he spent on her, but she was curious about his financial status, all the more so since she had discovered from Diane about his connection with the country's black market. Everyone knew that the black marketeers were making huge amounts of money. Myra had no moral scruples about what Nick might be doing. Why should she have? In this world it was every man for himself, and every woman with any sense knew that and made sure that she was with the man who was going places. That had been her mistake with Jim, marrying a man who was too 'good' for his own benefit, and thus for hers as well.

'Yeah, and since I'm a guy who likes value for his dollar you'd better make sure I get it, hon.'

'But how–'

'Hey...' Nick threw up his hands. 'No questions, OK? If you're gonna be my girl then you've gotta learn not to ask questions. Let's just say I've got several good deals going on.' He winked at her and patted his pocket. 'And I play a pretty good game of cards.'

He looked at his watch. 'Let's go get that drink. There's a guy I gotta see there in the bar. When he comes in, I'll give you the nod and you take yourself off to the ladies' room, OK?'

Obediently Myra agreed.

As they walked down the street towards the bar, Myra clung tightly to Nick's arm, her ring proudly on display. Jim, and the fact that she was still married to him, were pushed out of the way to allow her to enjoy her triumph. When a girl had the right kind of looks and the right kind of determination, and she knew how to use those assets, there was nothing she couldn't have, she exulted to herself. She could see herself now, stepping off the liner in New York, a GI bride arriving in her new home, the city that never sleeps.

'So we've seen the vicar, and I've shown you both round the church hall. I'm so sorry that Jess couldn't join us, Walter,' Ruthie, who was on the other side of Glen, apologised as the three of them left the church to walk back into the city. 'It's really kind of you to give up your free time to come to the church with us.'

'That's no problem, ma'am,' Walter told her politely.

'Don't be modest, Walter,' Ruthie teased him. 'It was very generous of you, especially when you'd planned to go to London for the weekend.'

'Your and Glen's wedding is more important. And besides, I've got plenty of time to catch the train,' Walter assured her. 'It doesn't leave until gone noon.'

It had been Glen's suggestion that they walk Walter back down to Lime Street to catch his train, and then that he should take Ruthie to Lyons' for something to eat, and Ruthie had been more than happy to agree. It was a real treat for her to eat out, even during these times of rationing and restricted menus. It made her feel so grown up and grand to be able to walk into the city on Glen's arm, her engagement ring giving that act respectability and acceptability. She had noticed the number of women who glanced at her left hand as they walked past them, just to check, as it were.

Not, of course, that everyone approved of the Americans or the girls who 'took up with them'; but Ruthie was too blissfully in love to let anything or anyone spoil her happiness.

'How long do you think it will be before your commanding officer sends for me to interview me?' she asked Glen as they all crossed the road together, easily dodging the lumbering trams.

'I don't know. I guess he thinks that making us wait will ensure that we're serious about one another.'

'But why should he think that we aren't?' Ruthie asked him anxiously.

The two men exchanged looks.

'What is it? Why are you looking like that?' she demanded.

'It's nothing, Ruthie, I promise. Only that we've heard that the army doesn't want a lot of guys rushing off to get married and then regretting it. It won't affect us.'

Myra knew the minute she came out of the ladies' and saw Nick's face that something was wrong. He was on his own, the two spivs who had been waiting for him when they arrived obviously having left. He was pacing the worn carpet in front of the empty bar and she paused in mid-step. Something about his pent-up rage reminded her of her own father. He too had clenched his fists like that when he was annoyed. But when someone crossed her dad, it had usually been her mother who had been the one to suffer. Myra swallowed against the sour bile of the memories.

Herself sitting alone in her narrow bed in the darkness, listening to her mother begging her father not to hurt her, followed by the sound of blows and then her mother's low moans of pain – or, even worse, those times when there had been no sound at all after the slam of the front door closing behind her father as he stormed out. Then she would tiptoe to the top of the stairs in the darkness and wait there, holding her breath, just in case he came back ... listening desperately, wanting to hear the sound that would tell her that her mother was still alive. Only when she was sure her father wouldn't come back had she gone slowly downstairs, avoiding the stair that creaked, feeling her way in the darkness until she was standing outside the kitchen door. When she pushed it open she knew what she would find. It was always the same: her mother, still curled up in the ball she had rolled herself into to protect herself, the smell of blood and fear filling the kitchen. Once there had been the smell of something else, something sickening and shocking, and that time she remembered she had nearly slipped in the darkness on the blood that had flowed from her mother. Her mother had sent her round for their neighbour that time and then told her to go to her room, but even buried beneath the thin bedclothes, Myra had still heard her mother's low moans of anguish as she gave birth to the dead child that would have been Myra's brother.

Angrily Myra pushed the memories away. Why was she thinking about that now? It had no place in her life, the life she was going to live with Nick,

303

a life that meant fancy diamond rings and staying at the Savoy Hotel, and she was a fool for thinking that just for a moment there had been an expression in Nick's eyes that made him look like her father. So he had a bit of a temper on him. So what? He had passion, and it was that passion that made him want her so much. And she needed him to want her, if she was to make her dreams come true. Nick was hers. She could control him; she had already proved that, she reassured herself. And after this weekend, after she had let him have a taste of what he wanted – and only a taste, mind – he would be even more mad for her than he was now.

'Come on,' Nick demanded, jerking his head towards the exit.

'What's wrong?' Myra asked. 'Half an hour ago you were on top of the world.'

Nick removed a pack of Camel cigarettes from his pocket and lit one up for himself without offering her one. Myra's mouth thinned but she didn't say anything.

'Half an hour ago I hadn't been messed about by some wise guys who think they know how to play the game better than me. Well, if they think they're going to double-cross me and get away with it, they're gonna learn they're making a big mistake. Come on, let's get out of here.'

Throwing down the barely smoked cigarette, Nick ground it into the floor with his heel, an expression on his face that made Myra suspect he wished it was the face of whoever had double-crossed him.

All she cared about, though, right now was them

getting on that train. London! It wasn't New York but it would be a darn sight more exciting and glamorous than Liverpool, surely. She felt on top of the world. Everything was going her way and working out just as she had planned. Nick was hers, and she had the ring to prove it. She looked down at it, happily oblivious to the fact that somewhere in the desert she had a husband who thought that the ring he had given her – a ring given in church and with solemn vows – meant that she was his. Nothing could go wrong now. Jim would come round and see things her way. She would get what she wanted from him; she always had. Nick's bad mood was just a minor and brief inconvenience. By the time they reached Lime Street, he would have forgotten about whatever it was that had annoyed him. She certainly wasn't going to let his bad mood spoil her happiness at the weekend and in the future. Everything she wanted was within her grasp now – all of it: America, New York, her longed-for glamorous life as the wife of an American. And not a poor American either, she acknowledged, taking another thrilled look at her ring. Let Diane try to tell her to watch out now, she thought triumphantly, too wrapped up in her own excitement to be aware of the bleakness of the empty bombed-out streets surrounding them as they made their way to Lime Street.

'No, don't let's go that way,' Ruthie objected, hanging back when Glen headed towards the shortcut to the station through an area of bombed-out streets.

'Why not? It's quicker,' he pointed out.

Reluctantly Ruthie gave in, unwilling to explain even to Glen how much she disliked walking down the now-empty streets with their solitary intact houses and the mass of rubble where other homes had once been. There was an air about the place that always upset her, and she couldn't forget that people had died here, killed by the bombs that had ripped apart their homes.

The street was empty, and their footsteps echoed on the pavement. As they reached the place where another street cut across their route, a young woman coming along it, who had turned as she rounded the corner, to say something to the GI who was with her, would have collided with Walter if he hadn't put his hand out to stop her. The young woman looked up. Ruthie, recognising her as Diane's co-billetee, was about to greet her when, to her shock, the GI with her suddenly took hold of Walter and pushed him back against the wall, growling, 'Get your hands off my girl.'

Shocked by the violence that had erupted out of nowhere, Ruthie looked at Myra, expecting to see the same horror mirrored in her eyes but instead Myra merely looked bored.

'Glen...' she began, worriedly.

But Glen was already moving closer to the other two men, attempting to get between them and Ruthie could hear him demanding tersely, 'Let him go, Mancini.'

'Let him go? Oh, I'll let him go all right, but not until I've taught him a lesson he won't forget in a hurry. No farm kid comes on to my dame.' He swore at Walter, before thrusting his knee hard into his groin, causing Walter to grunt and double over with pain. As Walter did so, Nick smashed his fist into Walter's stomach and then hit him again on the jaw.

'Accuse me of running a fixed crap game, would you, farm kid? Well, here's what you get for interfering in things that ain't none of your business.'

'Oh, make him stop. Please make him stop,' Ruthie begged Myra frantically, tears pouring down her face as she turned towards Walter, who was now crouching down on the pavement, holding his stomach whilst Glen stood protectively in front of him, squaring up to Nick, his own fists raised.

'Want some of what your friend got, do you?' Nick threatened Glen.

'Come on, Nick,' Myra demanded, her earlier good mood vanishing. 'We'll miss the train,' she warned him. She had no wish to have her trip to London brought to an end before it had started because Nick had got himself involved in a fight.

Nick, though, was ignoring her. 'Get out of my way,' he told Glen savagely, swinging a hard punch at him.

Glen staggered back, blood pouring from his nose and his lip cut. Ruthie gave a small cry of distress and left Walter to run to him.

'Come *on*, Nick,' Myra demanded impatiently.

A group of boys had appeared at the top of the street, kicking a football, and one of them called out, 'Hey look, a fight.'

Frantically Ruthie tried to stem the blood

pouring from Glen's nose with her handkerchief. Walter was still crouching on the floor behind her, and at first when she heard the sickening crunch she didn't realise what it was. It was only when Walter gave a thin scream that she turned round and saw to her horrified disbelief that the other GI was kicking him whilst he kneeled there on the ground, unable to defend himself. The GI aimed another kick at him, sending Walter sprawling, his head banging against the kerb as he fell, whilst the GI followed him, still trying to kick him.

'For pity's sake, make him stop it,' she screamed frantically to Myra, as Glen pushed past her, throwing himself between the other man and Walter's now inert body, and received a heavy kick in the groin himself for doing so.

From further up the street Ruthie heard the sound of running feet and the sharp shrill noise of a whistle. White-faced, she saw with relief that several policemen were running towards them.

'What's going on here?' a sergeant, Ruthie recognised, demanded as he reached them.

'Oh, Officer, please ... this man needs help,' Ruthie wept, watching anxiously as two of the policemen hurried to Walter's side.

Glen was sitting on the pavement beside him, having just been sick. Worriedly, Ruthie went to his side, trying to offer him what comfort she could.

The sergeant frowned and looked over to where Nick and Myra were standing together on the pavement.

'Leave the cops to me,' Nick mouthed warningly to Myra.

'I'm sorry about this, sir,' Nick announced respectfully. 'I did try to stop them. But I guess when two guys are determined to have a fight over a woman, especially when one of them has been insulting the other's girl–'

'Sarge, I reckon we're going to need an ambulance,' one of the policemen interrupted. 'One of these guys is in a pretty bad way.'

'So you and this young lady aren't with the others then?' the sergeant asked Nick.

'No, we were just walking down the street minding our own business and talking about our trip to London, weren't we, hon?' he asked Myra. He had tucked her arm through his own and now when he smiled at her he gave it a hard squeeze.

'Oh, yes...'

'So what happened exactly? Were they fighting when you saw them?'

'Not fighting, but it looked like they were exchanging some pretty strong words. The younger guy had his hand on the other guy's girl's arm and, well, I guess that was what sparked him off. Of course I tried to stop them, but I couldn't get them to listen. Seems to me there was some kind of vendetta going on between the two of them from the way the older guy was going at it.'

He broke off to glance at his watch, then said to Myra, 'Hey, honey, just look at the time. We're gonna miss that train of ours if we don't run. You know what, Sergeant? I reckon this is a job for the army's MPs, if you don't mind me saying so. They know how to deal with this kind of thing.'

'Thank you, sir. Now if you'll both just give me your names and where you can be found, I can

309

send you on your way.'

Ruthie hadn't even realised that Myra and her partner had gone until the sergeant crouched down beside her where she was worriedly dabbing at the blood still pouring from Glen's nose. His eye was half closed and his split lip was swelling up, whilst poor Walter looked even worse.

'Harry's run down to the ARP post to tell them to send a runner for an ambulance,' one of two policemen standing with them told the sergeant.

'Well, you'd better go after him and tell them to alert the American MPs as well,' the sergeant told him grimly before squatting down beside Glen and saying curtly, 'Now I appreciate that this young lady is your girl, but that's no reason to go half killing some lad.'

Ruthie stared at him, her eyes rounding. 'No, you've got it wrong,' she protested. 'It wasn't my Glen who—'

'Sarge,' the policeman who was bending over Walter broke in urgently. 'Come and take a look. I reckon this lad here's condition is more serious than we thought.'

PART THREE

August 1942

TWENTY-ONE

Normally she looked forward to her day off, Diane admitted, especially on a sunny Saturday like this, but on this occasion she would have given anything to be at work with the busyness and the other girls' conversation to act as a deterrent against her thoughts. Even having Myra around would have been preferable to being on her own right now.

She hadn't been able to sleep, lying awake instead, thinking about poor Eddie Baker Johnson and his family. Tell the truth, she admonished herself mentally, you weren't just thinking about Eddie, were you? She looked down the row of vegetables she had offered to weed as a small repayment to Mrs Lawson's widower neighbour for his kindness in keeping them supplied with freshly grown food, leaning on the hoe he had loaned her, her expression haunted by the events of the previous day.

It was almost lunchtime and the sun was hot. She lifted her hand to brush a stray lock of hair out of her eyes and to her chagrin felt them fill abruptly with tears. Because a young man she had only met once had died? Because the major had kissed her? Or because she had kissed him back and that knowledge both angered and shamed her?

So what if, for a few seconds, she had let her

guard slip, she told herself crossly as she dug the hoe into the weeds, slicing off their heads with a sense of great satisfaction, as she contemplated destroying her memories of her own unacceptable behaviour with the same thoroughness. But while the hoe might cut the heads off the weeds, their roots were still intact, unseen beneath the surface, waiting to spring into fresh life. What was she trying to tell herself? That a *kiss* had roots? That just trying to cut off her memory of it wouldn't stop her from... This was ridiculous. There were no 'roots' to what had happened. No history of past longing or future desire. No *life* outside that single event. It had been a simple error of judgement; a reflex reaction to the dreadful sadness of Eddie's death. It wasn't, after all, as though she had never witnessed similar behaviour in others. War did strange things to people. It brought them together in situations they would never have experienced or shared in peacetime; it created an immediacy and an intimacy that led to ... to the major kissing her and her kissing him back?

Forget about it, she told herself angrily.

If only it were that easy. Her inability to 'forget about it' was what had brought her out here so early in the morning, after a broken night's sleep in the first place, desperate to force herself to do something, anything, that would banish yesterday from her mind for ever.

It was gone eleven now and her muscles were beginning to ache. She had reached the end of the row, and Mrs Lawson had promised her the luxury of adding Myra's allocation of hot water to her own, which meant that she could wash her hair *and* have a bath, and she was certainly ready for both, she thought, as she returned the hoe to the small wooden shed at the end of the allotment and started to make her way back to the house.

Mrs Lawson was very proud of the fact that her house had its own bathroom; one of their landlady's biggest fears was that the Germans would bomb Chestnut Close and destroy her precious bathroom.

Mrs Lawson was just leaving when Diane walked up the front path, explaining that she was going to spend the rest of the day with a cousin.

'Might as well enjoy the sunshine whilst we've got it,' she told Diane, adding, 'And our Sarah's got some soft fruit she wants me to help her to pick for jam making.'

With the house to herself, Diane stripped off her allotment-grubby working trousers and old blouse, putting them on one side to take downstairs to the back scullery where the washing was done either in the stone sink or the old-fashioned copper, if it needed a really hot wash or was too big for the sink.

Pulling on her dressing gown, she gathered up her precious supply of toiletries. Her mother had sent her some Pears soap for her hair, which Diane suspected was black market; she certainly felt guilty when she used it, but the alternative was to use boiled-down scraps of old soap bars, which, as everyone who used them knew, left the hair lank and slightly sticky, no matter how much one rinsed in cold water. With no lemons to bring a shine to her blonde hair she had taken to using a small amount of cider apple vinegar instead. One of the girls at her last posting had also been a natural blonde and had recommended it, and Diane had managed to buy several bottles from a country pub landlord.

She had her bath first, scrupulously making sure she didn't use more than the allowed depth of water. Had Myra been here to witness this she would have laughed at her, Diane knew, having seen the clouds of steam billowing from the bathroom on those occasions when Myra had made use of Mrs L's absence to sneak an extra bath.

A few drops of the carefully hoarded Essence of Roses scent that had been one of her pre-war twenty-first birthday presents made the water smell heavenly, and if she closed her eyes she could almost imagine she was twenty-one again, that there was no war, and that she was at home in her parents' comfortable semi, the smell of her father's favourite steak-and-kidney pie supper floating upstairs, along with the gentle hum of her parents' voices. But there was a war, and somewhere across the Atlantic, Eddie's parents would be going about their own lives, not knowing as yet that their son was dead. Diane tried to imagine how she would feel in Eddie's mother's shoes but it was almost impossible.

She gave a small shiver. Her meagre allowance of water was going cold already, or was it yesterday's memories that were chilling her skin and acting like a leaden weight on her spirits?

Climbing out of the bath, she wrapped herself in a towel and started to wash her hair, carefully rationing the hot water for two thorough washes, and then using cold for the rinses. Only when she was sure that she had removed all the soap did she fill the basin again with cold water and add some of the cider vinegar, wrinkling her nose against the pungent smell.

At least it was effective, she told herself five minutes later as she made her way to the bedroom, her squeaky-clean hair wrapped in the towel she had tied turban-style around her head, a faint dusting of talcum powder giving a soft pearlised sheen to her skin. Despite her fair hair, her skin tanned easily and the summer had given her legs a good colour, which was just as well because she certainly didn't have the money for black-market stockings, even if she had been prepared to overcome her scruples in order to buy them.

Of course, there were other ways of obtaining them now that the 'Yanks' were here, and all the girls had heard tales of GIs waving one stocking in front of a girl and then telling her that she could have the other to go with it in return for a kiss or two. And then, of course, there were her uniform stockings, dreadful thick lisle affairs that itched like mad in the summer heat.

Half an hour later, dressed in a pre-war sundress of white cotton overprinted with yellow buttercups, Diane went to sit in the garden to let her hair dry off in the sunshine, determined to lift her spirits.

Myra let out her breath in a private sigh of relief as the guard started to slam the train doors, in preparation for it leaving. They were on their way at last. Now, nothing could stop them from reaching London. She glanced at Nick, who had thrown himself into the window seat next to her. She had been furious with Nick for fighting with Walter, fearful when the police had arrived that it would mean an end to their trip, but he was a quick thinker, she admitted, and he had certainly managed to convince the police that the incident was nothing to do with them. She hadn't been too pleased, mind, when she had discovered that she might not be allowed to travel on the train with him because it was reserved for the American forces, but again Nick had dealt quickly with the problem. He'd been angry at having to part with a five-pound note, from the thick bundle he had produced from his pocket, in order to get her on the train. And once they were on it he had complained loudly and angrily that he had already traded a favour to have a blind eye turned to her presence. His good humour had returned, though, when he had laughed at the sight of her wearing the soldier's coat she had been told to put on to get on board the train, and she had been quick to hand it back. Myra didn't like being laughed at.

Now, through the carriage window she could see a British soldier running down the opposite platform where the train was ready to leave.

Reaching for the leather strap to let down their own window, Nick called out tauntingly, 'Learned to run like that at Dunkirk, did you, buddy?'

The other GIs in the compartment with them got to their feet, jeering and making catcalls as the train pulled out with the British soldier, who had now turned to glare at them, red-faced and obviously furious. He looked so enraged that for a minute Myra thought he was actually going to try to board their train. He was, she noticed, wearing the insignia of the Desert Rats, Jim's unit.

'Quit riling the natives, why don't you, guys?' a lone GI in the opposite corner drawled wearily as their own train set off, distracting the men and causing them to switch from catcalling to whistling and cheering.

They were off. Myra looked down at the ring on her left hand, and smiled to herself.

'Why don't you get yourself off home, love?' the police sergeant suggested to Ruthie. The MPs, who had arrived in their Jeep, screeching to a halt in front of them, the two men in the back jumping out before the vehicle had even stopped and coming to them at a run, had quite intimidated Ruthie. But they had gone now, taking both Walter and Glen with them.

'I still don't see why they had to take Walter all the way back to Burtonwood instead of taking him straight to Mill Road Hospital, when it would have been so much closer,' Ruthie fretted worriedly.

'Well, that's regulations and the army for you, lass,' the policeman told her calmly.

The MPs had been so brusque and rough in their handling of both Walter and Glen that Ruthie had been shocked, but Glen had managed to reassure her that there was no cause for alarm.

'But they were acting as though *you* were the one who attacked Walter, and they wouldn't

319

listen when you tried to tell them about that other GI,' Ruthie had whispered worriedly to him, clinging to his hand over the side of the Jeep whilst the MPs spoke with the police.

'We can sort all that out when we get back to camp. The most important thing now is getting Walter back there so that he can get some treatment,' Glen had reassured her.

'You'll let me know how he is, won't you?' she had begged him.

'You'll be hearing from me just as soon as there's any news,' he had promised her, giving her a tender loving look that made her ache to throw herself into his arms and refuse to let him go.

'I wish the police hadn't let that other man go,' she had fretted.

'I guess they didn't have any choice. Mancini isn't the kind of guy who lets others tell him what to do. But don't worry about it: the MPs will catch up with him when he gets back to camp.'

'But he was trying to say that it was your fault and that you attacked Walter,' Ruthie insisted.

Glen had laughed then. 'Not even Mancini can get away with that. Who's going to believe him when Walter tells everyone what really happened?' he had told her.

'But why would anyone do such a thing?'

'That's the kind of guy Mancini is,' he had answered with a small shrug. 'He's got a grudge against Walter because Walter caught him out running a rigged card game – that's cheating to you, hon,' he had explained with a tender smile. 'And my guess is that it wasn't the first time either. Mancini has a crowd of guys around him that like to play for high stakes and he seems to win more often than he loses.'

'But he was the one who was in the wrong in the first place, not Walter, for cheating at cards.'

'Men like Mancini don't think like that, sweetheart. He's a real bad lot, and that's for sure. He saw his chance to pay Walter back and he took it. There's more than one poor guy wishing now he had never met him, nor got involved in his poker games.'

'Oh, Glen...' Ruthie had sobbed, clinging to his hand at the side of the Jeep right up until the last moment.

She knew that he was right, of course, and once Walter had recovered he would be able to tell the authorities himself about the attack and who had instigated it.

'Don't you want to take a ... a statement from me or anything?' Ruthie asked the sergeant forlornly, after she had watched the Jeep until it had finally disappeared.

He shook his head. 'That's not up to us, love. It's out of our hands now. It's American military business, you see. There's this new law just been passed saying that all American citizens here in Britain are subject only to American law.'

'I can't believe such a terrible thing has happened,' Ruthie told him shakily.

'Aye, well, love, that's the way it is sometimes wi' soldiers. Get a bit of drink inside them, they do, and then...' the sergeant gave a tired shrug. 'You get yourself off home,' he repeated.

What a horrid way to have cut short what

should have been such a happy day. Poor Walter had looked so dreadfully unwell, and no wonder after the way he had been attacked. Now, walking slowly home on her own instead of with Glen, shock set in and Ruthie discovered that she was shaking from head to foot, unable to blot out what had happened. Her life had been a sheltered one; she had never imagined that one man could attack another so viciously, never mind expected to witness such a thing. Had her Glen been the one to launch an attack like that on another unprotected man – which, of course, she knew he would never do, not in a million years – but just *supposing* that he had, she knew she could never have behaved in the way that Myra had done and she certainly couldn't have walked casually away with him, not saying a word when she had heard him trying to blame an innocent man. What Glen had said was true, though, she comforted herself. Walter would be able to put the record straight and tell the authorities exactly what had happened.

She felt a bit guilty about not joining up with the others and going to see the vicar about Ruthie and Glen's wedding, Jess admitted, but she hadn't had any choice, really, not having been invited to her mother's second cousin's eldest's wedding. That had been a surprise invitation and no mistake. Officially the reason for the hastily arranged wedding was supposed to be the fact that the groom was about to be posted abroad, but the reality, at least according to her mother, was that the bride had confessed to *her* mother that she had missed her monthlies twice in a row.

Since the groom was a friend of Billy's it was more than likely that he would be there, and that alone would have been a good enough reason for her not to want to go, but family was family, Jess reminded herself, and she couldn't let her parents down by not turning up. She had thought about inviting Walter to go with her, but her own sense of what was right and fair had told her that if *she* had been the girl Walter had back home she wouldn't have liked to think of him going out with someone else, even if it was entirely innocent. Having a few dances with him at the Grafton was one thing, but asking him to partner her to a family event was very different.

It was lovely sitting out in the garden in the sunshine, but her hair was dry now, and her weekly letter to her parents written, and Diane was guiltily aware that instead of reading her landlady's copy of *Picture Post* she ought to be washing her uniform blouses ready for the new week. Getting up, she closed the deck chair and carried it down to the shed at the bottom of the small garden, returning to where she had been sitting to pick up *Picture Post* and take it back inside with her.

She had just put her foot on the first step of the stairs when she heard knocking on the front door.

Expecting the caller to be someone wanting to see her landlady, she went to open the door. But standing on the doorstep, his Jeep parked outside the gate, was the very last person she had expected to see.

'I got your billet address from your captain,' the major told her brusquely. 'After yesterday I felt there were things we needed to discuss, in private, and that couldn't wait until you were back on duty.'

Diane had known, of course, that there would be something like this to endure; had known it from the minute the major released her after that kiss. What was more, she had been preparing herself for this conversation, but what she had not been preparing herself for was that the major would come here to see her. But then she was not really familiar with the behaviour of guilty married men anxious to make sure that their misdemeanour wasn't going to have unwanted repercussions, was she?

'Our landlady doesn't allow us to have male visitors,' she began primly, but Major Saunders refused to be put off, shaking his head in rejection of her words and placing one foot in the open doorway and one hand on the open door itself. With those shoulders he probably wouldn't have any problem at all in bursting open the door, if necessary, Diane decided as she added with what she hoped sounded like cool self-possession, 'There really wasn't any need for you to go to the trouble of coming to see me, Major. I'm not a green young girl, you know.' Just to underline her point, she lifted her chin and told him determinedly, 'Let's not beat about the bush, shall we? I expect you've come here to warn me against reading anything foolish into what happened between us yesterday, but I can assure you

324

that a warning isn't necessary–'

'The hell it isn't,' the major interrupted her savagely, causing a hint of betraying pink colour to flush her face, but other than that Diane managed to hold on to her control. She wasn't going to allow herself to be intimidated or silenced by his anger.

'No, it isn't,' she continued. 'I know exactly why you've come here and what you want to say to me.'

'Is that a fact!'

Diane took a deep breath, ignoring the grim look she could see darkening his eyes. Avoiding looking at his eyes altogether would be a good idea, she told herself since, as she had just discovered, it was impossible for her to look at them now without remembering the shocking surge of emotion that had gripped her when she had looked up into them and seen how different they *could* look.

'You've come here to remind me that you have a wife and that you are a married man. Furthermore, no doubt, you want me to understand that you intend to remain married. You want to tell me that the simple act of kissing me means nothing to you and that I would be wise to make sure that it means nothing to me. You don't want to hurt me, of course, but you feel you have a duty to make the situation absolutely plain to me. Since we may on occasion have to see one another through the course of our service to our countries, it makes sense to clear the air now so that there won't be any misunderstandings. We are both professionals, both old enough to realise that sometimes things happen in wartime that cannot be related to our lives or our real feelings outside the war arena. These "things" are best forgotten by both parties since they mean nothing. A brief kiss shared in a moment of tension is not something you feel proud being a party to, but it did happen, and therefore you feel obliged to make sure that I am not harbouring any foolish ideas...'

She was running out of breath, and out of courage, Diane admitted, and the major's silence was unnerving her so much that she was starting to feel slightly shaky. But she wasn't going to stop until she had made it totally clear to him that he had no need to worry that she might have been silly enough to think that his kiss 'meant something'. She took another deep breath and then concluded hurriedly, 'In short, Major, you want us both to behave towards one another as though that k– as though what happened between us did not happen. Well, that's fine by me. In fact, you could have saved yourself the trouble of coming round here because the truth is that since it didn't mean anything whatsoever to me I had as good as forgotten the whole incident anyway.'

There, she had done it. Diane was so engrossed in her own relief that she was totally unprepared for what happened next. At some stage the major must have stepped over the doorstep and into the hallway, and certainly he must have removed his arm from the door as well since he could hardly have kicked it closed behind him, enclosing them both in the hallway, if he had not done so. However, she had not registered either of those acts but she was certainly registering his current one. Indeed, it would have been impossible for her not to do so since he was wrapping her in his arms, and holding her so tightly that the medals on his jacket were pressing into her skin.

'It's a good theory,' he told her grimly, 'but it's the wrong fit. Try this for size instead.'

Diane tried to protest, but it was too late. The slight discomfort of his embrace was forgotten as he started to kiss her. And not just a little 'let's be friends' kiss either; not even an 'I'm an angry man, and I'll kiss you if I want to' kiss, Diane acknowledged dizzily. This was a real man-to-woman, 'I want you badly' kiss, the kind of kiss that couldn't be faked, the kind of kiss that her lips must have been sorely missing, to judge from the way they were responding...

Somehow the major had swung her round so that she was leaning up against the door, his body a hard weight against her own. She ought to put a stop to this, and right now. Her brain was demanding that she do so, but her body seemed to have developed a will of its own. It had been so long since she had been kissed like this ... held like this ... wanted like this, Diane acknowledged. So long since...

She gave a small gasp that could have been a protest when the major lifted his mouth from hers. His hands were cupping her face, forcing her to look up at him. The heat she could see in his gaze was transferring itself to her own skin, making her face burn.

'I've been wondering what you'd look like with your hair down,' the major told her softly. And then before she could say anything he kissed her again, slowly and tenderly this time, so that her

327

heart bounced crazily against her chest wall, sending her a message as potentially damaging to her future safety as any German bomb.

'Now,' he told her when he finally released her, 'don't tell me again that any kiss we share means nothing.'

Diane could feel the backs of her eyes burning with emotion. What was wrong with her? This was crazy. Hadn't she learned *anything* from what had happened with Kit? And this was worse – a hundred, no, a thousand times worse – because Lee ... the major, was *married*.

'I don't want this,' she heard herself telling him emotionally. 'We can't ... you're married...'

'Do you think I don't know all that?' He was still holding her, pulling her into his body now, and cradling her as tenderly as though he did understand what all of this was doing to her. 'Do you think I didn't tell myself the first time I set eyes on you that what I was feeling wasn't something I had any right to be feeling?'

'The first time you saw me?' Diane protested. 'But you were so hateful to me.'

'Believe me, that was nothing to the way I behaved towards myself. I swore I'd be all kinds of a fool to get the hots for a pair of blue eyes and a mouth so perfect that just looking at it made me want.' His voice had dropped and become soft and slurred with a need her body immediately recognised. 'And then I saw you at that dance hall, drunk as a skunk, and coming on to another guy–'

'I was not coming on to him. I thought ... I thought he was Kit.'

'I didn't care who you thought he was, all I cared about was that it wasn't me you were looking at like that with those big blue eyes. I told myself to get a grip; I reminded myself of all the reasons why what was going through my head was unthinkable, and then I found out that the two of us were going to be working together on our own.'

'You could have asked for someone else.'

'Yeah, I could. Doesn't it tell you anything that I didn't?'

Diane closed her eyes helplessly, caught up in the undertow of her own emotions and desires. *You know that you wanted this,* an inner voice was telling her, *you know you've looked at him and wondered ... imagined...* Yes, yes, she had done those things but not because she had ever envisaged anything like this.

'You're married,' she reminded him tersely. 'I can't... Even if I wanted to ... to ... I *couldn't;* not knowing that you'd be cheating on your wife.'

'Let me tell you something about my marriage and my wife. Six months ago I found out that she'd been cheating on me with the guy her folks had wanted her to marry all along. We would have been divorced by now if she hadn't decided that it wouldn't look good for her to "divorce a man about to go to war". And making sure she looks good in every single way matters one hell of a lot to Carrie. In fact, you could say it is *all* that matters to her.'

'You sound as though you hate her,' Diane told him unsteadily.

'Sometimes I think I do. I know she certainly hates me. She's told me so often enough. That's what happens in a relationship when you both realise you're tied to a person who has turned out to be not the person you originally thought they were. Speaking as a man, I guess it's easier to blame the woman than to accept the fact your balls got in the way of your brain.'

His frank speaking should have shocked her, Diane knew, but instead it seemed to create a shared sense of intimacy between them, as though they had both already accepted that they had a relationship that allowed that kind of frankness.

'I didn't just come round here because I wanted to kiss you again,' Lee continued.

Diane looked at him.

'I was worried about you after yesterday. What you did yesterday for that kid was one of the bravest things I have ever seen.' He drew her closer and somehow it felt natural and right to let him.

'You had me shit scared, I can tell you. Just thinking of what would have happened to you if that plane had gone up kept me awake half the night, whilst thinking about how it felt to kiss you kept me awake the other half,' he told her with a small smile.

'I ... I'd wondered about writing to Eddie's mother,' Diane told him in a valiant attempt to switch their conversation over to a less personal topic. 'I've been trying to put myself in her place but of course I can't. I don't know if it will help her to know that someone was with him, or whether knowing that his last words were for her will be too much for her to bear.' She bent her

330

head, turning her face into the major's shoulder to muffle the emotion seizing her by the throat. He smelled of cologne and sweat, and that earthy combination sent a charge of longing surging through her. It had been so long since she had known the intimacy of a man's hold.

'You shouldn't be here,' she told him, to punish herself for her forbidden longing. 'My landlady will probably throw me out when she gets back and hears how long your Jeep has been parked outside.'

'We don't have to stay here. I'd planned to take you out so that we could talk properly. I've got a picnic and a blanket.'

Diane's heart missed a beat. 'No ... we can't,' she protested.

But the major was ignoring her, smiling down at her as he told her firmly, 'Yes, we can. Come on.'

TWENTY-TWO

'Not brought Walter with you, then?'

Jess almost choked on her lemonade. She hadn't heard Billy coming up behind her and now, as he obligingly thumped her on the back, he said jovially, 'I know you, remember. You'll be hiccuping in a minute if I don't do this.'

'I haven't hiccuped since I was six years old,' Jess fibbed. 'And no, I haven't brought Walter with me. This is a family occasion, after all,' she added, pointedly looking over to where the curvaceous blonde Billy had arrived at the church with was standing talking to one of Billy's friends.

'Quite right,' Billy told her approvingly, irritatingly oblivious to the meaning of her comment. 'Have you asked Walter yet about that photograph I saw in his wallet?'

'You had no right to go spying on him like that.'

'I wasn't spying. I just happened to see it when I picked his wallet up off of the Grafton dance floor.'

So that was how he knew about Walter's girl.

'No, I haven't, and what's more I'm not going to,' Jess informed him, answering his original question. She could see no reason for letting him know that she wasn't going to ask Walter anything, because she didn't need to, because Walter had already told her all about Marianne and how much he loved her and hoped that she would wait for him.

Billy's reaction to her stubbornness wasn't what she had been expecting, though. Immediately the laughter died out of his eyes. He gave her a sharp look, his voice filled with an unfamiliar mix of disapproval and severity. 'I'd never have put you down as the kind of girl who goes out with a lad whose got another girl somewhere else, Jess.'

The cheek of it! For a minute she was tempted to tell him how wrong he was about her and Walter, but why should she tell him anything? He could think what he liked. She knew the truth, she decided stubbornly, and that was all that mattered.

'What I do is no business of yours,' she snapped back at him instead. 'I don't go telling you who you should see and who you shouldn't, but if I was to...' she paused deliberately.

'If you was to what?' Bill encouraged her.

Jess's mouth compressed. 'I'm not saying, 'cos it isn't any of my business, but if you was to ask me then I might just have to tell you that when a girl shows off her chest like that Yvonne you've brought here with you is showing off hers, then there's bound to be trouble.'

'Got a lovely figure, Yvonne has,' Billy responded appreciatively, with a happy sigh that made Jess want to throw a bucket of water over him.

'Lucky thing your Denise's ma noticed how much weight she was putting on before it was too late,' Billy added, changing the subject.

Jess gave him a suspicious look, but she still couldn't resist demanding, 'And what does that mean, when it's at home?'

'Nowt, only that if she'd have got much bigger she'd never have got into that frock she's wearing,' Billy answered innocently.

Jess wasn't deceived, but decency made it impossible for her to say to him that she knew perfectly well that he was referring to the fact that Denise was very obviously pregnant, and that if her mother hadn't realised that fact, her new son-in-law could have been out of the country and unable to do the decent thing and marry her.

'There you are, Billy lad. So what's all this about you joining the bomb disposal lot?'

This was her chance to slip away before Billy

asked her any more awkward questions about Walter, Jess acknowledged, and the only reason she wasn't doing just that was because her feet in her new pair of second-hand shoes were killing her. She'd told her mother that the silver dance shoes she'd bought her from a Red Cross sale would be too tight, but her mother had said that they were so pretty that it had seemed a shame not to get them and that Jess could rub a bit of Vaseline into her feet to make them more comfortable. It hadn't worked.

'I didn't join so much as get meself ordered into the bomb disposal lot,' she could hear Billy saying affably.

Very deliberately she waited until they were on their own again before telling him sharply, 'And that was a big fib you went and told your Uncle Fred, 'cos my dad told me that you hadn't been told to go joining the bomb disposal lot at all, and that you'd volunteered, because he'd heard it from your sergeant. I dunno why you had to go and do summat as daft as that, I really don't.'

'Perhaps I did it because I wanted to show you that it isn't just them ruddy GIs who can be heroes.'

Jess stared at him. Suddenly with one sentence Billy had changed the landscape of their relationship for ever.

'Show *me?*' she half stammered. 'Why would you want to go doing summat like that?'

'Why do you think?' Billy challenged her grimly.

''Ere, Billy, you said you was going to tek me out somewhere special. You never said nowt about bringing me to a ruddy wedding.'

334

Billy was looking at Yvonne as though he could hardly remember who she was, Jess recognised with a sudden surge of satisfaction. Not that she believed any of that fancy talk of his for one minute. She knew better than to fall for Billy's flattery.

'Hey, cabbie...'

Myra winced as Nick let out a piercing whistle but it certainly caught the taxi driver's attention.

'Savoy Hotel, buddy,' Nick told him as he threw both his own and Myra's overnight bags into the back of the taxi.

Already the taxi rank was a seething mass of uniformed Americans, all in search of a taxi. Their driver was about to set off when another GI called out, 'Hey there, any room in that cab for another passenger?'

'Only if you're going to the Savoy, mate,' the taxi driver called back.

'Then my luck's in. That's where I'm going too – at least it is now,' he grinned, adding, 'Mind if I join you?' as he opened the door and climbed in without waiting for a reply.

He wasn't army, Myra could tell that. He had a bit of a look of an Italian about him, what with his dark hair and his olive-toned skin. She glanced uneasily at Nick, not sure how he would take this intrusion. Along with the other men in their carriage he had been drinking for most of the train journey to London, and had even disappeared at one point, telling her he had some business to attend to, returning grinning from ear to ear after an absence of over an hour to show her his win-

335

nings from a poker game in another carriage.

He didn't seem too bothered about the presence of the other man, though, even offering him a cigarette.

'Up for the weekend, are you?' the man asked Nick as he accepted it.

'Yeah. And you?'

'Yeah. I'm ready for a bit of R and R. Name's Joe, by the way,' he told Nick, extending his hand. 'Joe Cavelli.'

'Nick,' Nick introduced himself, shaking this hand. 'Nick Mancini.'

'Stayed at the Savoy before, have you?' Joe asked.

To Myra's pique, he had glanced at her once and then looked away, totally ignoring her, and Nick was just as bad, she fumed. He wasn't making any attempt to include her in the conversation and hadn't even bothered to introduce her.

'Nope, but I've heard it's an OK place.'

'Sure, it's a real home from home, but without the steaks and the malt.'

Myra had had enough. She wasn't used to being ignored and she didn't intend to get used to it. 'We've heard that the Savoy's band, the Orpheans, are just wonderful to dance to. We're looking forward to having a really romantic couple of days, aren't we, Nick?'

Very deliberately she played with her new ring, and gave Nick a slow smile. There! That should do the trick and let Joe know the situation and that three was a crowd. He had certainly registered the ring, because he was frowning as he looked at it. If he was in London by himself he had probably been hoping to pal up with Nick and he was frowning because now he realised that all Nick's time would be taken up with her, his fiancée.

Myra hadn't been to London before, but after Nick's comments to her about New York when they had first met she was very much on her mettle not to look as though she wasn't used to city living. The truth was, though, that London was much bigger than she had imagined and much busier as well, with people hurrying this way and that, and with Americans in uniform looking so at home that the city might just as well have been theirs.

Their driver turned into the Strand, and then suddenly there was the hotel. Myra caught her breath, her eyes rounding with excitement and awe as she saw the doormen in their uniforms, decorated lavishly with gold braid.

'I'll get the fare,' she heard Nick saying to Joe as one of the doormen stepped forward to open the door for her.

It was seldom if ever that Myra allowed herself to feel at a disadvantage, but as she saw the guests hurrying in and out of the revolving doors, the women dressed in the kind of clothes that set them far above someone like her, even if those clothes were war worn and no longer new, and wearing jewellery, Myra drew in her breath. If only the girls she worked with could be here to see her now.

Nick and Joe, still talking, had caught up with her.

'See ya around, bud.' Joe was shaking Nick's hand. 'And if I do we can have a few beers together.'

Not if I have anything to say about it you won't, Myra thought to herself, as she slipped her hand possessively through Nick's arm, refusing to let him pull away.

'Anyone would think you didn't want to be with me,' she told him as they went inside. 'Ignoring me like that in the taxi. If that's some kind of New York custom...'

However, as they stepped into the ornate foyer to the hotel, her annoyance was forgotten, overwhelmed by the elegance of her surroundings. From somewhere she could hear the faint sound of piano music and the even fainter chink of china, coming from the large room she could just glimpse at the end of the corridor. From where she was standing she could just about see some of the ornate plasterwork and one of the mirrors reflecting the group of women seated on a velvet-covered banquette beneath it, talking and sipping their tea. One of the women – about her own age – was wearing the uniform of a Wren officer, whilst the others were wearing elegant afternoon frocks and costumes. They were all wearing smart hats, and they all had refined cut-glass accents. As Myra watched, one of them removed a cigarette holder from her handbag and fixed a dark-coloured cigarette into it, which Myra guessed must be a black Russian cigarette. One of the other women said archly, 'Sobranies, my dear. Aren't you the lucky one? I smoked my last pack for ever ago.'

Laughing, the woman smoking put down her

cigarette to drawl, 'My dear, all one needs is to know the right people. Do let me introduce you to our little man.'

The Wren officer frowned and told them both coolly, 'Personally, I'd never knowingly buy anything black market.'

An approaching waiter cut off Myra's view of them but what she had seen had been enough to have her spinning round, her eyes bright with excited pleasure.

'Oh, Nick, this is wonderful,' she told him impulsively.

'It sure is, hon,' he agreed.

Naturally, given the fact that they weren't actually married, she left it to Nick to go to announce their arrival and check them in, seating herself demurely on one of the elegant sofas to wait for him.

He wasn't gone very long, returning grinning and holding up a set of keys.

'Suite one-o-one. Com' on, babe, let's go and hit that mattress.'

'It's tea time,' Myra protested, pouting, 'and I'm hungry.'

'Yeah, I'm hungry too, sugar, but it ain't for "tea".'

There was a warning note in his voice, and a look in his eyes that Myra knew it would not be wise to ignore. She wasn't looking forward to what she knew lay ahead. The physical act of sex was just that, so far as she was concerned: a physical act, and one that, if the truth were known, she did not really care for and certainly did not enjoy. It was simply a part of what she had to offer a man in exchange for what she wanted from him. She had never experienced the urges she had heard other women describing, and she didn't want to. She couldn't imagine why any woman *would* want to. After all, controlling a man meant controlling oneself as well, and not being swept away by 'passion' and letting him get the upper hand. Right now she would far rather have been sitting down to afternoon tea, wearing a pretty frock and showing off her new ring, knowing that other women were looking at her with envy and their men with a desire that would make the women even more resentful of her. Myra liked knowing that other women thought of her as a threat. It meant that she had a power over them, and she liked that. Right now, though, she felt more sulky than powerful. She might have wanted Nick to herself, but that wasn't because she wanted to spend the weekend alone with him in a hotel suite.

'You said we were going to have fun,' she reminded him with a little girl pout. 'I thought you meant you'd be taking me to the theatre and out dancing ... so that we could celebrate our engagement.'

'Yeah, yeah, and so we will, but right now the kind of fun I want is the kind that comes with a double bed and a beautiful broad.'

Diane sat on the tartan rug, within view of the pretty small lake at Ellesmere, the little town almost on the borders of Cheshire and Wales. Lee had driven her through it when he had been looking for billets, although in reality it was too far out and she had said at the time how lovely she had thought it was, with its black and white buildings and its sense of being a world away from the war. Although they were too far away to see the faces of the occupants clearly, she could hear the laughter coming from the rowing boats on the lake and the splash of the oars of the amateur oarsmen, most of them young men rowing their girls. This was an English summer at its best, surely, with the smell of grass, and the lazy hum of worker bees filling the air around them. Ellesmere was undoubtedly a place for lovers, just as summer was a time for lovers, but she must not think about that, no matter how ironic and painful it was that Lee had brought her here. If only she were free simply to relax and enjoy everything that Ellesmere and its lake had to offer, but sadly she was not. Her arms wrapped tightly round her knees, she was looking straight ahead, but she wasn't really seeing the view. Instead her thoughts were focused on what she knew she had to do.

'We can't do this. We mustn't do this, Lee. We ... we can't be together,' she burst out miserably.

'Why not?'

'How can you ask me that? You know why not. You're married.'

'My marriage is over, and that's not just some line I'm shooting you, Di. It's the truth. Look, I didn't want this to happen to us any more than you did. In fact, I swore I wasn't going to let it happen. Hell, I damn near busted a gut fighting not to let it happen, but since it has ... surely you can see that we'd be fools not to take what we've been given? Be honest with me. How many people get to feel like this?'

'Plenty of them, from what I've heard.' Diane's voice was metallic and thin with pain, as she struggled not to let Lee see just what his words were doing to her.

'No, not plenty of them,' he corrected her. 'Very few, I would guess. This for us has come against all the odds – you know that as well as I do.' He reached for her hand.

Diane tried to snatch it away but he wouldn't let her.

'Don't try to tell me that you don't feel the same way I do.'

'It doesn't matter how I feel. Can't you see how wrong it would be?' she protested with despair. 'No matter what you say about your marriage, you *are* married.'

'And you're still in love with a guy who dumped you.'

Diane drew in her breath as she tried to stop the pain gripping her. 'Yes,' she agreed, after she had finally exhaled, 'yes, I am.'

'But you still want me...'

She wanted to refute what he was saying so badly that it hurt, but she knew that her own honesty wouldn't let her.

'You love him but you want me,' he persisted. 'You know what I think? I think you're afraid to admit that you might have stopped loving him because you're afraid of admitting that you could have started to love me.'

'No, that isn't true.'

She sprang up, shaking her head in angry denial, oblivious to the curious looks she was attracting from the other couples who had come to this lake on the outskirts of a Cheshire village, with its tranquillity and the privacy it afforded eager lovers.

'This can't happen, Lee. It mustn't.' She was perilously close to breaking point. 'We both know all about the temptations for a married man going off to war, when he's far from home, and we both know too what happens to the women who are foolish enough to get involved with them: wartime "wives" who are no such thing. And what if you are lying to me? What if your wife really does love you? Do you think I could live with myself if I thought I'd been responsible for causing that kind of pain to another woman; a woman who has the right to ... to everything?'

'You know what you're doing, don't you?'

When she didn't make any response, the major continued thickly, 'With every word you're saying you're making me fall deeper in love with you, Di.'

'Well, you mustn't. You *mustn't*. All we can ever be is ... is two people fighting together to win this war. Nothing more than that. Nothing!'

The starkness of the silence between them strained her nerves, the echoes of her emotional words dying slowly on the air as though to reproach her for what she was destroying.

'If that's what you want?'

She could hear the heaviness in his voice and she could feel it too in her own heart, but she had to do the right thing.

'Yes ... yes. It is what I want...'

She couldn't look at him. If she did he would see that her heart was breaking. Why did this have

343

to happen to her? Wasn't it enough that she had lost Kit? Did fate have to compound that blow by making her fall in love with a married man?

'I ... I want you to take me back to Liverpool.'

It was only just gone six o'clock and the long light summer evening stretched ahead of them, but Diane knew she couldn't trust herself to spend it with Lee. Not and keep the vow she had made to herself. How could this have happened? How could she have gone from thinking of him as someone whose dislike for her she returned, to someone she ached for and longed for, heart and body? It was the war that had done it, of course; the war, and the knowledge that life was frighteningly brief, that the man you held in your arms tonight might be dead tomorrow, that happiness had to be snatched from the jaws of fear and death and taken on the run before it was lost.

She bent down to start packing away the remains of their picnic, stiffening as she felt Lee kneel down next to her.

'Tell me something,' he demanded as he folded up the rug. 'If you hadn't known that I was married, what would your answer have been then?'

'Whatever it would have been, it wouldn't have altered the fact that I was still helping you to break your marriage vows,' Diane told him quietly. 'The only difference is that you would have been deceiving me as well as your wife.'

Myra lay on the bed staring up at the ceiling. It was over, thankfully. She could hear the sound of Nick showering in the adjoining bathroom, cursing without any heat at the inefficiency of the shower, and then starting to whistle cheerfully.

There would be bruises on her body tomorrow, her arms where he had gripped her too tightly and her breasts where he had squeezed and kneaded them, convinced that he was giving her pleasure. A 'gift' he had made her pay back with interest. She grimaced and wiped her hand across her mouth. She had been too startled to refuse when he had grabbed hold of her hair and pushed her face down towards his groin. Jim would never have expected her to do anything like that. Her whole body had stiffened in rejection. He had obviously not sensed how she was feeling, though, too carried away by his own arousal either to notice or, she suspected, care how she felt. But then Myra had grown up with a father who, via his treatment of her mother, had taught her that men were selfish and did not care about the women they professed to love, wanting only to have their own needs met.

She watched now as he came into the bedroom, naked from his shower. His body was heavily muscled and dark with body hair. There were scars on his arms and one low down on his belly.

'Don't worry, baby cakes,' he had told her when he had seen her looking at them. 'I'm still alive, but the guys who left me aren't. They're lying in New York harbour in a block of cement. No one double-crosses the Mancini family and gets away with it.

'Still feeling hungry?' he asked her now suggestively.

Myra shielded her eyes with her lashes so that

345

he wouldn't see the look of angry rejection in them. Forcing a pout she reminded him, 'You promised to take me out dancing.'

'Sure, and so I am, but you gotta get dressed first.' He picked up his wallet and removed several five-pound notes.

'I want my girl to be the best-looking girl on that dance floor tonight, sugar plum, so you go down to the beauty shop and get yourself the works. Take as much time as you want. I've got a guy I need to meet up with to talk over a bit of business.'

And he wanted her out of the way whilst he did so, Myra recognised. Well, if that was what he wanted, he could have it – at a price.

'It will take more than a visit to the hairdresser to make me look as glamorous as the other women staying here,' she told him, with a deliberate sigh.

As she had hoped, Nick peeled off several more notes.

'Here, take this and go buy yourself something pretty,' he told her. 'Ask the doorman. He'll know where you can get what you want.'

Forty pounds. Nick had given her forty pounds – an absolute fortune. Her dislike of the sexual intimacies he had demanded was already almost forgotten.

TWENTY-THREE

'Are you all right, Ruthie, only you've hardly said a word, and what with you and your Glen going to see the vicar on Saturday I thought you'd have bin chattering nineteen to the dozen, telling us all about it,' Jess teased Ruthie, her expression changing as she looked at her properly and saw her red-rimmed eyes. 'Oh, you and Glen haven't had a fall-out, have you?'

The bus taking them to work swung round a corner, causing Ruthie to fall heavily against Jess.

'No, it's nothing like that,' she told her miserably as she straightened up.

'So what is it then?'

'It's just... Oh, Jess,' tears flooded from her eyes, 'the most dreadful thing's happened. An awful fight... Poor Walter's been badly hurt and...' As quickly as she could, Ruthie explained what had happened.

'You mean that GI that Myra's walking out with beat poor Walter up for no reason at all?'

Ruthie could hear the shocked indignation in Jess's voice.

'Glen said it was because Nick has a grudge against Walter because he'd seen him cheating at cards. There's a group of them in the platoon, apparently, that all play cards together, and they bet and drink heavily. Glen says that it's always leading to trouble and fights. But I still haven't told you the worst thing.'

'What "worst thing"?'

Ruthie bit her lip and said wearily, 'When the police came, Nick told them that it was Glen who had been hitting Walter, and she – that Myra – backed him up. By the time the MPs got there they'd gone. This Nick with Myra had told the police that they'd got a train to catch. I tried to tell the police that it wasn't true what they'd said about my Glen being the one to hurt Walter, but they wouldn't listen. Glen said it didn't matter because Walter would be able to tell them what happened once he was well enough. The policeman asked me if they'd been drinking because he could smell it on their breath, but it was only a bit of something Mr Brown, our neighbour, had given them after we got back from seeing the vicar...' Tears welled in Ruthie's eyes. 'Glen said he'd be in touch with me as soon as he could, but I haven't heard anything yet.'

'Well, it's only been a few hours, hasn't it?' Jess pointed out practically. 'Seeing as it were only yesterday dinner and we're on an early shift today. Oh, but poor Walter. I wish I'd bin with you. I'd have had something to say to that Myra, telling lies like that,' she announced robustly. 'She's a fool if she keeps on seeing that Nick now. If it was me I'd have bin off like a shot the first time he showed me that he had a nasty temper.'

Ruthie gave a small shudder. 'It was so frightening Jess. Glen tried to stop him but he just kept on kicking Walter and he hit Glen too.'

'Now don't you go getting yourself upset about it all over again. If your Glen told you not to worry then that's what you must do. You look like you haven't slept a wink.'

'I haven't,' Ruthie admitted.

'You shouldn't have come in this morning.'

Ruthie gazed at her wide-eyed. 'I ... I couldn't stay off. After all, there isn't anything wrong with me, and it wouldn't be right, would it?'

'Well, it won't be right either if you fall asleep in the middle of filling one of them shells and end up with TNT all over you, will it?' Jess told her firmly, as the bus pulled up at the factory gates.

She was feeling doubly guilty for not going with Ruthie and the two men to see the vicar now, Jess admitted as they all stood up to get off the bus. Poor Ruthie was so gentle and unworldly that she simply wasn't up to coping with something like this. The poor kid would probably have nightmares about it for weeks, Jess thought compassionately. And as for poor Walter, it was just as well that his girl back home didn't know what had happened to him. She'd be worrying herself sick, just as *she* would if it had been... Now what was she thinking? Just because Billy had told a whopping big fib about joining the bomb disposal lot because he wanted to impress her, and just because he had snatched a dance with her before Yvonne had come storming over demanding that he dance with *her*, that didn't mean ... well, it didn't mean *anything*, Jess told herself firmly, and it was high time she got that through her own silly head and her even sillier heart.

Ruthie tried to focus on the normal morning routine of changing out of her own clothes and

349

into her overall, tucking her hair up into the cotton cap provided for that purpose, as she got ready to go into the cleanway area. All around her the other girls were doing the same, meticulously removing anything they were wearing containing metal because of the danger from the TNT.

'Here, give us the key to your locker a minute, will you, Ruthie?' Maureen whispered quietly, sidling over to her. 'Only I've bin promised a bit of stuff for the kiddies, like, for Christmas. Just a few tins...'

Ruthie winced, lifting her hand to her forehead, her head was aching with worrying so much. If only Glen would just get in touch and tell her that Walter was all right and that he had explained what had happened, but she knew she mustn't worry. After all, Glen had told her not to. Instead she should think about their wedding and how happy they were going to be. How long would it be before she and Glen were interviewed by his commanding officer? Two months' notice of their planned wedding date, Glen had told her he had had to give. They had told the vicar that and so he had suggested the third Saturday in October, which gave them a bit of extra time.

'Are you listening to me?' Maureen demanded impatiently.

'Yes, of course I am,' Ruthie told her. 'Only you know I don't approve of black-market things,' she reminded her uncomfortably.

'Oh, that's just typical of someone like you wot's got a GI boyfriend,' Maureen snapped angrily. She had adopted the fashion amongst some of the girls for keeping a piece of her hair free of her cap so that the TNT could turn it yellow – or if one's hair was very dark, orange.

'You'd never get me doing nowt like that,' Mel had sniffed critically. 'Who wants everyone knowing that you're working in munitions?'

'Aye, and just think about what could happen if a chap leaned over to offer you a light for your cig, with them TNT fumes dying your hair,' Leah had grinned.

Personally Ruthie couldn't take to the fashion at all, and was only too glad to protect her hair from the effect of the TNT. It was bad enough ending up with yellow-tinted skin.

'It's all right for you, isn't it? You don't have to go wi'out nothing. I'll bet he brings more than a few tins when he comes round your house. I'll bet there's chocolate and stockings, and ciggies and all sorts gets given to you, all stuff wots on ration, and you're getting it for free. And then you've got the nerve to go telling me that I shouldn't have a bit of black-market stuff for the kiddies wot's cost me an arm and a leg.'

As usual, Ruthie acknowledged, as she gave in and handed over her locker key, Maureen had managed to make her feel both in the wrong, and very selfish.

'Please make sure you give me the key back, won't you?' Ruthie asked.

The woman who had been covered in TNT was back at work, her face and hands looking very red and sore.

'That'll teach her to go nicking,' Ruthie heard one of the other women remarking with obvious

351

satisfaction as she glared at her.

Perhaps she was too soft-hearted, but she couldn't help feeling sorry for her, Ruthie admitted, even though she could understand the anger of those whose things she had taken.

When would she hear from Glen? She could hardly bear the waiting, but she knew she would have to do so.

She had hardly slept last night, Diane admitted, as she stepped out into the early morning sunshine, and that meant that for two nights running now, thinking about Major Lee Saunders had kept her awake.

She had done the right thing, she knew that. But that hadn't stopped her from lying awake thinking about the sweetness of his kisses. Sweeter than Kit's. She couldn't compare them, and she wasn't going to. Kit had ditched her because he no longer loved her. But Lee... She mustn't start weakening. She mustn't! She was in uniform and on duty now, she reminded herself sternly as she reached Derby House. She had made it plain to Lee that she couldn't and wouldn't help him to break his marriage vows. But what if he refused to accept what she had said; what if he tried to persuade her to change her mind? Was she strong enough to remain steadfast? She would have to be for both their sakes and for the sake of the woman to whom he was married.

The sight of a familiar face up ahead of her in the queue to show passes provided a welcome distraction.

'Susan!' Diane exclaimed, hurrying up to the

other girl. 'It's good to see you back.'

'Thanks.'

Diane tried not to show how shocked she was by the change in Susan's appearance. She looked thinner and older, with a bleakness in her eyes that couldn't be hidden, not the lively self-confident girl who had first greeted her on her arrival at Derby House at all.

'I'm so dreadfully sorry,' Diane said, helpless to say anything more.

'Yes. He was a good man. One of the best. He tried to ... to hang on, but in the end it was too much for him. He'd been in the water too long, you see, and ... they amputated his toes first and then the lower part of his leg. But then...' Her whole body was shaking, heaving with the pressure of the tears she was refusing to cry.

Overwhelmed with compassion for her, Diane drew her into a secluded corner, keeping her arm protectively around her.

'Oh God, Di, I am so glad that he died. Isn't that a shocking thing to say? I loved him but I wanted him to die! Not for me but for him. Can you understand that? I couldn't bear to see him dying inch by inch, you see, as they cut him to pieces bit by bit...'

Diane didn't say a word as she held her and tried to comfort her. What words were there for her to say, after all? Pity had gripped her by the throat anyway, silencing anything she might have wanted to say.

'They said at the hospital that they'd sign me off for some compassionate leave if I wanted, but I'd rather be here, back at work. At least that way I feel that I'm doing something to help get this war over with so that other men don't die like him.'

'He'd be so proud of you for being so brave,' Diane whispered to her, whilst she wondered inwardly if she could have done the same if she had had to sit at the bedside of the man she loved and watch him die. To her chagrin the face she could see inside her head was Lee's, not Kit's: Lee, with his blue eyes dark with pain and the desire for death, his body racked by pain. Stop it, stop it at once, she commanded herself shakily. Take a leaf out of Susan's book and bury yourself in work to forget the pain.

TWENTY-FOUR

Myra stiffened as Nick cursed.

'Asshole English rubbers, they're bloody useless. For a start, they ain't big enough.' He dropped the split rubber and opened a new packet.

It was just gone ten in the morning, and they were still in bed in their suite. Officially Myra had her own room, since the suite possessed two bedrooms, but of course, as she had known he would, Nick had insisted she share his bed.

He had woken up half an hour ago, complaining about the lack of proper coffee, and saying that the band they had danced to the previous night had been nowhere near as good as a New York band. Myra had come to learn that Nick had to be coaxed and flattered out of these bad

354

moods, so she had smiled at him and put her arms around his neck, telling him how much she was enjoying herself and how wonderful he was.

Now, as a result of that, she was going to have to lie here and let him have sex with her, but at least that would put him in a better mood. It was a pity it was Sunday otherwise they could have seen a few more of the 'sights', but at least she had her lovely new dark red rustling taffeta frock, bought from a woman who had arrived at the hotel with a selection for her to try after she had done as Nick had suggested and 'asked the doorman'.

She had felt as good as any film star last night in her new frock with her hair done, and her engagement ring sparkling away. It was a pity that she hadn't had a few rows of pearls to wear round her neck like some of the other women she had seen when they had finally gone down to dinner, but at least she had had the satisfaction of knowing that she had been the prettiest woman in the room. Nick had said so himself. Her smile faded as Nick gave up struggling with the new 'rubber' and reached for her impatiently.

'I guess you know what to do anyway, don't you, sweet stuff?' he said thickly as he climbed on top of her.

Unenthusiastically, Myra closed her eyes. She would need more new clothes than just her taffeta dress for when she went to New York. Of course, she would buy everything new anyway when she got there, but she wanted to arrive looking right. Nick grunted as he thrust into her, and she drew in a sharp breath. She felt slightly sore still from yesterday. Nick was much rougher than Jim had been, but that was because he felt so passionate about her, Myra comforted herself. This intimacy, uncomfortable and unwanted by her as it was, was in reality a small price to pay for what she would get in return, once she was his wife, and they were living in America. And not just in America, but in New York. She gave a soft sigh of pleasure, causing Nick to grunt approvingly and thrust harder.

'And I were warning our George about 'oo he goes talking wiv, now that he's joined the ARP 'cos you've only got to read the papers to hear about what's going on. There was that fast society piece wot was interned the other year, that Lady Howard, on suspicion of spying.'

'I should think that your George is pretty safe, though, Elsie,' Jess laughed. 'He doesn't do much hobnobbing wi' Winnie, after all, does he? And I can't see that Lady wotsit taking a trip down to the Dog and Duck, even if she hadn't been interned.'

They were on their break in the canteen and whilst everyone else laughed good-naturedly, Elsie looked ruffled. 'It's all right you laughing, but I'm telling you, it's not for nothing that the government keeps on telling us to "keep mum".'

'Isn't it your birthday this week, Alice?' Jess asked one of the other girls.

'Yes, it is.' She extended her wrist proudly. 'My Ian brought me this watch back when he was home on leave. Real gold, it is,' she told them all as she showed off the bright shiny new timepiece. 'Bargained for it himself, he did, in one of them bazaar places they've got out there in Egypt.'

'Well, you want to take it off when you have a wash, Alice, only you're getting a real funny-looking tidemark,' one of the other girls sniffed. 'Proper green, it looks,' she added as everyone at the table stopped eating their dinner to lean forward and look closer at the telltale mark just showing beneath the shiny gold watch.

''Ere, if you trying to say I don't wash?' Alice began indignantly.

'Never mind about washing, you mek sure you don't forget to put it back in your locker before we go back to the cleanway,' Mel warned her. 'Otherwise, gold or not, we'll all be going up in smoke, seeing as it's metal.'

'I'm not that daft,' Alice told her scornfully. 'I only got it from me locker just so as I could show it off. I'll be putting it back in before I go back.'

'I tell you wot, seeing as it's your birthday, Alice, how about us all going out to the Grafton this week?' Jess suggested. 'The rest of us'll club together and treat you, won't we, girls?'

Ruthie, who had been on the verge of saying she'd rather not go, felt obliged to nod instead. It wouldn't be right not to pay her share of the treat, she admitted, even if she didn't feel much like going dancing without Glen.

'That's that settled then,' Jess announced. 'We'll all meet up outside the Grafton on Wednesday. We can have a bit of something to eat first. Wot's up?' she asked as Alice frowned suddenly and began to scratch at her wrist.

'I dunno. It's me wrist, it's itching that much it's fair driving me mad. I reckon me watch is a bit on the tight side. Ruddy hell, there's the bell gone. How come the dinner hour goes that fast it feels like no more than five minutes, but when you're working every hour feels like it's going on for ever?' she grumbled as they all started to get up from the table.

'Sit down, Wilson. I just thought I'd have a few words with you post last week's dreadful accident. Major Saunders will be filing an official report to the American authorities, of course. Both he and the local rescue services have already reported on the role you played and your bravery,' Group Captain Barker smiled approvingly.

'I didn't think about being brave,' Diane admitted. 'I just didn't want... When you've worked with airforce men and you've seen... He was so young...'

To Diane's astonishment the Group Captain passed a clean white handkerchief across the desk to her, telling Diane bracingly, 'That's the spirit,' when she blew her nose to halt the tears that that been threatening to overwhelm her.

'Major Saunders told me this morning that you had requested the young airman's address so had you could write to his family.'

Lee had been here at Derby House? Diane's heart did a steep dive and then crash-landed, mirroring her swift surge of excitement followed by the disappointment of knowing he had not tried to see her.

'I ... I wasn't sure whether or not it would be the right thing to do,' Diane collected herself enough to respond. 'I thought initially that his mother would want to know, but then maybe that kind of knowledge might be too much for her to bear.'

'My advice to you would be for you to write your letter. The major's suggestion, which I thought a wise one, was that it should then be handed over to someone close enough to the family to know whether or not it was appropriate for them to see it.'

Diane nodded in acknowledgement of the wisdom of this suggestion.

The Group Captain paused, then continued, 'There is another matter I need to discuss with you, I'm afraid.'

Diane could feel herself starting to tense.

'I am aware that you requested a transfer from your previous post for personal reasons.'

'Yes, that's correct, ma'am,' Diane agreed, not sure what prompted her question.

'You were engaged to an airman but the engagement was broken?' the captain persisted.

Diane nodded again. What was all this about? A terrible thought struck her. Without realising what she was doing she got to her feet, asking anxiously, 'It's not ... nothing's happened to Kit, has it, ma'am?'

'Not so far as I am aware. Please sit down.' There was more kindness than authority in the Group Captain's voice.

A little shakily Diane subsided back into her chair.

'War brings us into contact with situations and choices which we would not normally be called on to deal with, all the more so when we are female. As your superior it is part of my job to be aware of the pressures that young Waafs experience, and when necessary to offer them guidance and advice.'

What on earth was the captain leading up to, Diane wondered.

'We all know how quickly *friendships* are made in a war situation, when people are working closely together under conditions of extreme pressure, and how easily, when that friendship is between a man and a woman, it can turn into something ... deeper.' The captain paused and looked down at her desk. 'I confess that speaking like this to my girls is not an aspect of my job that I welcome. After all, we have all been young, and it is fair to say that we should all have a right to our private lives. However, in wartime, the security of the country has to come before the luxury of personal privacy.'

The security of the nation? Diane's eyes widened. What on earth was the Group Captain talking about?

'The security of the nation is not always about the obvious,' the Group Captain continued, 'or the necessity to remember that our private conversations could become the property of spies. Sometimes it can be about things that are less easily definable, things such as the moral strength of a country, and the importance of that strength for the way it binds the people of that country together. It is part of our role here in the services to make sure that we women, who are in uniform and thus a highly visible part of our country's womanhood, are above reproach where our own

360

morals are concerned, and that we set an example for the fellow members of our sex to follow.' The Group Captain placed her elbows on the table, steepling her fingers together as she looked towards Diane. 'You will be aware, I am sure, that there have been reports in the press of a certain kind of behaviour by some British women with regard to our American allies,' she continued, whilst Diane could feel her face starting to burn with a mixture of guilt and shame. 'Major Saunders is, I would imagine, a good soldier, and a good man. My own dealings with him have certainly inclined me to think so. However, I would have to be blind,' the Group Captain continued wryly, 'as well as deaf, if I were not aware that so far as my girls are concerned he is also a very attractive man. The kind of man, in fact, that any young woman would be flattered to have paying her attention.'

Diane swallowed mutely.

The Group Captain stood up. 'I *do* understand how you must feel, my dear. You have been let down foolishly, in my opinion, by one young man, and naturally, when a man like the major takes it into his head to show you the kind of flattering gallantry the Americans are famous for... However, the major is a married man, even if his wife is over three thousand miles away.'

Diane wanted to jump up and run away but of course she couldn't do anything of the sort. Instead she bent her head, and said uncomfortably, 'I have already discussed this with ... with the major, ma'am, and ... and we have agreed that to avoid people misconstruing anything, it would be better...' Ignominiously, Diane could feel her voice breaking.

To her astonishment, Group Captain Barker put her hand on her shoulder and said quietly, 'There, there, my dear. I do understand that this can't be easy for you. I did think of offering you another transfer, but I am already three girls down and, to be blunt, I simply can't afford to lose a young woman of your calibre as well.'

A transfer! Diane's heart skipped a beat. But not at the thought of never seeing Lee again, she assured herself.

'It's inevitable that you and Major Saunders will come across one another in the course of your duties, but you're a sensible girl, I know that, and I can rely on you to remember your responsibility to the uniform you wear and to doing what's right. Now! I've taken up enough of your time, so you'd better run along and get back to work, and we'll say no more about any of this.'

'Thank you, ma'am,' Diane managed to respond woodenly before standing up and saluting.

'Are you OK now, only you looked a bit green when you came out of the Group Captain's office,' Jean said solicitously.

Diane gave her a wan smile.

'I can guess why, of course. After all, everyone's been talking about it.'

Diane stiffened, and then relaxed when Jean continued, 'It was frightfully brave of you to do what you did and go to that fly boy. I don't think I could have done it.'

'You'd be surprised what you can do when you

362

have to,' Diane told her dismissively, quickly changing the subject by saying, 'Susan told me about her husband this morning.'

'Yes, she's in a terrible state, although she's pretending not to be. It can't be easy for her being here when we've got another convoy on its way to Russia. She must be thinking every minute of her husband. Thank God my chap's on radio ops and not on active duty. Mind you, the best thing of all is to be like you. Being heart whole and man free makes life a hell of a lot easier. Plus you get to play the field and have some fun,' Jean told her with a meaningful wink.

'Me watch... It's gone...'

The frantic anxiety in Alice's voice, had all the girls close to her, including Ruthie, look up from their own work.

'Don't be daft, Alice,' Jess told her bracingly. 'It can't be gone. You were only showing it off to us at dinner.'

'It *has* gone, I tell you,' Alice insisted, tears filling her eyes. 'Someone has gone and nicked it, that's wot.'

'How can it be gone when it's in your locker?'

'Well, that's it, see.' Alice admitted. 'I didn't put it in me locker on account of not having time. I left it in me bag hanging up on me peg.'

'You did what? You dafthead, that was just asking to have it taken.'

Several female heads swung accusingly in the direction of the woman who had been caught out stealing before now.

''Ere, don't you lot go blaming me again, 'cos it

363

weren't me,' she objected immediately, bristling defensively. 'And wot's more, my Wilf says he's going to come down here and knock a few 'eads together if anyone starts mouthing off any more lies about me.'

'Someone had better go and have a look in her locker,' one of the other women called out sharply.

'Give over, you lot,' Jess chimed in. 'Lizzie would have to be daft to go thieving now after what happened. Come on, Alice, and stop that blubbing. What you had to bring it here for in the first place I don't know. Not when we all know that we can't wear watches when we're working,' Jess pointed out.

'Aye and not when we all know there's thieves about as well,' Maureen told her witheringly. 'You wouldn't catch me leaving anything valuable like a gold watch lying around for someone to take. I reckon your husband is going to have summat to say to you when he gets home next.'

'Oh, give it a rest, will yer, Maureen,' one of the other women demanded grimly. 'There's no call to go rubbing it in. Now see what you've done,' she accused her when Alice began to cry noisily.

'Coo, tek a look at that, will yer?' Lucy called as the girls queued up to leave the factory, nodding in the direction of the US Army Jeep parked outside the gates.

'Maybe it's your Glen, come to drive you home,' Jess teased Ruthie, as she showed the duty guard her ID.

Ruthie followed her, holding out her own ID, and then looking at the duty guard in bewilderment when he told her sharply, 'No, not you.'

'What's up? What's going on?' Lucy demanded.

'You Ruthie Philpott, are you?' the guard asked Ruthie, scrutinising her ID, 'because if you are, there's someone waiting to see you.'

'It *is* Glen,' Jess, who had hung back with Ruthie to find out what was going on, squealed triumphantly, when the guard nodded in the direction of the waiting Jeep.

Ruthie felt her heart lift with excitement and delight as she hurried over to the waiting Jeep, escorted by a group of her curious and giggling friends.

Only when she reached the Jeep she could see that there were two men inside it and that neither of them was Glen.

'Are you Ruthie Philpott?' the one in the passenger seat stopped chewing his gum to ask her.

Numbly, Ruthie nodded.

'Colonel's orders. We've got to take you back to camp with us.'

'He'll want to see you about you and Glen getting married, Ruthie,' Jess hissed. 'Go on. You go with them,' she urged. 'I reckon your Glen must have bin telling them how impatient he is to get married to you,' she teased.

Neither of the soldiers in the Jeep was saying anything, and their silence made Ruthie feel uncomfortable. She couldn't help thinking how much nicer it would have been if Glen had been able to come to get her himself, but perhaps that was against the rules.

'What about my mother? She'll worry when I don't get home at the usual time.'

'I'll stop off on me own way home and tell her for you,' Jess promised. 'And if you get to see Walter, don't forget to tell him how sorry I am that he got hurt,' she added, as the soldier standing by the rear door of the Jeep held it open for her so that she could scramble into the back.

By nature Ruthie was not used to talking to strangers, so she was in a way relieved when the two soldiers didn't try to engage her in conversation, and even more relieved that the noisy rattling of the Jeep prevented her from hearing more than the odd ripe word from their low-voiced conversation, with its frequent bursts of laughter. The world inhabited by men was still an alien and rather daunting world to her, and she instinctively retreated into herself away from it, daydreaming happily instead about the future she and Glen would share once the war was over. She felt she already knew his family, especially his mother and his sister, and she couldn't wait to meet them in person. Even her mother had seemed to perk up a bit recently. She had really taken to Glen, her pale thin face flushing with happy colour when he was there. Glen himself had assured her over and over again that his family would make her mother welcome, and even their doctor had told her that he thought a fresh start away from her sad memories would be good for her mother.

What kind of questions would the colonel, Glen's commanding officer, ask her? She knew her face would be on fire if he asked her if she loved Glen and intended to be a good wife to him. Glen had warned her that she would be asked about how fit she was to become an American citizen, and he had been told he would have to provide proof to show that he could support her after the war.

'Not that that will be any problem,' he had assured her, 'because we'll be living on the farm with my folks.'

It wasn't very comfortable sitting in the back of the Jeep, and Ruthie learned very quickly to hold on to the side of the vehicle to prevent herself from being bounced from side to side. By the time it came to a halt at the checkpoint to Burtonwood she was in such a fever pitch of nervous excitement that she no longer noticed her numb backside.

'Visitor for the CO, 720 Engineers,' the driver of the Jeep announced laconically.

'OK, take her through,' the guard responded.

Ten minutes later, when she was still in the Jeep being driven wherever it was she was supposed to go, between newly built hangars and all manner of other buildings, Ruthie was beginning to feel dizzy. It simply hadn't occurred to her that Burtonwood would be so huge. As big as a small town, she decided.

The driver finally brought the Jeep to a halt outside an anonymous-looking building. But not so anonymous that there wasn't a soldier with a gun standing protectively 'on guard' right outside the door, Ruthie noticed as the Jeep door was opened for her.

Even more alarming than the soldier on guard, though, was the way she was walked between the two straight-backed soldiers, as they marched towards the doorway, firmly saluting the guard.

'Person of one Miss Ruthie Philpott, safely delivered for the CO, Sarge,' the driver of the Jeep announced to the man coming out of the building.

'This way, miss.'

She was hardly being given time to draw breath, Ruthie reflected, and she still hadn't seen Glen.

'Excuse me,' she began timidly. 'I was just wondering ... my fiancé...'

'CO's office is two doors down, miss. Just take a seat, please, and I'll let him know you're here,' the sergeant told her without answering her.

'Miss Philpott?'

Ruthie jumped to her feet as the door opened and Glen's commanding officer stood looking down at her. He was tall, with iron-grey hair, and a different kind of American accent from Glen's.

'I'm Colonel Forbes, Private Johnson's commanding officer,' he introduced himself.

A little uncertainly, Ruthie shook the hand he extended.

'Please come in.'

'Glen told me that you'd be sending for me, to talk about us getting married,' Ruthie told him shyly as she took the seat he indicated and watched as he went round the large wooden desk and then sat down opposite her. 'I was hoping that he would be here.'

The colonel was frowning. 'There seems to have been some mistake,' he told her brusquely. 'This isn't about any wedding. The reason I asked for you to be brought here is much more serious than that.'

TWENTY-FIVE

'You're late, love,' Jess heard her mother call out from the kitchen sink as she opened the back door.

'Yes, I had to call round at Ruthie's. I promised her I'd tell her mother that she'd been taken off by some GIs.'

'What?'

'Only joking, Ma,' Jess laughed as her mother turned round. 'You should see your face; it's a picture. Ruthie's bin taken over to Burtonwood so that her Glen's CO can interview her to make sure she's good enough to marry a Yank.' Jess pulled a face to show what she thought of this.

'Well, I never did! That's a fine thing to happen to a decent English girl,' Jess's mother announced indignantly. 'Did you hear that, Colin?' she called out through the open kitchen door into the parlour, telling Jess without waiting for her husband to answer her, 'Billy's just called round to see your uncle. He got called to his first bomb this afternoon. Made Colin laugh his head off when he were telling him all about it, he did. Why don't you go in and say hello to Billy, love, and tell your uncle that I'm making a fresh pot of tea.'

Jess hesitated, but she knew her mother would start asking awkward questions if she acted like she didn't want to see Billy. Thought the sun shone out of his backside, her mum did. Taking a deep breath, she walked into the parlour.

'Mum said to tell you that she's making a fresh brew,' she told her uncle, bending to drop a kiss on the top of his head, before saying casually, 'Oh, hello, Billy. I didn't see you there.'

'Billy's just bin telling me about this bomb he dismantled this afternoon. Tell our Jess what you were saying about it blowing off, and making a real stink, Billy,' her uncle chuckled.

'Uncle Colin!' Jess protested, putting her nose in the air and pretending to look disapproving.

'Oh, go one wi' yer, you like a good laugh and you know it,' he chuckled.

'Aye, well, it stank like it were as ripe–' Billy began

'Billy...' Jess warned him

'It was your uncle as asked me to tell you about it,' Billy reminded her innocently. 'Anyway, what kept you? Your mam was just saying she won- dered where you'd got to.'

'I had to call round at Ruthie's to tell her mam that she'd bin taken up to Burtonwood to see Glen's commanding officer. Oh, and I never said, Ma,' Jess called out guiltily to her mother who was still in the kitchen, 'but Walter's bin in a bad fight.'

'Walter?' Her mother came bustling through to the parlour, wiping her hands on her pinny. 'What? A nice quiet lad like that, fighting?'

'Well, from what Ruthie was telling me it wasn't Walter's fault. Seems like he got set on by that GI wot's taken up with that Myra who Diane shares with.'

'Diane? Is she the one that got that funny drink

given her?'

'Yes, that's right, Mam. A really nice sort she is, a lady, but not a nose-in-the-air posh type. According to what Ruthie had to say, this Nick – that's this Myra's GI – had been caught cheating at cards by Walter, and he'd got a bit of a grudge against him on that account. Ruthie said she had never seen anything so scary in her life. And wot's worse, when the MPs arrived this Nick tried to make out that it was Glen who had bin the one wot started it all.'

'So how's Walter now?' Billy asked.

'Ruthie said she'd find out whilst she was up at Burtonwood.'

'He'll be all right, lass, don't you worry,' her stepfather offered comfortingly.

'Told you about his girl back home yet, has he?' Billy challenged her.

'That's between me and him and no one else,' Jess answered sharply.

'Exceptin' his girl back home,' Billy retorted.

'Our Jess would never take another girl's chap, would you, Jessie?' her mother defended her firmly.

'Well, are you going to tell us about how clever you were disposing of this bomb or not, Billy?' Jess demanded without answering her mother.

Billy gave a dismissive shrug. 'There weren't that much to it, really. It were only a little 'un. I reckon the sarge had kept it waiting there so as we could have a bit of a practice on it. Down by the allotments on Lansing Street, it was, right in a patch of ruddy nettles. Up to me backside in 'em, I were. You should see the stings I've got.'

371

Jess gave him a dark look, whilst her mother laughed and shook her head mock scoldingly, and told him affectionately, 'Give over with that teasing of yours, Billy, and tell us about the bomb.'

'I thought I was doing,' Billy responded with a wink at Jess's stepfather. 'Well, like I was saying, it was right in the middle of these ruddy nettles, and then when we'd got to it we had to dig down all around it, but careful, like. I mean, you don't want to go shoving a spade into one of them things.'

'Oh, Billy...' Jess heard her mother gasp as she went pale and put her hand to her mouth.

'No, it's all right, I'm only joking, Mrs H,' Billy reassured her quickly. 'What really happened is that them of us wot have just started with the section had to report to this bit of land wot the Royal Engineers keep specially for training new lads. They had this bomb there. Put it back together, they had, but with the TNT taken out and a bit of sand in instead. A one-hundred-kilogram bomb, this was – just a baby, really – and they have this fuse wot they call a number fifteen fuse, you see...'

Her parents were both silent as they absorbed what Billy was saying, leaving Jess free to look at him as well as listen. He was like a kid that had been given a new toy, she decided crossly, not someone who was dealing with something that might go off at any minute and kill him.

'This number fifteen fuse was the first one the Germans used. Nothing to it, there is, not really, not once you know how to deal with them. You

372

have to depress these two spring-loaded plungers wot are on the fuse head and then take out the fuse. We all had to have a go at doing it and the sergeant said as how I was the fastest.'

'Where are you going, Jessie?' Jess heard her mother ask as she headed for the door.

'I'm going up to me bedroom. I've got better things to do than listen to a lot of talk about bombs.'

Her heart was beating so fast Jess had to put her hand on her chest to calm it once she was out of sight. Just listening to Billy talking like that had made her feel so sick and frightened for him. Why did he have to take such risks? But that, she conceded, was Billy all over. And one of the reasons she felt the way she did about him.

'...And they've got this band at the Savoy, that's called the Orpheans, and you should have seen the frocks the women there were wearing, and the jewels. You'd never have thought there was a war on down there in London – not like up here. Nick wanted to go to Madame Tussaud's, but it was closed, but he showed me where the American Embassy was and we went to this club he'd heard about...'

Diane closed her eyes, wishing that Myra would leave her in peace. Her head was aching and her eyes felt as though they had had sand rubbed in them. She might have been the one to tell Lee that they could never be anything to one another, but today, a day without seeing him at all, had seemed to be one of the longest and most miserable days

373

of her life, even without what the captain had had to say to her.

'You're not listening to me, are you?'

Diane opened her eyes and looked across at Myra, her expression changing when she noticed the ring Myra was wearing for the first time.

'It's my new engagement ring,' Myra told her proudly. 'Nick gave it me before we left for London.'

It was the most vulgar-looking ring she had ever seen, Diane decided, but even if it hadn't been, she was worried Myra was getting herself in too deep.

'You can't mean to wear it in public at work, Myra,' she protested.

'Why not?' Myra demanded.

'Why not? Because you are already married to someone else,' Diane reminded her.

'That's finished, and I'm engaged to Nick now. Did I tell you about the frock he bought for me? Of course, it's too good to wear for going out up here, but it will come in handy when I'm sailing to New York. Oh, and here's your blouse back.'

As she handed it over, Diane saw that one of the buttons was loose, and that it had been torn from the fabric.

'Nick got a bit too keen,' Myra smirked without a trace of embarrassment or apology. 'You'll be able to mend it.'

Maybe she would, but she knew she could never bear to wear the blouse again, Diane decided, in distaste.

TWENTY-SIX

'What ... what do you mean?' Ruthie stammered. 'I don't understand.'

'I understand that you were a witness at the fight that took place between Privates Johnson and Stewart this last Saturday.'

'No. I mean, yes, I was there, but it wasn't Glen and Walter who were fighting, but Walter must have told you that. Glen said that he would as soon as he was well enough.'

The commanding officer looked at her with a very grave expression. 'Regrettably Private Stewart never recovered consciousness and died of his injuries shortly after his return to Burtonwood.'

Ruthie couldn't believe it. Her shock was so great that she felt it reverberating through her like a physical blow.

'Walter is dead? But he can't be,' she stammered in protest, unable to accept that someone as kind and gentle as Walter could possibly die in such a cruel and pointless way. 'He's going to be Glen's best man. He can't be dead.' She was shaking, she realised, tears springing to her eyes.

Colonel Forbes frowned down at the leather blotter on his desk. 'I'm sorry you've had such a bad shock, but I'm afraid it *is* the truth.'

Ruthie shook her head. 'I can't believe it ... poor Walter. He was so kind and so...' She had to bite down hard on her lip to stop herself from crying.

'It seems so unfair. He hadn't done anything wrong. Does Glen know?' she asked, her heart suddenly giving a trip beat as she registered the colonel's silence. 'Where is he?' she asked more anxiously. 'When can I see him?'

The commanding officer's mouth compressed. 'Private Johnson is in solitary confinement and under armed guard.'

'What! No ... you can't... But why?' Ruthie demanded piteously.

'Private Johnson stands accused of the manslaughter of Private Stewart and that is why–'

'No, no, that isn't true. Glen would never have hurt Walter. He was his friend. He tried to protect him.'

'I have a report here from the British police officers who were first on the scene, stating that both Private Johnson and Private Stewart had obviously been drinking. Is that correct? You were with them the morning before the fight, I understand. Is that true?'

'Yes. We'd gone to the church to see the vicar about ... about the wedding, and the vicar offered Glen and Walter a glass of elderberry wine, as a bit of a toast, like. Please, let me explain what really happened,' Ruthie begged the colonel, telling him before he could refuse, 'It wasn't Glen who hurt Walter, it was ... that other American who was there. Glen said he did it because Walter had caught him out cheating at cards.' Tears spilled from Ruthie's eyes whilst the commanding officer looked on impassively.

'If by "the other American" you mean Private Mancini,' the colonel said impassively, 'he came forward as soon as he heard about Private Stewart's death, to explain what he had witnessed. According to both him and the statements he and his girl gave to the police at the time, they happened upon the fight purely by chance.'

'That's not true,' Ruthie protested. 'He started it. He came round the corner and he saw poor Walter and then he just hit him.'

'Private Mancini just hit him. Just like that? For no reason? Come now, miss, I appreciate the fact that you want to protect Private Johnson, but you can't really expect me to believe any of this,' the colonel told her sternly. 'And I should warn you that even though you are not an American citizen, when Private Johnson is called before his court martial, it is more than likely that you will be obliged to appear as a witness, under American law. You will then be under oath and any lies–'

'I am not lying!' Ruthie interrupted him, her normal timidity overwhelmed by her anxiety for Glen. 'What I said is the truth. He ... Nick was the one to attack Walter. Why would Glen want to do such a thing anyway? He and Walter were friends.' If Walter wasn't alive any more to speak up for her Glen, then she would have to do so for him.

'This is the United States Army, miss, and here we take any accusations against our soldiers very seriously,' the colonel explained patiently. 'The whole of the platoon has been questioned about the relationship between these two privates, and I have to tell you that quite independently two men have come to me and told me that there had already been an argument between the two men over a poker game debt. Gambling is, of course, forbidden but that doesn't stop some of the men doing it. The reason it's forbidden is that it leads to exactly the kind of situation we have had here – men drinking and fighting, and ending up getting themselves in one hell of a lot of trouble. Now I'd like to take a statement from you, if you please, stating in your own words, exactly what happened, from the minute you first saw Privates Johnson and Stewart on Saturday.'

'Very well, but you won't make me say that it was Glen's fault and I won't be lying either,' Ruthie told him fiercely. 'Glen doesn't play cards for money. He told me that his parents don't approve of that kind of thing, and neither does he.'

Slowly and carefully, her voice trembling as she fought for the right words, she started to tell Glen's commanding officer what had happened. It wasn't easy. Several times she had to stop because she was too overcome by her emotions to continue.

'What ... what's going to happen to Glen? Those other soldiers didn't tell the truth, and it's because of them–'

The colonel was standing up. 'Thank you for your co-operation, Miss Philpott. My sergeant will see to it that you get a ride back home.'

As though by some sleight of hand, the office door opened and the sergeant was standing there waiting to escort her out.

Diane took a deep lungful of air. Walking past Chestnut Close's allotment might not have had

378

the same soothing effect as her favourite childhood walk through the Hertfordshire fields and
then along the river bank, but at this time in the
evening, when the air was still warm from the
sun, there was just enough scent of the countryside in it to make her feel that if she closed her
eyes she could almost be in the safe comfort of
her childhood home. And she needed that
comfort very badly at the moment. Apart from
anything else, she doubted that she could have
stood another minute of Myra's boastful description of her weekend in London. But was it wise
to give herself the opportunity to dwell on her
own feelings? She paused to lean on the gate that
led into the allotments. Beyond them a goods
train, heavily laden, chuffed slowly towards the
railing siding in Edge Hill, known locally as 'the
Grid Iron', sending thick white clouds of steam
up into the clear evening sky. They were well into
August now, but thankfully it would be the end
of October before the clocks went 'back', losing
them extra hours of daylight saving light. The
deprivations of living in a country at war were
somehow all the more hard to bear in the winter
months, with the darkness of the blackout at
night and the shortage of fuel with which to keep
warm. But maybe she should think forward to
the winter. Maybe by then she would have found
a way to deal with the heartache that was causing
her so much misery now. She was doing the right
thing, she knew that, but those who believed that
'doing the right thing' automatically outweighed
the pain of not being with the 'wrong' person had
no idea at all of how it really felt. Her whole body

ached with the most desperate longing for Lee. Even her skin yearned rebelliously for his touch, whilst her heart did a series of victory rolls at the mere thought of seeing him.

Why should she consider his wife, when the future was so very uncertain? Would she really miss those few, to Diane, precious days that might be all they could have together? Would her life be any the worse for Diane having had a small handful of moments to call her own? She need never know, and so could hardly miss them, whereas Diane would have them to cherish for as long as she lived, a precious gift, wrapped away like fading rose-scented love letters and locked in the most secret compartment of her heart. The Group Captain might have given her a direct warning that her and Major Saunders' relationship was already under scrutiny but everyone knew that there were ways and means by which a determined couple could be together without their intimacy being betrayed.

She opened the gate and walked into the allotments, unwilling to return to the house and Myra's unwanted company.

She was halfway along the narrow path that skirted round the allotments and then divided them between that part traditionally used for growing food and that smaller part on which, before the war, the allotment holders had created small gardens around the huts they used to store their tools. Slowly these gardens were now being converted into new vegetable beds, mainly planted with potatoes to break up the soil, but a handful still had their pretty gardens.

Out of the corner of her eye Diane noticed that someone was sitting huddled up in the corner of a bench in one of them. She was about to walk away, not wanting either to disturb them or to have them intrude on her own unhappy thoughts, when she realised that the other person was Ruthie and that she was obviously in great distress.

Not giving herself time to change her mind, she picked her way over to her, more shocked to see the look of bleak despair in her eyes than by the sight of her tear-blotched face.

'Ruthie, what's wrong?'

Ruthie started up guiltily, and then subsided back into her seat when she recognised Diane. She had come here to try to compose herself before she went home, but instead, she had ended up becoming totally overwhelmed by her distress.

'It's Glen,' Ruthie told her brokenly. 'He... Walter's dead and Glen's going to be court-martialled but it wasn't his fault.' She started to sob uncontrollably.

Worried, Diane sat down next to her, taking hold of her hand. 'Stop crying, take a deep breath and tell me properly what's happened,' she instructed her calmly, using the manner she would have used to a raw new recruit.

To her relief Ruthie did as she had told her, although it took many stops and starts before Diane was able to get the full story from her and make sense of it.

What Ruthie told her filled her not just with shocked disgust for Nick and Myra, but also with a deep sense of unease. She knew how things worked in the tightly controlled environment of rules and regulations that was the armed services, and just how difficult it would be to convince Glen's superiors that he was the victim of an injustice when his platoon mates were lying to protect Nick. It was obvious to Diane that Ruthie was telling the truth, and she suspected that initially, when they had lied to the police, Nick had assumed he would find some way of wriggling out of any charge brought for fighting with a comrade. Walter's death, though had altered things. Whoever was convicted would be facing the death penalty. Poor, poor Ruthie – no wonder she was distraught.

'Look, dry your eyes,' Diane told her.

'I can't tell Mum what's happened. She's really taken to Glen and she's been so much better since him and me got engaged. It's been like a bit of a miracle, and even our doctor has said how much she's improved. She hasn't gone out once looking for Dad, like she used to. I don't know what it's going to do to her if I have to tell her about Glen. It will be bad enough telling her about Walter.' Fresh tears filled her eyes. She turned to Diane, twisting her damp handkerchief between her fingers as she sobbed, 'Why did this have to happen? And that Myra – how could she lie like that?' Hope suddenly flared in her eyes. 'You wouldn't have a word with her, would you ... tell her what's happened to my Glen? Oh, please say that you'll help us?' she begged desperately.

Diane hated to disappoint her but knowing Myra as she did she doubted that Myra would agree to do anything that would damage her chances of getting to America. She couldn't bring herself to destroy Ruthie's hopes, though.

'I will speak to her,' she agreed, 'but only if you promise me that you'll stop crying and go home.'

'You mean it. You really will try to help us?' Ruthie breathed.

'I mean it,' Diane assured her.

'Promise?' Ruthie begged, suddenly more a little girl than a young woman. Her vulnerability tugged at Diane's own heart.

'I promise,' she agreed.

'I've just seen Ruthie,' Diane announced without preamble as she entered the shared bedroom.

'Ruthie, who?' Myra asked her. She was lying on her bed, smoking, her eyes narrowed in contemplation of the smoke ring she had just blown, but Diane wasn't deceived.

'You know perfectly well who I mean, Myra. That GI Nick beat up has died.'

Myra sat up, stubbing out her cigarette. 'You're lying!'

'I wish it wasn't true but it is. He died at Burtonwood – after you and Nick had left for London, having told the police that it was Glen who had been fighting with him.' She paused deliberately. 'But that wasn't true.'

'Is that what she told you? *Ruthie?* Because if it was–'

'Yes, Ruthie did tell me and I believe her.' Diane stopped her firmly. 'I saw the way Nick was behaving towards Walter at the Grafton, just in case you've forgotten. He's got a dreadful temper, Myra, and you can see just from looking at him that he's the kind who'd carry a grudge.

Glen and Walter were friends, everyone knew that, and by lying about what happened you could end up in an awful lot of trouble.'

What she was doing was rather underhand, Diane knew, but she soothed her conscience by telling herself that her not letting Myra know that Nick had somehow persuaded others to lie for him as well was in a good cause.

'If you ask me, him dying had nothing to do with Nick hitting him. I reckon that it was hitting his head on the pavement that must have done it, not him having a bit of a scrap with Nick.' Myra gave a small shrug. 'And that makes it just a bit of an accident. It could have happened to anyone.'

Diane breathed out slowly. 'Well, if that's the case then you need to tell the police about it, don't you?' she told her firmly. 'There's no sense in someone being blamed – wrongly – for Walter's death if it was an accident.'

'I'm not saying that was wot killed him, I'm just saying that it could have been,' Myra backtracked immediately. 'And besides, I've already given the police a statement. I can't go telling them that I want to change my mind now.'

'You could say that you got mixed up a bit,' Diane told her, refusing to give up. 'After all, with all that was going on, no one would be surprised by that.'

Myra looked at her speculatively. 'Why should you be so keen for me to do anything? After all, it's no skin off your nose what happens, is it?'

'No skin off my nose? I should have thought it would be a heavy weight on *your* conscience,

Myra, if a man got accused wrongly of killing another man because you hadn't told the truth.' Diane knew immediately that she had said the wrong thing.

'What do you mean, "accused of killing"? If you think I'm going to go saying something to the police that would get Nick into trouble–'

'You're the one who's going to be in trouble if you lie about what happened, Myra,' Diane warned her. 'After all, Ruthie was there as well, and she saw what happened too.'

'Much good that will do her.'

Diane looked at her. There was nothing for it, she was going to have to do something she had no desire to do at all, but she had no other option.

'Have you told Nick yet about Jim?'

The effect of her question was every bit as dramatic as she had guessed it would be. Myra leaped off the bed and reached for her cigarettes, her hand trembling as she lit one.

'If you're trying to threaten me–' she began.

'I was simply asking you a question,' Diane told her. 'You've talked non-stop about Nick and that rock he's given you,' she nodded in the direction of the ring Myra was wearing, 'so naturally I wondered if you've told him yet that by rights you should be wearing another man's wedding ring on that finger. That's what happens when you tell lies, Myra. They have a habit of coming back to haunt you when you don't want them to.'

For a moment Diane thought she had won and that Myra would give in and agree to tell the police what had really happened, but then to

Diane's disappointment she burst out angrily, 'Don't think I don't know what you're doing but it won't work. If you're that keen to get someone else blamed for that Walter's death it must mean that Glen is in a lot of trouble. Anyway, it's like Nick said to the police, we were just coming round the corner, minding our own business... And as for Jim, you go ahead and tell Nick if you want. It won't make any difference to him.'

Not now it wouldn't, Myra decided triumphantly, because with Walter dead that meant that Nick needed her to support his story. A wife couldn't give evidence against her husband – she remembered reading that somewhere or other. Nick had no option but to marry her now, she decided smugly, and Diane was a fool if she thought she was going to threaten her into changing her story.

Diane watched with a sinking heart the way Myra's expression changed. She had gambled and lost, she could see quite plainly. But she had promised Ruthie that she would help her, which left her with only one option. She would have to talk to Lee and ask him if there was anything he could do – perhaps speak to Glen's commanding officer on his behalf, or at least suggest that he looked more closely into the stories of the men supporting Nick's allegations that Glen and Walter had had a quarrel. Her heartbeat accelerated as though it was a plane on the runway and about to lift off on a dangerous mission. Or was it simply taking wing and soaring with joy at the thought of being with Lee, no matter how bleak the circumstances?

TWENTY-SEVEN

'If Major Saunders comes in today, I wonder if you would mind, please, giving him this note for me?' Diane tried to look far more composed and professional than she felt as she handed the sealed note she had spent so long agonising over last night to the duty sergeant on the desk in the foyer of Derby House.

The sergeant was eyeing her rather suspiciously. 'Would this be a personal letter?' he asked her disapprovingly. 'Because–'

'In a manner of speaking, yes, it is,' Diane smiled with what she hoped looked like frankness. 'Major Saunders was kind enough to provide me with the address of the young pilot who crashed out near Nantwich, so that I could write to his parents. I wanted to thank him.' The truth was that she wanted to see him but of course she wasn't going to tell the sergeant that.

The sergeant's expression was relaxing, the nod of his head almost approving, Diane noticed guiltily, but she had to keep her promise to Ruthie, didn't she?

Ten minutes later, when she stepped into the Dungeon, she was swept into more than enough work to keep Lee out of her mind, though, of course, it didn't. With each swing of the doors opening her concentration was broken as she looked up anxiously, hoping to see him.

The morning passed, she could barely eat her lunch, and then it was back to work, monitoring the positions of the Mosquito planes protecting the convoys. The minutes and then the hours ticked by and she was just on the verge of giving up hope when she looked up and saw him walking towards her.

'You wanted to see me?'

Diane nodded. 'But not here...'

There was a narrow corridor that led to a seldom-used storeroom.

There was no valid reason for either of them to be there, but Diane couldn't tell Lee what she needed to say in the middle of the busy Dungeon.

The minute they were on their own he started to reach for her, groaning, 'You don't know how much I've missed you. I don't know what's made you change your mind, but whatever it is...'

For a second Diane allowed herself the luxury of leaning close to him and letting herself daydream – but only for a second. Pushing herself away from him, she told him quickly, 'This isn't about us, and I have not changed my mind. In fact, the Group Captain has made it clear to me–' she broke off. There wasn't time for her to talk about their own situation.

'I don't know whether or not you've heard about it yet, but there was a fight in Liverpool over the weekend, as a result of which a young GI has died.'

'Yes, I've heard about it,' Lee frowned. 'But what's it got to do with us?'

'Nothing. That's what I'm trying to tell you, Lee. This isn't about us. Myra and Nick Mancini lied about what happened on Saturday. Myra has as good as admitted that to me, although she isn't prepared to say so publicly, and because of that an innocent man is being blamed for Walter's death.'

'What does this have to do with us?' he repeated

'Nothing, except that I've promised to do what I can to help Ruthie – that's Glen's fiancée. She was in a terrible state last night, having been taken up to Burtonwood thinking she was going to be interviewed by Glen's CO prior to him approving their wedding, only to find that her fiancé was under armed guard for the death of his best friend, because Nick Mancini has put pressure on some of his platoon buddies to support his claim that Glen and Walter fought over an unpaid gambling debt. The poor girl is distraught. The truth is, apparently, that Walter caught Nick cheating at cards and said so, and because of that Nick had a grudge against him. Glen's CO won't listen to Ruthie and, of course, none of the others are going to admit they are lying. You're the only person who can help them, Lee. You could speak to Glen's CO, let him know what's been going on and then he can–'

'Stop right there,' he told her sharply. 'First off, what you're asking me to do is against army protocol; second, you've only got this Ruthie's word for it that the others are lying; third, if you knew anything about the US Army you'd know that getting a decision overturned because it was based on a pack of lies that were accepted as truth is harder than turning base metal into gold.'

'Hang protocol! We're talking about a man's life here, Lee,' Diane protested. 'If Glen is found guilty he'll be facing the death penalty. We can't let that happen to an innocent man. You must see that.'

'Listen, what I see is that even if he is innocent – and I'm not saying that he is – even if his CO were prepared to listen to me and order a full inquiry, Mancini sure as hell isn't going to admit that he's lied and corrupted the truth by putting pressure on others to lie as well, when he knows if he does, *he's* the one who's going to be looking down the wrong end of a death sentence. That stands to reason.'

Diane knew that he had a point but she still persisted.

'The only way he can have persuaded the others to lie has to be by threatening them. They probably didn't realise when they agreed what they were doing to an innocent man. Lee, please.' Diane reached out pleadingly and put her hand on his arm.

To her shock he shook her off, his mouth tight-lipped with anger. 'When I got your note and I saw the way you looked at me when I came through to the Dungeon, all big eyes and soft lips like you wanted me so much it hurt, I thought you'd changed your mind about us, that you'd realised how precious and special what we could have together would be, but you were just putting it on, weren't you? All you wanted was to use me to help your friend. How far were you prepared to go to do that, Di? All the way to my bed?'

Overwhelmed by her feelings, Diane would

have slapped his face if he hadn't grabbed hold of her wrist.

'If you knew anything about me – anything at all – then you'd never say anything like that to me,' she told him passionately. 'You'd know too that sometimes a person shows their love more by what they do not do than what they do, and that loving someone sometimes means sacrificing your own feelings for their protection. If I wanted to help Ruthie it's because I know how I would feel if I were in her shoes and the man I love was in Glen's.'

Lee had relaxed his grip of her wrist and she pulled herself free of him, turning on her heel to walk away.

She had almost reached the end of the corridor when she heard him say rawly, 'God dammit to hell, Di,' followed by the sound of him walking swiftly towards her.

She didn't turn round because she couldn't. She was too afraid to let him see what was in her eyes. She felt his hands on her shoulders and stiffened as he turned her round, and then kissed her almost savagely.

'No,' she began but it was too late, her body was already saying 'yes'.

Lee was breathing as though he'd run a race when he finally released her and she knew her own heartbeat was ragged with the intensity of her emotions, as she clung to him, torn between her need to be with him and her need to punish herself for giving in to it.

'OK, I'll see what I can do,' he promised her, adding, 'I can't give you up, Di, and I don't intend to. We need to talk properly.'

'Not here,' Diane objected. 'We can't.'

'No... Look, what about meeting up at that dance place the day after tomorrow?'

'The Grafton, you mean?'

'Yeah.'

Diane nodded.

TWENTY-EIGHT

'Jess, I need to talk to you.'

The quiet desperation in Ruthie's voice made Jess frown. What on earth was wrong? Surely Glen's CO hadn't refused to let them get married?

'Go on then,' she encouraged her as she finished pushing her hair up out of the way, ready for work.

'I meant in private,' Ruthie whispered, glancing over her shoulder.

'Well, let's hang on here a minute until the coast is clear, then,' Jess suggested, waiting until the others had left the cloakroom before saying, 'OK, what is it?'

'It's Walter. He's dead.'

Jess stared at her in shocked disbelief. 'He can't be,' she protested. 'You told me he'd just been knocked about a bit. How can he be dead?'

'He is. He died at Burtonwood,' Ruthie insisted. 'That's what Glen's CO wanted to see me about, not ... not me and Glen getting married. He wanted me to make a statement, because ...

because he says that it's because of Glen that he died.'

Whilst Jess stared at her in disbelief, fresh tears spilled from Ruthie's eyes, swiftly followed by the words spilling from her lips as she told Jess what had happened.

'You mean that that Myra deliberately lied?' Jess's voice was sharp with incredulous anger. 'By golly, if she were here right now I'd be letting her know what I think of her.'

'Diane has said that she'll have a word with her and try to get her to tell the truth.'

'Huh...' Jess began, about to say in no uncertain terms just what chance she thought Diane had of succeeding, when she saw the strain in Ruthie's eyes. There was no point in upsetting her even more, she decided. The poor kid was having a hard enough time of it as it was. For herself, it was only just beginning to sink in what had happened and that Walter was dead.

'Poor Walter. I think I need to sit down for a bit,' she confided to Ruthie. She may not have loved Walter in the way that Ruthie loved Glen, but she had liked him and she had thought of him as a friend – a good friend. She raised her hand to wipe the back of it over her eyes and brush away her tears. Who would tell Walter's girl? She hoped that someone would. She pictured herself getting a letter telling her that Billy was dead, that he had died whilst she had been going about her own daily business and she hadn't known anything about it. A feeling gripped her like someone twisting a sharp knife inside her chest. It was so intense that she actually lifted her hands to her chest and pressed them against it. What a truly dreadful thing to have happened. And poor Ruthie, to have to cope with hearing that, because of other people's lies, her Glen was going to be accused of causing Walter's death.

Jess was still grappling with her shock an hour later as she went through the motions of filling her shells, her movements automatic and neatly efficient. Unlike Ruthie's, she recognised, as she looked up from her own work to see Ruthie's hands trembling so much that she spilled some of the TNT.

Going over to her, she told her gently, 'Come on, let's get this wiped up, otherwise you'll end up with burns.'

''Ere, have you heard the latest?' Mel interrupted them excitedly, ignoring the warning look that Jess was trying to give her to alert her to the fact that Ruthie needed a bit of peace and quiet. 'They're going to search everyone's locker, on account of that Alice's watch going missing. Mind you, I'm not surprised. I told the foreman meself that I thought they ought ter do summat like that. They announced it whilst you two were still in the cloakroom. Said that we all had to line up at dinner whilst they went through everyone's locker. Cor, look at you,' she laughed when she saw Ruthie's white face. 'One look at you and they'll have *you* pegged down as guilty and no mistake.'

'Give over, will you, Mel,' Jess told her sharply. 'Can't you see that Ruthie's got enough to worry about? Not that she's any need to worry about

Alice's ruddy missing watch. We all know that Ruthie wouldn't take it.'

Mel sniffed and tossed her head in the air. 'Well, as to that...'

Before she could say any more, the foreman walked onto the shop floor, accompanied by one of the managers. Automatically all the girls stopped working.

The manager looked angry, and his voice was sharp and clipped as he informed them, 'A theft has been reported, and since we treat this as a very serious matter, a thorough search of everyone's locker and outdoor clothes pockets will now be conducted. For this purpose you will all go to your lockers and stand in front of them whilst the foreman and I open them and check their contents.'

Immediately a low buzz of speculative conversation broke out amongst the girls, swiftly silenced by the manager, ordering them into single file to march out into the yard and then across to their cloakroom area.

Each worker was made to line up opposite her locker and face it whilst the manager went down the line, one worker at a time, demanding her key and then unlocking her locker and searching through it.

It was a laborious process, and there was an uproar when, halfway through it, the foreman announced that because of the time lost they wouldn't get a proper break.

Ruthie's locker was the next to be inspected. Not that she cared. She was too wrapped up in her despair over Glen to think about anything else. Numbly she handed over her key, watching obediently as the locker was opened and the bag containing her personal belongings removed.

There was nothing there should not have been amongst them, and the manager was just on the point of putting the bag back when he stopped and frowned, holding it in one hand whilst he reached deep into the locker with the other.

'What's this?' he demanded ominously, holding up to Ruthie the box filled with packets of sugar, which he had removed.

Automatically Ruthie looked at Maureen, but the other girl was refusing to look back at her. Ruthie could feel her face starting to burn.

'I ... I...' She swallowed hard. What could she say. It was obvious that the sugar was black-market goods, and not just one packet but a whole boxful.

Jess looked on indignantly, willing Ruthie to tell the manager that it wasn't her who had put the sugar in her locker, but Maureen, but to Jess's dismay, Ruthie looked too shocked and distressed to think of defending herself.

'I'll see you about this in my office later,' the manager told Ruthie grimly before handing the sugar over to the foreman for safekeeping and going on to the next locker.

Miserably Ruthie watched as the manager moved on down the line.

'Why didn't you tell him that you was the one who put that ruddy sugar there, instead of letting Ruthie take the blame?' Jess hissed angrily to Maureen.

''Oo says I did?' Maureen returned challengingly, lifting her hand to scratch at the raised rash of red lumps on her wrist. Jess stared at them, her eyes widening as she remembered Alice saying that her watch had made her itch, but before she could say anything to Maureen the foreman was ordering them to get back to work.

It was only when they were all back at their benches that Jess realised that Ruthie was missing. At first she assumed that she had gone to the ladies'; but when five and then ten minutes went by without her returning, she began to worry, remembering how shocked and distressed the other girl had been.

'Ruthie's gone missing,' she told the others. 'I'm going to go and look for her, so cover for me, will you? And as for you,' she told Maureen sharply, 'if I were Alice I'd be asking to compare that rash on me wrist with the one you've got on yours.'

Maureen's face turned a dark shade of red, but Jess didn't stay to argue with her. She really was worried about Ruthie.

The girls weren't supposed to leave the factory during their shift without permission, but no one had tried to stop Ruthie as she stumbled across the yard and out through the gate in a state of anguished shock. It felt as though her whole world had been turned upside down and all the happiness Glen had brought into it extinguished. Her sensitive nature made her shrink in shamed distress from the notoriety she knew she would gain from the sugar being found in her locker. It would be almost as bad as actually being branded a thief. But nothing like as bad as what had happened to Glen. Tears filled her eyes as she wandered aimlessly down the street, not knowing where she was going and not caring either, just knowing that she couldn't bear to stay at the factory with everyone talking about her behind her back.

Jess saw her from the factory gate and called out her name, but Ruthie simply kept on walking. Jess hesitated. By rights neither of them should have left the factory and they would both be in trouble if they were found out, but Ruthie, of course, would be in the worst trouble because of the sugar. She needed to come back and be persuaded to tell the manager who had really put the sugar there. Jess glanced back towards the factory gates. She could always tell the foreman that Ruthie hadn't been well and had had to go home. He would guess the truth, of course, but at least it sounded better than having it discovered that she had just walked out. And she would be there to tell him about the sugar. She took a step back towards the gate. Ruthie had almost reached the end of the road. She looked so forlorn and vulnerable. She would be crying her eyes out and worrying herself sick about her Glen. She wasn't really in any fit state to be on her own.

Jess shook her head as though regretting her own folly, and set off after her.

'I'm not going back, Jess. I can't... Not with them all thinking ... what they will be thinking.'

'Well, whose fault is that? You should have told the manager about Maureen.'

'How could I? It wouldn't have been right.'

'Of course it would. Do you think she'd keep mum to protect you?' Jess challenged her. 'Oh, come on then.' She gave in when she saw how genuinely ill Ruthie looked. 'Let's get you home. Then I'll go back and tell the foreman that you were taken bad.'

'You don't have to go with me,' Ruthie protested.

'Not half, I don't,' Jess told her bluntly. 'You should see yourself. You look as sick as a cat.'

Jess was on the bus on her way back to the factory, having seen Ruthie safely home, when they heard the explosion. A dull crump, followed by a series of sharp ear-shattering bangs that caused the bus driver to stop the bus and the passengers to fling themselves to the floor.

'Bloody hell!' the large woman who had been sitting next to Jess puffed seconds later, as they all got apprehensively to their feet. 'Ruddy Hitler's getting a cheek on him, bombing us during the ruddy day...'

'It ain't Hitler, it's the ruddy munitions factory,' someone else called out.

'Look.'

All the passengers crowded to the side of the bus and looked towards the factory where they could see flames and smoke pouring from part of the building.

Jess's heart slammed into her ribs. Her friends were in that factory. Automatically she started to push her way past the other passengers to get to the bus door.

''Ere, mind where you're putting yer feet,' one woman objected.

'I've got to get to the factory. I work there,' Jess told her frantically.

'Sorry, miss, but you can't do that,' the conductor informed her, blocking, her exit. 'ARP'll have the whole place cordoned off by now, just in case Hitler has dropped a bomb on it. Course, if you ask me it's more likely to be one of them fifth columnist spies wot's done it,' he announced, referring to the news items they had all read concerning Hitler's spies within the country. 'Must have infiltrated the place, like we're allus being warned, and then gorn and blown it up.'

''Ere, my niece works up there,' another passenger said worriedly, followed by two more saying anxiously that they had family there too.

By now the whole bus was in an uproar, with the conductor barring the exit and saying that it would be more than his job was worth to let anyone get off.

'Don't be daft,' someone protested, but the screams of sirens as fire engines raced past them towards the factory, followed by police, proved his point that no mere civilians would be allowed close to the place.

One of the passengers started to cry noisily, but all Jess could do was stare blindly towards the smoke and flames.

'I left me overalls in me locker, and there'll be hell to pay if they get damaged,' she told the woman standing next to her. 'Dock me wages for them, they will.'

'Sit down for a minute, love,' the woman told

her in a kind voice, adding gently, 'You've had a nasty shock, I dare say. Lucky you wasn't up there, if you ask me.'

Jess shook her head. The munitions factory was huge, and all the workshops separated from one another just in case of any kind of accident or incident. Everyone who worked there knew how dangerous the TNT was and how little chance they would have of surviving if their workshop ever took a direct bomb hit.

Another fire engine raced past the stationary bus, followed by an army lorry.

'I expect they'll have the bomb disposal lot up there. Bound to get them, if you think about it,' one man commented knowledgeably. 'I wouldn't do their ruddy job for all the tea in China, I wouldn't. A lad down the road from us was wi 'em. Lasted four weeks, he did. Blown to bits. Told his mam that all they'd found were his little finger.'

Jess made a strangled sound deep in her throat. Please don't let them send Billy there, she prayed. Please, please don't let them.

'Where the 'ell do you think you're going?' the conductor demanded as she wriggled past him before he could stop her.

''Ere, you come back,' he yelled after her as she started to walk and then run towards the factory, but of course she didn't pay any attention to him.

The ARP wardens, aided by the police, were turning back everyone who tried to get close to the factory, warning them that as yet they had no idea what had caused the explosion. The factory had obviously been evacuated because Jess could see where, on the other side of the road, the women were standing huddled together in their overalls.

'Well, it weren't no bomb being dropped,' Jess heard one man saying firmly as she wriggled her way to the front of the crowd gathered at the end of the street. 'Mind you, I can't say I'm surprised. What else does the bloody government expect if it lets a load of daft women loose with explosives,' he added with contempt.

Several of the other men in the crowd were agreeing with him until one of the ARP men stepped forward and told them grimly, 'That's enough of that kind of talk. My youngest works in munitions and ruddy hard work it is, an' all. And I'll tell you now, mate, without our womenfolk doing their bit, our lads wouldn't have no shells to fire at ruddy Hitler, and that's a fact. If you think it's so easy then how come you're out here gawking and not working in there yourself?'

'Here, there's no call to go on like that,' the other man retaliated, quite plainly wrong-footed. 'I can't go doing no work like that. Got a bad leg, I have.'

The crowd, ready to side with him a few seconds earlier, had now turned against him, its low murmur of anger growing louder as everyone looked towards him, giving Jess the chance to slip past the ARP warden and dash behind the nearest fire engine.

'Here, love, you can't go in there,' one of the firemen called out as he caught sight of her, but Jess had gone before he could reach her.

Her heart was pounding sickly. The air was full

of smoke and the smell of TNT. The factory gates, normally closed unless deliveries or collections were due, stood wide open, and there was no one in the small guardroom by the gate the girls used to get in and out of work.

Several fire engines were drawn up close to the shed where Jess had worked, soaking it with arcing plumes of water to try to put out the flames.

Dodging the busy men, Jess finally made it to where the munitions workers were standing.

'I work in number three shed,' she told them, demanding anxiously, 'What's happened?'

'Number three shed?' one of the women responded. 'Well, you won't be working there no more, love,' she told her. 'Blown sky high, it's bin. And as to what happened, you know as much as the rest of us, doesn't she, Doris?' she asked the woman standing next to her, raising her voice above the sounds of the hoses and the running engines, and men shouting commands.

'Oh, aye, that's right. Mind you, I've just heard summat about one of them women working there starting it all by sneaking out for a smoke. Chucked her fag down when she thought she were going to get caught by the foreman, right into some ruddy TNT.'

Jess knew, of course, that what she was being told was only supposition but, even so, a chill of horror ran down her spine. One small explosion of TNT would have led to more and bigger ones, and the girls in the shed wouldn't have had a chance, especially if it was true and the girl who had caused the initial explosion had been standing just outside the doorway. Unwanted and violent images were already forming inside her head, the faces of those she knew she would never see again, not laughing and joking as she knew them but instead contorted with horror and fear, knowing what they were facing. How many seconds of that terror had they had before that final explosion that had blown them to pieces? Ten? Twenty? She had gone icy cold but sweat was pouring down her body. And what if there hadn't been one final explosion but several smaller ones, whilst they ran screaming and desperate, seeking some way of escape...?

As though she had read her thoughts, Mabel suddenly told her grimly, 'Lord knows but they must have bin desperate, trapped inside there. I know how I would have felt. We was in number five shed when we heard the explosion and our foreman had us outta of there that fast, and thank God he did.'

'I heard one of the women from six shed saying as how she'd heard that they was taking women down to the ambulances wot had tried to get through the fire. She said that they was coming all on fire and that their skin was hanging off their bones, and that the smell...'

Jess put her hand to her clammy forehead. She felt sick and faint and filled with a huge, furious burning anger. She lurched away from the women, ignoring their calls to come back as she dodged past an ARP man, who had turned away to talk to an exhausted fireman.

'Called in the bomb disposal lot, they have. Much good they can do,' Jess heard the fireman saying grimly. 'If this fire gets round to that shed where they've got all them shells stocked the whole of ruddy Liverpool will be going up in smoke.'

'We was told they'd brought in as many lorries as they can to get them shells out,' the ARP man was saying.

'Aye, well, they've sent the bomb disposal lot round that side. Rather them than me. They'll be the first to cop it if the fire spreads over there. If we get a ruddy early onshore evening wind, that will be it. It will fan the flames and we'll have no chance.'

The bomb disposal men. That meant Billy.

Oblivious to everything and anyone else, Jess started to make her way round to the storage area for the shells, muttering under her breath as she did, 'That Billy, he's got no more sense than to go and try to be a ruddy hero. What does he know about TNT or shells? All he'll be thinking about is going down the Grafton and telling some daft girl about how he saved the munitions factory. Huh, how he blew himself to bits, more like, although how he's going to be telling anyone that once he's gone and got himself killed I don't know...'

The men working to control the blaze were too busy to notice her, and her knowledge of the factory enabled her to reach the shed where the shells were stored without being stopped.

As she rounded the corner of one of the other sheds and looked towards it, she came to an abrupt halt. Where she had expected to see the familiar sight of several of the factory buildings, there was now only rubble and an empty space into which fire hoses were pumping arcs of water.

On the other side of this devastation she could see where several men, wearing the insignia of the Royal Engineers, were grouped together. One of them was bending over, fastening his shoe laces.

Jess's heart turned over slowly and painfully inside her chest. It was Billy, she was sure it was, but she still didn't let her breath out until he straightened up. A huge rolling wave of relief picked her up, carrying her with it so that she had no awareness of running towards the men, no awareness of sobbing out Billy's name, no awareness of anything at all really until Billy turned round and then started to run towards her, snatching her up and then holding her so tightly that she could hardly breathe whilst he said chokily over and over again, 'Ruddy hell, Jess ... ruddy hell. I thought you was dead.'

He kept on hugging her tightly whilst Jess hugged him equally tightly back. She could taste the salt of his tears mingling with her own and see the tracks they had made on his smoke-blackened face.

'Ruddy, ruddy hell ... Jess,' he kept on saying brokenly until she told him breathlessly, 'Give over saying that, will you?'

'I thought you was in that number three shed,' he told her. 'I thought you was gone like them other poor things.'

'Poor things. Daft things, more like, for getting themselves killed like that,' Jess contradicted him angrily. 'Why did they have to go and let summat like that happen to them? I only have to turn me back for a couple of hours, and they go and get themselves killed.' She could feel the anger bubbling up hotly inside her, like jam in her mam's jam-making pan, suddenly boiling upwards in a surge of unstoppable fury. Deep down inside herself she knew that what she was feeling was unreasonable but somehow she couldn't stop the angry words from spilling out whilst Billy held her as though he would never let her go.

'There must have been a couple of them wot's alive, Billy,' she pleaded, 'and that had the sense to get out in time?'

His arms tightened round her, giving her the answer before his gruff, 'I'm sorry, Jess.' He wiped one hand across his eyes whilst still holding on to her with the other.

'I thought you were dead, an' all, I really did. Felt like me own life was over, I did,' he told her hoarsely. 'Didn't seem as though there was any point to it any more wi'out you to scrap with. You must have had someone up there looking out for you – ruddy hell, you must,' he swore, looking skywards meaningfully.

'It was on account of Ruthie. I had to take Ruthie home. She had an upset,' Jess stumbled over the words and then broke off and pulled back from him, fresh tears filling her eyes.

'Oh, Billy, I'd almost forgotten. Poor Walter ... he's dead.' The way Billy was looking at her hurt her physically for him. 'It's all right,' she heard herself telling him shakily. 'Me and Walter, we were only friends really, but I still feel on his account, dying like that after he'd been beat up by that Myra's GI. Oh, that poor girl he was

407

sweet on, Billy. I hope that someone thinks to let her know what's happened to him.' She shivered, despite the heat from the still burning fires.

''Ere, Billy, stop that canoodling and get yourself over here. Orders are we're to get back to base, seeing as there's nowt else we can do here now that they've got the last lorryload of shells out of the way,' one of the other men called out.

Immediately Billy's hold on Jess tightened as though he didn't want to let her go.

'You'd better do as he says.' Jess gave him a little push and, disengaging herself from him, suddenly started to feel more like her normal self.

'And you'd better take yourself off back home. Your mam will be at her wits' end worrying about you,' Billy reminded her with a sternness with was almost proprietary. And she realised how much she liked it.

TWENTY-NINE

Diane tried not to think of the reason for the acrid taste in the air as she walked up the path to her digs. A sombre mood of mourning had enveloped the whole city following the explosion at the munitions factory, and it seemed that everyone you spoke to knew someone who had died in that inferno. Every day one heard heart-rending stories of young children who had been left without mothers, parents left without daughters, husbands without wives and serving men without sweethearts.

'Here, there's a letter for you,' Myra told her as she walked into the kitchen. Taking the envelope, Diane turned her back on her without speaking. Myra had made several attempts at getting her to act as though nothing had happened, but Diane was too disgusted by what she had done to want to have anything to do with her.

'Still on your high horse, are you?' Myra sniffed now. 'Well, suit yourself then.' When Diane didn't respond she added sharply, 'Anyway, I don't see why you get so hot under the collar about something that doesn't affect you.'

Diane put down her letter and turned round. 'When someone tells the kind of lies that mean that an innocent man's whole future is put at risk, then it affects everyone who knows about it, whether or not they are personally involved,' she told her curtly, adding in exasperation when Myra shrugged sullenly and turned away from her, 'Doesn't it mean anything to you that Glen is being accused of something that was nothing to do with him because of your lies?'

'I never said I'd told any lies,' Myra denied. 'It's you that's said that.'

Refusing to respond, Diane picked up her letter and headed for the stairs. Myra was quite plainly already dressed for going out for the evening, which suited her because she was going out herself – to the Grafton to meet up with Lee. Her heart thudded with guilty excitement.

Her letter was from her mother, which rather surprised her because she didn't normally write

409

mid-week. She sat down on her bed and opened it, quickly scanning the first few lines almost absently and then staring at the letter in disbelief, as she went back to the beginning and read it again.

Darling, I have thought long and hard about telling you this but your father and I have talked it over and we feel that we can't not tell you.

Kit came to see us over the weekend. Of course, your father was all for refusing to let him step over the threshold to begin with but in the end he gave way.

Kit asked us to pass on to you his apologies for the pain he caused you. He said he couldn't explain himself fully to us without having explained himself fully to you first, which of course we could both understand. However, he did say that there is an explanation he wants to make to you and an apology he needed to give to you.

Oh, my dear, if you had seen him. He was still very much our dear familiar Kit and yet at the same time he has changed, become more thinking and less carefree, I would say, more a man who has gone through the awful experience of war with all that that means rather than a boy who sees it as a kind of great adventure.

He asked – so humbly and sweetly that it moved me almost to tears I have to admit – if we would give him your address so that he could write to you. Your father and I talked this over and we decided that we could not do that without asking you first what you yourself wanted. We know how hard these past few months have been for you and what you must have suffered, even though you have been so very brave and kept this to yourself.

We cannot advise you, darling, your dear old parents who have never had to face what you modern young people are having to live with day in and day out. Daddy and I both liked Kit very much, but what is important to us is that our darling girl is happy, and that when she marries it is to a man who puts her happiness before everything and anything else. My feeling as a mother is that your happiness is more important to me than anything else. You have not said so to us but as your mother I have detected in your recent letters a certain note of light-heartedness I was beginning to fear you had lost for ever, and I have wondered if this is because you have met someone special.

Much as we like Kit, it is you, my darling, who is closest to our hearts. If you want us to give Kit your address then that is what we shall do. If you don't then you may be sure that we shall respect that.

Your loving mother

Diane's hands had started to tremble.

She put the letter down on the bed and walked over to the small window, looking out of it but not seeing anything other than the images forming inside her head – Kit's face, Kit's smile... She closed her eyes, but now she could hear his voice, soft with love, warm with laughter ... and cold with rejection, she reminded herself fiercely. She opened her eyes. She must not give in to sentiment and let Kit back into her life. He had hurt

411

her so badly ... so very badly. What was to say that he would not do so again if she was foolish enough to let him? And besides, what about Lee? Lee, whom she was due to meet at the Grafton in less than a hour, she reminded herself firmly, picking up her mother's letter and putting it back in its envelope.

The queue outside the Grafton had started to move forward. Jess reached for Ruthie's hand and held on to it tightly. Neither of them had wanted to come here tonight, the night they had planned to celebrate Alice's birthday, but both Ruthie's neighbour and Jess's parents had insisted firmly that they must.

'It's the only way, lass,' Jess's stepfather had said gently. 'I know how much the loss of them as you worked with grieves you, Jessie girl, but sitting at home cryin' won't bring them back. Life is for livin', Jess, and, ruddy hell, that's what we all have to do these days. Look at them wot's just gone...'

'Don't, Uncle Colin,' Jess had protested, her eyes red from the hours she had spent crying.

'Your uncle's right, Jess,' her mother had backed him.

'I can't go out dancing with them not even in their graves yet – what's left of them,' Jess had stormed.

'I'm not saying that it is not right and proper that you should mourn them,' her stepfather had told her, 'but what I say is that from now on it's up to you to do their living for them, Jessie. And that's a big responsibility. But if anyone can take on that responsibility then it's you. It will need a strong pair of shoulders to carry them with you through life, lass, and a big strong heart to go with them. The day you get wed, the day you hold your first kiddie in your arms, those days you'll be thinking of them young lasses that will never do those things, and in a way you'll be doing it for them and in honour of them. That's what happens in wartime, Jess. Them wot dies can only live on in the memories and the living of them wot lives. So you just dry your eyes and go out there and dance for them all, my girl, because that's the very best thing you can do for them.'

It wasn't just them feeling the sombreness of what had happened, Jess acknowledged, as she looked at the shadowed expressions of the others going into the dance hall. And what about poor Ruthie, standing next to her? She might have survived but her Glen was still accused of Walter's death. She reached for Ruthie's hand and squeezed it.

'I feel awful coming here,' Ruthie told her emotionally. 'It seems so wrong.'

'I know,' Jess agreed, 'but we have to do it for Alice, Ruthie, and especially all those lost souls. How's your mother taken it?'

Ruthie gave her a weary look. 'She's bin bad but not as bad as she could have bin. She hasn't been doing any of that going out wandering around looking for Dad, but she was sitting in her chair last night, just rocking to and fro, and staring into space just like she did when we first lost Dad. She keeps asking for Glen as well. She's got it into her head that he was at the munitions factory. She

413

was asleep when I came out. I wasn't going to come, but Mrs Brown said that I should.'

Jess squeezed her hand sympathetically, wondering whether or not to say what she was thinking.

'You know, Jess,' Ruthie told her huskily, 'I can't help thinking about that watch of Alice's and how it went missing and wondering...'

Jess squeezed her hand more tightly. 'I've bin thinking exactly the same thing meself,' she admitted. 'And you know what else? I reckon I know who stole it.'

Ruthie stared at her.

'I've bin thinking about it a lot. I reckon it was Maureen.'

'No! She wouldn't,' Ruthie denied, but even as she spoke she knew deep down inside herself that Jess could be right.

'She was scratching at her wrist, wasn't she, just like Alice had been doing, and, well, I allus thought there was summat a bit "off". Look at the way she let you tek the blame for that stuff she'd got hid in your locker.'

'But even if she stole Alice's watch she would never have taken it into the cleanway,' Ruthie protested.

'No, not deliberately, but mebbe summat happened and she had no choice, or she forgot about it. I'm not saying what happened were on account of her, mind, I'm just saying that I wouldn't be surprised.'

It was a horrible thought but Ruthie couldn't deny that it was a possibility.

'So you did come. I was just about to give up on you.'

Diane whirled round. 'Lee!' And then wished she hadn't as she realised how close her small movement had brought her to him.

'Watch out,' he warned her, as he reached out, placing his hand on her shoulder to draw her out of the path of a group of men making their way to the bar.

'Do you know how much I wish that right now I had you all to myself?'

'You mustn't say things like that to me,' Diane protested.

'No? Then what should I say? What a surprise, Wilson. I never expected to see you here.'

'We shouldn't be here together like this, Lee,' Diane told him huskily. 'We both know that.'

'No, we shouldn't,' he agreed, surprising her. Immediately she looked up at him and then realised her mistake when he bent his head and whispered to her, 'We should be somewhere on our own.' He lifted his hand to tuck a stray curl of hair off her face and his fingertips stroked the soft flesh just below her ear, making her shudder. He leaned closer to her. 'Somewhere where I could take you to bed,' he added softly, stroking his knuckles gently along the vulnerable skin of her bare throat.

'Lee. Don't!' she begged him, almost choking on the words.

'Don't what?'

'You know what,' she told him emotionally.

'I've booked us a room for the weekend,' he told her abruptly.

415

Diane stared at him, not believing what he'd just said. 'Where...?' That wasn't what she had intended to say at all! And she had no idea why she had said it.

'A small inn tucked away in one of those Cheshire villages we drove through.'

'You were very sure of yourself, weren't you?' she challenged him whilst she struggled to come to terms with what was happening.

'I've always been sure of myself where you're concerned. Sure of my feelings for you and how much I want you,' he responded.

Why was she hesitating? It wasn't because of her mother's letter, was it? Because of *Kit*? Deliberately Diane hardened her heart against her ex-fiancé, reminding herself of how much he had hurt her. If she really meant what she had said about not letting him back into her life then perhaps she *should* spend the weekend with Lee. She would never be able to go back to Kit if she did. Her bridges would have been well and truly crossed then, and not just crossed but burned behind her as well. Inside her head she could hear her father's voice and see her mother's smile. They had liked Kit so much, welcomed him into the family, looked forward to him becoming their son-in-law, and now he had been to see them and... She looked at Lee and took a deep breath.

'When ... when do we leave?' she asked him bravely.

She could feel his hand tightening on her arm and see the hunger in his gaze.

'Bring a case with you on Friday. We'll leave as soon as your shift finishes. That will give us the whole weekend together,' he told her hoarsely.

'No one must see us leaving together,' Diane warned him.

He frowned. 'The way I feel about you isn't some hole-in-the-corner affair, Di.'

'Maybe not, but you are married.'

'Yeah, and to the wrong woman.'

The conversation was going down a route she didn't want it to take. She started to shake her head, but before she could say anything Lee drew her closer.

'Let's dance,' he suggested.

Diane nodded, unable to speak.

'You haven't said yet whether or not you managed to talk to Glen's colonel,' Diane reminded Lee ten minutes later, sitting opposite him and lifting her drink with one hand whilst beneath the tabletop she held Lee's hand with her other.

'No, I wanted to talk about us first,' Lee replied. 'I did speak to him though.'

'And?' Diane begged him anxiously, her hopes rising.

'He's a colonel and the guy's commanding officer, Di, whilst I'm merely a major.'

She sank back into her seat, trying to contain her disappointment for Ruthie.

'However...' Lee looked at her and squeezed her hand, 'I guess after what you said to me I kinda put myself on the line a bit and pressured Hal more than he really liked, but in the end he agreed that the matter needed looking into and the two guys who gave evidence have been approached.'

'Oh, Lee.' Diane's eyes were sparkling with delight and pride. 'I knew you'd be able to do something,' she told him.

'You've got a hell of a lot more faith in me than I have in myself. However, like I said to Hal, we can't afford to make the mistake of accusing and then punishing an innocent man and letting a guilty man go free, even if it does mean having to wade through some pretty messy stuff to get to the truth. Will you quit looking at me like that?' he mock complained. 'First you get me so turned on on the dance floor that I can't walk without looking like I'm suffering from a war wound.'

Diane giggled.

'And now the way you're looking at me is making me wish I'd booked that room for tonight.'

'The weekend's only two more days away,' Diane whispered shakily. Right now she was feeling that she didn't want to wait herself. Dancing with Lee, feeling his body pressed hard against her own, snuggling up to him whilst he took advantage of the lower lights over the dance floor to slide his hands down over her back and then back up against whilst he kissed her, had reaffirmed everything she already knew about the way her body felt about him.

'Two days,' Lee groaned. 'Hell, right now two hours is one hour fifty too long.'

'Now, I *know* that you're exaggerating,' Diane told him, trying to sound stern, but laughing instead, as she instructed him, 'Tell me about Glen.'

Lee groaned again. 'You Brits sure are hard-hearted women. Here I am, trying to make love to you, and all you want to do is talk about some other guy. OK, OK,' he gave in when she looked at him.

'Hal, his colonel, has personally interviewed the two guys who claimed to have witnessed his quarrel with the dead man.' Lee paused. 'I shouldn't really be telling you this. Technically, it's against regulations but he promised them that he'd make sure, if they told him the truth, it wouldn't come out how he'd gotten hold of it, and off the back of that they opened up and admitted that they were so deep in debt to Mancini that they were forced to agree to lie for him. They're now on immediate transfers, to protect them as much as anything else, and Mancini is going to be facing a court martial, but at the moment it's all under wraps and Mancini has no idea what's going on. The colonel wants to get all his ammo together before he confronts him.'

'But he does believe Glen?' Diane asked anxiously.

'Yeah. There's no doubt about who's the guilty one.'

'So what will happen to Glen now?'

'Once Mancini has been charged and put under guard, Glen will be given a full discharge, and a clean bill of health, and by way of compensation for what he's been put through his colonel is going to give his permission for him to go ahead and get married.'

'Oh, Lee! Can I tell Ruthie? She's here tonight. Poor girl, she's been through such a dreadful time these last few days, what with all this business and Walter's death and then – well, you won't know about this – but she worked in a munitions factory workshop where there was a terrible explosion earlier this week. Everyone working there was killed in the blast. Ruthie would have died too if she hadn't gone home from work not feeling well.'

'Jeez...' Lee swore under his breath. 'Poor kid. Well, I guess you can tell her, but you'll have to tell her as well that she's to keep it under her hat for now, bearing in mind what I just told you about Mancini.'

Diane gave him a tender smile and said lovingly, 'I've just had a better idea. Why don't I bring her over so that you can tell her? She's only over there on the other side of the dance floor. I should warn you that she's a bit on the shy side, but something tells me that she's far more likely to believe you than she is me.'

'Well...' Lee looked dubious, but then when Diane squeezed his hand he laughed and said, 'OK... I guess I'd agree to anything to have you smile at me like that, Di.'

'Wait here.' She released his hand and stood up. 'I'll go across and fetch her.'

'Ruthie?'

Both Jess and Ruthie looked up from their silent contemplation of the dancers when Diane touched Ruthie lightly on the shoulder.

'I was sorry to hear about ... about what happened,' she told them both quietly.

'I keep feeling that it's wrong for me and Jess to be alive,' Ruthie said miserably. 'It's as though somehow we've cheated, and...'

420

'Major Saunders has had a word with your Glen's colonel,' Diane told her calmly, overriding her despair. 'And he wants to talk to you about it, if you can spare a minute.'

The immediate change in Ruthie's expression was heart-wrenching. Diane watched the hope flare briefly in the girl's eyes, only to die away again as she looked across the dance floor.

'It's no use, is it?' she asked Diane. 'He can't do anything.'

'You need to talk to him yourself,' Diane told her.

Ruthie looked uncertainly at Jess. 'I don't like to leave you on your own.'

'Don't be silly,' Jess told her robustly. 'I'll be fine.'

'Dance?'

Jess looked up, Billy's voice bringing her out of her dark thoughts.

'I ... I've promised Ruthie I'd wait here for her.'

'She doesn't look like she's about to come rushing back any time soon,' Billy told her drily, glancing over to where Ruthie was talking animatedly to the dark-haired American major sitting next to Diane.

'I need to talk to you,' Billy added, 'about Walter.'

Jess discovered that her mouth had suddenly gone very dry whilst her hands had gone very clammy.

'Why would you want to do that?' she demanded warily.

421

'Oh, I'm just so happy. I can't thank you enough.' Ruthie put her hands to her burning cheeks, her voice breaking with emotion. 'I almost feel as though I can't let myself believe it, just in case.'

'Of course you can believe it,' Diane assured her gently. 'Lee wouldn't say it if it wasn't true.'

'That's right,' he confirmed.

Ruthie smiled beatifically and then stopped, her eyes filling with tears. 'Oh, but I shouldn't be feeling like this, not when...' she gave a small shudder. 'It seems so wrong to be happy with all those poor women and girls gone and poor Walter too.'

Diane exchanged looks with the major. He was beginning to appear slightly impatient and very much as though he wanted to have her to himself.

Touching Ruthie lightly on the shoulder she told her in a kind voice, 'You must try to look on you not being there as something that was meant to be, Ruthie.'

'Meant to be?'

'Yes. You see, if Glen hadn't been accused of being responsible for Walter's death, you wouldn't have been so upset that you had to go home from the factory, would you?'

Ruthie shook her head.

'And then you and Jess would have perished with the others,' Diane persisted. 'So you see, you surviving must have been meant, and that means that you owe it to those who didn't survive to make the most of what you've been given.'

'You mean that because of them I have to be happy?' Ruthie asked her uncertainly.

'Absolutely,' Diane confirmed. She'd never felt surer that life needed to be seized with both hands. And she would do just that this weekend.

'Why do you think I want to talk to you about him?' Billy asked Jess.

She heaved a sigh. They could go on and on round the houses like this for the rest of the night without getting anywhere.

'I don't know,' she told him. 'So why don't you tell me?'

'All right then, I will.' He took a deep breath. 'Why did you let on to me like you and Walter was together?'

'I did no such thing,' Jess denied immediately.

'Yes you did.'

'No I didn't.'

They had stopped dancing now and were facing one another. Jess had her hands on her hips and Billy was glaring at her in exasperation.

'Give over,' Billy demanded. 'You made out like you was sweet on Walter, clinging to his arm and looking up at him all daft-eyed and that.'

'I never.'

'Yes you did.'

'I'm surprised you had time to notice how I was looking at Walter wi' all them girls of yours fawning all over you all the time,' Jess challenged him, changing tack.

'What girls?'

Billy looked and sounded genuinely perplexed but Jess wasn't going to give in.

'Them girls wot you're always flirting with, and don't say that you aren't, because you are.'

'Well, don't you tell me that you weren't flirting with Walter neither.'

'I never! Me and Walter were just friends. He was lonely and he wanted someone to talk to about his girl on account of having to leave her back at home without having a chance to say goodbye to her properly like.'

There was silence for a few seconds as they glared at one another, and then Billy said gruffly, 'Well, you should have said summat to me then, shouldn't you? You know, like telling me that he was just a friend, and you knowing he had a girl at home.'

'What? You've got your nerve, Billy Spencer! Why should I go telling you anything of the kind? Huh! We all know now what would have happened if I had. The next thing, I'd have known, you'd have bin telling everyone that I was sweet on you and acting like I had to make sure you knew I was free for if you wanted to ask me out.'

'Don't be daft.'

Another silence. But a different one this time. Billy shuffled slightly towards Jess and when she didn't move back he reached out and took told of her hand.

'If *you* was to say that you were sweet on *me*, Jess...'

Jess looked back at him. She felt as though she was trembling on the edge of something that was both exciting and dangerous, something she longed for and yet at the same time feared.

Billy was pulling her gently closer to him and she wasn't resisting. She looked into his face and her heart did a cartwheel.

'Jess ... I know this might not be the time but–'

'Billy! There you are. I've bin looking everywhere for you. You owe me a dance, remember?'

Jess stiffened as the other girl came up to them, deliberately turning her back on her whilst she leaned towards Billy, acting as though Jess just wasn't there, never mind having her hand held by him. Abruptly she pulled her hand from Billy's and turned on her heel, ignoring him when he called out to her to stay. Stay here and wait in line for him behind someone like that? He'd got a nerve, and she'd got more respect for herself!

She could see Ruthie making her way back to their table. Determinedly, she hurried over to her and said, 'I don't know about you, Ruthie, but I'm ready for me bed. I reckon I've had enough here, what with all that's happened this week, an' all.'

'I'm ready to leave as well,' Ruthie confirmed. She couldn't wait to get home and give her mother and their neighbours the good news about Glen.

THIRTY

'Ready?'

Diane nodded without being able to look at Lee as he took her small case from her and put it into the back of the Jeep.

They had both agreed that it made sense to meet up away from Derby House and its prying eyes, but that didn't stop her from feeling somehow uncomfortably shabby about the manner in which she had deliberately let the others think she was going home to see her parents for the weekend before making her way to her prearranged rendezvous with Lee on Wavertree Road. There was no reason for her to feel like this, she reassured herself. It wasn't as though she had had to hang around on a street corner, advertising her intentions by putting her case at her feet, after all. Lee had been waiting for her.

No reason? What about *Mrs* Saunders, Lee's *wife?* Wasn't she any kind of a reason for her to feel guilty about what she was doing?

Lee was opening the passenger door to the Jeep for her.

'Have you any idea how damn much I want to kiss you?' he told her thickly.

Immediately her pulse quickened, whilst a now-familiar heat flooded her body. This was so different from what she had felt for Kit. Then her sexuality had been unknown, and untested. She had been inexperienced, knowing only that her desire for Kit, her love for him, were driving her on to make that leap into the unknown that was womanhood, in Kit's arms. Afterwards, as a woman – Kit's woman – she had grown used to the hot ache of her desire for him and her yearning for those stolen nights – sometimes merely stolen hours they had shared together as lovers.

Now she was already a woman, experienced, knowing the desires of her body and what fed them. The hunger she felt for Lee's touch wasn't the excited urgency spiked with uncertainty that belonged to a virgin, but the awareness of her own deepest self that belonged to a woman who had known physical love.

She and Lee would be meeting physically as equals. Her need for him was a woman's need for a man, not a virgin's need for the experience of sexual intimacy, or to 'give herself to the man she loved' that she had felt with Kit. How naïve that girl seemed to be to her now, how naïve, and impossibly morally pure, because that Diane, that girl, would never even have contemplated experiencing, never mind satisfying, her physical desire for a married man. She would not even have accepted that it was possible for a woman to feel that kind of hunger in its own right. For her, the sexual act had only been acceptable when it was the result of a woman having fallen in love and being loved back by a man who was free to give and take that love. She would never have accepted that physical sexual desire could be something a woman could feel simply because she was a woman and because she was missing what she had once had, because she was afraid that this war might take from her the right to be fully that woman.

'My guess is that we'll be there in about an hour and a half – can you wait that long to eat?'

Ridiculously after what she had just been thinking, Diane could feel herself suddenly blushing because she knew that her appetite wasn't for food.

'God, I'm so hungry for you, Di,' he told her in a low groan, his words mirroring her thoughts. 'You're all I've been able to think about since

427

Wednesday night.'

Myra grimaced in distaste as she made her way along the down-at-heel street in the fading daylight. With its boarded-up houses and general air of neglect and abandonment, the whole area had an atmosphere of sullen brooding resentment spiced with danger. It reminded her in many ways of the atmosphere at home whilst she had been growing up. Angrily she shrugged aside that thought. Just as soon as this war was over she would be leaving all of this behind her. There wouldn't be streets like this one in New York: streets where houses had been bombed and left empty, where hostile dark shapes, human and animal, slunk along in the twilight, anxious to keep out of sight but still ready to turn and fight their corner if they had to. Myra's grip on her handbag tightened. Nick had no right to expect her to come to places like this, she decided, conveniently ignoring the fact that Nick had not summoned her to the bar and that it was her own decision to come there and look for him, because he had not, as she had expected, been in touch with her since their return from London. Apart from anything else, she needed to see him to tell him about what Diane had had to say to her. Once they were married there would be some changes made and no mistake. It was all very well him claiming that it was business that brought him to this dank sunless street, with its fetid smell of corruption and fear; there must be other 'business' he could make money from, surely. Wrinkling her nose in disgust, she started to walk down the worn stone steps that led to the bar.

In the well at the bottom of the steps a woman with brassy dyed hair was leaning against the brick wall, smoking.

''Ere,' she called out to Myra as Myra made to pull open the door. 'This is my pitch. Tek yourself off and go and find your own.'

Ignoring her, Myra stepped into the bar.

Unlike on the other occasions she had been here, this evening it was busy, the air thick with smoke, men crowding round the bar, whilst a couple of women of the same type and profession as the one she had seen outside were sitting at one of the rickety tables. As Myra surveyed the room, a man standing at the bar turned to spit on the floor, catching sight of her as he did and nudging the man standing next to him. Within seconds every man at the bar, or so it seemed to Myra, had stopped talking to turn and look at her, except for the man she had come here to find. He was continuing with his conversation as he kept his back to her. Because he didn't want to acknowledge her? Myra smothered the anxiety she could feel uncurling deep inside her, and walked quickly over to him. He was wearing civvies instead of his uniform, and the man he was talking to was the same American he had met here once before. He gave her a hard unwelcoming look before nudging Nick and muttering something to him as he slipped him a package.

'What...?' Nick began tersely as he turned round and saw her, but Myra was determined to have her own way.

She shook her head, stopping him, then told

him, determinedly, 'I need to talk to you, Nick – but not here.'

'Hey, look, can't you see that I'm in the middle of a business meeting here?' was his response.

Myra had no intention of giving in, though.

'This is important, Nick. It's about what happened the other Saturday before we went to London ... remember?' she warned him.

The two men exchanged looks.

'We can't talk in here,' Myra told Nick.

'Go ahead, Nick,' the other man said, still ignoring her. 'I'll be in touch – usual place.'

How quickly he melted into the shadows, Myra noticed. One minute he was there, the next he had gone, or so it seemed.

'I'm surprised you haven't been in touch with me before now,' she said to Nick as he hurried her out of the club, and up the stone steps, 'especially seeing as we're engaged now. I've been thinking about that, Nick,' she added, 'about me and you being engaged.'

'Well, don't think about it,' Nick snarled at her, 'because there ain't no point.'

'What's wrong with you?' Myra demanded, put out. 'And why are you out of uniform?'

To her shock he turned on her, winding his fingers tightly into her hair.

'Ouch,' she protested. 'You're hurting me, Nick.'

'Am I? Good. Maybe that will teach you not to come poking your nose in where it isn't wanted.'

Myra was outraged. 'Not wanted! You weren't saying anything about me not being wanted when you gave me this.' She waggled her ring finger.

'Did you tell anyone you were coming here?' he demanded, ignoring her comment.

'No. I would have told Diane, but she was acting all uppity about that Walter going and dying that I didn't bother,' Myra sniffed disparagingly. 'Look, Nick, when you and me are married–'

'Back off, will you?' he told her.

Back off? Myra stared at him. 'You can't tell me to back off,' she started to bluster, 'not with us getting married.'

Nick started to laugh. 'Me marry you? Are you crazy?' he taunted her, looking contemptuously at her. 'There's no way I'd tie myself to a dumb broad like you. Broads like you come a dime a dozen in New York, and no way does anyone marry them.'

Myra's heartbeat slowed ominously and then started to beat far too fast at what she recognised in his look. Suddenly and very clearly she could see her chance of fulfilling her dream slipping away from her. Nick was her passport to that dream and to the future; without him... She forgot that she was already married and that she wasn't in a position to marry him; in fact she forgot everything other than the agonising pain she could feel bursting into life inside her as destructively as ignited TNT. 'But you said–' she began.

'Said, schpred,' Nick shrugged dismissively, as he let go of her hair. 'I ain't the first guy to spin you a line to get you into bed and don't try telling me I am. There's no way a dame, who gives it out like you do, doesn't know what it's all about.'

'You don't mean that... You've ... you've got to

431

marry me,' she burst out in her panic, 'otherwise...'

Nick stopped chewing his gum, his body suddenly completely motionless and emanating such an aura of menace that Myra started to shiver.

'Otherwise what?' he demanded without taking his gaze off her.

She wasn't going to be frightened by Nick, Myra told herself staunchly. If anyone was going to be afraid then it was him.

'Diane's already been asking me questions about what happened on Saturday. If you want me to keep on lying for you, Nick, then you are going to have to marry me. After all, it's the only way you can be sure I won't say anything, isn't it? It's against the law for a wife to testify against her husband.'

Myra was still smiling when Nick closed his hand round her throat and started to squeeze it.

'You stupid broad,' he snarled savagely, ignoring her attempts to claw his hand away. 'Do you really think I'd let you do that? And as for me marrying you,' he turned his head to one side and spat out his gum, releasing his hold on her throat just enough for her to be able to breath properly. 'There ain't no way I could marry you, sugar. You see, I've already got a wife. Yeah, and she knows her place and how to keep her mouth shut when she's told, which is a hell of a lot more than you do.'

Nick was married! Myra didn't want to believe it but she could see that he was telling the truth. The bitterness of her disappointment boiled up inside her like raw acid eating into her pride and her self-control.

'So I guess that leaves only one way for me to shut you up now, doesn't it, sweetness?'

Nick's voice had become as softly caressing as the fingers he was stroking down her bare throat, but Myra wasn't deceived. She started to shiver violently with sick fear, trying to push him away, but he was far too strong for her.

'It's no good,' he told her silkily. 'I ain't letting go.'

'If you hurt me then that will get you into even more trouble,' Myra warned him desperately.

Nick laughed. 'No way! I'll be out of the country before they find you, sugar. It's all arranged. In fact, Carlo is waiting for me a couple of streets away right now.'

Myra looked at him, only now realising the significance of his being in civvies, and then remembering the man he had been with when she had walked into the bar, and the package she had seen exchanging hands.

'No, Nick, please,' she begged him. She could hear the sound of people leaving the bar and she prayed that they would look up the alleyway and see them.

'You'll be just another dame who got too friendly with the wrong guy,' he told her, smiling. 'A good dame gone bad who gets what she deserves...'

He was squeezing her neck so tightly that she couldn't breath. She tried desperately to claw at his hands but he kept on squeezing, and then suddenly he banged her head back against the wall so hard that the last of her breath escaped from her lungs in a tiny sigh like a punctured tyre. He let her go, watching as she slid down the wall, leaving a thin smear of sticky blood behind her as she did so, before he turned and walked away.

'Well, it isn't exactly the Ritz.'

Diane looked at Lee across the small room with its sloping eaves.

Down below them was the taproom of the pub and the conversation from it drifted upwards through the floorboards in a muted hum of male voices. Just off the bedroom was an even smaller room containing a wash basin, whilst the lavatory was along the corridor and down a flight of stairs. The bed itself looked comfortable enough, though: high, and so wide it almost filled the room, its patchwork quilt faded and soft to the touch.

'We've got everything we need here,' she answered him quietly, and was rewarded with a fierce glow of passion illuminating his gaze at her.

'A room, a bed and thou,' he misquoted ruefully. 'Have you any idea just how special you are, Di?'

'I'm no more special than any other girl,' she denied.

He shook his head. 'You do not begin to know just *how* different you are. For a start, you haven't complained yet about the room not having a closet, or a bathroom, you haven't told me that you need to go visit a beauty parlour before you can do anything else, nor have you suggested that it would have been better if I'd booked two rooms, so that you'd be spared the discomfort of having to share a room, never mind a bed, with a sweaty, uncouth soldier. And that's just for starters.'

'Oh, Lee.' Instinctively she went to him, leaning her head against his chest and putting her hand on his arm, wanting to comfort him.

'Are you really sure you don't mind about this place?' he pressed her. 'It seemed kinda romantic when I planned it, but I guess I might as well have offered you a night in a hayrick,' he grimaced, as he looked up at the thatched roof.

'This *is* romantic,' Diane assured him. 'You're here and so am I. We're alone, with a bed. What could be more romantic than that?'

'The kind of hotel that can provide a large steak, a bottle of good red, a sprung dance floor and a decent dance band?' he suggested.

'Trimmings,' Diane scoffed. 'And you'd probably have found that someone you knew was staying in the same hotel, and that they wanted you to join them, and that–'

'OK, OK,' Lee grinned, wrapping his arms around her. 'You win. We're in the right place; the best place; the only place we could possibly want to be...'

As he spoke he started to kiss her, slow lazy kisses strung out along her jaw and then her throat as he walked her backwards towards the bed until she could feel it behind her.

'God, but I want you,' he groaned as he stopped playing and cupped her face, kissing her fiercely and possessively.

This was what she had wanted and yearned for, Diane told herself as she closed her eyes and clung to him, kissing him back. As she leaned into him she could feel the thick ridge of his erection and her body quivered. Not with the nervous apprehension with which it had quivered when she had first permitted this intimacy with Kit, but rather with eagerness and impatience.

Lee was sliding his hands inside her jacket, caressing her body over the top of her blouse. She could feel the callused heat of his palms against her breasts through her clothes. Her nipples tightened with the tiny quivers of sensation sensitising them, that same sensation miraculously mirrored deep down inside her body, making her want to melt into him and press herself up against him just as hard and close as she could. She arched her neck, inviting the caress of his kisses, wanting to moan out her pleasure but careful of the reality of the bar downstairs. Would the bed squeak like the one she and Kit had once had, and which had made them collapse with laughter after their third attempt to defeat its giveaway springs. In the end they had put the eiderdown down on the floor along with the pillows, and made love there rather than risk the ribald comments they knew they would have to face if they went ahead in the bed. Kit swore that one of his friends had put the landlord up to giving them that particular room.

This bed was blissfully silent, though, she acknowledged when Lee lowered her back onto it and she sank into its delicious softness.

He undressed her slowly and tenderly, kissing her in all the right ways and places, not hurrying things, but at the same time not drawing them out too long either. She liked the way he moved so efficiently and naturally, familiar enough with female clothes not to fumble, but not so used to the female form that he didn't register a flattering appreciation at each freshly revealed bit of her.

She liked it even more that he undressed himself when she wanted him to do so, whilst encouraging her to make as free with his body as she wished.

He was more heavily built than Kit, but then of course he was older, with more flesh padding his muscles, and more body hair, but she liked it that he was different, she told herself. It meant that she wouldn't be thinking about Kit whilst she was with him.

Was her own high-breasted, narrow-waisted, pale-skinned body different from that of his wife? Was he looking at her full, creamy-fleshed breasts with their dark nipples and imagining another woman's breasts? Diane pushed away her disturbing thoughts. They had no place here in this bed with them, just as those other partners had no place here. Here in this room, this bed, it was just them and the way they felt about one another; the way Lee made her feel when he lay next to her and cupped her breasts in his hands, looking down at them as though he thought he was observing a small miracle; the way she felt about the fact that they were sharing an intimacy that once she had thought belonged and would always belong exclusively to Kit.

A huge lump suddenly and inexplicably formed in her throat. How had she managed to travel so far down this road, which prior to the war would have been one she would never have imagined would have any place in her life?

Kit had wept the first time they had made love. For the men who had not come back with him, for the beauty of her body and for the perfection of their love, he had told her. And she had wept too, just listening to him.

Kit. Out of nowhere the pain came and slammed into her, taking her breath, numbing her body and then ripping it apart with fresh pain.

Lee was leaning forward to kiss her breasts. Abruptly she wriggled away and then sat up.

'I can't,' she told him bleakly, filled with too much guilt to be able to look directly at him. 'I can't do it, Lee. I'm sorry. Please take me back.'

For a moment she thought he was going to argue or, even worse, actually try to force her. She held her breath and his searching gaze, and then exhaled as he gave a brusque nod.

Ten minutes later they were dressed and ready to leave.

'Which of them was it?' he asked her heavily, breaking the silence. 'My wife, or your ex?'

'It was Kit,' Diane admitted, uncomfortably aware that, having come this far, the existence of Lee's wife would not have been enough to stop her. Facing up to the truth about oneself with such brutal honesty wasn't easy, but she owed Lee that much at least.

'I wasn't going to tell you but I've had the offer of a transfer. I guess now I'll accept it,' he informed her.

Tears stung her eyes. Even now, a part of her wanted to turn back and tell him that she had changed her mind. The question she had to ask herself, though, was how was she going to feel when all this was over and she looked back? Which would she regret most – having an affair with him or not having one?

Only time could give her the answer to that, she told herself as Lee held open the door for her.

''Ere, Cedric, hang on a sec.'

The two men had been the last to leave the bar, and now one of them turned into the alleyway, drunkenly intent on taking advantage of the blackout to relieve himself. He staggered forward and then recoiled as he almost stumbled over Myra's body.

'Ruddy hell, Cedric, bring that ruddy torch, will yer?' he called out shakily. 'There's summat here.'

His companion shone the torch down the alleyway onto Myra.

''Ere, I don't like this. Let's scarper.'

'We can't do that. She's still alive – look, she's breathing. You wait here, I'll go and get help,' Cedric, abruptly sobering up, told his companion.

'I can't see no breathing. She looks like she's a goner to me. Why don't we–'

'Stay here,' Cedric repeated.

Half an hour later, when the ambulance arrived, summoned by the ARP unit Cedric had alerted, one of the ambulance crew gave a low shocked whistle.

'She might be breathing now,' he said, 'but from the looks of her it's the morgue we'll be taking her to. Someone's really laid into her, and no mistake.'

THIRTY-ONE

'They'll be putting the clocks back in another couple of weeks. I'm not looking forward to them dark nights with this blackout still going on, I can tell you.'

Diane smiled sympathetically as she listened to her landlady.

'Going down the hospital later on to see Myra, are you?' Mrs Lawson asked.

'I expect so.'

Over the last few weeks, following on from the shocking news that Myra had been found up a back alley behind a seedy bar, unconscious and so badly beaten up that initially the doctors hadn't thought she would live, they had been taking it in turns to visit Myra as often as they could.

'Do you reckon they'll ever catch up with that GI wot beat her up and killed that poor Walter?'

'I doubt it now,' Diane told her landlady.

Diane knew from Ruthie, who was now blissfully counting off the last few weeks to her November wedding to Glen, that it was believed that Nick had either managed to leave the country or was living somewhere in England under an assumed name with the help of his connections with the American Mafia, although Ruthie had also stressed that Glen had been warned that the US Army did not want to have public attention drawn to this connection, and that officially Nick was simply recorded as AWOL – absent without leave.

It had been raining on and off all morning, a thin drizzle, which, combined with the mist that had rolled in over the Liverpool bar, was giving the whole city an air of closed-in grey, dank misery. It was Diane's day off but she did not feel in a holiday mood as she huddled up inside her uniform greatcoat, worn to protect her from the weather despite the fact that she was not on duty.

She had become such a regular visitor at the hospital that the porter on duty recognised her, giving her a cheery smile.

During her early days in Mill Road, Myra had been put in a small side room on her own, such had been the severity of her injuries and the doctors' belief that she could not survive them.

Now, though, she was in a bed in a large ward surrounded by other female patients, several of whom called out chirpy 'hellos' to Diane when she walked in.

Because they were both in uniform and because Myra had no family to come and visit her, the normal rules about visiting hours had been stretched to allow for Diane's on-duty hours, but she tried, apart from a few exceptions, to keep to them. Today, though, was one of those exceptions.

From her bed halfway down the ward, Myra raised her hand in welcome. Poor Myra, Diane reflected sombrely as she reached her bed and pulled out a chair to sit down next to it. She had paid a dreadful price for her foolish infatuation with Nick Mancini. Her hair had started to grow back now after the doctors had had to shave her

441

head to deal with her wound, but she was not the girl she had been, and had lost that sharp self-confidence that had so marked her out before.

She looked anxious and upset, and Diane could see that she'd been crying.

'What's wrong?' she asked her sympathetically. 'You haven't been having those bad nightmares again, have you? Only if you have you should tell Sister, because she said–'

'No,' Myra said. 'Well, at least, it feels like a nightmare, and I wish that was all it was and that I could wake up from it.' Her eyes filled with tears, and she bit down hard on her bottom lip to prevent them from overflowing. 'I'm having that bastard's kid,' she told Diane starkly. 'I've been sick for a while, and they've thought it was something to do with ... with what happened, but then they asked me if there was any chance I could be carrying, and I had to say yes, so they did some tests and I am. I can't believe it. It was only the once without a French letter, and even then...'

Diane didn't know what to say. She was astonished after what Myra had gone through that she had not lost the baby she was carrying, and privately couldn't help thinking that it might have been for the best if she had. What was more, she suspected from Myra's reaction that she felt the same way. Not that either of them could ever say so, of course.

'And as if that weren't bad enough I got a letter from Jim this morning – the first I've had from him since they wrote to tell him what happened to me. He's due back on leave any day now and he says he's ready to talk about us having a divorce.' Myra gave a bitter laugh. 'He'll be the one wanting to divorce me when he sees the state I'm in and he finds out what's going to happen. That means that me and Nick's little bastard are going to be managing on our own.'

'But you've got your mother,' Diane protested. 'I know she hasn't been able to come and see you but—'

Myra shook her head. 'She won't want to know. Settled now, she is, with her cousin, living in some boarding house down Brighton way. The last thing she's going to want is me turning up on her doorstep with a bastard grandchild.'

Diane didn't know what to say. She reached for Myra's hand, patting it awkwardly, whilst reflecting inwardly on how easily the situation Myra was now facing – being a young woman carrying the child of a man who had deserted her – was one that was becoming increasingly common. And one she could potentially have been facing herself if she had gone ahead and had an affair with Lee.

But she had not done, had she, and if sometimes at night she lay in her bed and ached with loneliness and need, well, at least she could comfort herself with the knowledge that she had done the right thing.

'Have they said yet when you'll be able to come out of hospital?' Diane asked.

'Another couple of weeks,' Myra said, looking off into the distance, obviously fearing what the future held.

'There's Billy waiting for you,' Ruthie told Jess

443

unnecessarily, giving her a nudge as they walked out of the church hall where they had been to check up on the final arrangements for Ruthie and Glen's wedding.

'I don't know why,' Jess responded grumpily.

Ruthie laughed.

'What's that for?' Jess challenged her.

'Well, if you can't see that Billy's mad for you, Jess, then you want to go and get those eyes of yours tested,' Ruthie told her with the forthrightness that had come with the new confidence Glen's love for her had given her.

'Huh. He might make out that he is, but then that doesn't mean owt, not with a lad like Billy.'

'Maybe it's up to you to make it mean something, if that's what you want,' Ruthie suggested.

Jess stared at her. 'What, me go chasing after him, you mean? Not on your nelly.'

Ignoring her grumpiness, Ruthie replied cheerfully, 'What I was meaning was that if that was what you wanted, you could perhaps give him a chance to come chasing after you instead of pushing him off all the time. If that's what you was wanting...'

'Well, it isn't,' Jess snapped, but Ruthie was well aware of the yearning look in her eyes that she couldn't quite conceal as she looked towards where Billy was standing waiting.

Ruthie knew that she would never ever forget how close she had come to losing Glen. He had brought so much happiness to her life that it was only natural, surely, that she should want her friend to have the same happiness. Even when that friend kept on claiming that it wasn't what she wanted.

'I've got to go,' she told Jess. 'Glen will be waiting for me at home.'

'Hang on,' Jess began, but it was already too late: Ruthie was hurrying away from the hall, leaving her standing on her own with Billy between her and the gate.

She watched as he came towards her.

'Bin sorting out the wedding, have you?' he asked her.

'No, I was looking for the Majestic Picture House and I took a wrong turning,' Jess told him witheringly.

'Vicar still in there, is he?' Billy nodded toward the church hall. ''Cos if he is, how about you and me going and having a word wi' him and asking how he fancies doing us as well?'

Jess's face was difficult for him to read.

'Doing us as well? One day, Billy Spencer, them jokes of yours are going to get you into big trouble,' she warned him angrily, making to walk past him. But as she did, Billy reached out and caught hold of her arm, stopping her.

'Who said anything about a joke?' he asked her abruptly.

Jess could feel her heart pounding like one of those bomb fuses Billy was always talking about to her stepfather. She felt a bit like a bomb inside, as well, she admitted – a bomb that was about to go off!

'I mean it, Jess,' he continued seriously. 'I'm fed up wi' us messing about.'

'Us messing about...' Jess began and then was forced to stop as suddenly Billy took hold of her.

'Stop it, Billy,' she protested. 'You're nearly squeezing the breath out of me, holding me so tightly like that.'

'Well, I'm going to go on holding you tightly, and I'm going to kiss you as well,' Billy told her ruthlessly. 'And I'm going to keep on kissing you until you tell me that you and me are going to get married.'

'You can't–' Jess began.

'Oh, yes I can,' Billy told her softly, and then proceeded to kiss her so thoroughly that she felt as though she could no longer think, never mind try to speak.

Ten minutes later, as they stood wrapped in one another's arms, Jess looked up into Billy's eyes, her own bright with love and happiness.

'You'll have to marry me now,' Billy said with great satisfaction, ''cos Mrs Harris, three doors down from your ma, has just walked past and seen us. By the time you get home the whole street will know.'

Jess assumed a serious expression. 'You're right there, Billy, there's no help for it now. We've got to get wed. Not that I want to wed you, of course. Not if you're going to keep on kissing me like that.'

'Like what? Like this, do you mean?' Billy queried.

'Mmmm ... yes ... just like that,' Jess sighed happily as she snuggled closer to him.

The evening's visitors were filing into the ward. Myra looked towards the door, her heart thumping heavily as it had done every visiting time for the last few nights since she had received Jim's letter.

Knowing that he was due home and planning to visit her, Diane had told her that she and Mrs Lawson, her only two other visitors, would time their visits so as not to come during proper visiting hours until after she had seen Jim.

'Not that seeing him is going to do me much good,' Myra had told Diane. How could it do, she reflected miserably now. Jim had already as good as told her he was going to agree to a divorce, and that was the last thing she wanted or needed now, with no lover to turn to and an unwanted baby on the way. Agree to it – he'd be the one forcing a divorce on her once he found out what had happened, and no mistake, Myra admitted.

Her stomach, already tied in knots was even more so as she saw Jim's familiar figure coming through the doorway, his cap under his arm, his greatcoat hanging off his too-thin, desert-worn frame. His sunburned face was creased into an expression of self-conscious embarrassment as he clutched some flowers and tried not to look at the women in their beds as he made his way along the ward.

'Jim,' Myra called out to attract his attention.

'My, your 'usband looks a fine chap,' the elderly woman in the bed next to her own leaned across to whisper. 'One of them desert rats, is he – Monty's boys?'

Myra had just finished confirming that Jim was indeed, when Jim himself reached her bedside.

'Sit down, Jim,' she told him after a nurse had

447

bustled up to remove his flowers. 'I ... I got your letter.'

'Aye, and I got the one the 'ospital sent me, saying as you had been in a right bad way,' he told her. 'Got a bone to pick wi' them, I have. They should have let me know the minute you was brought in here, instead of waiting until you was on the mend. I'd have put in for compassionate leave and been home long before now if they had.'

'I said not to,' Myra told him, avoiding looking at him.

'Well, they had no business paying any attention. It's not right, me not being here, me being your husband, and all. Give me a right old shock, it did, when the letter came and I read it.' He had reached for her hand and somehow or other, without meaning to, Myra had let him take it. Now suddenly, with her hand held firmly within the warm safe clasp of his, her throat had started to ache with pent-up tears. She could feel them pressing against the backs on her eyes, and despite all her attempts to prevent it doing so, she could feel one of them escaping and running down her face.

Surreptitiously she tried to brush it away, but Jim saw her.

'Aw, come on,' he chivvied her. 'I haven't come here to start upsetting you and reading the riot act, Myra. If it's a divorce you want then–' he broke off as Myra started to sob, her whole body shaking convulsively.

'Gawd, woman, what the hell have I said now,' he protested. 'I'm giving you what you was wanting and you start bawling your eyes out.'

'I'm pregnant.'

Myra expected Jim to let go of her hand immediately but he didn't. Instead he gripped it a bit harder.

'This chap, is it?' he asked her valiantly. 'This GI you've taken up with that wants to marry you?'

Myra shuddered. 'He never wanted to marry me. It was a pack of lies, all of it. Even the ring he gave me turned out to be a fake, and besides...' her voice dropped to an agonised whisper, 'he was the one that put me in here, Jimmy. He beat me up real bad,' she confessed, 'worse than Dad ever did Mum.'

Jim had clenched the hand that wasn't holding hers into a tight fist and there was a hard fiery look in his eyes.

'By God, when I get hold of him...'

'He's gone, scarpered, no one knows where. I've been such a fool,' Myra wept. 'Such a ruddy, ruddy fool.' She shook her head. 'Even if he were to come crawling back here now I wouldn't have him back. No, sir, I wouldn't,' she announced vehemently.

'So what *are* you going to do?' Jim asked her gruffly. 'You've got the kiddie to think of now, after all,' he pointed out, nodding in the direction of her bedding-covered body.

'Do you think I don't know that?' Myra demanded with a return to her old sharp self. 'I'm the one that's going to have the ruddy thing. A proper disgrace that's going to be and no mistake. Me with no husband and a kid about to be born.'

'No husband, my left foot. Of course you've got a ruddy husband,' said Jim indignantly 'Still married to me, aren't you?'

Myra stared at him. In the place of despair and misery suddenly there was the tiny beginning of hope.

'You won't want me now,' she told him, 'not after what I've gone and done. And if that weren't bad enough I'm carrying the kid to prove it. It's a pity it wasn't my stomach he thumped; then I might have lost it.'

'Aw, Myra, don't say that. Poor little blighter, it isn't its fault. 'Sides, who's to know whose kid it is anyway if you and me stay together?'

Myra's eyes widened. 'You don't mean that,' she told him. 'Why should you take another man's kid on?'

Jim said quietly, 'It's like this, see, Myra. I never told you 'cos you allus said that you didn't like kiddies, but seemingly on account of me having mumps as a lad I can't have no kids of me own, so me being a dad to this one you're having – well, it will be like there's summat good come out of this war for me. I'm not saying that it didn't feel like someone had ripped my guts out when you told me that you wanted to leave me for this other chap, and I'm not saying neither that I didn't want to punch his lights out and give you a piece of me mind, because I did. But you and me, Myra, well, I reckon we belong together, and when this kiddie comes along, it will be our kiddie, and I promise you this: I'll love it like it were me own, Myra, because it will be me own ...

450

not a little bastard but a little Stone…'

Myra was laughing and crying at the same time, hiccuping in between her tears and laughter as she clung to Jim and tried to tell him what she felt.

For some reason fate had relented and given her a second chance. All these days she had been lying here, knowing what a fool she had been to give up a good man like Jim; a kind man who loved her and who made her feel safe, just for the sake of a bit of excitement with a man like Nick. Her longing for a glamorous life in America was gone, as though it had been some kind of dream she had now woken up from. And she had changed too, grown a conscience that she found inconvenient at times – times such as now, for instance.

'I can't let you do this, Jim,' she told him. 'You'll end up hating me. It's not right, you deserve better.'

'No, it's *you* who deserves better, Myra – you and me and our baby, and I'm going to see that we get it, just as soon as this war's over. I've got to thinking out there in the desert, and I've been making a few plans. I've saved up a fair bit and I've got a bit put by now. There's a chap out there who told me that he's planning to buy himself a little house now whilst the war's still on and he can get one at a good price, and that's what I'm going to do. A nice house with a bit of a garden for our lad – or lass – somewhere decent where we can have a fresh start … summat a bit posh, like, so that you can have your bit of a show-off… I know what you're like. So what do you say? Shall we give it a go?'

'Oh, Jim, I don't deserve a good man like you, I really don't,' Myra sobbed as she wrapped her arms round her husband's neck and kissed him with passionate gratitude.

Diane sniffed the crispness of the autumn air as she walked down Chestnut Close through the blackout. She had called at the hospital to see Myra on her way home from her shift and had been regaled with Myra's almost giddily excited story of Jim's visit and their plans for the future.

Whilst she was relieved and happy for her, Diane admitted that deep down inside, the ache of her own loneliness hurt very badly. She had a long furlough coming up soon and she planned to go home to see her parents. That should cheer her up a bit, she told herself firmly, as she stepped up to the front door.

She was just about to use her key when it opened inwards, to reveal Mrs Lawson, dressed in her hat and coat, ready for going out.

'You've got a visitor,' she told Diane importantly. 'I've put him in the front parlour – and mind, I'll be back in a couple of hours.'

Before Diane could say anything she had stepped past her and was hurrying down the pathway.

Light was streaming out from the hallway, reminding Diane that she was breaking the blackout regulations. Hurriedly she stepped inside and closed the door.

A visitor. *He* was in the parlour. A little uncertainly she turned the door handle and pushed open the door.

'Di...'

'*Kit!*'

'Oh God, Di, I've missed you. I've missed you...'

He had sprung up from the armchair when she opened the door and now she was in his arms and he was kissing her, fiercely, possessively, passionately, in all the ways she had so long remembered and longed for, just as though nothing had happened. No, not as though nothing had happened, Diane recognised dizzily as she tried to focus rationally through the delirious pleasure of being back in his arms.

She had changed and so had he. He even felt different: harder, thinner, his face careworn.

'My darling, darling girl, I have missed you so much. Please say that it is not too late for us. I've been badgering your poor parents for your address and it was only when your father let slip that you were coming home next weekend and I threatened to camp out on their doorstep that he finally relented and told me where you were.'

Her father was a sly old fox, Diane decided giddily, and that 'slip' had been no accident, she suspected.

'Di, say something,' he demanded emotionally.

'How can I when you won't stop kissing me?' Diane protested.

'You mean when I *can't* stop kissing you,' Kit corrected her. 'You don't know how much I've dreamed of your kisses, Di, how much I've longed for them and for you. Tell me it isn't too late for us.'

He had released her now, and Diane stepped

back from him.

'I ... I don't know,' she told him honestly.

The look on his face echoed the pain in her own heart.

'I've got to be honest, Kit. It wouldn't be right if I wasn't.'

'But you still love me,' he insisted. 'You wouldn't have kissed me like that if you didn't.'

'Yes, but ... but I'm not sure I believe any more that love on its own is enough. There has to be ... trust ... and...' She shook her head. 'It hurt me so badly when you broke our engagement without any kind of explanation or ... or anything, Kit. And now you're here, telling me ... saying...'

'You're right,' he agreed with unfamiliar humility. 'I'm rushing things and jumping out mid-flight without a parachute, and expecting you to jump with me. That's because I'm so eager to get back down to earth and be with you, my darling. As for what I did, I can explain if you will listen.'

'Of course I'll listen.' She was forcing herself to smile but inwardly Diane was steeling herself for what she felt sure was to come. Even after her own relationship with Lee it still hurt unbearably to think of Kit rejecting her for someone else, even if now he had decided that that person no longer mattered and he wanted her back. Was that wanting her back enough to build a life together on, or would she always be worrying that ultimately there might come another time when he wanted to break his vows to her and go AWOL for a while?

'It was that last mission we flew before the prof bought it,' Kit told her, referring to a member of the squadron who the others had nicknamed 'the

Prof' because of his love for crossword puzzles. 'You remember the one?'

'Yes.' Diane did remember it, but she didn't know why Kit was asking her if she did with almost painful intensity.

'Well, the thing is, that it wasn't a Luftwaffe plane that shot him down, it was one of our own, one of the squadron,' he stressed.

Diane felt that she needed to sit down. 'But that's not possible,' she protested. 'That couldn't happen.'

Kit grimaced. 'That's the official line but the reality is that we all know that it can happen all too bloody easily, even if we never talk about it. When you're up there caught up in a dogfight, with the sun shining right down on you and planes everywhere, you see someone coming up behind you and your immediate reaction is to go into the attack. The truth is that it could have happened to any one of us, and in the confusion who's to know? It just so happened that I was behind the Prof and I saw the whole thing.' His voice had dropped and he wiped his hand over his eyes.

Diane's heart ached for him and her immediate instinct was to go to him and hold him, but she sensed that he needed to cleanse what was obviously a festering wound within himself fully, no matter how painful that process, and that she would not be helping him if she rushed in with offers of comfort to hide away what needed to be removed.

'None of the others in the squadron saw what happened, and ... nothing was said when we got back.'

Diane bit her lip. She knew that Kit's deliberate avoidance of naming the pilot responsible for shooting down his own comrade was to protect that pilot.

'I couldn't say anything myself, but ... hell, Di, you know how it is. We were all filing our reports, and the report was that the Prof had been shot down in combat. I had to go along with that, but I also had to fly in the same squadron as the chap who had shot him down. I began to think that there'd be another accident but this time it would be me. I couldn't think about anything else. Apart from the poor old Prof. He shouldn't have died. He should still have been alive. I kept thinking that he might do it again and that I should say something if only to protect the rest of the squadron, but then I kept thinking about him and how it was a mistake anyone could make. I didn't know what to do. It ate into me. I started thinking that the reason I'd seen it was because I was going to be next. Every time I went up I believed I wasn't going to be coming back. I kept thinking about you and how it was unfair of me to keep you tied to me when I was a goner – a dead man – and so I did what I thought was best for you. I gave you your freedom. I couldn't tell you the truth, you know that. I couldn't.'

Yes, she knew that he could not have betrayed a fellow squadron member by revealing the truth, and she knew too that she did understand how he must have felt, how tortured and afraid and how very alone.

'I knew you wouldn't accept that I wanted to break our engagement without a reason so I ... I started acting like the fool I would have had to have been to have thought any other girl could come anywhere near rivalling you.'

'I understand what you're saying,' Diane told him. Of course she did. The loyalty between members of a squadron was intense and sacrosanct. It had to be because their lives depended on one another. So when one of them was responsible for the death of another, then the clash of loyalties had to be unendurable. 'But what's changed?' she asked. 'Why are you telling me now what you couldn't tell me before?'

'The pilot concerned came forward and spilled the beans. Told the Wing Co that he couldn't go on any longer carrying the guilt,' he told her simply. 'He's been discharged – full honours. There's no point in muck-raking and, poor sod, he's punished himself enough without anyone else doing it for him.

'His going brought me to my senses and made me see what had happened for what it was – an accident, not a warning that I was going to be next. All I want now is to get back to where I was with you, Di. That and for us to get married as soon as it can be arranged. No more being sensible and waiting until the war is over. I've spent too many days and hours without you now not to want to cherish every single minute we can spend together and to want us to share them as man and wife. If you'll have me back, that is?'

Diane took a deep breath. 'There's been someone else,' she told him, striving to keep her voice light. 'He... I... He is married and so, because of that and because ... because I couldn't bring

457

myself to share with him what somehow I still felt belonged only to you, we didn't go through with it. But I planned to, Kit, and I wanted to,' she told him with painful honesty. 'And I'd be lying if I said anything else. Kit,' she protested as he crossed the space between them and took hold of her, wrapping his arms around her.

'Now I'll tell you something,' he said hoarsely. 'All those other girls – it was all just a great big sham, Di, a lot of talk and noise in public but nothing in private, because, like you, I just couldn't, not with anyone who wasn't you. Please tell me you'll take me back.'

For her answer Diane laced her hands either side of his face and held it tenderly whilst she raised herself up on her tiptoes and kissed him.

For a few seconds he let her, and then he took the control from her, holding her and kissing her with fiercely thrilling sweetness that melted her bones and dissolved all of her pain.

'My landlady will be back in a few minutes,' she warned him breathlessly, half an hour later.

'Good. She can be the first to congratulate me on our re-engagement,' he teased her. 'Which reminds me. Your mother said to tell you that she's had a word with the vicar and he's said he'll have a talk with us on Sunday about a date for the wedding.'

'A date for the wedding. Is that all? I thought she'd have had the wedding dress, the cake and the whole thing sorted out by now,' Diane laughed.

As he bent his head to kiss her, Kit told her softly, 'She has.'

EPILOGUE

'Well, I don't know,' Jess marvelled, easing off her shoes and wriggling her toes in front of Ruthie's mother's parlour fire. 'Who'd have thought that first time me and Ruthie met up wi' you at the Grafton, Diane, that we'd all be here now wi' all three of us getting wed before Christmas?'

'It just goes to prove that you never can know what's round the corner,' Diane agreed. 'Especially in wartime. You'll be the first of us to be married, Ruthie.'

With only a week to go before Ruthie and Glen's marriage, the three girls had been busy all day checking all the arrangements, and now they were relaxing over the much-needed cup of tea and some toast, which Ruthie's mother had made for them, before going round to spend the evening with her neighbour.

'Your mam's come on ever such a lot just recently, Ruthie,' Jess commented. 'You'd never know her for the same person now.'

'No, I know. Our doctor says it's a little miracle. He reckons that having Glen around, and me and him getting married, has done her the world of good. Time was when I was that worried about her, I even got to thinking that she might try to do away wi' herself or summat.'

'Well, you don't need to worry any more,' Diane to her gently. 'Not now you've got Glen.'

459

'I still can't believe my own good luck,' Ruthie smiled happily, before adding, 'It's ever so nice of you to put off taking up your transfer back down to where your Kit's stationed so that you can come to me and Glen's wedding.'

'I wouldn't have missed it for the world,' Diane assured her. 'It was really kind of you and Glen to include Kit. He's going to come up on Friday, and then we can travel back down to Cambridge-shire together afterwards. Don't forget, will you, that Kit and I want you all to come down to our wedding?'

'And then you'll have to come back up here for mine,' Jess reminded her, before turning to Ruthie to say, 'I'm going to miss you when you go off to America.'

'That won't be until after the war is over, and that doesn't look like it's going to be any time soon. Glen says that I mustn't worry about it, because his family will make me and Mum really welcome, and, of course, I'll have him.'

'Aye, and probably a baby bouncing on your knee as well by then,' Jess laughed. 'You should hear my Billy. You know what he's like.' She rolled her eyes and laughed. 'He keeps on saying that he reckons we should have a honeymoon baby. I can't say as I'd mind. I haven't got the stomach for working on munitions any more, and there's no work conscription for mothers with young kiddies.'

Diane listened to them without making any comment. There were those who said that they couldn't think of bringing a new life into the world in such perilous times; women who said practically that they did not want to face bringing up a fatherless child as a widow, but she suspected that Ruthie and Jess felt as she did herself – that with the coming of a new life there also came hope for the future. For her there was also the matter of her duty to the uniform she wore, and the work she was trained to do. She and Kit both had roles to play in the war and they had agreed that they would try to wait to start a family if they could.

'Have you heard anything from that Myra?' Jess was asking her. 'That husband of hers is a fool for tekin' her back, if you ask me.'

Diane could see the way Ruthie was looking away. She certainly didn't blame her for not feeling sympathetic towards Myra after what she had done.

'He loves her and I think that Myra recognises now how lucky she is to have him. What happened to her has changed her.'

'Well, she certainly needed to do some changing,' Jess broke in.

'Yes, she did,' Diane agreed. She couldn't help feeling glad for Myra's sake, and that of the child she was carrying, that Jim was prepared to stand by her, even if she sensed that the other two thought she had been undeservedly lucky.

'Come on, girls,' Jess announced determinedly, refilling their teacups. 'Let's have a toast.'

'What to?' Diane asked her.

'To the future, and the end of the war, and, of course, the Grafton,' Jess grinned. 'And to us, the Grafton Girls.'

The publishers hope that this book has given you enjoyable reading. Large Print Books are especially designed to be as easy to see and hold as possible. If you wish a complete list of our books please ask at your local library or write directly to:

Magna Large Print Books
Magna House, Long Preston,
Skipton, North Yorkshire.
BD23 4ND

This Large Print Book for the partially sighted, who cannot read normal print, is published under the auspices of

THE ULVERSCROFT FOUNDATION